We Two Together
A Novel

'A heartfelt evocation of times past and places remembered, We Two Together *beautifully captures the exquisite pain of first loves and first losses. The writing brims with passion for art, music, poetry and boys, and deftly portrays the formative experiences that build the foundations for a life.'*

Michael Langan, author of Shadow is a Colour as Light is

'An unusually honest and open-hearted welcome into an exclusive world on many levels. Freddie is a wonderful guide – engaging us in his coming of age and a love story, which changes the context of family history permanently and for the better. A rare achievement especially in a first novel.'

Leonora Rustamova, author of Stop! Don't Read This

We Two Together

A Novel

James Lomax

Matador
Unit E2 Airfield Business Park,
Harrison Road, Market Harborough,
Leicestershire. LE16 7UL
Tel: 0116 2792299
Email: books@troubador.co.uk
Web: www.troubador.co.uk/matador
Twitter: @matadorbooks

Paperback ISBN: 9781803137636
Hardback ISBN: 9781803137643

British Library Cataloguing in Publication Data.
A catalogue record for this book is available from the British Library.

Printed and bound by CPI Group (UK) Ltd, Croydon, CR0 4YY
Typeset in 11pt Minion Pro by Troubador Publishing Ltd, Leicester, UK

Matador is an imprint of Troubador Publishing Ltd

In memoriam M.C.F.L. (1950–1970)

*In her journal she writes: 'Out of extreme narcissism, I want to
see my past set down on paper and in that way, be as I am not.'*
Annie Ernaux, *The Years*

*What could he do but accept the disturbing extent to which
memory was fictional and hope that the fiction lay in the service
of a truth less richly represented by the original facts.*
Edward St Aubyn, *Some Hope*

Prologue

Giles reached for his mobile.

'Hi Sam…Yeah, I'm good thanks. Look, I've found something and I'm not sure what to do.'

'Something among Uncle Freddie's things, you mean?'

'That's right. I've been going through all his papers. Not just as his husband. It's my job as his executor. Anyway, I've found a stash of letters written to you and obviously never sent. Long letters. More than 20 of them.'

'What! When did he write them?'

'They start about five years ago, seemingly after you'd both been to an exhibition at the Hepworth in Wakefield. He says he promised to write to you after he'd had a 'minor convulsion', as he calls it, in front of one of the pictures.'

'Oh, yes. I forgot all about that. But I remember it now.'

'It must have been about the time Freddie and I first got together. I'd no idea what he was doing scribbling away in his study for hours on end, and never liked to ask in those days.'

'Why on earth did he never send them?'

'Search me. But I've got an idea – although I don't want to share it with you until you've seen them. Then we've got to decide what to do: keep them here, or with you, or even destroy them – although I think that would be a pretty beastly thing to do. There are things in there...'

'OK. You'd better send them by Recorded Delivery. Emma and I will have a look at them when we can.'

'Will do. And please give my love to your mother. She was obviously very upset at the funeral. It was lovely though having you and the children here for a few days. Made the place seem like a real home again. I'll be interested to hear your thoughts.

Bye for now, Sam.'

1

30th March 2020

My dear Sam,

I'm relieved to hear that you and Emma and the children have escaped London now that Lockdown is upon us. Being with your mother in Sussex should be much more sensible for everyone. Let's hope we can all get through this crazy time unscathed.

Did she mention that I've got a lodger, and won't be here on my own, thank goodness? He's called Giles Harbord and we've declared ourselves an official Bubble for the duration. We met at a conference a few weeks ago when he told me he was looking for somewhere to stay while he finishes his PhD. Since we got on so well I've offered him a room here and in return he's being very helpful in the garden and sorting out some of my things. He said he knew you slightly from Uni when you were both in the Art Film Society. It seems you had different views on Derek Jarman's films – among other things! He's been a great blessing as it's turned out, since it wouldn't have been much fun 'socially isolating' on my own, with only Tarquin here snapping at my heels for walks we're not allowed to take. I've promised Giles a trip to Rome together, to celebrate, when it's all over.

*

You'll remember I promised to write to you explaining why I had a minor convulsion at the Hepworth Gallery last year when we saw that picture and heard the poem. I told you it was a long story, so here is my opening shot. It will probably be the first of many letters; I don't know at this stage just how many. I hope you will keep them. When (and if!) you eventually inherit the Queen Anne secretaire I suggest you stuff them into one of the internal drawers where the other family papers are kept. Who knows; if I get past Letter 1 and make a decent job of it this could be a contribution to our family's history.

I hope that everything I'm going to write will be more or less accurate. Like a lot of people of my antiquity, my long-term memory seems to be getting better as I get older – or maybe it's just my capacity for wishful thinking? 'Recollection in tranquility' indeed! But it's perfectly true that I find it easier to remember things from over fifty years ago than from this morning – you need only ask Giles.

*

I wonder if I had a premonition as I was waiting for you to arrive off the London train that day a few months ago? I was a little early and walked to the end of the platform keeping Tarquin on a tight leash. From there I could see the relentless tides of traffic washing back and forth over the Calder Bridge. On one side was the medieval bridge chapel, all ogees, pinnacles and crockets, like a folly in an illuminated manuscript. On the other, the spartan blocks of the Hepworth, the symbol of Wakefield's hoped-for Renaissance. Two temples, 500 years apart: one dedicated to faith, the other to art, each making their separate bids for immortality.

As you stepped off the train, I'm afraid the first thing I noticed was that you'd cut off your ponytail at last! You told me you'd done it to celebrate your thirtieth now that you'd joined the ranks of the 'young middle aged'.

'Welcome to the club,' I said, and I caught you looking at me to check I was joking.

It often takes a little time for us to settle back into our banter, but we always enjoy sparring with each other in front of works of art, don't we? That was why we'd arranged to meet to see the exhibition 'Alan Davie and David Hockney: Early Works'. I'd hoped this show might be nicely provocative but, as you'll remember, it completely knocked me for six.

That labyrinth of white spaces! We'd just about got attuned to the large semi-abstract canvases when we turned a corner to be confronted by a picture of shocking crudeness: two indeterminate figures attempting to kiss, one arm reaching out to grasp the other against the wall of – possibly – a urinal? It was splashed haphazardly with obscene slogans and love hearts. The picture was deliberately *art brut*, of course – a homage to Jean Dubuffet, maybe? And all the more startling coming from Hockney who draws as beautifully as Ingres. Then I saw the title: *We Two Boys Together Clinging*.

Oh my God, those words! I knew just where they came from. And a moment's inspection of the canvas showed me that all the lewd graffiti were the lines from Walt Whitman's defiant poem. I gasped inwardly in surprise and recognition.

'What do you make of this?' I managed to ask, playing for time.

'Is it "cottaging", 1960s style?' you almost joked. 'It's raw... but quite tender... nice soft blues, pinks and greys – are they symbolic? ... What's all the graffiti trying to say?'

'Let me read it for you.'

I knew it off by heart, of course. How could I ever have forgotten a single word?

'We two boys together clinging,
One the other never leaving,
Up and down the roads going,
North and South excursions making,
Power enjoying, elbows stretching, fingers clutching,
Arm'd and fearless, eating, drinking, sleeping, loving.
No law less than ourselves owning, sailing, soldiering,
thieving, threatening,
Misers, menials, priests alarming, air breathing, water
drinking, on the turf or the sea-beach dancing,
Cities wrenching, ease scorning, statutes mocking,
feebleness chasing,
Fulfilling our foray.'

All those participles came rolling out – all twenty-four of them, I remember now – in quick succession: 'clinging... clutching... drinking... sleeping... loving...' They sounded like hailstones dropping heavily into a basin of still water, making ripples, bouncing back from the edge, crashing into each other, creating a storm of confusion.

I had to sit down. You took my arm and helped me to a bench nearby. You asked what had upset me. Was it the picture? Or the poem?

It had been *me*, the sound of my own voice bringing up those words and images from so long ago, which had confounded me. They were coming on too quickly to focus: moments of joy, and then one of inexpressible sadness. There we were again, We Two Boys, dressed up to the nines, standing in front of the mirror before my eighteenth, my arm across his shoulder, saying nice, sweet, boyish things to each other; then he and I lying in the grass, me overwhelmed by his beauty, his closeness, and the sound of his voice, so rich and gritty.

As we passed through the foyer, there was a video

with Andrew McMillan reciting the Whitman poem in his strong South Yorkshire voice and with a twinkle in his eye. I remembered how I had envied those boys in the poem, and still do – especially now! How brazen they were! They'd been so happy with each other and their adventure; they didn't give a damn about where they were heading, or what they were doing. But we, the readers, are left hanging in the air wondering. What was their story? Did they get away with it? How did it end?

We took our lunch trays into the garden and sat ourselves on the paved terrace surrounded by raised beds carefully planted with shrubs and spring flowers. Huge, empty, Piranesian warehouses loomed over us.

'Come on, Uncle Freddie, I want to hear about that poem,' you said. You added, smiling, with a hint of forgivable prurience, as if to coax me further, 'I'm very broad-minded, you know.'

I laughed and said you'd certainly need to be once I got started. I told you how the poem had been adopted by me and my first love as our special 'motif' or 'national anthem', all those years ago. How the two of us had dreamt that we might be like those two boys, living our own picaresque adventure, creating a self-contained little world without caring about anyone else.

As I was speaking, I felt an overwhelming need to articulate something, almost anything, to express what I was now feeling. Then I heard a voice in my ear, barely a whisper:

'Go on, Freddie, tell Sam the whole story. You must do it. Remember that last night when you were together. You thought your love had made you immortal; here's your chance to tell it.'

Now I come to think of it, perhaps it was the voice of my long-suffering guardian angel who I'd been neglecting for the past half-century.

*

And so, Sam, let me take you back to the third week of September 1966, the year England famously won the World Cup. The autumn term at Upton Abbey School was just beginning. Most of us who lived in the South were on the specially chartered train – with some of GWR's most battered carriages – leaving Paddington for Stroud via Cheltenham. My friends, all of us sixteen-year-olds in Ambrose House, had purloined a whole vacant compartment for ourselves, locked the door and pulled down the blinds on the inside. The banter and bragging were only to be expected after two months' holiday as we put our feet up on the seats and puffed away on our last 'legal' cigarettes – 'gaspers' or 'fags', we called them. The atmosphere soon became agreeably warm and fuggy.

My offering was a typically pretentious bottle of lukewarm duty-free Asti I'd brought back from Sicily where I'd been staying with Galbraith's family in Taormina. We prised it open with a loud plop, to great acclaim, and then handed it round, everyone drinking straight from the bottle trying hard not to be outwitted by the resurging bubbles.

'Is your sister still seeing Waybrook?' asked the ever-hopeful Scrope.

'You're telling me,' I replied. 'He came to stay for a whole week's sailing at the cottage. I had to share my room with him and his revolting socks. He and Pippa were going around together all the time. But I think she's getting fed up with his moods.'

'Perhaps I could start writing to her?' he asked, looking expectant.

'You could try, but I'm not sure she'll answer. She can be very picky.'

Poor old Scrope had been waiting in the wings for the past six months. I didn't have the heart to tell him that with his glasses and terrible acne he wasn't exactly your mother's type. As for Waybrook, I always thought he was an arrogant smoothie.

He probably despised me equally as an irredeemable pervert. But we had to put up with each other as our mothers were like sisters.

This group was what I called my 'mainstream' friends, some dating back to my time at prep school and mostly from the extended Catholic cousinhood, which, even at this late date, provided a certain tribal identity. My other, more exotic, half-foreign friends must have been returning to school by alternative routes. Our talk was all about girls, parties, water-skiing, where we'd watched The Match on TV and all the rest. I was thankful to be part of this, although in the back of my mind I wasn't always comfortable with everything this camaraderie represented. It was simply that I knew I was a bit different from the others, and to be fair, most of these fellows recognised that. No one seemed to mind, since by now we'd all become very used to each other. I knew perfectly well what my difference consisted of but didn't know yet where it was leading. Whether or not I'd be able to stand up to the inevitable consequences was still an unknown.

No one else in that compartment knew it, but there was one person in particular whom I was truly aching to see again. My heart beat faster every time I thought of him as we drew closer to Upton. Might he have changed in the past two months? What would be his attitude now he'd become Head of House?

The windows had steamed up so much that even with the blinds raised it was impossible to see the passing landscape or the towns that hardly any of us would ever visit by choice. A raucous sing-song got going, including the 'Eton Boating Song' with some alternative and highly improper lyrics.

How different this was from my train journey home from Sicily a few weeks ago, entirely on my own, after my father – your dear grandfather, Sam – had refused to buy me an air ticket because of the additional cost. I well remember feeling indignant but could hardly complain. I spent most of the journey standing in the passage, my imagination in overdrive as we tore past places with such romantic associations: the Bay of Naples, the Roman Campagna, the Ligurian Riviera, then over the Alps via Milan and Domodossola (what a beautiful name!) and on to Paris. How familiar that route was to become in a few years! Just as exciting was the unfamiliar *frisson* as I let those dark-eyed Italian boys brush past me, especially the young soldiers, giving me a courteous '*Permesso*'. I couldn't resist taking a backward glance as they strode down the passage with supreme assurance, admiring their elegant figures, so tantalising in their neatly pressed khaki trousers and shirts.

After being decanted into the waiting coaches at Stroud for the last leg of the journey, this unwieldy cargo finally disgorged itself into the main quad at Upton. The sun was getting low but was still strong enough for the fine Gothic-revival buildings and the abbey church to cast their long shadows over the gravel. Just at that moment the familiar sound of the triple peals for the Angelus rang out – the call to midday and evening prayer reminding us, and the world, of the Incarnation:

The Word was made flesh
And dwelt amongst us.

Alas, that day its sublime message was lost in the prevailing confusion.

By the time everyone had orientated themselves, found their new rooms or dormitories and unpacked their trunks, it was time for supper. This was followed by an extended free time until the bell for the bedtime routine. In Ambrose all seventy boys assembled in the main dormitory, a big open-vaulted interior, standing beside their bed-cubicles. My new berth this term was almost de luxe, with its own side window and fitted chest of drawers, situated about three quarters of the way around the perimeter, thereby reflecting my recent advance in seniority. Those who slept in the adjoining juniors' dormitory, or the older boys with their own rooms, crowded around the two doors. A background hubbub prevailed, with some light ragging among the more spirited individuals taking advantage of the duty prefect's distraction.

A general hush descended as the housemaster, Dom Gabriel, adjusting the cowl of his monk's habit, entered the dormitory accompanied by Fitzpatrick himself, the new Head of House, and the six house prefects.

At last; this was the moment I'd been waiting for. My heart leapt as he came into view – the boy, now surely a man, with whom I'd been smitten last term. Those feelings of intense admiration came rushing back. He seemed to have become even more untouchably handsome since I had last seen him over two months ago, if such a thing were possible. Now he was sporting his new dove-grey double-breasted waistcoat – a sartorial detail of immense prestige, endowing him with an aura of heroic glamour. How often I had dreamt of the day when *I* might be able to wear this prized item reserved only for this most senior of roles. His acolytes, the house prefects, looked utterly pedestrian in their equivalent versions in black. Everyone else had to make do with standard single-breasted black waistcoats worn under our morning suits: plain black jackets, pin-striped trousers, white shirts, stiff collars and black ties.

The task for the Head of House was to carry the silver asperges bucket containing the holy water, walking behind the housemaster as they processed around the dormitory blessing the assembled company. Dom Gabriel would dip the *aspergilium*, or sprinkling brush, into the bucket from time to time, then wave it in the air in different directions, hoping everyone would receive a good dowsing. It was a symbolic cleansing of our sins of that day before we proceeded shortly to our bodily ablutions in the washrooms below. A side-benefit – it was hoped – was that we might be strengthened against the nocturnal temptations of the Devil.

As he set forth Dom Gabriel began the '*Miserere*':

'Have mercy on me, O God, in your kindness...'

We all took up the rest of the psalm, reciting it from beginning to end by which time he had circumnavigated the whole dormitory. Dom Gabriel's new liberal regime had recently ordained that it should now be said in English instead of Latin. That was a shame, in my view – an early example of my highly selective counter-culturalism and weakness for lost causes.

As the little procession approached my cubicle I tried to catch Fitzpatrick's eye. Last term, more than once, he had reciprocated my longing glances with truly beatific smiles. Today...

Oh no! What a disappointment! What cruelty!

All I got was an icy stare.

That night I fancy my pillow was wet through with the tears of rejection and my bedclothes dishevelled with the restlessness of fury. Alas for the disappointments of youth!

More to the point, it is Dom Gabriel who is the more significant player in this story. I admired him very much, although I had been a bit shy of him in my first year or so. He was still youthful, even in our eyes, and with his dark curly hair and knowing smile, was one of the most popular and charismatic of the school's seven housemasters. He smoked a pipe, and his panelled study, with its deep leather easy chairs, always reeked deliciously of his favourite St Bruno brand. Of course, the pipe was a subterfuge and a thoroughly un-monastic affectation. But it allowed him a moment of drama as he paused to relight it during a tricky conversation, using slow deliberate hand movements, sometimes stealing a glance at his now-flummoxed interlocutor. Before he'd become a monk he'd read

English at Cambridge, supervised by the great F.R. Leavis, and been Secretary of the Union.

Most boys understood implicitly how his celibate monastic status gave him a unique bond with each and every one of us. All his paternal instincts were directed towards us, his adopted family. Some boys just never 'got it', however, and thought all the monks were closet paedos. In those more innocent times, strangely enough, there were no serious grounds for anyone to believe that. Thirty years later, of course, the evidence began to stack up. Most of us still believe it was just a case of one or two 'bad apples'. But it's been enough to ruin their reputation forever.

Depending on each boy's 'attitude' – which could be pretty volatile – Dom Gabriel would be acknowledged with signals varying from a guilty glance to broad grins. I'd just learnt I was to be in his and Dom Benet's group for my second-year sixth-form English: Milton (*Comus*), Shakespeare (*The Tempest*), Yeats, E.M. Forster and Henry James. I was raring to go.

*

Next morning at precisely seven o'clock the duty house prefect burst through the double doors into the dormitory, switching on all the lights simultaneously, and ringing a large brass handbell with sadistic vigour. The chorus of groans and whimpers emanating from under the crumpled bedclothes expressed a predictably adolescent response to this unwelcome reveille. After a third warning by the exasperated prefect the worst and slowest offenders would have the sheets and blankets summarily ripped off their beds. There was more than a whiff of testosterone and other suspicious rancid smells, which the prefect did his best to dispel by throwing open the nearest windows. Only the most determined ephebophile could relish such a scene.

An equally unsightly routine now followed as the entire

school made its way from every direction towards the abbey church for Mass. The yawning, resentful teenagers, some with stiff collars left undone, others with shirt-tails hanging out, were sprawled across the rush-bottomed chairs trying to make themselves as comfortable as possible. If anyone had their head in their hands, they certainly weren't praying.

After what seemed like an age without sustenance, we'd be ravenous for breakfast, usually consisting of vast quantities of hot porridge, bacon, eggs and baked beans, bread and marmalade, all washed down by gallons of sweet milky tea. (Consult the Jennings books for the general picture – or even Harry Potter.) By which time most boys had pulled themselves together sufficiently to gather in their house dayrooms for a short assembly.

In Ambrose this was another huge draughty room with a ping-pong table at one end and a billiards table at the other. Around the sides the robust Arts and Crafts panelling contained built-in lockers while the space between the windows was filled with a dusty trophy cabinet. There were a couple of big lumpy sofas, battered easy chairs and window seats, and two large oak tables on which were strewn the daily newspapers and a few carefully vetted glossies including *The Illustrated London News*, *Punch* and *Paris Match*. Dim portraits of ecclesiastics and a giant crucifix clad the upper walls. The house record player, an indestructible Dynatron capable of truly ghetto-blasting volume, and the single black and white television were the most prized fixtures. Their use involved an impenetrable Byzantine protocol.

For the morning house assembly everyone ranged themselves in a wide arc centred on the housemaster who would stand with his back to the trophy cabinet. Tradition decreed that the most junior boys stood to his right and the most senior to his left, with everyone else taking up their places in between. My position in this unofficial *placement* was therefore towards the centre, veering slightly towards the left of Dom Gabriel.

Within my sightlines I could distinguish a wide gamut of youthful physiognomies. They were principally Anglo-Saxon but with a few Latin, Asian and African variations, reflecting the school's catholicity. Near to me was Lee from Hong Kong, short, wiry and inscrutable – incredibly bright, with a scholarship for Harvard in the offing, and a sprightly little hooker in the scrum. Next to him was his close friend de Courcy, nephew of the French Prime Minister, tall and handsome with classical features, beautifully mannered and obviously destined for the Quai d'Orsay. In total contrast was Clementi, congenitally obese but transparently good-natured. His father owned a string of ice cream vans in Scotland and was the generous sponsor of our periodic 'feasts'. The urbane but tough Lascelles, from Barbados, had had a difficult start but was now becoming our star turn in the inter-house boxing tournaments.

Fitzpatrick was there of course, next to Dom Gabriel. I could hardly bear to look at him after last night. But, summoning up courage, I raised my eyes to take him in. To my relief, there was nothing at all – no rush of affection, no swelling of the heart, no impulse to grab his attention. Instead, all I saw was a medium-sized boy, fumbling about with today's agenda, definitely out of his depth in his new role. *Pathetic!* How blind I must have been, how foolish. Thank goodness that was all over with.

But I had a lesson to learn: nature abhors a vacuum.

I continued looking around me. Other examples of youthful expression included the cheeky subversiveness of Langton, positively proud of having been overlooked as a prefect; the air of supercilious entitlement of the elder of my two cousins in the school, Scarisbrick Ma, one year older than me; or the painful timidity of some of the younger ones, like sad little Dodsworth, standing opposite, always seemingly on the point of tears, poor boy.

Yet the overall impression was one of resignation; most people would probably admit to being not-entirely-unhappy and prepared to make the best of it. Ambrose was well known as a liberal and easy-going place. Its civilised, even quite sophisticated, ambience was largely Dom Gabriel's personal achievement. Floggings by him were now almost unheard-of and the prefects were no longer allowed to administer physical chastisement at their own discretion. Without bragging about it, we Ambrosians were quite proud of our overrepresentation among the past and present holders of prizes in the music, art and literary fields, as well as our better-than-average ratings in the inter-house sports ladders. No wonder I'd done my utmost to switch to this house having heard of unpleasant tales in the one to which I had originally been assigned.

As if to compensate for the uniformity of our school outfits, it was the way we lavished attention on our hairstyles and sideburns that betrayed our individualism and general trendiness. Most of us wore our hair as long as the recently liberalised rules allowed, unthinkable only five years ago: Buttricks and some of his cohort had adopted Beatles-style mop-tops or 'curtains' since last term – not very flattering in my eyes. One or two, like Kutchinski and Acton, had cultivated a suave swept-back poetic look, which I rather admired, imitating Rupert Brooke or even Oscar Wilde. At the opposite end of the spectrum, a very few ultra-conservative types, including Dillon and O'Brien – probably anticipating their future in the Irish Guards – wore their hair super-short with a sharp parting, slicked back with hair cream shining as glossily as their shoes.

Close beside me were my contemporaries, in mid-career. On the whole we were an unremarkable lot, most of us now having reached our full height but some still needing to 'fill out', as my mother would say, leaving us looking slightly disproportionate.

I myself had long legs, well-formed thighs and a fleshy, rounded bottom, which seemed to attract some not-always-unwelcome stroking and pinching in the showers.

Don't be too shocked, Sam; such gropings were par for the course and quite flattering, I suppose! Perhaps my easy acquiescence of such attentions was a discreet acknowledgment that I was a not-entirely-closeted Homo. Although I never went so far as to positively invite admiration, unlike some.

*

My *amour propre* – at least concerning my appearance – had received an unexpected fillip during the holidays. I was on my way home from Hurlingham on the Underground still wearing my tennis kit. Sitting opposite me was a tall, hippyish fellow, with long blond curly hair, who kept smiling at me and looking me up and down. His hand was embarrassingly just a little too close to his crotch and I tried not to look. As he opened and closed his manspread our knees would knock and I'd feel a nice little shudder pass through my body and something moved under my jockstrap. I kept trying to look away, but it was no good and I found myself smiling back.

As we approached Earl's Court he stood up to leave. He leant over towards me, giving me a wink, saying softly,

'Bye for now, gorgeous.'

I felt so flattered that I couldn't resist giving him a winsome little smile. Perhaps that was why, just as he was stepping off the train, he looked round at me again and blew me a kiss. For a split second I was tempted to get up and follow him; what an adventure that might have been! It became a subject of many nocturnal fantasies! But panic set in, and I stayed put. Later I realised he was obviously stoned, but even so I felt tremendously heartened. I swore to myself I'd never be so feeble again.

*

Since this was the first assembly of the new school year, I was not the only one keen to inspect the new intake of boys, now 'fags', who had moved up from their year in the Junior House. The lineup of a dozen boys standing opposite me in different profiles and attitudes briefly resembled the sculptured frieze of a classical temple.

For goodness' sake, Sam, don't confuse the word 'fag' in this context with the American meaning of the word, or, heaven forbid, 'faggots'. Or even how it was used as slang for cigarettes. In the English public school tradition 'fags' were the junior boys who were assigned to the seniors and prefects – their 'fag-masters' – to do small errands like cleaning shoes, making tea and so on. It was supposed to give each a sense of responsibility for the other. In principle it was quite a good idea but it often led to resentment, or alternatively to some quite overintense relationships. The question of whether institutional 'fagging' – excuse the inelegant phrase – should be abolished was a perennial one in the school debating societies.

Among the new boys standing opposite me there was one who immediately stood out: shortish, smooth-skinned, fine jet-black hair, an oval face, and big, inviting doe eyes. He was looking directly across at us with a cheeky smile, suggesting he knew all about his potential charms. He was indeed a prize 'lush', as these particularly attractive pubescent boys were known, capable of ravishing or breaking many hearts by granting or withholding real or imagined favours. My overly precocious friend 'Pips' Phillips, standing next to me – evidently having stolen his sister's eye-liner (later confiscated) – saw the direction in which I was looking and whispered loudly in my ear,

'My dear, he's called Rowse – pronounced "Rose", don't you

know. "'What a pretty boy! Such an impertinent air!" as the divine Marcel once said.'

My other friend, Williamson, overhearing him added, imitating a Cockney rudeboy,

'Cor! 'E'll be the new 'owse tart alright. Looks as though 'e'll be up for it, too.'

But it was the boy standing next to the new house tart, and to whom he was now speaking, that caught my eye. He looked really, really interesting, and somehow different from the usual ideals of ephebic beauty. He seemed a little older than his immediate neighbours, and taller, his face with graceful tapering cheeks, a honey-coloured complexion, wide-set eyes and a softly modelled nose. His hair was thick and curly, slightly tousled, with some locks flopping casually across his forehead. But there was more to him than a mere shallow prettiness; it was his expression of detachment, a sort of pensive melancholy, that made him stand out so strikingly. In a flash I was reminded of the unknown Renaissance prince, the poster boy for the recent exhibition of Florentine portraits at the RA seen all over the London Underground that summer. I'd been mesmerised by that elusive image, constantly obscured by passing trains, or just out of view as I ascended or descended the escalators. Here was his long-lost brother – right here in front of me – sharing just the same intangible allure, inviting respect and deference and – once I looked closer – yes, *complete adoration.*

'Who's the fellow next to young pretty-pants?' I asked Pips, without taking my eyes off the vision ahead of me.

'That's Shipton. But he's much too serious for you, BoyO. You wouldn't stand a chance.'

I bristled inwardly and felt like giving my supposed friend a kick. Do people still think I'm a frivolous airhead? Dammit, I think I'd be quite a catch.

Ignoring him, I continued staring at the boy. All of a sudden a burst of bright autumn sunshine streaked diagonally across the room, right in front of where he was standing, as though a searchlight had been switched on in the wings. I watched as it caught a million little shimmering particles glistening in the air, rising and falling, enveloping the boy in a translucent haze.

And then I really saw him.

In that brief moment, emerging out of that mirage of ethereal light he seemed transfigured: no longer just an icon or poster boy, but the living and breathing embodiment of manly beauty and youthful innocence.

Deep within me I felt a sharp pain, as though an angel had shot an arrow or plunged a dart into my heart making it burst and bleed. I felt my body shiver, and then a numbness as my mouth became parched. The angel was whispering in my ear as he pierced me again and again,

'This Is Him. He's The One For You. Go For Him!'

I averted my eyes for an instant, attempting to resist the boy's magnetism. Looking up to gaze across again I became conscious of his autumnal, thoughtful eyes, and the set of resignation in his mouth; did they not suggest a vulnerability, an unresolved inner life? How I'd love to know how he was coping with those hopes and fears that swirled around in the hearts and minds of us teenage boys: identity, loyalty, faith, ambition... desire... and love.

This near-supernatural epiphany dissolved in slow motion as he turned to his neighbour once again. That look of distance and sadness vanished as his face lit up in the momentary animation of a smile, making his eyes bigger and sparkling, and his mouth expose a dazzling set of white teeth between his dark red lips.

I groaned inwardly as the angel made another thrust.

The boy must have sensed something, even at that distance. I saw him look across the room, searching for the source of the unseen power I was directing at him. Our eyes met, and, for a second they locked. Now I willed him to hold my gaze so that he'd remember me, mark me out from the crowd. I managed a quivering smile and then a little nod of my head; his acknowledgement was a reticent half-smile, but so sweet I thought the remains of my heart would finally break up. Then he blushed and looked down at his feet. I cursed myself for having made him feel uneasy. Now all I wanted was to hold him and comfort him, put my arms around him and tell him I'd meant him no harm.

Who could he be? Where did he come from? How could I find out more about him?

From that moment I made it my business to discover everything I could, looking at notice boards, checking lists, and asking discreet questions here and there. He was Paul Shipton, fourteen years old, soon to be fifteen, good at sports and likely to be in the Colts teams. He was obviously bright, being in the top fifth-form streams for English, History and French.

My heart sank as I realised we were unlikely to meet with much regularity in the innocent routines of school life. I would have to be creative in finding ways to encounter him. Whatever happened, I still needed to be careful not to attract undue attention, either from the authorities, or even – at this stage – from some of my friends and contemporaries. In matters of the heart there were certain complicated and unwritten rules to be observed. I'd had my fingers burned once before and had learnt my lesson. Since then, I'd tried hard – despite myself – to remain well within the bounds of the 'conveniently broadminded' attitude of this side of life at Upton.

His Christian name, Paul, took on wonderful evocations and resonances as I spent hours daydreaming about him, repeating his name over and over in my head, sometimes whispering it softly to myself, or even saying it very quietly out loud, as though calling and yearning for him. It was a slightly unusual first name at this time. But for me, right now, it meant him, uniquely him. I came to love its euphony; the short, sweet monosyllable expressed a magical combination of sounds, both hard and soft – with its sharp first consonant, the soft diphthong of the two elided middle vowels, almost a soft 'a' and the final consonant, which seemed to die away: 'P... AU... L...' In my daydreams I would pronounce it longingly in French: *Pŏl* – quiet and mysterious; or in Italian: *Paolo* – sexy and exciting.

Sam, it's been more than fifty years and I still find it impossible to describe this encounter objectively. Just remembering it now, and writing about it, has unnerved me so much that I have to break off.

*

Who has ever been able to describe, let alone recapture, their feelings the moment they first fell in love? I just didn't know what had hit me; it was something completely outside my experience. All I could do was to abandon myself to this transcendence, praying it would lead me to where I wanted to go. I knew instinctively that I had been in the presence of Beauty Incarnate. Not just a beautiful work of art or of nature, like a beautiful song or a sunset, but a living, breathing, beautiful being.

Now all I could think about was how to possess the boy, to hold him in my arms and gaze at him forever. I desperately wanted to smother him with gifts; to give, give and keep on giving to him, recklessly, extravagantly. Maybe such crazy generosity would result in a smile from him, at least. But then it wasn't long before more carnal feelings kicked in: desire, no less; and later still, more noble feelings – love, surely.

Some may say that, as a sixteen-year-old, I must have been ready for it, on the grounds that if I couldn't fall in love with a girl – because there were none – it was only natural that I should fall for a boy. That may have been true in principle, and it was a theory many people clung to, but it needed to be tested. Which it was, in due course, as we'll see.

*

How can anyone call public school life 'privileged'? The damage that many of these places caused, and the bullying and abuse that went on, have been written about often enough. Even in the most enlightened places, like Upton, it was the mental cruelty of some of the boys that had the most devastating effect – until, somehow, the victims learnt to live with it. At prep school the physical discomforts had been even worse: cold showers every morning for example – a minimum of ten seconds under the slow, freezing drips. Real torture! There was no telephone in the whole place, and all letters were censored. Even the lavatory paper was rationed to four sheets per boy each morning! At Upton at least there were two payphones for about 600 boys. But there was almost no privacy, sleeping in dormitories until you got your own room in your last year or two. And as for the lavatories, 'the bogs' as they were called... I could go on and on! And the cost to our parents was approximately the same as a new family car each year, for both your mother and me. You can imagine the sacrifices all this entailed for many parents; yet to have done anything less for their children would have been unthinkable at the time.

The strange thing was that all this squalor was wrapped around in intimations of great beauty at almost every turn: the huge golden-stoned abbey church itself – a vision of medieval glamour come to life; the Arts and Crafts school buildings; the landscaped grounds; the plainchant of the monks; the treasures of the library; and all the opportunities that were on offer –

music, art, drama. And of course, the beautiful young men into whom we were morphing.

With my love,

Freddie

P.S. Sorry, but I'm going to postpone sending this first letter for the moment; I need some time and space to mull over some of my confessions before committing them to you irretrievably!

2

My dear Sam,

My first letter – still unsent, I'm afraid, but I'm going to plough on anyway – ended with my trying to recapture something of the intensity I'd felt when I first saw Paul that morning. It was a truly life-changing moment but, as I hope I've implied, it didn't exactly come from nowhere. Looking back now, I can see how it was the inevitable result of many things I'd been finding out about myself over the years.

If I were to identify a precise date when I made the first of these discoveries, I would pinpoint early September 1959. I was nine years old, and the country was in the grip of a general election campaign with Harold Macmillan claiming, 'You've never had it so good.' That slogan certainly didn't ring true for me! The summer holidays would soon be over, unfortunately, and I would have to return to my loathsome preparatory school on the south coast. Perhaps as a reward for sticking it out there over the past year – but also to take my mind off my imminent return – my parents had decided to take me with them to Spain for the last fortnight of the holidays. I had been thrilled, and my excitable nature was in high expectation of new sights, sounds and experiences. Your mother, Sam, being two years younger than me, was sent off to ride Shetland ponies in Wales, accompanied by Nanny Doreen.

In those far-off days my parents always preferred to take the car, a somewhat elongated Vauxhall Velox – turquoise, with lots of gleaming chrome, quite stylish now I come to think of it – and cross the Channel on the Folkestone–Boulogne ferry. Having disembarked, my father would manoeuvre it onto the double-decker trailer that brought up the rear of the waiting overnight train to Lyons. Once this – to my anxious eyes – precarious and time-consuming operation had been achieved we would make a dash for the celebrated Restaurant de la Gare Maritime, the proud holder of a single Michelin rosette.

For all its reputation the restaurant was not luxurious. This first time, as I entered, I was taken unawares with the sudden blast of humidity, which made my glasses steam up. My young nostrils were filled with the rich combination of meaty and fishy effusions wafting from tureens brimful with soups and ragouts. The tables had crisp white linen cloths and napkins, constantly being laid and relaid by busy waitresses in black dresses, little white pinnies and strange old-fashioned *chignon* hairdos. Others were scurrying around carrying enormous covered dishes or balancing piles of finished plates on their arms. They were making a great deal of chatter with a proprietorial air – either trying to move the customers along, making up *l'addition*, or flirting with the regulars. In contrast to these almost demonic figures were the elegant young waiters, in their little bow ties and immaculate long white aprons, bringing drinks to the tables with an insouciance I could only admire.

Then there were the fellow diners. Glancing round, I guessed that perhaps half were English, heading for the *wagons-lits* like us, mainly young-middle-aged couples like my parents. There were almost no other children; after all, it was the very end of the school holidays.

The other half looked as though they might be locals, maybe even regulars, some obviously at 'their table': burly late-middle-aged gentlemen with their napkins tied under their chins, unashamedly tucking into their favourite dishes; a pair of handsome but sallow-faced young *curés* in *soutanes* with soft briefcases on the floor beside them; a group of mighty French *grand-mères*, shapeless in their enveloping black coats, which spread down to the floor, their multiple chins wobbling in animated conversation. Complete with their battered felt hats, I was reminded of Grandma in the famous Giles cartoons from the *Daily Express*.

Then there were the younger French couples – so different from their English counterparts, not just in their clothes and body language, but deep in conversation, entirely wrapped up in each other, with eyes for no one else. The men were dark, intelligent-looking, conversing with much gesticulation and shrugging of shoulders. The women were small but with sharp features, beautifully dressed and made up. Somehow, in the way they looked at their men so darkly, holding their cigarettes so effortlessly and elegantly, they seemed not only to engage with them completely, but also to control them. I thought I'd try imitating their hand movements one day when no one was looking; it would be good practice for when I started to smoke myself. How different they were to the pretty English ladies sitting nearby with their more muted gestures and expressions.

I looked on in horror and amazement as my parents tucked in to half a dozen *escargots à la bourguignonne*, swimming in oily garlic and smelling sweet and sickly. I played reluctantly with the strange and slightly obscene *saucisses de Strasbourg* in front of me. Their rather bland taste was compensated entirely by the delicious *frites*, such as were completely unknown in England, let alone at my prep school, where bog-standard plain greasy 'chips' were rationed – as though a treat – to just once a week, with our Friday fish. For pudding I loved the idea of an *îsle flottant*, or a *baba au rhum*, but my mother assured me they would make me sick, so I stuck to a chocolate ice cream.

'Now we're in France, Freddie,' said my father, with a waiter standing nearby holding a bottle of red wine, 'would you like to try a glass of wine if we dilute it with water, just like all the French boys and girls?'

I didn't really like the idea. For one thing it was an alarming-looking colour, seeming to match my mother's vivid red lipstick, its shade described on the little cylinder with the beautiful French word *cramoisy*. But I sensed this was something of an occasion and I shouldn't ask for Ribena, let alone a glass of milk, either of which I would have greatly preferred.

'Chin, chin, darling,' said my mother as we lifted our glasses.

'Here's to your first glass of wine, Freddie,' echoed my father. 'And I hope you'll enjoy many more as you get older.'

I took a sip from my glass. It tasted rather bitter. I was tempted to pull a face, but again I knew this was supposed to be a treat, a rite of passage perhaps, and I'd better pretend to enjoy it. Anyway, it had turned a pretty rosé colour.

'You can't trust the tap water in France, Freddie, even less in Spain.' He said we'd be stocking up with bottled water next day. I thought how ridiculous to pay for something that fell out of the sky for nothing.

My mother suggested I might practise my French by shopping for our picnic tomorrow: bread, cheese, ham, perhaps an apple tart. I felt a little alarmed at the responsibility but agreed provided they weren't too far away in case I needed help.

I quite liked French at school, taught by a magnificent tri-lingual, somewhat emotional half-Polish colonel. He insisted that the whole class learn the irregular verbs by rote, reciting them all together out loud as though we were on parade. I loved the sound of the words, the way they rolled their r's, the vowels with their different accents, and the subtle way they left the last letter silent. Sometimes their phrases sounded so much more expressive than in English: *double entendre* and *bien aisé* were some of my favourites, as was *tête à tête*. I also had a mini boy-crush on my comic book hero, the fresh-faced young detective Tintin, with his cute little turned-up fringe.

Perhaps another reason my parents had decided to take me on this holiday was because I was quite good at keeping myself company and had no need to be constantly supervised or entertained. My headmaster had indeed written of me in a recent school report, '*Frederick has decided what is going to be "his world", leaving all else to be just not "his business"*.'

This may have been prescient in many ways, and if it implied an indifference to those school activities I found disagreeable, like team games, especially football, or, in the classroom, mathematics or science, he was entirely correct. But I hope he did not mean an insensitivity to other boys or to people around me. If so he had definitely – and not for the last time – misread me. Certainly, the shock and brutality of boarding school life had had the effect of making me clam up, becoming defensive and jealous of my own space. The snatching away of all the familiar and happy routines of home life had at first bewildered me. Being naturally affectionate, I found there was a huge gap in my heart waiting to be filled by someone with whom I could share my enthusiasms, little pleasures and secrets, someone to lark about with, and show off to.

And so we clambered on board the *wagons-lits*, and found our sleeping compartment. There it was, that indefinable, oily smell, forever afterwards associated with the SNCF and evoking long journeys to new and strange places. It was very different to the suffocating smokiness of English trains always taking me to predictable destinations, some welcome, others definitely not. As it was still just about daylight I wanted to stand in the passage to look out at all the new sights of the French countryside. My father tried to disillusion me by telling me it wasn't like England at all; they didn't have fields and hedgerows, and most of northern France was just one big flat plain. Southern France would be far more memorable.

'But will it still be light when we pass through Paris?' I asked, hoping I might at least be able to glimpse the Eiffel Tower or the Sacré Coeur and earn some esteem from my friends when I told them back at school.

'I'm afraid it'll be nearly midnight and you'll be in bed by then. Anyway, it won't be very interesting, as we arrive at the dirty Gare du Nord, then the train goes around the back streets to the Gare de Lyon before heading south.'

This was all a bit disappointing. At the beginning of the holidays, way back in July, my father had taken me up to the West End to see the new film *A Tale of Two Cities*, with the wonderfully dark and handsome Dirk Bogarde and the delicately petite Dorothy Tutin.

I had been transfixed by the story and had begged him to buy me a children's edition of the book to read to me in bed. I loved snuggling up to him in my pyjamas so that I could catch the delicious lemony aroma of his hair oil, bought by my mother and me from a tiny shop in the Burlington Arcade for his Christmas present. Then, when he'd finished, I'd enjoy the ticklish feel of his moustache on my soft cheek as he kissed me goodnight. I would slide under the bedclothes to dream of the beautiful châteaux and elegant ladies being rescued by handsome young fellows.

Even better had been *Gigi*, with the unbelievably *soigné* Louis Jordan being driven in his elegant landau in a lavender suit and a shiny top hat. Paris seemed to encapsulate everything that was smart and stylish, where all the men were impossibly romantic and all the pretty ladies 'had an interesting past' (as my mother put it – whatever that meant). I had pestered my parents endlessly to take me to Maxim's to see all the glamorous people when I was old enough. As my mother said, more than once, and only half in jest,

'What an *impossible* child you are, darling!'

I rather enjoyed being impossible, sometimes.

I never slept very well on the *wagons-lits*, despite proper sheets, pillows and blankets, and their being much more comfortable than the couchettes in which we travelled to Switzerland after Christmas. Although the constant movement and rhythmic noise – *clackety-clack, clackety-clack*, like Nanny Doreen's knitting needles – was semi-soporific, I kept waking up, especially whenever we jolted to a stop, wondering at what exciting place we had arrived.

Next morning we disembarked at Lyons into the warm blast of the Midi, jolting uncomfortably over the cobbled streets as we left the town heading south. Then came the vineyards each side of the Rhône valley. There was still no motorway so it was slow going as we passed through every town and village, stopping at traffic lights and pedestrian crossings. No wonder we were only intending to reach Arles for the night. With luck we'd reach the Costa Brava by evening the next day. At a small village we stopped for coffee, sitting outside in a shady square while I was sent forth to find provisions for our picnic lunch. I must have acquitted myself well as I had no need to call for my parents.

Somewhere between Valence and Montélimar the temperature rose quite noticeably, and the sun became more intense. Sitting on the back seat of the car in my ruckled-up linen shorts I could feel my bare thighs getting sticky against the leatherette, and further up, my crotch becoming a bit moist under my summer aertex briefs; it wasn't at all unpleasant.

All the while I was looking out of the window, partly open to allow the breeze to keep me cool while I relished the new sights. Then, suddenly, there it was: a huge billboard proclaiming,

'*Ambre Solaire: comme la nature!*'

There was a group of maybe eight happy, smiling young people playing netball on a golden sandy beach with a deep azure sky behind them. They may have been in their late teens or early twenties but they all, of course, had perfect bodies. The girls were in bikinis and the boys wearing skimpy swimsuits of a new kind from Australia known as Speedos ('budgie smugglers'!), which made their bodies look like elegant sculptures. They had been artfully choreographed so that they each presented themselves at a slightly different angle: a couple were full frontal, another in half-profile, while one girl and one boy showed their backs. There was a girl reclining on the sand in the foreground, propping herself up with her elbows, while beside her was a boy sitting upright. They were all tanned to an almost uniform golden honey colour, the effect enhanced by the pastel shades of their swimwear.

The girls' bodies were slim without being skimpy, and rounded in all the right places, their cleavages modelled beautifully by their bikini tops. Nothing very remarkable there, as I had seen my mother and her friends so attired many times before. But it was the boys who made me look twice; had I ever seen such dazzlingly beautiful bodies, with their wide shoulders, manly chests, tight, shapely bottoms, curving legs and muscled arms, some of them straining in the effort to reach the ball, while others relaxed as they watched?

Then I recognised him. One of the boys looked just like my good friend Eddie: tall, dark, curly-haired, with his strong and supple body now more tanned and handsome than ever. He was looking directly out of the picture and straight at me with those kind, gleaming eyes, as if to say,

'Come on, Freddie, come and join us.'

*

I remembered it all now – just three years earlier, on the beach at Stanley Village in Hong Kong. We would drive down from our house in the garrison on the hill and go swimming. Our little party would invariably consist of me and your mother, our stand-in nanny, the eighteen-year-old Shawna, and Shawna's boyfriend, Eddie, who was a National Service squaddie. He was also my father's batman.

We would pitch ourselves on the beach near a shady breaker and clamber into our bathing gear. Eddie and I would race to get into the water first, he always letting me win, pretending to have a problem with his sandals. As I ran towards the water, he would chase me from behind, and with a dolphin-like dive, plunge into the sea and disappear. I'd be worried and confused until he re-emerged from the waves a few yards ahead of me, shouting,

'I spy sharks! Sharks!' causing me to panic and go rushing to the shore. Of course, I knew there were no sharks at Stanley; there was a big 'safety net' of meshed chain several hundred yards across the bay. But Eddie loved playing on my excitability, and anyway the possibility of danger made it more exciting.

By this time I'd be getting a bit overwrought, and it would take Shawna's reassurance and Eddie's mock apologies to calm me down. Now we'd go back into the water more sedately and Eddie would give me another lesson in the American crawl; I had already mastered the breaststroke while we had lived at the seaside in Wales. To prevent the middle part of my body from sinking under its own weight Eddie would hold me up as I floated on the water, placing his big hands on the flat of my tummy and allowing my arms and legs to move backwards and forwards while he walked along beside me, waist-high in the sea. His hold on my body was wonderfully reassuring as I made great speed splashing along happily. In no time I was able to report to my parents that I felt ready to compete in the Regimental Gala at Shek O.

Just as much as the swimming, I loved playing in the damp semi-viscous sand near the water's edge, making castles, fortified villages, canals and rivers, even bridges. I could occupy myself for hours like this, while my imagination invented new scenarios populating these miniature structures. It would all be over when the tide came in, of course, and I would watch my handiwork slowly disintegrate and give way to the little waves as they crept up the shore and then drew back, like a series of miniature tsunamis. All the time I had to be on the lookout behind me, as Eddie was very inclined to come up and sweep me off my feet, carrying me off into the sea and plonking me down head first into the water. I would be wriggling to be set free, yet loving every minute of it as his strong arms held me firm next to his hairy chest.

I really loved Eddie; he had a plain wide-open face, big brown eyes, a sharp mouth from which came forth little witticisms in his broad Yorkshire accent. I especially loved his short, dark, curly hair, which he would let me try to uncurl when we sat on the sand afterwards, drying ourselves. His wide chest was full of humps and bumps, and he would show me how he could make his arm muscles bigger by clenching his fists, expanding his chest and moving his arms higher, revealing a little knot of deliciously smelly hair under his arms, which I would tickle for him. I was fascinated by his firm pink nipples, which I once tried to pinch until he slapped my hand away, giving me a frown. Perhaps I had overstepped the mark just the once. I really admired the little V-shaped clump of dark hair on his chest, which then spread down in a line towards his belly button and disappeared into his swimming shorts. I wondered if I would start sprouting some hair on my chest soon and whether it would look just as manly and attractive as Eddie's.

And he was such fun. He was always smiling and laughing, teasing me and making us happy. When the time came for us to leave, he would drive us back to the house in the jeep and say goodbye. This always made me sad, and not a little jealous of Shawna who I knew would be seeing him later, on her own.

Why, oh why couldn't he be with us all the time, perhaps even instead of Shawna? He had become my big brother and a longed-for companion, so much more of a hero than anyone else I knew, and someone I wanted to grow up to be like. Although I loved your grandfather, Sam, of course, I could never think of him – often so strict – in the same way. I could never forget the big wallop he gave me the previous Christmas when, at my most excitable, I had waved around his prized bottle of single malt whisky in front of all the grown-ups. It had ended up smashed on the floor and with me being sent to bed early in disgrace.

One afternoon as we were packing up our things on the beach I felt so overcome, so bereft at leaving Eddie, that I snuggled up next to his long brown legs and hugged them. When he bent over to disentangle me, I whispered in his ear,

'Can I kiss you, Eddie?' He looked at me full in the face, and then ruffling my hair, said very tenderly and quietly,

'You're a dear little laddie, Freddie. Alright, just this once,' and I put my soft lips against his stubble.

To my intense joy he kissed me back, his lips tasting of salt and smelling of the sea.

*

As we continued our journey ever southwards into the Midi, these memories of Hong Kong and Eddie kept returning. Alas, our time there had been for only one year. Your grandfather, as you know, had been there, in the army, at the time of the Japanese invasion and among the last to surrender on Christmas Day 1941. He had endured three and a half years as a prisoner of war in the notorious camps, suffering appalling hardships alongside his comrades, and about which he never spoke. He had survived to return to England, to marry my mother – your grandmother – a rising choreographer and ballet mistress at Sadler's Wells. Fifteen years later – the time of which I am writing – he had been posted back to Hong Kong to supervise the decommissioning of the ordnance that had been so ineffective, alas, against the Japanese.

Immediately after our return to England he had retired from the army and somewhat reluctantly become a stockbroker. I always knew he'd have preferred to become a country prep school master, like many of his ex-army colleagues, but my mother insisted on living among her theatre friends in London. We'd set up home on Campden Hill, and the following year bought a pretty thatched cottage just outside a village at Chichester Harbour. Nanny moved back in with us, defaulting to the role of housekeeper and general minder. In truth I became a little embarrassed to admit that we still had a nanny in the house until I explained to my schoolfriends that my mother was often ill. In any case, my mother had never been interested in the kitchen, so Mrs Drake did all the cooking in London and Nanny at the cottage. Nanny loved baking and made the most delicious cakes, even teaching me how to make cupcakes to take to my friends' birthday parties. I'd spent a year at a smart little pre-prep school in Notting Hill Gate, and then been sent to my boarding prep school on the south coast. The sole reason for my parents' choice was because my father had been there thirty years previously, as had my uncles and cousins.

*

Over the next twelve months I often thought of those young people playing on the beach while I was lying in my bed in the dormitory back at school. I remembered vividly their sun-drenched bodies, their happy expressions, and wondered if I would see them again when we returned next year, as my parents had promised, and this time with your mother.

Sure enough, the following September we repeated the same routine at Boulogne and Lyons. As we were speeding down the new motorway, there they were: exactly the same boys and girls in just the same balletic staging on the beach. I nudged Pippa to look, but she just grimaced, and continued pointing her head out of the window on the other side. Then came another, and yet another, like old friends now.

Another twelve months passed, and I still couldn't forget my friends on the billboards. I often wondered if I would ever have such a beautifully proportioned body as the boys', and whether my sister would become as shapely as the girls. Then, one day I found myself asking whether I would *prefer* to be among the boys, or the girls, on that beach. Who would I want to sit with, chat to, and secretly admire after our game of netball? Which of them would I like to spend more time with if I had the chance? Who did I find the most attractive? I was pretty sure of the answer. But I reckoned I'd better put off a decision until I saw them again.

This time, our third visit, I awaited them anxiously as we passed Valence. There was the first one; I looked, and instantly my eyes fell on the boys. There was no question about it. I was captivated by the manliness of their bodies and the confidence with which they disported themselves with just a pair of Speedos covering their middle so neatly and snugly. I couldn't help wondering what they look like if they took them off.

As we drove on south, the hot sun beat down on the car and, despite the open windows and the breeze, it was very warm, and my thighs were again sticking to the leatherette. Again, I could feel my crotch becoming damp with the heat, as I thought, and a little tingling sensation in my cock. It was *very nice indeed*, and I was tempted to put my hand down to stroke or scratch it, but thought better of it with my sister sitting beside me and bound to make a snide comment.

Then I realised that this nice sensation only came on when I thought about the boys, and especially when I fantasised about the contours beneath their skimpy briefs. I was a little horrified at first, knowing full well that boys are supposed to admire girls, and not each other. I tried to think about the girls and their curvy breasts and shapely figures. But it was no good; it was only the boys who produced this effect between my legs. Now, at last, I admitted to myself what I had probably always known:

I preferred boys.

The years passed and I never changed my mind. Strange, intensely pleasurable dreams just before dawn confirmed my inclinations. At the beginning, of course, I said nothing. However, it wasn't long before I discovered I wasn't the only one who felt like this.

With my love,
Freddie

3

My dear Sam,

I'd arrived at Upton aged thirteen and on the crest of a wave, having achieved some of the best results in the country in the Common Entrance exam, or so I was told. It had been a complete reversal of everyone's expectations of me at my first prep school.

I had been an odd little boy, nervous and excitable, subject to wildly alternating bouts of precocious self-confidence and introspective self-doubt. Maybe it was the result of the ultra-strict regime imposed by my Irish nanny who was with us until your mother was born two years later. Then we'd moved to Wales and Nanny Doreen took her place. I'd been terrified of the dark, heaping my affection on my teddy bears, always keeping them close to me. Of course, I idolised my glamorous but distant mother, but Nanny Doreen was easier to love as she was chubby and tactile, always kind, and a great cook. I gained a reputation for being excessively polite and formal, abnormally anxious to please everyone around me. This, alas, sprang not from any innate good nature, but from fear of the consequences if I didn't.

The shock of arriving at prep school and being deprived of all family affection, all my little comforts and certainties in life, had resulted in humiliating scenes of bed wetting – having to own up to the school matron next morning – weight loss, a complete inability to concentrate or master my new lessons, let alone participate in team games. To this day I still carry the marks of some of the self-harm I inflicted. In bed at night, or secretly on my own, I'd be overcome by homesickness, blubbing my heart out.

However, after a year – at the time my parents first took me to Spain – I'd carved out my own little niche and things had begun to improve. I fell in love with the Church, and was thrilled after my father told me we had had a real martyr in the family, surely a saint, who had been starved to death 'in his chains' in the Tower of London under Queen Elizabeth. From then on I loved all the exotic trappings, the bells and smells and the dressing up. I became an expert on the lives of the saints, especially the martyrs. It was a great comfort to be part of this universal family in which I believed, so naively, that everyone had a place, and everyone knew their place. I became a model altar server, knowing all the Latin responses at Mass off by heart. St Dominic Savio, the newly canonised boy-saint and patron of youthful purity, became a major crush. Aged nine, I took his name for Confirmation and had a big poster of him stuck on the inside of my locker which I used to kiss when no one was looking. I just loved his sad, girly face with his melting eyes lifted up to heaven.

I hated football and rugger and boxing of course. My reputation was just about redeemed by winning the Under 11s Cup for swimming and for being a recklessly hard-hitting batsman at cricket.

The importance of success in the Common Entrance exam for admission to public school at thirteen was drummed into everyone ceaselessly. Failure or even mediocre marks might result in being refused admission to one's parents' first choice of school, in my case Upton Abbey, and the terrible indignity of having to go to a 'minor' public school. My future at Upton could not be presumed upon despite my family's history of loyalty. My Anglo-Chilean great-grandmother had been a major benefactress to the abbey church thanks to her speculations during the War of the Pacific. But that was nearly a hundred years ago.

My prep school headmaster's nickname could almost have been Whacko! for all his enthusiasm for physical chastisement. He used either a cane on the bare bottom or, for lesser offences, a leather belt on the hand. It was after I'd been given six-of-the-best for reading *The Sunday Times* (not apparently post-prandial Approved Reading), left behind after a visit by my parents, that they finally realised my education was not being best served there. I was sent to a new, small school, sometimes unfairly described as a 'crammer'.

It was the best move my parents could have made. From almost the very first day I blossomed. Within six weeks I had been made Head Boy. In truth, I don't think there was much competition, and it didn't seem to make much difference except that I sat at the top of the table in the dining room. There were only about thirty fellow schoolboys, with a schoolboy–teacher ratio approximately four to one, so all but the dimmest were able to shine. We were housed in a ramshackle Victorian country mansion; the owners were an old army colonel, deaf as a post, and his alarming blue-stocking chain-smoking wife always dressed in slacks. They ran the place almost as though it were a big informal house party. The dormitories consisted of just four or five beds in each, with carpets and curtains, and proper cupboards for our things. There was no official uniform or organised games; as long as we were in sports jackets and ties, we could wear whatever we liked. Classes took place in the mornings; afternoons were spent messing about in the woods or going to the café in the village for hot chocolate and cakes, and evenings spent in prep.

On Sundays we could catch the train home for the day, taking the pre-Beeching branch line and changing at Crawley, allowing us enough time to buy the *News of the World* and follow the latest in the Christine Keeler saga (we're talking 1963). Of course, the paper was quickly binned once we got to Victoria. I was particularly interested as a couple of my mother's friends, one of them a duchess, went to Stephen Ward for their back problems.

Actually, Sam, I found that whole saga only mildly titillating. My real interest in sex was taking off in other directions. At this stage it was mainly a fascination with my own changing anatomy and that of my peers whenever I caught a glimpse of them.

How well I remember that business between O'Malley and me, aged twelve. I used to be mildly jealous of his cock when I saw him in the showers and wondered how much bigger it got when he played with himself. One day when we were alone, I managed to steer a rather smutty conversation round to the point where I could suggest, 'I'll show you mine, if you show me yours.' We found a quiet study room where, after some preliminary banter, he yanked his out from his flies and showed me how it grew and got stiffer as he played with it – much more than mine when I did the same as we compared them.

Still, I wasn't too discouraged and soon found my own apparatus began to respond more happily to the attention I paid it. I continued wondering whose among my friends I'd like to have a closer look at, and maybe – heaven knows – get to hold if I played my cards right. Perhaps I should organise a secret competition to see whose was the biggest and best; from various remarks I overheard I had good reason to think it might be quite popular. All this was despite being reminded that 'offences against purity' could be mortal sins and lead to eternal damnation unless confessed pronto.

These priapic obsessions began to merge with more romantic feelings. One of my favourite dreams was to be adopted by a handsome new daddy who would spoil me beyond my wildest imaginings, transporting me somewhere tropical and exotic, like Tahiti (I'd just seen *South Pacific*). I'd go swimming and diving into deep pools of clear blue water fed by torrential cascades rushing down a steep waterfall. My new daddy would find me lovely slim brown boys, just starting to sprout little tufts under their arms and on their chests, tummies and thighs. They'd always let me climb and sit astride them as we messed around, letting me touch them all over and kiss their full luscious lips.

I hope these detailed revelations are not too shocking for you, Sam? I warned you in advance that you needed to be broad-minded to read this story, and this is only the first and tamest, I'm afraid. If you find them awkward or embarrassing – coming from a dirty old man, albeit your uncle – you can always skip past them. But I hope you'll understand that I include them as part and parcel of my growing-up odyssey.

I'm afraid girls didn't feature in many of these fantasies, except as bit parts, and as a foil to the boys. They would be charming and graceful and kind, but then leave us alone when we wanted them to.

*

My new self-confidence was enabling me to enjoy the company of my parents' friends much more, especially those of my mother, many of whom were still involved in the theatre world. I particularly enjoyed going to the smart lunch parties at Aunt Helena's enormous house in Holland Park. She wasn't really an aunt at all, just a distant relative, but she was my mother's best friend. They had both been in Noel Coward's long-running *Sigh No More* during the war, before my mother went on to Sadler's Wells. There were always interesting people at her house: actors, actresses, agents, impressarios, writers and musicians.

I loved following their conversations and became mesmerised by their often-exaggerated way of speaking, their expressive gestures, their flamboyant clothes and general air of effortless sophistication. Despite their being – or perhaps *because* they were – sometimes rather catty about each other, I thought they were so clever and smart. I soon found myself imitating their speech and mannerisms back at home and among my friends at my new school. It certainly dawned on me that half the men at least were probably Homos, or 'Pooftahs', as my father (who never went) called them, invariably with a half-smile, half-sneer across his face. But for me that was no great worry, rather it added to their fascination. I was always the polite schoolboy deferring modestly to my elders and betters, always addressing the men as 'sir', or married ladies as 'Mrs X or Y, or Lady Z'. In return everyone was very kind to me.

My precociousness reached its peak during the Christmas holidays before going to Upton when, as usual, we'd joined a large party of cousins and friends for skiing in St Moritz. It was here that I first compromised my true instincts by snogging with a girl for the first time. This was with my sister's friend Annie, who I liked very much in the normal course of things. It happened on the dance floor *après ski* when the music had gone smoochy, the lights turned down and everyone around us was at it. It was nice feeling our lips touching, although I think I may have been a little rough with her. Neither of us really knew what to do next. For both of us, I think, it was something that had to be done so as not to feel left out. Even afterwards, when we started writing to each other, I think we both knew we were being complicit in fulfilling others' expectations of us, particularly our competitive fellow schoolfriends. After a brief pang I was happy for her when she took up with another boy at our rival school in Yorkshire.

*

My crest of a wave crashed with overwhelming force barely one month after my arrival at Upton. What happened next was the defining trauma of my adolescence.

I thought I was doing rather well, making new friends and enjoying the atmosphere of my new school. The Junior housemaster, the worldly-wise Dom Alban, had shown me his special favour by inviting me to sit next to him in the refectory and plying me with questions about St Moritz where he used to go skiing in his youth. It was, however, a dangerous compliment, giving rise, unbeknown to me, to resentment and jealousy from boys who had obviously taken against me.

On that Sunday morning, Dom Alban delivered his pre-Mass homily, taking as his theme the evils of gossip and spreading rumours. He said it had come to his notice that there was a certain, unnamed, boy in the house about whom unpleasant stories and innuendoes were circulating and he wanted this stopped immediately.

I thought no more about it until after lunch that day when I realised, to my intense horror and pain, that the victim of this campaign was ME! It came in a blinding flash when I asked a couple of boys who I thought had been friendly enough if they would like a walk later to The Rock, a couple of miles from the school.

'No. We're not going anywhere with a fey pansy like you. You can get lost. We don't want anything to do with a nancy boy.'

Something within me just crashed. I was seeing stars, as though someone had just punched me in the face. My mouth went so dry that my tongue almost seized up.

'What makes you say that?'

'You talk like one,' came the reply. And that included waving my arms around, exaggerating, sounding affected and having 'strange expressions'.

I was speechless, flabbergasted, reduced to total silence, and just slunk away. There was nothing for it but to try to find some others who I might join for the afternoon walk. My overtures elsewhere were rebuffed with equal cruelty.

I realised I had miscalculated badly. The witticisms I'd learnt at Aunt Helena's theatrical lunch tables clearly had not transposed well to the Junior House refectory. Here I was, someone who had begun to enjoy life and imagined he was quite well liked, a former head boy of his prep school, now reduced to a friendless 'loner', ostracised by his contemporaries. There was no physical bullying; I was too tall and well-built for that. Instead, this was full-on mental torment. From now on it was enough that people gave me strange looks in the passage, turning away from me if I tried to engage with them, seeing them mutter under their breath when I tried to speak up in class. I felt so miserable and humiliated – beyond tears. It might be true that I was all those things they said, but it was their merciless 'outing' and the resulting loneliness that now plunged me into deepest despair.

Thus, almost overnight I went from being an outward-looking, confident boy – admittedly with some silly affectations and expressions – to being silent and withdrawn, distrustful of my surroundings and companions. My world really had fallen apart and everything I had begun to enjoy about my new school had become intimidating and full of risk. I seemed to lack any resilience, becoming intensely self-conscious, desperate to avoid drawing attention to myself, and ashamed of who I was. Within days I became reconciled to the fact that I had no friends or allies and was not likely to make any. On no account could I talk or write to my parents about it; it would have been a terrible admission of failure. I had to become used to the unbearable sadness of my solitary walks, being a nonentity, shunned in the classroom, and always last to be picked for a team on the games fields. I overheard someone say that cross-country running was a sure remedy for Queerness and so, in a half-hearted attempt to cure myself, I took it up. I knew in my heart it was pointless.

For the first time I had to admit to myself that I really was an incurable Homo and that everyone probably knew it.

My only hope was that my isolation might be temporary. Some of my old and loyal friends from my first prep school would be arriving in a couple of terms. They knew me well enough, and I just hoped I could rely on them, if I could hold out that long. And maybe the mental bullying would die out when we all dispersed to our senior houses.

Meanwhile there was one solace in all this misery. Just as I had turned to the consolations of religion during my agonies as a bewildered new boy at prep school, so now I found myself irresistibly drawn to the mysterious yet comforting presence of the magnificent abbey church. It seemed like a loving father reaching out to me. At night or at dusk its dark recesses invited me to explore deep within its rich, numinous secrets. As I drifted through its different parts, new spatial perspectives opened up in every direction. Best of all were the aisles behind the monks' choir and the high altar, the architect Thomas Garnet's masterpiece. That was where the side chapels and altars were situated, with their various changes of level and sightlines, the steps leading up to the iron screen in front of the Lady Chapel, and down into the lugubrious depths of the crypt. Its Gothic-ness might have inspired fear in some, but for me it was permeated with a sense of mystery and peace. I loved gazing upwards at the soaring vaults, at the rich mouldings of the columns and the banks of carved saints dimly seen above the altars. Presiding over the steps to her chapel was the statue of Our Lady, illuminated at night from below with rows of flickering candles. Their moving light caught the gold fleurs-de-lys on her blue mantle and the flashing brilliants in her crown. She almost came alive for me in this radiant luminosity, her lips forming a serene smile as she held the Infant Jesus in her arms. Everywhere this sense of transcendence was heightened by the lingering fragrance of beeswax and incense which wafted through the air in the twilight hours after Vespers.

It was here that the confessionals, the 'sin bins', were to be found.

One evening, having been sent to Coventry by my peers in the refectory, I was desperate for a friendly voice – somewhere, anywhere. I found myself in the confessional of Dom Placid. He was not one of the monks who had regular dealings in the school as a teacher or housemaster, possibly being less worldly than some of his brethren. In any case he was now somewhat elderly, and with his pure white hair, his serene and happy smile blending with his soft sing-song Irish voice, seemed to exemplify everything one looked for in a holy man.

I whispered my usual laundry list of sins: impure thoughts (generic), selfishness, thinking badly of others, failing to concentrate in my prayers. He was of course facing away from me behind the grille in the partition. After I had finished, he turned slightly.

'Tell me – you must be a new boy – are you happy here at Upton?'

'Yes, of course... but, that is... no... not really. In fact, not at all, Father.'

I felt the tears coming into my eyes, the first time I had allowed this to happen since the beginning of my ordeal.

'Yes, dear boy, I can tell. You can cry here without feeling bad about it and let it out; don't be ashamed or frightened. You can talk to me. I have no idea who you are, but I could tell straight away that you are not happy. What has happened?'

And then I told him how my world had fallen apart with the stories that had been told about me and how I hated myself and was so ashamed of what others thought of me.

'Listen to me now. What happened to you is horrible, to be sure, and should never have been allowed. The boys who spread these rumours should be punished – and if they haven't been already, they will be later in life. Their evil attitude will catch them out one day. Not that I am concerned about them. I am concerned about *you*.'

He continued, 'Tell me, what name do your family call you by? I don't want to know your surname, or how you are known in the school. But do you have a nickname that I could use if you want to come and talk to me again, so that I know it's you?'

'I'm Fred, or Freddie to my family, Father.'

'Now listen to me, Freddie. What you have to remember is that we are all created in the image and likeness of God. We are all part of his family – his creation. Everyone and everything that has ever been created and has life – including the natural world – is "different", and part of our Heavenly Father's immense diversity. That means you and me, Freddie; how boring it would be if we were all the same! So you must never be afraid of being yourself.

'So, let me give you some advice. There is only one person in the world in whom we can put our complete trust, one friend who will never let us down, or ever abandon us. And that is Jesus, the Son of God himself. He loves you like no one else, he lives in you, he wants to be your very closest friend and companion, your elder brother. Do you have an elder brother, Freddie?'

'No, I don't, Father. I wish I had.'

'Well, then, there you are, to be sure! Jesus just wants to be with you wherever you are. He wants you to talk with him as though he were right there beside you, all the time.

'Let me suggest something to you. Whenever you feel down, or alone, or just want to speak to someone, just say these words to him, from the depths of your loving heart – and I can tell that you have a loving heart, Freddie – "Jesus, I love you." Say it slowly and repeat it as many times as you like.

'You'll be amazed. You'll get a response back from him, *immediately.* He'll reply, "Freddie, I love you too. Don't be worried, we'll get over this. All that matters is that we are close."

'I'll give you your Absolution now, dear boy. But please come back and tell me how you are getting on. Next time just say, "It's Freddie here, Father", and you can tell me. Once you know that Jesus is looking after you, you will feel so much happier, and so strong that you could conquer the world.

'One last thing, though. You must pray that he will send you good and faithful friends whom you can trust and be comfortable with. And, yes, you could ask him for a special friend with whom you can become close and share with, even more fully, if it is his will.'

I'm not sure I immediately took in this last suggestion, or its implications. Drying my eyes, I managed to thank him and say I'd be back again soon.

Leaving the confessional there was already a small queue building up outside which I had obviously caused by my lengthy session. There were a few scowls and nudges between the waiting boys, but I wasn't bothered. I made my way to the side chapel of the Sacred Heart and knelt in the prayer desk, looking up at the statue of Jesus with one hand in blessing and the other pointing to his exposed chest. He looked serenely beautiful, and I knew instantly that he loved me. Things were never quite as bad again.

Sam, in hindsight it would be easy to dismiss all this as a kind of sublimation for my real need of physical affection. That may well have been true, but somehow – at the time – it worked.

With my love,
Freddie

4

My dear Sam,

My crisis and depressed state had not made me entirely inert. I managed to summon up enough mettle to ensure that when I left Junior House after two terms I was moved to Ambrose, the most liberal-minded senior house where none of my prime enemies were destined. There was much huffing and puffing by the authorities and my family who wanted me to go on to Gasquet where all my relatives had been. But my determination paid off, and over the next few terms I slowly emerged from my difficulties, learning to be circumspect in my choice of friends and more careful in how I presented myself to the world. There was less waving of hands around, fewer and quieter exclamations and altogether less exaggerated behaviour.

Some of my natural cheerfulness slowly reasserted itself. I had found a way of 'fitting in', being unremarkable if not quite a nonentity, definitely not sporty but also not particularly bookish or academic. I got through all my O-Levels (bar Maths) much better than I expected and that gave me more confidence. During my first year in the sixth form I made a wider group of 'mainstream' friends, although my close circle were definitely more 'exotic'. I was drawn to the latter because they were more interesting and more fun, and they seemed to enjoy being with me. Phillips – 'Pips' – was the most outrageous – deliberately effeminate and provocative. He'd been bullied, like me, but had sailed through it all with his impenetrable self-belief and tart repartee. Rosedale was half French, a natural aesthete who spoke with Gallic inflections and turns of phrase as second nature. Galbraith was half Sicilian, and glorified in being an unapologetic wop, always in tinted glasses and stinking of *Pino Silvestre Vidal*. Williamson was utterly charming on the surface and became a favourite of my mother's, but had a mind as filthy as a sewer. Each of us had travelled by different routes to the realisation that we were all irredeemable Homos and we might as well try to enjoy it.

How did this admission square with the loyalty most of us felt we owed to our Catholic identity? Had we not all been brought up – at great cost – to be faithful to our religion and heritage, which held the activities of such people to be beyond the pale? My problem was exacerbated by the unnatural practices I would exercise on my own body, accompanied by unspeakable fantasies, for which the only remedy was instant confession. We'd be assured that if we persevered we would be rewarded and our urges would disappear. It wasn't very convincing. We knew that one day there would be a clash and we'd have to make a decision.

*

Anyway, a more liberal attitude held that salvation was not just a question of agonising over our own personal problems – 'polishing up our souls' or 'navel gazing' as one of the younger monks put it. We needed to take a wider view. It was instilled into us that there was no such thing as privilege without responsibility. We heard how some of the monks – whom we never met – were working in the poor parishes of Liverpool, and others had recently gone to South America to start an experimental mission. Dom Gabriel continually, but gently, made us aware of questions of social justice and the opportunities we should take to share our gifts and blessings.

One day, after I had been chastised for bunking off instead of showing up for a Cadet Force inspection in the driving rain, he said to me,

'I could overlook your dislike of army games and sport in general, McNaughton, if I knew you were doing something useful instead.'

Just a few days later my friend Pips and I were having one of our long walks. He was on his usual tack, sharing his mildly titillating fantasies about his latest crush: how he'd fallen out of love with the silent Zermanski who'd obviously given him the brush-off, and was now fixated on Scott-Martin, the supremely elegant head of Addison, who he was sure had made a pass at him. Perhaps he'd join the Debating Society and be able to ogle him at close quarters. What did I think? I didn't like to tell him that with his effeminate rhetoric he'd lose every debate he ever tried to speak in. Anyway, I'd long since learnt to discount half of his so-called conquests; when it came to specifics, he was usually extremely vague. I was always a bit wary of confiding in him, knowing he'd be incapable of keeping a secret.

We were passing a group of old stone cottages and, being desperate to change the subject, I stopped to speak to the old lady in her front garden attempting to cut back the brambles.

'Are you boys from the college then?' she asked in her broad West Country accent.

We admitted we were.

'Do you know Father Placid? He used to be our parish priest here years ago. Such a lovely man.'

'Oh yes,' I said. 'We know him very well. I quite agree with you.' The ice had well and truly broken.

'I'm Elsie,' she said.

'I'm Fred,' I answered, 'and this is my friend Stephen.'

We both tried to contain our giggles; the discreet allusion to *Round the Horn* had been involuntary, although Elsie gave no indication that she'd recognised it.

She was obviously having some trouble in reaching the brambles and weeds, so Pips offered to give her a hand. We took the shears and secateurs and in twenty minutes had made great progress. Putting all the debris into a wheelbarrow we took it round the back of the cottage to make a pile for a future bonfire. When we saw the state of her rear garden we couldn't help offering to come back next week, maybe with some friends, to see what we could do.

That's how The Conclave was born.

We got Dom Gabriel's enthusiastic approval for us to visit Elsie again. He gave us all the welcome chitties excusing us from games. In no time we'd found other neighbours of Elsie's who needed help one way or another and soon there was a group of about eight fellow Ambrosians, visiting the elderly in the villages nearby to chat with them and offering to do any odd jobs. We always went in small gangs, and by the end of our first term we'd even redecorated the kitchen of a housebound old sailor. He loved watching us, giving us cups of tea and reminiscing about his travels. He told us he'd never married. Pips of course picked up on it straight away, later inferring he was the local paedo.

'But never mind, darling. Safety in numbers, especially among sailors.'

We decided we should meet in the evenings as well, and it was quite a coup to get Dom Edmund, the handsomest and most charismatic of the junior monks, to chair our sessions. Someone would read out a leading article or a piece from a journal or newspaper for us all to discuss. It opened our eyes to many things, and often the conversations became quite personal, with guarded confidences being shared. As a result, we all got to know each other pretty well, and new, strong, and sometimes intense, relationships were forged there. Later we started inviting outside speakers to come and share their knowledge and experience with us on wider subjects. It all bore fruit in many ways, often years later.

*

But to return to the story, I kept asking myself how was I ever going to meet and engage with Paul? I was utterly preoccupied with finding ways to see him, speak to him, get to know him, make him turn his elusive smile on me. But I knew full well that to give the game away too soon by seeming *too* keen, *too* contrived, would be disastrous. Despite – maybe because of – all my frustrations, I was intoxicated by my new obsession and wallowing in how out-of-control my feelings were for him. Never had I felt so *alive*, or had such a craving to *be with*, to *possess*, someone. Surely there was no other word for it but love? I was determined not to be the shrinking violet in this scenario which was causing such havoc in my life. *I* was going to be the one to manage its progress to my very best advantage and on no account leave anything to chance.

For starters I made a point of finding the whereabouts of his private locker, an obvious place near to which he might be found from time to time. It was in one of the wide passages near the dayroom, alongside the deep window seats in which boys would often sit reading or socialising during free periods, especially after supper. I could easily be walking past without drawing attention to myself.

It took three attempts. At last, there he was on his own, lying across a window seat with one of the O-Level set books which I recognised as *Antony and Cleopatra* propped up against his knees.

I sauntered towards him, hands in pockets, trying to disguise the palpitations raging within me.

'Hello,' I said. 'I'm McNaughton. You're Shipton, I think?' I could feel my mouth going dry already, and a tingle rising up my spine. My goodness, my heart was beating so fast and so loudly I wondered if he could hear it.

He looked up, a bit quizzically. 'Yes?'

I tried to smile as I asked, pointlessly, 'Is that *Ant and Cleo* you've got there? Are you in Dom Benet's class?' I sat down beside him in the remaining space on the window seat, forcing him to shift and draw his knees up closer to his chest. I was shaking all over – but the die was cast.

He turned the book over, keeping his finger in the place he'd been reading.

'That's what it says here. I'm trying to get to the end before our class tomorrow.' He sounded a bit surly and defensive, even a bit annoyed. Yet there was a slight flicker of a smile at the edge of his mouth.

It was the first time I had heard his voice at close range; until now I'd had to strain my ears to catch anything he might have been saying.

I was beguiled; it was a wonderful sound – slow, gritty and luxuriant, quite different from the lazy drawl of some of his contemporaries.

From this close vantage point I could study his face minutely. His skin had a golden honey radiance, as pure and soft as a girl's, without blemish, and tempting to touch. Looked at full-on, his cheeks tapered downwards gracefully to his softly modelled chin, almost like a Raphael Madonna. I dared to look directly at his eyes; they were big, set deep and wide apart, like beautifully shaped almonds, his lids framed by dark curly lashes, moving expressively as he looked me up and down. The whites of his eyes were pure ivory, the irises a pale brown flecked with green jasper, his pupils deepest black. I felt their intensity as they stared back at me. Then, with a single blink they would be transformed to reveal a capacity for compassion, tenderness, even a hint of laughter. His dark red lips were so sensuous: the upper one an elegant ogee-cupid's bow, the lower one more cushioned and luscious, suggesting a tantalising poutiness. Their combination was irresistible; in my imagination they were crying out to be smothered in kisses, over and over, ten million times.

He was quite simply the most beautiful being I had ever seen.

I looked up and down his semi-recumbent figure, oh so tantalisingly close to me, one leg now draped to the floor, the other still bent at the knee. I tried to imagine the glorious mysteries that must lie imprisoned behind the formless pin-stripe trousers, the ill-fitting black jacket and the crumpled white shirt. How I wished I could slowly, slowly undo the buttons to reveal the unseen miracle of his body, and then to touch him – his arms, his shoulders, his chest, his legs, his thighs, his… – and then turning him round… to run my hands down the length of his back to his bum… to fondle its roundness… and then to stroke the undulating form of his high insteps, hidden within his lace-up Oxfords…

There was an almost Mediterranean sultriness about him, a superior kind of voluptuousness – his darkness, his languid posture, his air of detachment – which I found so compelling. Merely by looking directly at me this Renaissance prince – my Bronzino poster-boy-come-to-life – had totally unnerved me, a mere prole, daring me to explain myself to him.

But I had to pull myself together, so I continued, 'I was in Dom Benet's O-Level class two years ago. I didn't like him to start with; I found him rather precious. He was very sarky about my "fine writing" as he called it. He didn't like my purple passages which I always thought were rather good –

actually.' Oh God. Was I sounding a bit of a prick? I carried on relentlessly.

'He made me take the part of Enobarbus:

> *"The barge she sat in, like a burnish'd throne*
> *Burn'd on the water; the poop was beaten gold*
> *Purple the sails, and so perfum'd, that*
> *The winds were love-sick with them, the oars were silver..."*

I especially liked the next bit:

> *"On each side her*
> *Stood pretty dimpled boys, like smiling Cupids..."'*

Shipton didn't seem to think that was terribly funny, so I held back from giving the leery smirk that usually accompanied these lines. Even so, he seemed to be relaxing a bit.

'That's impressive.' His dark red lips parted in a little smile showing his sparkly white teeth. 'Yeah, he's got me to take the part of Antony, and I've got to make love to Cleopatra in the shape of Scarisbrick Mi. He's not exactly my idea of "*my serpent of old Nile*", he said with a grimace.

Lucky Scarisbrick bloody Mi, the younger of my two cousins at the school. You undeserving little piece of shit.

I thought I'd better take the conversation forward in a less contrived way. I asked if he had seen the recent film *Cleopatra* with Elizabeth Taylor, Richard Burton and Rex Harrison. He said he'd been to see it in Leeds with his mother and sister. He'd found Elizabeth Taylor pretty hot.

'Oh?' I made no further comment but continued,

'You know, you've got a touch of Richard Burton about you, a slightly softer version perhaps. Did anyone ever tell you? You've got some of the same features and colouring – "movie star looks"!' I said laughing. 'Except of course Richard Burton has a high forehead, whereas you disguise yours with those floppy locks.'

It was a gamble. I could have misfired terribly but, thank goodness, he took it the right way. Instead of glaring at me, which is what I dreaded, he lifted his right hand to sweep back his fringe to reveal his high forehead without a single line or crease to spoil its smoothness. It was like lifting a veil. In an instant his face, indeed his whole persona, had lost much of that air of mystery, and had somehow opened up, become lighter, more transparent.

'There,' he said, 'any better?' A reluctant smile crossed his face.

He kept his hand in place just long enough for me to consider the effect before withdrawing and letting his curly mop fall down again like a curtain crashing down on a stage.

'No, no,' I said, 'maybe later. We like you just the way you are. Stick with the floppiness, for now anyway. It suits you better.'

He blushed, reaching out trying to slap the book at me, obviously trying to suppress a smile.

'No one's ever told me I look like Richard Burton before. You certainly know how to flatter a bloke. Go on with you.'

At that moment I knew I'd 'got it'! That look of his – which some might call sulkiness, disdain or even pouting – it was merely a mask for his *shyness*, obviously his weak point. Now *that* I knew I could cope with, maybe with some careful and affectionate teasing; it might be a long haul, but eventually his shyness could and would be broken down. If only he could place his trust in me and accept my offer of genuine friendship, maybe even more would come later.

It was obviously a signal to leave, and not to annoy him any further, even playfully. I stood up, and as I did so, I came out with it, entirely involuntarily:

'*Bye for now, Shipton.*'

It was *that phrase*, that parting shot which my admiring hippy had used before he blew me a kiss on the Underground that day and which I'd never forgotten. '*Bye for now, gorgeous!*' It had been *so nice*; it made me smile to think of all the possibilities it implied.

Oh goodness, now I'd used it for the first time on Paul. Had it sounded just a bit too familiar? Too presuming of another one-to-one engagement and a more fruitful conclusion? Yet it expressed everything I hoped for.

He gave me a sideways look, and a little smile came across his face.

'*Bye for now, McNaughton.*'

My heart leapt – those words; but do you *really* mean it, Paul? That you wouldn't mind seeing me again? You're even looking forward to seeing me again? *Then when? Where? How? Just tell me, for God's sake, tell me – NOW!*

That wicked little angel of desire had been plunging his darts straight into my heart all this time, piercing it with insistent, joyful incisions of hope, followed by prolonged and agonising withdrawals of suspense and unknowing. I was entirely in his hands; there was nothing I could do except abandon myself to his unbearable caprice. Far from swooning with the crazed and contradictory emotions he was assailing me with, I was fully alive as never before, hanging in the air in his power.

'Bring it on!' I implored him. 'If I have to suffer a thousand tortures for just one moment of joy, I can take it. Let me be the plaything of your probing, thrusting penetrations.'

Paul swivelled round to put his two legs back onto the window seat where I'd been sitting and gave me a dismissive wave as he looked straight back into his book.

I almost skipped down the deserted corridor feeling high as a kite, totally exhilarated, drunk with hope and expectation. I'd managed to speak to him, sit with him and made him smile and laugh. Did anything else matter in the entire world?

Later that night as I lay in bed I recalled and savoured everything I had seen and heard: the sensuousness of his beautiful face, every nuance, every change of expression, every flutter of his lashes or blink of his eyes, every square millimetre of his golden flesh. At the same time, I kept hearing the sound of that soft, deep, languid voice coming from those exquisite lips:

'*Bye for now, McNaughton.*'

As my consciousness dissolved into dreams, I became aware of the agitated rustlings of that pretty, beastly, little angel. This time he'd come to bandage the latest wounds he'd inflicted on me. His hands were consoling, delicate, persistent. I gasped at his ministrations as my body went into an orgasmic spasm. As he was leaving, he kissed me, smiling sweetly but so cruelly, whispering,

'I'm called Eros sometimes, Freddie – you lucky boy – and I've only *just started* on you.'

Whatever was in store for me?

With my love,

Freddie

5

My dear Sam,

Now that Paul and I were at last 'acquainted' I felt emboldened to give him more personalised signals in public. So, for instance, as I watched him from the touchline in the Colts hockey or rugby matches, I would give encouraging cheers: 'Well done, Shipton', 'Well played, Shipton'.

But I soon learnt there were certain things I could not presume upon, at least yet, such as when I ventured to give him an uninvited nickname: '... Well passed, Shippo!...' After the third time of shouting this across the rugby pitch he glared at me, sweating and panting while mouthing something inaudible which indicated he wasn't pleased. I hoped to goodness I hadn't blown my chances.

It was of course one of the most ancient taboos to call anyone by their Christian name at Upton, or indeed at any public school. It was all part of the masculine ethos, supposedly immunising us against any kind of close personal relationships. Strangely, it had exactly the opposite effect, making us invent nicknames that were even more indicative of friendship than using our first names.

They often began by being mildly insulting but had soon become covertly affectionate: 'Fog' (for Thicknesse), 'Ginger' (for Redknapp), 'Bunny' (for Hare), 'Pips' (for Phillips). Among the exotic brigade there could also be some not-unfriendly regenderings: 'Garbo' (for Galbraith), 'Roz' (for Rosedale), 'Berta' (for Roberts), 'Mo-Mo' (for Fitzmaurice) and 'Sugar' (pronounced 'Shugaah', for Monroe, after we'd all seen *Some Like It Hot*). I didn't seem to have one; it was only the half-Welsh Pips who called me 'BoyO'.

Seeing Paul on the games fields stripped of his regulation suit and clad in sports gear he looked almost eighteen months older, much closer to my age. His proportions seemed entirely 'right' just the way he was; when he grew everything would find its proper place and he would become a more mature, scaled-up version of the boy now in front of me. His face I could imagine becoming a little thinner, perhaps more modelled, exposing more of his bone structure. In my imagination I rhapsodised about his appearance in two or three years: even more handsome, taller and broader, 'filled out in all the right places'.

Until now my fantasies had been centred on a vague romantic *ideal* of his hidden nakedness. Now my imagination could extend itself, teased beyond endurance by the sight of his half-seen, half-unseen flesh. I had an unbearable longing to possess this perfect body – to overpower him and at the same time be overpowered by him. How I envied that rugby ball: the way he clung to it so firmly, and then passed it obliquely with an elegant, almost balletic leap sideways, his body suspended in the diagonal for a split second before crashing into the mud! If he had had an accident I would have been the first onto the pitch. How lovingly I would have tended him, better than any nurse, ministering to his every need. Yet at other times I dreamt of ravishing him, tying him up so tightly in his nakedness, having my wicked way with him as he groaned in agonising ecstasy. Afterwards I would be consumed with shame for violating the very thing I loved most. All this, I knew, was not just desire, but something less controllable, more elemental: *lust*. Eros was doing his work, smiling all the time as he plunged his darts deeper and deeper into my heart, twisting them as he did so, making me writhe in glorious pain.

I wasn't sure what my response to Paul's physicality was supposed to say about me and my tastes; in the broad spectrum of adolescent male beauty he probably occupied the middle ground. Certainly, he wasn't a delicately tender 'lush', nor yet a knight in shining armour. I had always been – as I remain – fairly catholic (dare I say it), and sometimes erratic, in my preferences. Perhaps his ambiguity meant I could find *all* men attractive and potential lovers if they had the right *je ne sais quoi*: a combination of sensuality, gracefulness, voice, presence, and of course, availability. All the right beeps on my gaydar.

I was obviously never going to make much of an impression on the games field, nor alas with music, one of his favourite extracurricular interests. Early on, I'd seen him with a guitar hung incongruously over his shoulder and I'd crept over to the music department to listen to him beneath a window, strumming away 'Can't Take My Eyes Off You'. The ballad struck me to the core and remained forever associated with him. But who could *he* have been thinking of?

However, I certainly wasn't giving up. There would surely be other ways to gain his attention, and over a short period of time I was encouraged by a gradual accumulation of small incidents.

He was studying the same subjects as me and covering much the same ground as I had two years previously. I reckoned I might be able to help him if he needed and would let me.

He was a conscientious student and I'd noticed that he sometimes went into one of the empty classrooms during the hour-long free time after supper. This was presumably to catch up with his prep, instead of gossiping with his friends, practising on his guitar, playing billiards, or going to one of the societies for debating, discussion, or music.

I thought there'd be no reason in the world for me not to do the same myself and 'accidentally' run into him. Thus, one evening, having seen him quietly gather up some papers and disappear into a deserted classroom, I let him settle in for a few minutes. Then, collecting my own stuff, I quite nonchalantly breezed into the room myself. Feigning surprise when I saw him sitting at a desk in a far corner I merely said,

'Oh! You're here too?'

Reassuringly, he didn't seem too badly put out.

'Yeah, just getting on with *Ant and Cleo* again. Dom Benet has set us a choice of essays and I'm having problems deciding.'

'I remember thinking it was such a fabulous play,' I replied, unbidden and possibly pushing my luck. 'Such drama, such strong themes and all in such gorgeous language... "*I have immortal longings in me*",' I pouted, giving a poor imitation of Elizabeth Taylor inside her pyramid. Paul couldn't possibly know what immortal longings *he* was giving me.

Even so, he seemed to be listening. Trying hard not to sound too boastful, I asked if any of my old essays would be any use to him. They were all in the exercise books in my locker gathering dust. His face lit up with genuine gratitude, but then a look of hesitation came over him.

'But maybe not. I wouldn't want anyone to think I was cribbing off you.'

I told him that, in my view, three quarters of the world consisted of plagiarists, and how – without being too cynical – one's success depended mostly on how well one disguised other people's ideas or put a different spin on them. He looked a bit nonplussed.

'Look,' I said, 'if you really want to grab the examiner's attention don't faff about. You've got to make your work stand out. Make him smile, make him remember you, allude to something a bit different even if it's slightly off the point. It's all about *connections*.'

I suggested that one of the best ways was to give casual and mildly off-beam cross-references. So, for example, there might be a question about Cleopatra's strategies. Since he had seen the recent film he could make a throwaway remark about how she had seduced Rex Harrison as Julius Caesar, playing the part of a sexy nymphette – as conceived in the G.B. Shaw play – and compare that with her more mature skills with Antony, as described by Shakespeare. If he wanted to be really clever, he could even make a reference to Tiepolo's famous picture of their meeting; it was illustrated in the Clarendon edition we were using.

Or again, I suggested, he could allude to Cleo in his History paper, giving his essays a fashionable feminist twist. For example, he could make a throwaway remark comparing her to Queen Elizabeth or Catherine the Great and how these women used their femininity to captivate men. Basically make the examiner think he knew a whole lot more than he really did!

'Although it's probably best *not* to remark, "How unlike the home-life of our own dear Queen!" I quipped, quoting another old queen, maybe Lytton Strachey.

That made him laugh, at last, so I continued, 'I'm usually knocking around in the classrooms after supper and don't mind having a chinwag if you wanted.'

'Hey, that would be kind, McNaughton. I'd really appreciate it. I need to get on top of all this.' My heart melted for him.

Soon afterwards I found a moment to drop my essays in his locker. I was tempted to have a snoop at some of his things but my conscience got the better of me, taking in only the photographs sellotaped onto the inside of the door. And a big handwritten slogan, from his favourite song:

YOU'RE JUST TOO GOOD TO BE TRUE

My God! I was convinced: that *had* to be me!

It would need a response, to be pinned to the inside of *my* locker door for him to see when he returned my books. It could only be another line from the song:

AND I THANK GOD I'M ALIVE

*

Indeed, there was a lot of pining, yearning and gazing over in Paul's direction that Michaelmas term, and in the Lent term following. At least a dozen times he caught me glancing over at him, longingly, at morning assembly or looking up from my book in the library and our eyes had met. At first he'd blushed and looked away but after that he had held my gaze with a guarded smile. My friend Pips saw what was going on and passed me a note written in a faux-Elizabethan script:

Smiles are of love the foode...!

I never discovered where he'd found that saucy little aphorism.

These days of course, Sam, I would probably have been utterly brazen and made him an offer, straight out, to be his boyfriend! But at that time it would have been unthinkable. Anything so overt would have been a *disaster*; he wouldn't have known how to take it, poor lad. Possibly it was unnerving enough that I, as an older boy, was giving him such undue attention, although he always appeared super-cool. If it got out that I'd propositioned him directly I'd have been thrown to the lions. No, I had to be patient, bide my time and work at it. Funnily enough there was a certain delicious *frisson* in having to proceed so gingerly and with such an unpredictable end result.

The nearest I got to a 'declaration' was composing a series of beautiful love letters and poems. I would lie awake half the night rehearsing how I could express what I felt, and then hours next day pouring out my heart and soul onto paper instead of getting on with my prep. In one of them, I remember, I suggested we run away together to the South of France where we'd live like beach bums all summer. Fat chance! I never sent them, thank goodness, heeding Pips's advice and experience. He'd once got into a lot of trouble and only escaped severe punishment as his were composed in Greek, in sapphic stanzas imitating the muse of Lesbos. I kept mine in a secure box in my locker. Maybe, if all went well, I might show them Paul one day. It probably made my writing style even more flowery, to Dom Benet's despair.

Oddly enough, despite all this time-wasting, my work didn't seem to suffer. If anything, it improved; my new intense feelings seemed to generate an energy and confidence I'd forgotten I possessed. My A-Level subjects were English, History and Geography and my tutors began to take more interest in me. Perhaps by falling crazily in love I had unlocked some neural pathways in the brain. One day some shrink can explain it all to me.

Once, and only once, I came across Paul in the showers. It was in the Lent term after he had finished a game of rugby while I had been on a cross-country run. The washroom was humid and steamy, the figures wandering in and out looking like ghostly shapes. I discarded my kit and reached the showers at the far end. All but one had a naked boy standing beneath, shampooing and washing his body. I went over to the unoccupied one and turned on the tap. I looked to my right and to my astonishment there was Paul. He was being drenched in water, with shampoo and soap cascading down his chest, his legs and his cock.

My heart missed a beat. I was covered in confusion and the prospect of an imminent erection.

'Hello there, Shipton,' I said, 'how was the match?' not having a clue who he'd been playing against.

He hadn't seen me until then, so he turned and as he shook

his head to one side to dispel the water, he gave me a sideways smile and a little wink – or was he just trying to get the water out of his eye? If it was the former… my goodness, '*What complicity! What first steps of sensuous delight!*' as Pips's friend Marcel once wrote in a different context.

'Hello, McNaughton. It was OK, thanks. We beat them 15-12,' was all I got in return.

'Great stuff!' I replied. He turned off the shower, gave his cock a little flick, and went into the washroom to retrieve his towel and dry himself.

Here was the real thing that I had been fantasising about for weeks, the full Monty, standing in front of me for a split second in all his beauty, enveloped in the soft-focus mist of the shower room. He was no anonymous ghostly shape but the very incarnation of the divine ephebe: Antinous himself in the clouds of Mount Olympus.

There was nothing exaggerated about him, nothing to suggest the vanity of an overdeveloped physicality; his sinuous forms were all in perfect proportion. The same golden hue of his skin extended over his whole body, with a tantalising paler section around his middle. His arms had finely contoured muscles, his shoulders and chest firm and proportioned, tapering inwards towards his Adonis belt and hips, with little flecks of dark hair down his abs towards his belly button. Emerging out of the density of his pubes his cut and perfectly formed cock, hung semi-flaccid, slightly off the perpendicular. Between his shapely thighs was his loosely hanging nutsack, just waiting to be grasped and fondled.

His *derrière* was equally irresistible. From the nape of his neck downwards there was a continuous elegant curve as it dipped inwards following his spine, and then outwards as it reached his bum cheeks which stood out proudly like a voluptuous plump peach, rounded, slightly furry, and so fleshy, so invitingly touchable. In between, his mysteriously dark crevasse tempted one into regions unknown. What pleasures awaited me if I could ever gain admission to his garden of delights!

The world now assumed a wonderful radiance. His naked image became etched indelibly on my heart and in my mind. I tried hard to repeat my visits to the showers at the same time as him, but rarely with success. But the memory of that single vision was enough as I daydreamed of holding him in my arms, kissing his lips, caressing his neck, holding his bum, making love to his cock, giving him intimate, exquisite pleasure. But would he want any of this from me? Would he ever accept me? What did he feel about me? Would he ever come to desire me as much as I now desired him, and yes… loved him?

Each morning at Mass, often enough after my semi-somnolent hard-on had been relieved, voluntarily or involuntarily, I would have feelings of remorse, anxiety and shame. The fantasies, the chronic obsessions – surely these must constitute a massive accumulation of mortal sins? Was I betraying my Heavenly Father irreparably, and Jesus, my faithful older brother, as well as the Church, my spiritual home? If so, should I even ask my parents to remove me from the school to root out this 'occasion of sin', the source of so much anguish and temptation?

But I was in love. Everyone taught that God is Love, and that we ourselves must love in order to become sons of God. And furthermore, our bodies were temples of the Holy Spirit; so how could it be sinful to worship them? I was utterly confused.

I tried to pray about this, and the answer came back: go and seek advice from the one person who understood you so well when you were in a crisis a couple of years ago – Dom Placid.

Filled with apprehension I sent him a note.

He replied immediately, saying he hadn't seen or heard from me for some time and had been wondering how I was getting on. He suggested a date and time, but already I was asking myself why was I making such a fuss? Was I being self-indulgent in seeking this dear old fellow's attention? Why not just 'man up' about my problem and either go with it, enjoy it, or dump it?

It was too late to call it off, so I duly met the good monk at the gate into the monastery gardens, usually strictly out of bounds for the boys. He could not have been more charming with his soft Irish accent echoing the openness of his face, his shock of white hair, white eyebrows, pink complexion and kind, dark eyes. His simplicity and transparent holiness were utterly convincing; I'd heard that quite recently he had received the Great War poet Tristram Montefiore into the Church.

It was quite cold and he was wearing a full-length black cloak over his habit, and a black beret, giving him the look of a venerable French *curé*.

I was nervous and dry-mouthed as we exchanged our pleasantries. But he exuded such calm and confidence that I just came out with it bluntly when he asked what he could do for me.

'Well, it's this, Father, and no one else knows: I've fallen in love with another boy, about eighteen months younger than me.'

Then it became a torrent: 'Is it a sin? Should I try to resist it? How can I live with this condition which I'm told is *unnatural*? Am I betraying everything I've been brought up to believe?'

'Heaven be praised,' he replied, to my great surprise. "Tis a great gift from God to fall in love, to be sure. The fact that it's a boy makes no big difference; if you were out in the world, with young ladies around you every day, you would probably feel the same towards one of them. One day you will fall in love with a beautiful young lady, to be sure.'

'But, *I'm* not so sure about that, Father. You see, I've never had feelings like this for a *girl* before, and I know in my heart that I've always preferred boys.'

He seemed completely unfazed. 'Don't be too hard on

yourself, Freddie, or think your feelings are set in stone. Keep your heart open to whatever the Good Lord sends you.'

He said he knew just how I must feel, and I could believe him; as though someone switched on all the lights in a darkened room, how I wanted to be always with the boy, spoil him, hug him, hold him. It was something completely normal and happened to everyone – a time of great joy in the short term, but more often ending in pain and disappointment.

'Now let me give you some advice. Remember what we've been trying to teach you: God is Love, as St John, the disciple who was beloved by Jesus, tells us – just as he is all Truth, Beauty, Goodness, Wisdom and Holiness. What you're experiencing now, being in love, is nothing less than an echo of God's Holy Spirit within you. I told you once before, Freddie: we've all been made in the image and likeness of our God, our Heavenly Father, and when you are in love you are reflecting something of His eternal nature and His unconditional love for *you* – His very own creation – unique in His eternal universe.

'But now the most important thing for you is that you should reciprocate God's love by loving your friend in the same way – unconditionally and with complete integrity.'

He explained what he meant: not 'objectifying' him, not making him into an *idol* to worship; nor trying to *control* him by showering him with gifts and affection, and thereby expecting – *demanding* – a reward from him and his total dedication. I needed to be patient and kind, understanding – even anticipating – his needs, and above all, to be forgiving if he caused me anguish or disappointment. I would soon know if he reciprocated my feelings. If he didn't, then I would have to accept it and if I *really* loved him I would still wish him well. The Good Lord would find someone else for me to love. On no account should I give way to jealousy, 'the biggest enemy of love', which made people incapable of future relationships, turning them into angry monsters, incapable of reason, let alone forgiveness or the operation of grace.

'But what if my love for him *is* reciprocated, Father?'

'Then you will be truly blessed, dear boy, and if it is the will of our Heavenly Father, everything should fall into place and you will become truly happy with a real, genuine and intimate love for each other.'

I just couldn't help myself. 'But what *then*, Father?'

'*Then*, dear boy,' he hesitated, 'if it happens naturally, and both of you are ready, you should be able to share your love for each other fully.' The dear man almost looked lost for words for a moment, but then, quite spontaneously, he looked into the middle distance and came out with it.

'Some people say we should sublimate these strong, difficult, feelings and burying ourselves in great causes, like "marrying" Holy Mother Church, and remaining forever celibate, being content with "loving friendships". But I'm not sure that isn't just avoiding the issue and postponing a natural conclusion.'

He hesitated again before turning to me with a smile of resignation and a shrug: '*If two people love one another, then who am I – who is anyone – to judge?*

'So, dear Freddie,' he suddenly became more cheerful, 'be prepared, persevere, be faithful, and with God's grace everything will come out right.'

I thought that was the end of the matter and that he obviously didn't want to discuss it any further.

But then he made a strange remark: 'It's possible, too, that you may have to perform an act of great courage or heroism for your friend one day, something that will prove your love and demonstrate it to all the world.'

I was taken aback. 'What sort of thing do you mean, Father? I'm not really the heroic type.'

'Oh, I can't possibly tell, and it may never happen. But, for example, you may have to be a witness for him, speaking out for him, even risking everything – your life and reputation – for his sake.'

There was one final thing. I must not confront him with my feelings until I knew for certain that he felt the same; I might frighten him and ruin a potentially beautiful friendship by rushing at it. *And* – and this was painful – I was not to be the first to lay an affectionate hand on him; he was the younger and more vulnerable of the two of us. It would be up to *him* to show if *he* was ready for me. Dom Placid was quite vehement on the subject and made me promise.

He paused before continuing, 'What I'm going to do for you – since you asked my advice – is to write out a little passage from St Paul for you to keep in your wallet or somewhere where you can look at it from time to time.'

It was getting late, and there was a distinct chill in the air as he gave me his blessing. I knew a great burden had been lifted from my shoulders now that I'd been heard and understood. I felt like giving the dear man a hug, and I'm sure he would have let me, but something held me back. Instead, I went on my knees in front of him, on the muddy path, and bowed my head. Tenderly he put his two hands over me and gave me his blessing.

Next day I received an envelope; inside it there was a plain postcard and a message written on one side in an elegant italic hand:

Love is always patient and kind; Love is never jealous;
Love is not boastful or conceited; It is never rude and
never seeks its own advantage; It does not take offence or
store up grievances… Love never comes to an end.

1 Corinthians 13: 4-5, 8

*

So, Sam, you can see how genuinely enlightened these good monks were. They were the opposite of the generally perceived image of RC priests with their ignorance, hypocrisy and pharisaical attitudes. Although they had taken the celibate path for themselves – and in due course we would come to understand why – they knew all about the stirrings in the hearts of young boys and how to deal with us! But it didn't take me long to wonder why this attitude wasn't the norm elsewhere. Would I have been so lucky if I'd been at a Jesuit or Christian Brothers school?

With my love,
Freddie

6

My dear Sam,

Easter was always the least satisfactory of our holidays. Exams were just a bit too close to be able to relax fully and the unpredictable weather often ruined any well-laid plans. This year, 1967, our time was spent alternating between London during the week and the cottage for long weekends. We never spent enough time at either, to my mind. At the cottage I purloined the garden room for my own exclusive use; I needed peace and quiet for revision. And more importantly, to daydream about Paul.

In London I started visiting the galleries and museums on my own, walking to them through the parks. My God, how I wished Paul was with me. But once there, I'm afraid, my eyes would be diverted by the slightly older French and Italian students in their slinky jeans and polo necks, hand in hand with their girlfriends. Until then I used to think I was the bee's knees in my tweed jacket, flannels and hush puppies. But now I wondered what it would be like to be as liberated as these casual fellows and divest myself of these trappings of identity. I was being pulled in two directions: one part of me envied the boys their freedom, but another part felt defensive of my loyalties.

*

The one major event that Easter was spending a few days at Pips's house in Bournemouth. His parents were genuinely kind and mildly amused at their son's eccentric effeminacy. His sister seemed to encourage him, letting him choose her clothes for her and approve her new perfume before we went to a party one evening. Years later, when Pips became seriously ill, we became great friends.

On my penultimate day I finally understood the reason why he'd asked me to stay: he desperately wanted to visit a pub 'with a certain reputation' which he'd never dared enter on his own. He'd heard it was *the* place to go on Sunday lunchtimes when it was full of colourful characters. We could probably get away with it as we looked just about legal. His furtive excitement was infectious and I'm afraid I had no misgivings. '*After all, what was the harm?*'

It was about five miles away, in a village, so we had to take a bus and pretend to Pips's parents that we were going to visit a National Trust house nearby. No objections were raised.

There were a few smart two-seater sports cars parked outside, suggesting that if one of us got lucky we might get a lift home perhaps by a circuitously amorous route. For a second I felt slightly panicky that we might get separated and I'd find myself adrift in a strange place. As we pushed open the door I was both excited and nervous. But it was all reassuringly old-fashioned: oak beams, big settles, horse brasses. I went up to the bar for two half-pints of cider, Pips finding us a table and a two-seater bench. The swarthy barman looked me up and down, and for a moment I felt intimidated by his shirt open to his navel, his hirsute chest and gold bangles. Before serving me he looked across to an old crone sitting on a bar stool in the corner with a gin and tonic; thin, grey hair in a beehive and lots of diamonds on her knuckles. She nodded to him, so he smiled knowingly as he pulled our drinks.

Back at the table Pips and I tried to disguise our virginal apprehension by smoking furiously and feigning animated talk, all the while sneaking glances at the men standing around the bar. Mostly they were about the same age as our respective fathers, 'silver daddies' Pips called them, smart but casual, in jackets, cravats and suede brogues, drinking Camparis or gin and tonics. Some were trying to chat up the much younger, pretty lads, propped up by the bar, more our age. I knew instantly that they were probably shop boys or office juniors brought here by their older admirers – 'dolly boys', again in Pips's immortal words. Despite all the attention being lavished on them they kept looking around, bored and distracted. One of them threw a pouty glance in our direction almost as though Pips and I were queering their pitch.

It didn't take long before some of the daddies started looking over at us in a friendly kind of way, turning to their neighbours and obviously talking about us. And then they'd give another look in our direction, this time with a hint of amusement. I'd only once been looked at like that before, by my blond charmer on the Underground last year. Recalling that lost opportunity, I plucked up courage to return their glances with a nervous little smile of my own.

Sam, you have to remember that we were complete novices at all this. I soon learnt that I had handled the situation all wrong, and that a cool indifference, blanking them out and playing hard to get, like the dolly boys, would have been the correct response. The men must have been amused and guessed immediately that Pips and I were making our début. Then I heard one of them make strange 'cluck, cluck, cluck' noises. They all fell about laughing.

Eventually a couple of them came over asking if they could join us. I got the dark one next to me, Kevin: early forties, shortish, but with a friendly round face and a bit tubby – which I didn't mind at all – with nice wavy hair, and slightly jowly cheeks, but lovely piercing blue eyes which seemed to look straight through me. He slightly resembled the actor Jack Hawkins. I became entranced with his full smiley mouth as we exchanged small talk which they must have thought suitable for a couple of posh schoolboys hoping to get laid. It was a bit patronising but we didn't care: where had I bought my amazing kipper tie?... Did I prefer Cliff Richard or Tom Jones?... Betty Davis or Joan Crawford?... Had anyone told me I looked like Anthony Perkins? Pips got the more handsome blond one, Derek, but I reckoned Kevin was nicer.

The talk got more relaxed after a second and then a third round, with a lot more eye contact and little flirty signals. At one point, when Pips was fully engaged with Derek, Kevin paused and turned his head to look mischievously and directly into my eyes, his mouth slightly trembling. I looked back at him, smiling, willing him on, to make me a proposition; maybe he'd invite me for a drive in his sports car? I'd heard that a ten-shilling note was the usual tariff or 'tip' if I agreed to be interfered with. *That* would have been quite a trophy! Or perhaps he'd offer to take me away on holiday pretending to be my uncle? What would my answer have been, I wonder, had not Pips intervened?

'We'd better be getting back. BoyO here has to go home to his Mama this evening.' I suspect Pips was getting fed up with *my* success – and *his* lack of it. Kevin looked away, disappointed. 'But *I'll* be coming back,' Pips announced. 'Maybe see you both again soon.'

Gosh, I was so annoyed I could hardly speak to him on the bus. It taught me a lesson: in future always go to these places of ill repute on your own. Then you can always leave *with* whom you like, and *when* you like.

A week later, when I saw him on the first day back at Upton, he came up to me in a state of high excitement, walking even more oddly than usual.

'You'll never guess. That Kevin of yours was *so* nice, such a big boy, and *so* thorough.'

'Don't tell me!' I said, fascinated, incredulous, spitting with curiosity.

'Yes,' he said, barely able to contain himself. 'My dear, IT happened. Last night. In his sports car. *My dear, I'm no longer a virgin.* Isn't it wonderful!'

*

For most of us the first six weeks of every summer term were passed under the dark clouds of impending exams: this year O-Levels for Paul and As for me. But once they were over the remaining time should have been idyllic. The grounds were looking at their best, the shrubberies still resplendent with rhododendrons, azaleas and sweet-smelling lilac, the sweeping lawns at their most verdant with the ancient cedars giving welcome shade against the hot afternoon sun. The wide terraces and playing fields were laid out in expectation of afternoon cricket and tennis matches. How reassuring were the shouts of 'Owzat!' or 'Thirty-Forty... Deuce', followed by a gentle clapping! From every viewpoint the abbey church closed off the scene, its tower reaching heavenwards into the azure skies, the bell pealing the call to the seven monastic Offices and the Angelus. Further afield the lanes and pathways of the countryside were alive with blossom and the smell of haymaking filled the air. Was I conscious then – or ever since, until now – of my good fortune in being at such a beautiful place at this beautiful time?

Now the air was filled with a certain festive buzz, heralding the satisfactory end of another year. There would be camping expeditions to the Brecon Beacons, long 'pilgrimage' walks to Hailes Abbey, theatre trips to Bristol and Stratford, and the cricket matches with Worthan and Appleford, our sister schools. It would culminate in the final long weekend for the Prize-Giving Festival which parents were expected to attend. The whole school would be on show: gymnastic displays, concerts from the musical societies, plays by the dramatic groups and art exhibitions by the *habitués* of the Art Attic. It would culminate on the Sunday with High Mass and a *Te Deum*, followed by prize giving and the headmaster's speech in the theatre. After lunch we'd all disperse homewards for two months' summer holidays.

It was considered poor show not to partake in one of these public-facing events, at least once in your school career. As I was hopeless at music, and couldn't draw (except maps, and these rather well), there was nothing for it but to volunteer for a play. I heard that the legendary Rappy was looking for a cast for *Twelfth Night* to be performed in the out-of-doors amphitheatre on the evening before Prize Day.

In a flash I knew what I had to do. Paul had already made his mark in one of Rappy's earlier productions while in the Junior House, and he'd once mentioned that he'd like another shot at acting. How about it?

The day after term began I met him in the dayroom. Had he had a good holiday? Not really. It seemed he'd been stuck at home like me.

'The only good thing was staying with Rowse in the Lakes for a week when we went out sailing most days.'

I almost choked. The very idea of tarty little Rowse having Paul to stay! What could they have got up to? Why couldn't he have stayed with *me* instead? I was trembling with envy.

'Oh,' I said. 'I didn't know you enjoyed sailing. You should come and stay with *us*; we've got a cottage down at Chichester Harbour and a dinghy that we mess about in. And you could meet my delightful sister and her friends,' I added with a smile.

I felt like saying, but didn't, 'I won't be taking you to places of ill repute like Pips took me to in Bournemouth. I'd want you all for myself.'

He looked back at me, his eyes dilating in genuine pleasure.

'Yeah, that would be nice. Are you sure your parents wouldn't mind?'

I told him they quite enjoyed having our friends to stay provided they 'fitted in'. It kept your mother and me occupied and was very little extra trouble. Nanny was there to do all the cooking and housekeeping. A new fantasy arose: Paul and me sharing my room at the cottage, going everywhere together on our bikes, snogging behind the bushes, swapping each other's swimsuits, climbing into bed together. I felt something move in my crotch.

I was determined not to lose him now that I'd got his attention.

'Are you going to be in Rappy's latest play? I hear he's doing *Twelfth Night* out-of-doors for Prize Day.'

'Rappy' was Dom Meinrad, a plump, roseate, tonsured monk and noted eccentric, of secretive nationality, possibly something *mitteleuropäisch*. He never tired of reminding anyone who'd listen that he once trod the boards of the Abbey Theatre, Dublin, and had been on first-name terms with the great GBS. His dimly lit cavernous study was clad from floor to ceiling with posters of his previous productions, the shelves full of signed first editions by his friends and boxes of scratchy 78rpm records.

'I'm not sure. I've got O-Levels and don't want to make a hash of them if I'm going to be in a play.'

'Oh, go on,' I said. 'I think *I'm* going to have a try.'

I hesitated for a moment before coming out with it. 'It would be really good if you were in it too.' Was I going too far, assuming a friendship which in truth was only in its infancy?

'Well, I might be persuaded, if he gives me a decent part. I'm not going to play one of those cross-dressing parts, whatever happens.'

'Nor am I going to play Malvolio,' I replied, 'I'd never live it down. Nor Andrew Aguecheek, let alone Toby Belch. I bet he gives you the part of Orsino, he's bound to,' I said enthusiastically, almost clapping my hands and already dreaming of his speaking those beautiful opening lines in that languid, dreamy voice of his:

> *'If music be the food of love, play on,*
> *Give me excess of it...'*

I'd loved the play's exaggerated love poetry since we'd studied it in the fourth form. The gender ambiguities and mistaken identities had seemed far-fetched then, but now I became fascinated by how Orsino fell in love with Viola while she was disguised as the boy Cesario. And what about the relationship between Sebastian and Antonio? What was going on there?

We duly presented ourselves at Rappy's audition, and of course he gave Paul the part of Orsino, the love-obsessed melancholy prince. I was awarded Antonio, Sebastian's rejected admirer. What irony! But never mind. To my intense relief there were no other friends of Paul's in the cast, nor indeed anyone else from Ambrose, so there should be plenty of opportunities for us to be thrown together.

A routine soon established itself: twice a week, in the hour-long 'free period' between supper and prep Rappy would take us through the play, scene by scene, act by act. In the final weeks the whole cast could rehearse more thoroughly in advance of a trip to the theatrical costumiers in Cheltenham. There would be a dress rehearsal and the final performance at five o'clock on the evening before Prize Day. As usual there would be an after-party at which a limited amount of alcohol was provided, but this was always, by tradition, supplemented by anything that could be smuggled in nefariously by the cast.

Even at our first read-through with Rappy it became clear that

Paul had an extraordinary feeling for the part; he had a way of drawing out the poetry and nuances of the verse which astonished us all, including Rappy. His naturally deep and languid voice could change effortlessly from melancholy to surprise, anger or action. With the more intense scenes he was able to animate his face, voice and gestures with ease and naturalism, compelling our attention at his every appearance, even though his was by no means the biggest part in the play. He was a complete revelation to everyone.

Rappy had suggested that we should all 'pair up' with another member of the cast to hear each other's lines when we got the chance, to act as prompts, and be sounding boards for each other. It seemed a heaven-sent opportunity, and without any inducement Paul suggested that he and I, being in the same house, should combine our efforts.

'You can keep me up to the mark, McNaughton. I'm no good if I'm left to my own devices.'

I was determined to help him as much as I could, now that my little plots to gain his attention had been achieved so providentially. At last we should be able to establish a genuine relationship, each of us with responsibilities for the other and with something in common to work towards. My dream was coming true; we were becoming part of each other's lives. At least that is what I persuaded myself.

*

Yet I was also aware of the precariousness of my situation and the potential danger of losing his affections before I had even started to earn them. Perhaps his newly revealed talents might lead to others' undue and unwelcome admiration; I needed to be more assertive in defining my status in his eyes. Who was I exactly? A friend? Yes definitely, by now; a mentor? Yes, so far so good. His *best* friend? Not quite yet. His special friend? Oh, if only! His lover? There was a *long* way to go!

I tried to conceal my longing for our sessions together in the empty Classroom XII, which we agreed would be our base for our rehearsals *à deux*. Here at last I could gaze at him unimpaired, study and memorise every pore of his skin, every bump on his nose, every crease of his lips, every curl in his tresses. Each time we sat opposite each other in close proximity I was thrilled to find something new and different about him. One time it might be the three tiny, delightful, amber freckles on his cheek below his left eye; another time, the half-moon cuticles on his pink fingernails; or yet again the little wrinkles that appeared on his temples when he laughed. The memory of them would haunt me until I could see them again.

It was the same with his voice, as I savoured each word, not just the rich cadences and varying modulations he brought to Shakespeare's great poetry, but our ordinary conversation and schoolboy banter. I wanted to worship at the source of this euphonic paradise, just to *kiss* him again and again on his mouth as he exhaled each syllable.

I can still see and hear him now, leaning against a desk, hands in pockets, tilting his whole body backwards, his head looking up at the ceiling with his eyes closed trying to memorise his soliloquies. He always wore his tie in a Windsor knot, and inevitably by evening it had loosened and fallen an inch or two below the collar stud. Once, when he had his eyes closed, I emboldened myself sufficiently to take hold of it, tighten it and slide it back to its proper place. I teased him as I did it, astonished and excited by my temerity.

'We can't have our "noble duke" looking scruffy, can we?'

'Oh, thanks.'

That's all I got, but as he said it so casually, he looked directly into my eyes with such affection I had never seen anyone give me before. At the same time the corner of his mouth quivered almost imperceptibly as though he wanted to smile. My nerve nearly failed me; I could do nothing except dive back into the pages of the book.

We'd spend hours discussing Orsino's character. Why was he so lovelorn? Did he *really* think music was the food of love?

'What sort of music?' I asked him, hoping to store up this information for future reference. 'What about *smiles* being the food of love?' I continued, remembering Pips's oblique message. What did Orsino think he was doing by trying to woo Olivia so hopelessly and vicariously through 'Cesario'? At what point did he realise he was *really* in love with Viola, the trans-dressed pageboy Cesario? Was it when he rhapsodised about the androgynous boy-girl's lips, 'as smooth and rubious' as Diana's? Shouldn't Paul actually *touch* 'Cesario's' lips at this point? Even *kiss* them? Wow! What would Rappy say to *that* new stage direction! How would pretty little Scarisbrick Mi (yes, him again, dammit) playing the part of Cesario/Viola, take it if it was suggested? My goodness, *I'd* be jealous as hell! Anyway, would it make any difference these days if Viola/Cesario turned out to be a boy after all?

When it came to rehearsing my part, the older Antonio, there were yet more coded references. Paul would take the part of Sebastian with whom Antonio was besotted. I would look him straight in the face and say my lines, *sotto voce*:

'*But come what may, I do adore thee so...*'

And later, defiantly:

'*And to his image* [me pointing to Paul], *which methought did promise Most venerable worth, did I devotion.*'

Was he taking it all in? I just couldn't tell. He asked me once, smiling but trying to be serious, if I thought this the first Homo love declaration on stage since antiquity?

'Mmm, probably,' I answered. 'But poor Antonio is betrayed by his best friend, and ends up on his own. It seems very unfair.'

My God, I thought, *I'm determined that's not going to happen to* me.

*

I wanted to find out everything about him: his family, his likes and dislikes, his hopes and fears. But above all, what lay deep in his heart. Now, at last, these meetings allowed us to open up about ourselves. He admitted that he didn't find it easy to confide in others or make new friends, yet somehow he seemed completely at ease with me! Had his air of cool detachment sent out messages to others that he was indifferent to friendship, not available, not to be messed with?

He wasn't that straightforward. He could be judgmental of those who fell short of his high standards, and there was a cynical and quite sarcastic streak in him. On the other hand, he could be very loyal to his few close friends. Perhaps this was why he was still hanging around that little whore Rowse who'd befriended him in Junior House after he'd arrived from his day school in Yorkshire knowing nobody? In some ways, though, I was glad he wasn't a total paragon; his blemishes somehow made him more human. They were something I could help eliminate to make him perfect in every way.

I heard how he and his younger sister were being brought up by their mother and living with their aged grandmother in Yorkshire. His father had not been heard of for several years, and his school fees were being paid by his childless uncle and aunt. Paul had felt deeply the absence of a father figure at home, or even an older brother, and he longed for the normality of the family life he had seen in the homes of his friends. He confided that when he was eight there had been terrible scenes when he had tried to run away from home to find his father who he thought must be somewhere in America; he had got as far as Leeds station before being returned home by the police. Now he felt under a great obligation to his uncle and his family to do well to fulfill their expectations. As he told me all this, sighing, and with a resigned look on his face, I wanted to hug him and adopt him as my younger brother.

He didn't know what he wanted to do in the longer term; perhaps he'd go to Cambridge, like his uncle, but he wondered if he'd be up to it, and, at this stage had no idea what he wanted to read. I told him that was also my plan, or rather, my father's ambition for me.

My heart really went out to him. I thought how much he must be missing by being so conscientious, so guarded and introspective, preoccupied with having to do well. I swore to myself I'd do anything and everything to help him. But I wondered at my capacity to be of any real use.

When I once asked, somewhat guardedly, about girls, he gave a slight blush and looked defensive. Yes, he'd snogged with a girl he thought he'd fancied for the first time at a teenage dance last holidays and quite enjoyed it, but there was no one special who he was writing to; that was the usual way our romances blossomed in those days. I wondered at that. Surely such a handsome boy must have admirers among his sister's friends? Had he put them off somehow? And if so, why? Most boys would have taken full advantage of their assets. Why wasn't he so keen? Was he a cold fish, or shy, or just 'not that interested' in girls?

At this date it was almost impossible to tell where his affections might lie. He never gave the slightest inkling he was attracted physically to any other boys; that was a big relief for me. I knew for sure he had other admirers in the school to whom he'd shown his easy contempt, thank goodness. No, *if* he ever had a boy-on-boy love interest in his life – and *if* that was to be me – I knew instinctively that he would be completely loyal and monogamous and that he would demand the same from me.

There must have been *something* about me that attracted him, right from the start, and he must have felt he could trust me. I don't think he ever imagined that I was an out-and-out predator and that all I wanted was to make a 'conquest' of him, hold him up as a trophy, and then dump him. He knew me better than that by now. If he had guessed at my feelings for him – and I was by no means sure that he had – I wanted him to know that he was not just another boy-crush. The day would surely come when I would have to tell him how much I loved him, worshipped him, wanted to give him everything I had, all that I was, to be always close to him, to become a part of his whole being and his life. I half dreaded, half longed for that day of revelation, but knew it was inevitable. I prayed that, in return, he'd be able to say the same to me.

What was he finding out about me, I wondered? Of course, I was putting my best foot forward trying to make him *like* me, perhaps trying too hard. Up until now I had been playing the part of the older, more sophisticated boy-about-town, perhaps a little patronising and imagining I was the big 'catch' with all my so-called wisdom and experience to offer.

But I knew in my heart of hearts that I was a bit of a fraud, and any sense of superiority wouldn't wash with Paul. It was no use my pretending to be someone I wasn't. I was only too aware that *I* was the lovelorn pursuer and *he* the pursued. I knew that overattentiveness might result in annoying him, but if I showed indifference he might walk away. Somehow, I needed to strike the right balance.

The best thing about being in love, as I now declared to myself to be, was the transformation of my self-confidence. Each new day offered endless exciting possibilities; everything was achievable and worth striving for. What a change from the dark early days when I had moped around in the background of life trying to be invisible. I discovered that some of those little eccentric characteristics for which I had once been bullied were making a comeback, although this time more discreetly. I was using my hands more as I spoke; my voice was more expressive; I was allowing my face to reflect my feelings; I was becoming bolder, answering back with what I imagined was clever banter, being flippant and witty. I was smiling a whole lot more. Thanks to the relaxed atmosphere of Ambrose, I was finding no resentment among my contemporaries to this new freedom. There was a real spring in my step, a feeling of elation that enabled me to be cheerful and think well even of the most unattractive boys or the most detached of the monks. It must have been clear to everyone that I was genuinely happy.

Miraculously, the more relaxed and genuine I became, the more Paul seemed to enjoy being with me. I was amazed and overjoyed when his face lit up sometimes when he saw me coming down the passage, and he'd often take the initiative in suggesting the next date for our 'rehearsals'. Sometimes he even seemed to be picking up some of my odd turns of phrase, even my mannerisms; or was he just mocking me in a friendly way? Maybe I'd been trying too hard to impress him and it was really the little things about me that he was drawn to.

What did I have to offer him? Looking back now, objectively, the answer was probably not much! But to be fair, I knew I could at least provide him with encouragement; I could share his anxieties and show him how to expand his horizons, engage with the world more confidently. He needed someone beside him to help him, to bring him out; I just wanted to be that person.

In the longer term, maybe I could transform his cynicism into something more positive – develop a sense of irony in him and humanise that air of cool detachment. I just wanted to make him *smile* a lot more, like I seemed to be doing.

He was affecting me in other ways too. The great explosion in my life that he represented was coinciding with concerns about how I was projecting myself to the world. Until now my identity had been somewhat blurred. I had probably been giving the impression that I was a semi-closeted appendage to my more interesting, oddball, exotic friends, but still relatively conformist myself. Just getting along with life as I found it and not very good at anything in particular.

This wasn't good enough. I wanted to develop my own unique identity, my own brand of 'being different' or 'otherness'. Alright, being a Queer (or a Homo as we more often called ourselves) was 'different' enough, and I wasn't afraid or ashamed of it by now, and even rather enjoyed it in the right context. But I was unsure how I should project this to the world; I knew I didn't want to identify as an effeminate pooftah, like Pips. I would never get away with it, and it would upset too many people, not least my parents. There must be some middle course for me that would neither offend by being too obvious, nor deny by being too closeted. I had yet to find a Queer role model, maybe somebody clever and sophisticated, say, like Noel Coward – although my mother assured me that 'he's a perfect bastard, darling' – or dark and alluring, like Dirk Bogarde in *Victim*: handsome, brooding, 'complicated'.

But there was more to me than just my sexuality; I wanted something extra to fire me up, something special to mark me out. I knew I had a creative side – there was a lot of my mother in me – but I hadn't yet nailed it. It wasn't anything obvious like art or music or drama, although I enjoyed all of these passively. Whatever it was, I knew it would be something linked to my

Queerness. Although I knew my father was disappointed that I disdained most team sports, and my mother that I was so unmusical, they seemed to tolerate my deficiencies hoping that a more defined personality would emerge in due course. I could probably bide my time.

Then I came to wondering what else this wondrous fifteen-year-old who seemed to be electrifying me might have to offer? In the grandest scheme of things the answer was simple: love, *of course*. Then, maybe happiness, for both of us, together, and *forever*.

But, in a more mundane way, and perhaps subliminally, I hoped that Paul could be the catalyst for bringing out those latent qualities I knew I possessed but which hadn't yet emerged properly: an ability to be kind, generous, engaging – simply to be *nice* to people. All of that had gone underground when I'd been thrust down that hole in Junior House. For too long I'd been on my guard, like so many monosyllabic adolescents. I was almost out of that slough of despair now, but I needed someone's strong hand finally to haul me to the surface and embrace me into the sunshine. That was going to be him. He could be the motivation behind my new identity.

*

These were all the thoughts that occupied me during the latter part of that summer term. What were his, I wondered? Was he changing? Was I having any effect on him? Yes: during the course of these two months I could see how he was slowly coming out of his shell, finding within himself a sensitivity he never knew he had, and becoming alive to everything around him. There had been one or two hints already, but late one summer evening I had a glimpse that we might, just might, be on the same journey together.

When the weather became warmer and the evenings longer, we would spend more time after supper lying under the giant cedars, enjoying the early summer sounds and the smells of newly mown grass, each of us rehearsing our lines and getting them word perfect. When it was time to go indoors, I would pick off any stray grass or bugs from his jacket, and he would do the same for me. My heart raced as he came so close to me, touched my clothes, allowing me to inhale a tiny suggestion of him, hardly daring accidentally to brush my hand against his. We would walk back silently together across the lawns, looking up at the great abbey church and its magnificent tower as its shadow lengthened and the air became cooler. I had a sense that he was feeling the same as me, tired but relaxed and happy.

As we sauntered slowly towards the side entrance, he broke the silence.

'You know, I find these evenings we spend out here really beautiful. I just wonder if it's not all a dream. Whether it's really preparing us to withstand all the ugliness and grief we're bound to discover out there,' pointing vaguely into the distance. 'I keep thinking I mustn't squander this time. I'm sure I'll never be so fortunate again.'

I nodded and looked towards him. 'Who knows what's in store for us, Shipton? But one thing's for sure: we can always *remember* this time. If life gets bad later on, we can at least relive some of these days in our imagination. No one can take that away from us.'

'Yes, I think that's what I mean,' he replied.

There was a pause. We were nearly at the door and had been walking almost shoulder to shoulder. We stopped and he turned sideways to face me.

'Anyway, thanks a lot for this evening... You know, I really like being with you.'

'And I like being with you, Shipton.' I hesitated before the next words, which I knew I had to say, and then took the plunge: 'I think you probably know that by now.' I looked him straight in the face.

For a second he turned to stare at the ground, then he looked towards me with a smile.

'It's ridiculous our calling each other by our surnames all the time. Won't you let me call you Fred, at least when we're together like this?'

What was I hearing? My heart missed a beat.

'I can go better than that,' I said. 'I'd much prefer if you called me Freddie. Only my family do that, but I'd make an exception for you. But only if you let me call you Paul.'

'I'd really like that,' he said, his eyes twinkling in the dimming light as he thrust out his hand for me to shake to seal our new relationship, then giving me a mock punch on my chest. It was his own very personal gesture of spontaneous delight, something that I came to know and long for.

Was this the first 'touch of affection' that Dom Placid had insisted must come from him?

A door had opened at last.

With my love,

Freddie

7

My dear Sam,

Now the exams were over the whole school seemed to breathe a collective sigh of relief. But for those committed to the end-of-term festival there was yet more work to do, with its own tensions and deadlines, yet not without its pleasures. The cast of *Twelfth Night* would gather more frequently with Rappy, and a great sense of camaraderie built up. This was quite a rare thing, cutting across different ages and houses, everyone enjoying a shared experience.

We had a lot of fun at the theatrical costumiers in Cheltenham trying out potential outfits. Back at school I suggested the matron add a few flourishes to Paul's black velvet doublet and cloak. We prayed for fine weather, which, in the event, we were blessed with. There was a decent audience from among the boys, the monks and the parents, including mine, seated on rugs on the stepped grass amphitheatre. Paul's mother and uncle were there, and he managed to introduce me briefly just before we disappeared to change. It all passed off pretty well, and – as I had anticipated – Paul took an unequal proportion of the attention and applause. He was the perfect Orsino, looking, speaking and acting the very incarnation of a Renaissance prince.

After taking our bows, and glowing with the applause, we removed the greasepaint and changed in readiness for the special supper laid on in one of the guest dining rooms. It was eight o'clock by now and we were ravenous, lapping up the kitchen staff's special fare polished off by strawberries and cream from the monastery gardens. Rappy's entrance into the feast bearing jugs of pale ale was reminiscent of a panto Friar Tuck and drew cheers from the cast. Even such mildly intoxicating liquor was unknown in the usual routine of the school refectory.

As we sat or stood around the room in small groups, we refilled our glasses as soon as they became empty and the atmosphere became increasingly euphoric. The headmaster, known as Whiskers because of his permanent five o'clock shadow, made his appearance to congratulate us. At last Rappy delivered his final thanks and left the room with the parting shot,

'Be sure to be back in your dormitories by ten o'clock for lights-out.'

Once the coast was clear Paul and I sprang into action. My parents had driven up from London in the Bentley and had been instructed by me to call at a farm nearby to collect two gallons of homemade scrumpy cider, which I assured them was traditional for the after-party. They were to leave it in the boot of the car in the quad for me to retrieve during a quiet moment in the afternoon. I had then hidden it in an empty locker near the guest dining room.

As we appeared with the heavy jars there were more cheers from the dozen or so boys who were still left. I knew from experience that the potion was incredibly powerful, and even one pint each, on top of Rappy's weak pale ale, would be enough to make any of us blotto. The taste was disgusting, sour and coarse, but just about drinkable if diluted with lemon juice. Even so, everyone was gulping it down, getting merrier and merrier, voices becoming slurred, faces getting redder, and anyone attempting to walk finding themselves increasingly unsteady. There were frequent visits to the nearby bogs. Mercifully no one threw up.

I had dreamt that in my inebriation I would be emboldened to say something to Paul that I'd never dared before; he'd have to respond one way or the other; we might get to touch, or even kiss. I had rehearsed endlessly the words I would use. Yet nothing was likely to happen while we were in the presence of the rest of the cast, however drunk we all became. Maybe later, on our way back to Ambrose, in one of the deserted corridors or crossing the quad in the moonlight. Following him into the bogs would be a final option; I've always been too fastidious for anything like that.

At quarter to ten a bell alerted everyone that the dormitory routine would be starting in fifteen minutes. We needed to get back.

Paul's usual languid voice had now become slurred and exhausted, to such an extent that it was difficult to make out what he was saying.

As we left the room he was staggering from side to side. I had to keep him propped up, with my arm under his shoulder, leaning him against my chest. He smelt of greasepaint, sweat and booze, a beguiling new sensation for me. I got him into the quad without falling over. But once outside in the night air he became a dead weight. Just in time I got him to kneel over a grating before it all came spewing out. Oh God, this was awful, but I had to get him to the dormitory as fast as I could. The vomit had partly cleared his stomach and he must have felt better, starting to move again and leaning against me as I held him upright. As we reached Ambrose there was just enough time to take him into the ground-floor wash house, throw some water over his face and grab him a glass of water before we staggered up the stairs to the dormitory. Dom Gabriel was waiting outside the door with the head of house, the prefects, and all the asperges paraphernalia and about to start proceedings. We rushed past and hurled ourselves into the room just in advance of them. Dom Gabriel looked daggers in my direction. I knew instantly that my chances of being made a prefect next term were now in ruins.

Paul's cubicle was diametrically opposite mine in this huge room in which some thirty boys slept, ten cubicles each side, and ten down the centre. The moment the '*Miserere*' was over, I could dimly make out that he was barely managing to change into pyjamas, then throwing himself into bed without even going down to the washroom. Within minutes he was motionless, fast asleep.

Our late arrival and disorderliness had not gone unnoticed by Paul's neighbour in the cubicles, his friend Rowse – Pips's 'pretty boy with an impertinent air' and Williamson's (correctly) predicted 'new 'ouse tart'. His extreme prettiness had not diminished in the course of nearly a year. With his dark complexion, cute size and exquisite proportions, his oval face, wide-set eyes, heart-shaped lips and fine lustrous black hair, he could almost have been taken for an expensive mixed-race rent boy, now I come to think of it. He knew full well I fancied him. Often he would give me a wink, or lick the corner of his lips, to which I would respond irresistibly with a smirk, finding it intensely provocative and maddening. How he squared all this with being a friend of Paul, so serious and conscientious, I could never fathom. Yet I had noticed that their behaviour when together, for instance on the rugby field, was perfectly normal. The whole cockteasing thing was obviously a great game for him.

Of course, Rowse was well aware of my attentiveness to Paul, particularly this term. There had been one or two snide whispers, barely audible, as we had passed in the passage, always delivered with his knowing little snigger, such as:

'Had a good session with Shipton today, McNaughton?', or even 'Been "rehearsing" with Shipton today, McNaughton?'

I wondered what, if anything, they said about me when they were together.

Tonight, after Dom Gabriel and the prefects had left, going to their own late-night end-of-term party with the headmaster, all sense of order in the dormitory deteriorated rapidly. The hapless and most junior prefect left in charge seemed unable to exert any sort of authority over this unruly and excitable crowd, exhilarated at the prospect of going home next day. Boys were wandering around in their dressing gowns, ragging and larking about; a pillow fight had broken out in one corner; some bottles of beer had appeared from nowhere.

Amidst all this chaos Rowse came sidling over to my cubicle and lay provocatively across the end of my bed, partly propped up by his elbow. I was in my pyjamas, sitting on top of the small chest of drawers by the window, looking longingly across at Paul's cubicle and watching the chaos unfold.

'You managed to get Shipton out stone cold tonight then,' he said, with his tarty little grin. 'Didn't anything happen?'

'I haven't got the first idea what you're talking about,' I said, archly, still with a slur in my voice.

'Bad luck this time,' and, as he said it, he put his hand into the gap in his dressing gown evidently scratching his dick. 'But Shipton's not the only pebble on the beach. What about someone else instead? Come on, McNaughton, admit it, you've always fancied me like hell.'

He stood up and looked at me again. 'Why not "come round and see me some time",' he pouted, in a fake Southern drawl trying to imitate Mae West, 'like tonight after the lights go out? Here's your big chance!'

He sauntered off to his end of the dormitory. After a few steps, twirling his dressing gown cord round and round, he gave just one backward glance towards me as I stood there dumbfounded.

'Well, why the hell *not*?' It was Eros again, egging me on. 'You've been waiting for something to happen for such a long time and here's an open invitation. It'll be nothing serious, don't worry.'

But I had so longed for my first romantic, erotic experience to be with Paul. Now, in my semi-drunken state, I was unable to resist; others might have been able to, but I was beyond caring or thinking of the consequences just at that moment. A thrill ran through my whole body at the thought of touching Rowse's beautiful skin, kissing those sultry lips and getting my hands on those tempting shapely limbs.

The duty prefect made a final effort to restore order before switching the lights out and leaving. The general chatter started up again; another pillow fight broke out; someone found they'd been given an apple-pie bed; more bottles of beer had appeared. I was able to go over to Rowse's cubicle without any comment or suspicion being raised.

It was a humid night and he was lying on his back under a single sheet, head propped up on his pillows. As I approached, he gave a huge grin, turned on his side and threw back the top sheet to reveal his naked torso. He patted the side of the mattress inviting me to join him.

It was a sight to savour, alright; his golden flesh seemed luminous in that midsummer half-light, one of his arms clutching at the headboard showing his muscles slightly strained and his dark tufted pits. His face was the very picture of seduction, looking at me with smiling come-to-bed eyes, his tongue licking his delicious half-open lips.

I defy anyone to have resisted.

I unbuttoned my pyjama top and let it fall to the ground, climbed in next to him as he moved over, his right arm now bent at the elbow, holding his head in one hand. But now he'd hooked me his expression changed, seemingly hardened. Somehow that made him even more desirable. I lurched forward in a frenzy to grab his pretty little face in both hands, to try to kiss him full on the lips, my mouth open and eager. But – Oh Hubris! – I only succeeded in battering at his teeth; his tongue was evidently *not* on offer. Maybe he wasn't expecting me to be so greedy. The bloody little tart seemed to be clamming up.

But I wasn't going to be put off so easily. I kissed and licked and tasted my way down his neck, his pecs, his chest, but thinking all the time of Paul and how this should be him. I felt my body tingling and my cock stiffen as I fumbled with his pyjama bottoms to thrust my hand inside.

But without any warning he propped himself up on the pillows.

'That's enough. You're pissed, McNaughton, and you stink of booze. Go away! And, by the way, I'm *not* Shipton.'

At that very moment there was a flash of torchlight across the bed. My goodness, the prefect had returned. I was done for. But, no: he just stopped for a moment and said, with a voice of weary exasperation,

'Oh, for goodness' sake, McNaughton, go back to your *own* bed, NOW,' and moved on.

I couldn't believe my luck. Maybe he'd been there himself in the past. I could only assume it wasn't worth his effort to make a scene: there was too much pandemonium for him to sort out. I'm sure his name was Walker, and he was considered a soft touch anyway. I scurried back as fast as I could but not without a quick glance in the direction of Paul's cubicle; all I could see was a humped mass under the sheets.

I was amazed at myself for being so daring. At the very least, now I knew I didn't have to spend the rest of my life as a pathetic onanist. Given another chance, and with the right boy – Paul of course – I'd have no more inhibitions. It had just been our hard luck that tonight the prefect had interrupted us (but thank God he'd been so pre-occupied otherwise the consequences would have been dire). I told myself that Rowse had seen him coming, and *that* was the reason I'd been thrown out, and not, as he'd tried to imply, because I was so drunk and clumsy. I refused to believe he'd been disappointed. Later, as I finished myself off, I had a wonderful time fantasising how it might have ended.

I woke up next morning with a headache and still feeling tired. In the cold light of day I dreaded how Paul would take it when, and if, he got to hear about last night's shenanigans. Would he be shocked, angry, disappointed? Somehow I doubted he would merely shrug it off.

Hell, I thought. *I've been so patient with you, so generous, so attentive – and all my plans have come to nothing. I had been at bursting point last night and it just happened to be Rowse who was on offer. I'd so hoped it might have been you – but you just weren't there.*

Leaving the dormitory on the way to breakfast I ran to catch up with Paul as we clattered down the parquet staircase.

'How are you feeling today?' I asked, adding, 'You don't seem too good,' looking sideways into his blurred eyes and pale face.

He gave me a sour look such as I'd never seen before. 'Pretty bloody awful, if you must know. Wherever did you get that scrumpy? It was a killer.'

'Oh, it came from a remote farm where they sell it at the back door for 2/6d a gallon. Mum and Dad could hardly get the car down the lanes they were so narrow,' I replied, desperately hoping that was all that was worrying him.

Now we were walking side by side, in the general surge through the hall towards the main refectory. I got the horrible impression he was trying to leave me behind by walking faster.

'More to the point, McNaughton...' he said, stopping in his tracks against the tide of boys bearing down on us from behind. He looked sideways at me, now with fury, sadness, incomprehension in his eyes.

'I'm truly appalled with what I heard you and Rowse got up to last night… I never thought you'd fall for his cheap little tricks; nor, I suspect, did he. I had you on quite a pedestal, you know.' His voice was almost hoarse as he barked out each phrase.

I felt a rush of panic. I could barely think straight. 'Oh, for goodness' sake. It was nothing, really nothing at all. He was being such a little whore. Besides, I was blotto, like you, and…'

Was he even listening? But now my panic was giving way to remorse. I could feel my eyes going damp.

'Is this going to affect the two of us, Paul?'

'I'll have to think about it. But I just can't bear the idea of you *pawing over and snogging someone else*, from what I'd heard, especially with Rowse.'

He paused. 'I suppose I've got too used to you. You've been *leading me on* to think that *I*… was… you know… your… your…'

He couldn't bring himself to finish. His exasperation had made him speechless. He looked up at me, his big brown eyes bleeding despondency and bitterness.

'God knows if I'll ever forgive you for making me feel like this.'

The penny dropped. How could I have been so blind? My instinct now was to reach out to hold him, to kiss him and cover him with my tears. But my mouth went dry with panic again. Whatever could I say?

'But, Paul, of course you were, still *are*, my most *special* of all *special friends*, if that's what you mean. You *must* know that, for goodness' sake.' I was almost choking. 'But you never gave me any hint of how you felt about me. I'd given up all hope.' My God, I was whining like a wretched child.

But surely I had a right to justify myself? My heart was pumping violently, blood surging round in my head, making me stumble over my words.

'Anyway, what do I owe you, for God's sake? I've given you everything I have, which isn't much, I know. But you seemed to be *taking* everything and *giving* nothing. If you weren't interested in me, why should I "save myself" for you? Why should I bother anymore if we're going nowhere? I needed to find someone else – *anyone* else – just at that moment when I felt most deprived of you.' Now I was angry, tearful and sorry, all at once.

'Come over here,' he said, turning round abruptly and going behind one of the giant Gothic pillars. 'Over here.' He was *ordering* me. The passing hordes had thinned out and only the odd stragglers were still meandering in our direction.

'*This* is how I feel about you, Freddie McNaughton.'

With a single, brutal thrust he lashed out his fist at my nose. There was a thud. I was seeing stars, stunned by the pain. My fury burst; in a split second I had become Neanderthal. But I was too late. He was gone, marching in the direction of the refectory, and I hadn't the will to go after him. Instead, I was left helpless, humiliated, clasping my handkerchief, trying to stop the flow of blood gushing from my nose.

At that very moment, Pips came up beside me, my angel incarnate.

'I saw that, you poor bastard! Shipton's gone pretty rough on you. Why did he go running off? Lovers' tiff?' he smirked. 'Did you say something?'

'Oh, Pips,' I almost blubbed. 'I've got to talk to you. I'm in such a mess.'

'Let Nurse Phillips administer her healing touch,' he said, starting to mop up the blood. He was surprisingly delicate and reassuring.

'Come on, BoyO. Chin up now, while we go into breakfast. We can tell everyone you walked blind into one of these pillars in your terrible hangover. Meet me behind the bogs afterwards. We'll have a gasper and you can tell me all about it.'

Pips was the most super-intelligent and perceptive of all my friends. Not for nothing he was to get a top Classics scholarship to Christchurch. Although his own emotional life was an exhausting rollercoaster of entanglements, he could see right through other people's relationships and knew just where they were going.

*

Later, at our insalubrious rendez-vous, I was still feeling sore as I helped myself to one of Pips's B&H fags. The surge from the first inhalation made me feel a whole lot better. I told him the whole saga. He'd missed the scenario last night as he'd been too busy flirting unsuccessfully with his latest, Langton, the ace spin bowler in the 2nd XI.

Pips looked at me with the earnestness of one who knows the answer to every problem.

'That punch of his means just one thing. Shipton's *so* crazily in love with you that he now *hates* you. It's jealousy, BoyO, pure jealousy. The surest but most dangerous sign of true love, despite what those monks say.'

His advice was to do nothing yet. No letters, no more apologies, make no overtures for another meeting.

'After all, you've both made your feelings pretty clear about each other, haven't you? You're *meant* for each other, you two.' In his view, Paul was an idiot to take my misdemeanour so badly.

'On the other hand,' he said, 'you've got to understand how he'll be seriously hurt. How would *you* feel if you'd seen *him* in bed with another boy – with your gorgeous friend Charlie Herbert, for example? Wouldn't *your* blood be boiling? Just think about it.'

'But I wasn't sure he felt like that about me,' I almost cried.

'You should have read the signs, BoyO. Didn't you say *he'd* been the one who asked to call you "Freddie"? And wasn't it *he* who suggested you had your little rehearsals *à deux*? You won't know this, but I've watched you two from the windows – when you were both lying under the big cedar in front of the abbey. My God, I thought, how lovely! How romantic! Two boys together, in love, without either of them having said anything to the other!'

Pips thought the air should be cleared after this little contretemps. Time was a great healer.

'Yes really,' he said. 'Within a week or two of next term. There's everything to hope for. I just know he'll forgive you. It'll be the sign of true love.'

I looked at him doubtfully.

'Yes, you two have a *duty* to become a lovely couple – just looking after each other, doing things together. You could be a really *positive* model for "particular friendships" between boys.'

I loved Pips for his well-meaning advice and gave him a smile and an affectionate kiss on the cheek – the first time I'd ever done that to a schoolfriend. His reaction stunned me. As he returned me a kiss, just missing my lips, he said,

'My God, darling. I can't tell you how long I've been waiting for *that* from you!'

*

But I wasn't so sure the air would ever be cleared, knowing Paul's stubborn contempt for those who failed to live up to his standards. I knew I was on a knife edge. I'd never tested his capacity for forgiveness before, let alone made him change his mind over something important. I was completely in his power.

It was just as well it was the last day of term. I managed to keep going sufficiently to show my parents the exhibitions, listen to all the prize-giving and speeches. But finally, as we drove away, I just crashed out in the back of the Bentley. They wanted to talk about plans for the holidays, but I kept my eyes closed, feigning sleep. I felt so bitter and sad; I'd messed everything up and probably lost the love of my life for good. *Is this what hell looks like?* I wondered. A thought kept passing through my head: maybe I should pack the whole thing in, and *demand* my parents remove me from Upton. If Paul was never going to forgive me, I'd rather be at the failing Comprehensive in Notting Hill where I could sink into everlasting obscurity.

With my love,

Freddie

8

My dear Sam,

After those disastrous events I should have been the last person to call 1967 the 'Summer of Love'. But you'll soon see how things turned out to justify that phrase for me, as well as the rest of the world.

Your grandparents had arranged for your mother and me to go to France for almost the whole two months' holidays. The excuse was that we should improve our French, but in truth your grandmother was still not well, and the prospect of having us at home – even with Nanny's help – was too much for her. When I pressed my father for an explanation he was always evasive: 'Change of life', is all he would say, almost under his breath, expecting us to understand. Without really knowing what he meant, Pippa and I would try to be sympathetic and keep out of the way. This time your mother went as an *en famille* 'exchange' (never reciprocated) to some cousins of cousins in Charente, and me as a paying guest at a château in Touraine recommended by a colleague of my father's.

I was still feeling pretty broody as I was put on the boat-train at Victoria only a week after returning home. I had been obsessing about how I might have lost Paul forever because of my stupidity. The hot summer afternoons had been spent on solitary walks in the park, dreaming about how the two of us might have been there together lying in the sun. The melancholy strains of *Sergeant Pepper* seeping out of every open door and window in London made me feel even more love sick.

*

Madame de Ferrand and the eldest of her two sons, the twenty-one-year-old Olivier, were at Tours station to meet me, under the clock as planned, with her small dachshund, Toto, on a long lead. She was a large late-middle-aged widow, jowly and somewhat hatchet-faced, no hint of makeup, wearing a grey raincoat down to her ankles which matched her thin tresses done up in a bun. Yet I soon discovered this *formidable* appearance belied a kind and motherly nature. Olivier, ever obliging and with a wide, smiling, open face, stuffed my bags into the boot of her DC and we bounced along the cobbled streets of Tours in a south-westerly direction.

The Château de Miré was a fine eighteenth-century mansarded country house, approached by an impressive avenue of chestnuts, with lawns to the front and rear, and an elegant but precarious balustraded terrace. Behind a screen of trees to one side lay the farmyard and its buildings, the domain of chickens, ducks and geese who would flap about bad-temperedly every time Madame swept past, honking at them in her ancient car. The front door was kept permanently locked except on Sundays when the lunch guests, which reassuringly always included *Monseigneur l'abbé*, would be admitted that way. Closer inspection revealed that at least half the château was uninhabitable. I was given a suite of three rooms, with grand but faded Empire furniture, and a private bathroom, but no hot running water. This was produced by a very small immersion heater, which took about ten minutes to heat up enough for an occasional shave. When I asked on arrival if I could have a bath, my hostess looked somewhat bewildered saying that certainly I could if I accompanied her to her cousin's house at Chinon in a couple of days. I soon learnt not to bother. It was an excuse to douse myself even more liberally with the latest Italian pong Galbraith had given me for my birthday.

On arrival I was introduced to Louis, Madame's nineteen-year-old second son – younger, darker, more Gallic and mysterious than his elder brother, with huge, languid, brown eyes and fabulous lashes. Gosh! I remember them even now.

He was bearing an envelope. 'A telegram has arrived for you, Frédéric.'

'Oh, but please call me Fred,' I replied in French, rolling the 'r' as best I could. I thought, *No, I'm not going to let you call me Frédi, until I know you a whole lot better.*

I looked at the envelope with dread, knowing its contents must reveal my A-Level results forwarded by my father, although I hadn't expected them so soon. I needed the privacy of my room before I could bring myself to learn my fate.

To my intense relief they were much better than I expected. In my depressed state I had been expecting the worst. Yet I knew that I had sharpened up quite noticeably last term, the effect of being in love, I suppose, and desperate to make some sort of impression on Paul.

When I broke the good news to my host family downstairs they were full of effusions, Madame calling for champagne. But before that, I needed to telephone my father. My reverse-charge call to England turned into a major event for the local telephone exchange; there were long silent pauses when I thought all was lost, but then numerous encouraging interjections – '*ne quittez pas... ne quittez pas...*' – before I finally got through.

I felt flattered as my father congratulated me so warmly. Ever since I'd been at Upton I'd been conscious that I didn't stand very high in his estimation. At last, here was a minor achievement of his son and heir in which he could take some pride.

'They're certainly good enough for a "redbrick", Freddie,' he said, not quite managing to disguise his lack of enthusiasm for such remote places.

'But no. I've already spoken to Whiskers and he agrees you should stay on at Upton, retake them and hope you get even better grades for Cambridge next year. Keep up the family tradition, dear boy. After all, you're barely seventeen and really much too young to leave school.' As if in benediction, he increased my allowance from £60 to £100 a year, backdated to my birthday last May. I loved my father's military decisiveness when it suited me! But he was already hinting he'd like me to read Law at university in due course; I wasn't too bothered then, let alone able to take in the implications.

I felt really buoyed up. Bugger Cambridge; I'd have another whole year at Upton to win back Paul. I decided *not* to ask to be removed to that failing Comprehensive in Notting Hill. Now that I'd eaten humble pie maybe Paul would forgive me, as Pips had prophesied, and we could start again. That night I dreamt of him lying beside me in Madame's great Empire bed, wrapping my arms and legs around the unfamiliar long bolster pretending it was him.

Olivier and Louis were both students at Tours. Their role as my hosts was undefined but Olivier took a bit of a shine to me, taking me out within the first few days shooting rabbits on the estate and driving me to see the magical château of Azay-le-Rideau nearby. The beguiling Louis, on the other hand, had little time for me, being fully occupied with a new girlfriend in the village.

On my very first Saturday the boys improvised a dance for their local friends in the barn beside the château. I helped rig up the Japanese lanterns, the trestle tables, the disco, and the sound system. I wondered how I would get on with a lot of slightly older lads and lasses. I swigged down a couple of glasses of red wine as the guests started to arrive: pretty blond girls with ponytails in slacks, handsome dark boys in jeans and tight T-shirts. They all seemed to know each other. Olivier and Louis introduced me to one or two of the girls and I jived along on the dance floor with them for the first half an hour to Sandy Shaw's 'Puppet on a String', Johnny Hallyday, and Mireille Mathieu. But it was soon evident they wanted to get off with the older boys. The snogging began and I withdrew to the side, knocking back another glass of wine, quite enjoying my detachment.

Olivier emerged from the shadows to sit next to me. He seemed concerned I wasn't hitched up with anyone.

He looked at me a little slyly, perhaps a bit drunk himself. '*Alors, tu n'aimes pas nos filles françaises, Fred?*' 'Don't you like our French girls then, Fred?'

'*Mais oui, bien sûr,*' I replied guardedly, feeling slightly offended. 'Of course I do.'

And then, with a knowing smile and twinkle in his eyes, '*Mais peut-être, en vérité, préfères-tu nos garçons français?*' 'But perhaps, in truth, you prefer our French *boys*?' It was asked without any trace of malice or teasing.

What had I got to lose? There was something in his voice that invited a truthful, even reckless answer. Go *on*, why pretend! You *deserve* something exciting to happen to you! You can do it!

'*Eh bien, peut-être c'est vrai,*' I answered, with a mixture of bravado and audacity. 'Well, maybe that's true.' I smiled back at him; why should I feel bad about it?

'*Ce n'est pas un problème, n'est-ce pas?*' 'It's not a problem, is it?' I added.

Olivier winked. 'I think you need a nice *petit ami* for your holiday here, Fred. Let me find you someone I think you'll like,' he said, getting up with a broad grin, and disappearing into the darkened recess of the barn.

I felt relieved at having been so brave. Maybe this would be the start of something big.

A minute later he reappeared, leading a tall, sinuous but elegantly proportioned and intelligent-looking boy, about my height, but obviously a year or so older than me. He had big wide-set eyes, delicately rounded lips, his skin a shade of pale olive and fine jet-black hair swept back across his forehead. He had an air of quiet confidence about him, and I knew straight away I was going to like him. Olivier introduced us and our eyes engaged meaningfully for a brief moment.

He sat down beside me, trying to look indifferent, then taking a swig out of his glass. We glanced sideways at each other. I watched as his long lashes seemed to move in slow motion. I felt a sudden thud within my belly followed by an irresistible need to smile, which, after a moment's hesitation, thank goodness, he returned. That was a relief!

We alternated our conversation in French and English. If anything, I took the lead, hopefully not being either too serious or too frivolous, and not giving too much of myself away. I gathered he lived in the village and was here this evening because his elder sister was a friend of the boys. His father was an architect and his mother a nurse at the hospital in Tours. He had just finished his *terminale* at the lycée and was going on to university in the autumn.

It is a cliché, I know, that French people, both men and women, often sound irresistibly sexy when they try to speak English. It was certainly true of Henri that night. As I listened and watched his expressive face and gestures against the soft light of the lanterns, I swore to myself I wouldn't finish the evening without at least having a snog with him. The mood in the barn was encouraging but even so we needed some privacy. I suggested we went outside for a cigarette.

We found a narrow bench. Henri made the first move and sat down, offering me a Gitanes as I remained standing. I leant over as he gave me a light, and we looked into each other's eyes silently once more. There was nothing else for it: I sat down next to him, making him shift very slightly. Both of us were in tight jeans and our thighs touched deliciously, neither of us making any effort to move them. I could already feel a stirring. *What next?* I wondered. My heart was beating frantically; I could feel my pulse racing ahead. We both looked over towards the château, taking in its crepuscular profile standing out against the orange streaks of the setting sun. The slow, sultry tones of Procol Harum's 'Whiter Shade of Pale' in the background combined with the dense humidity of the evening seemed to heighten an atmosphere *'brimming over with possibilities'*.

Just as the conversation went into a momentary lull, he looked towards me with a long steady gaze and slowly exhaled a gust of cigarette smoke directly towards me. I thrilled as I knew perfectly well what this signified. With equal nonchalance he reached out his hand to stroke my bare forearm which was resting on my knee next to his. A lovely little flutter ran through me, making me tingle from head to foot. I gave him a broad grin as he turned towards me with a quizzical smile, moving his leg against mine very slightly. I offered no resistance as he continued to run his forefinger over my hand and wrist, stroking the little bleached hairs backwards and forwards. His touch was very gentle, almost innocent, but his eyes were saying something I had never heard before: 'I think you're a very attractive fellow, Fred. What about it?' Mine were responding, probably with too much nervous excitement.

A moment later our faces were drawn together gently but irresistibly. I could feel nothing else but our lips touching, firm and eager, then our tongues. In a moment he had put one hand on my thigh while running his fingers through my hair, kissing my ears, cheeks and neck. His skin was wonderfully soft to touch, and as I kissed his neck I inhaled his enticing masculinity, a sultry mixture of deodorant and fresh sweat. How I had ached to do this with Paul, but it had never happened. Now, at last, I felt the full force of my desire welling up inside me and driving me on. I found I was irresistibly whispering, 'Paul! Paul!'

'Who is Paul?' asked Henri, looking annoyed and disentangling himself for a moment.

Oh goodness, I didn't want to foul this up quite so soon. I apologised.

'Paul is the boy I think about all the time.'

'But I am *Henri*, Fred, not Paul! Please, *please*, you must call me by *my* name, not someone else's!'

'I'm sorry, Henri. I love him with all my heart, but he's never allowed me to touch him. I think my chances are over now. We've just had a big row.'

To my surprise he looked genuinely concerned. 'Okay, Fred, I can understand. It's the same for me: I've only just broken up with Jacques who I thought was the love of my life. To be truthful, I'm still desperate for him.'

'So we're both in the same boat?' I asked, not expecting an answer as I drew him closer and put both my arms over his shoulders, looking at him straight in the face. 'Well, *I* think you're a great guy and very, *very* lovable,' and I gave him a big full kiss on his lips.

He must have appreciated my impulsiveness – maybe he was bemused at being with such an obvious *ingénu* and willing victim – for he returned me a kiss of such deep and slow passion as I had never imagined. He fumbled with my shirt, one hand undoing the top buttons, the other on my belt. Clearly this wasn't going to be *his* first time. Maybe, silently, he was calling me Jacques.

'Come on, let's find somewhere away from all this,' I whispered in his ear.

We walked through the farmyard and round the back of the buildings. Over to the side there was a small area enclosed by a tall hedge behind which there was an old caravan used by the farmhands for their tea breaks. I'd been in it before when exploring the grounds, and knew it had comfortable divans that converted into beds. There were a few lights coming from the château windows which helped to guide our way while the silvery glow from the full moon gave the lawn a sparkling luminosity. My heart was pumping away excitedly, partly with the sense of danger – would we be discovered? – but more in anticipation of unknown delights.

Thankfully the caravan was not locked. The moonlight filled the whole interior transforming its squalor into a temple for eager bodies. The lingering whiff of Gauloises and coffee permeated the air like incense after Mass.

Within seconds Henri was all over me, greedily kissing me on my mouth, on my neck and reaching into my shirt. We quickly stripped off, Henri helping himself to my shoulders, licking, then biting my pecs and nipples, pressing his face under my arms as I raised them high.

'*Laisse-moi te séduire, Fred, laisse-moi.*' 'Let me seduce you, Fred... let me...'

My goodness, even if I was only the vicarious object of his lust for Jacques it was wonderful – so flattering to be so desirable.

*

He smiled as he turned towards me. 'Are you alright now, *mon petit?*' he asked as he lay beside me, both of us enjoying the afterglow. At last I admitted it was my first time.

'I must be the luckiest boy in France tonight,' he said. 'All that passion of yours exploding like champagne! The other stuff will get easier for you the next time, and the time after, don't worry. I'll make sure – if you'll let me.'

I gave him a lascivious grin in reply. 'Yes, it's something I could get used to very easily. Especially with you, Henri.'

It was a hot and sticky night, and we were both sweating like pigs. Henri reached for a cigarette for each of us, lighting them between his lips, and offered me one. As he turned over to lie on his tummy, his face turned towards me, I could take in more soberly the beauty of his body in repose, the wonderful long double curve of his back, the creases under his plump, rounded buttocks, the furry darkness of his cleft, and the elegant contours of his thighs and legs. I ran my fingers down them all, tickling his hairs. To my surprise I felt myself getting hard again. He smiled and tried to smack my hands.

But it was getting late, and we needed to make our way back to the barn in case our absence was noticed. We dressed quickly and made our way stealthily past the side of the château. As we approached the barn it was obvious everything was drawing to a close. Henri's sister appeared out of the gloaming, and he introduced me to her. She looked at us almost threateningly. Did we look too flushed, perhaps even with a tell-tale smell of sex about us, easily recognised in the humid night air? In the distance I saw Olivier looking our way with a big smirk on his face.

Henri touched me gently on my bum and whispered, '*Bonne nuit, mon petit.* I'll ring you tomorrow.'

Hurray! My heart leapt. *He really wants to see me again!*

I found myself excited, reassured, and surprised all at once. But why should I feel like that? Why shouldn't someone find me desirable? I reckoned I had every right to be considered attractive and sexy. In the future, I now determined, I was going to make the best of my assets, learn from Henri how to be charming, seductive, and expert in making love. He was going to be the perfect, patient tutor and I didn't mind at all what he would do to me. I was longing to see him again, to kiss and explore his elegant, supple body and learn from him my own capacity for giving and receiving intimacies.

It was only when I was back in my Empire bed that I was struck with a moment of guilt. Just a day or two before I'd been fantasising about Paul lying here alongside me. What was I doing now with Henri? How had I managed to transfer my affections so easily – or was it only my lustful desires for a boy, *any* boy – like I had with Rowse? No, Henri was utterly different. Right now, it was only him I wanted to see and with whom I wanted to have passionate sex. I refused to feel bad about it; hadn't I been longing for Paul for over a year and never been bold enough? I'd learnt my lesson. And then a little voice – another messenger from Eros? – was telling me that this attractive boy *really* wants *you*. Seize the day! He isn't *The One*, but go with him, take him, learn from him!

*

Henri rang next morning soon after Madame and I had returned from Mass (where I had held back from going to Communion, duly noted by Olivier). I could almost see his lips moving as he spoke quietly and seductively down the phone. I sensed Olivier might be listening somewhere nearby and so remained deliberately evasive, agreeing to meet after lunch at the bar in the rue St Eustache and then to go for a bike ride along the river.

I was grateful for the intermittent shade of the great chestnuts as I cycled towards the village. My bum was still feeling slightly sore, but the narrow saddle had the nice effect of massaging it if I rode carefully. I was full of anticipation. Would Henri want more intimacy, or did he just want to be friends from now on? Did *I* want more intimacy? Of course I did, but this time I hoped it would be as slow, romantic and erotic as it had been fast, furious, lustful and even a bit painful last night. Would Henri ever allow *me* to take the initiative? How would it be for him? I was already imagining how I would undress him slowly, stroking, caressing and kissing him in all the right places.

He was there at the café, waiting for me, sitting in the shade at one of the small round tables on the pavement, with a glass of cold beer in front of him and another ready for me. That little gesture of kindness spoke volumes. I sat down opposite, and we beamed across at each other. His face was glowing with health, his eyes already penetrating me again lustily, yet so kindly. I didn't feel at all unnerved. *You really* are *such a fabulous guy*, I thought, *handsome, dark, serious, kind, and* really hot. *How good to know I can raise that look of desire in you.*

We talked and talked, lightly and flirtingly, mostly in French, although it seemed only fair to let Henri practise some of his English too. He told me all about the de Ferrands, about the late comte and his heroism in the War, about his own family and his hopes at university coming up soon. I gave him an account of *la vie en château* as amusingly as I could, and he took it all in the right spirit.

Eventually I braved it, trying not to sound too eager. 'I'm here until the beginning of September, Henri. Are we going to see more of each other?'

'Yes, Fred, I'd like that very much.' He looked straight back at me and paused. I could see his mouth open and his lips hesitate for a second before continuing, 'We could meet nearly every day if you like.' Now *that* was what I wanted to hear. What an invitation! What a declaration! I nearly choked as I replied with the biggest smile in my repertory,

'Yes, let's do that.'

But I needed to suggest that, for me, I wanted it to be something bigger than a mere passing friendship, however intimate.

So I continued, 'If we're going to become... *copains*... buddies... for the summer, Henri, I'd like you to call me "Freddie", like all my family do. I haven't heard it said in French before, so I'd love to hear it from you now. But only when we are together, not in front of Madame de Ferrand or anyone else, *compris?*'

He gave a big smile. '*Oui, bien sûr, mon Frédi... Frédi...* It sounds quite sexy!' The way he said it I felt properly gallicised. 'Come on, *mon Frédi*, let's find somewhere quiet along the river.'

He led the way as we rode our bikes along the towpath lined with tall shady plane trees, gently rustling in the breeze. I loved seeing him ahead of me in his pale brown shorts, leaning forward with his gorgeous bum raised slightly off the saddle, his elegant calves straining as he pedalled slowly and rhythmically. The belt of his underbriefs was barely peeping out over the top of his shorts. For a delicious moment I thought it might be a jock strap.

We came to a sloping grassy bank and a small pebbly beach. In the distance we could see the bridge, the end of the village, and the tower of the medieval abbey. Stepping gingerly over the shingle, the water felt cool and refreshing.

'We could go bathing further down the river one day, if you'd like. Have you brought your swimsuit to France? If not, you could always use one of mine.' The erotic possibilities struck both of us simultaneously, making us grin knowingly. The merest suggestion made something move.

We found a spot to lie in the grass under the welcome shadow of a chaste tree, looking across at the wide sweep of water moving slowly and inexorably downstream. The little wavelets were glinting in the sunshine like rows of diamonds.

'This is a great place to be with a great guy like you, Frédi,' he said smiling, lying beside me propped up by one elbow. No one had ever said anything like that to me before. I was lost for words as he started to sing quietly, looking at me, then at the river and then back at me.

> *'Ô beau pays de la Touraine!*
> *Riants jardins, verte fontaine*
> *Doux ruisseaux qui murmure à peine*
> *Que sur les bords j'aime à rêver.'*

The rippling murmur of the river provided a soft orchestration.

'What a lovely song! I'd no idea you had such a great voice.' I leant over and gave him a long kiss on his lips, holding his head in both my hands.

'It gets a bit sad later on, so I won't give you any more. I can tell you're a sentimental sort of boy!'

I plucked a daisy from the ground and tickled his nose with it.

'Let's just stick to poetry then,' I said, as a couple of lines from Baudelaire came to mind. They seemed to fit the tranquil warmth of the afternoon, our togetherness, and an atmosphere laden with erotic longing:

> *'Là, tout n'est qu'ordre et beauté,*
> *Luxe, calme et volupté.'*

He grabbed the daisy from me as I burst into laughter, Henri merely smiling. We rolled over each other, kissing, and holding each other tight. As I rested my head against his chest he gently stroked my hair. I could feel and hear his heart beating so closely and recognised the whiff of his sweat from last night. My body was aching for more; I was ready for anything.

'Here's another one,' he said, reciting the beautiful lines from de Vigny's poem, pointedly emphasising the last words of the first line:

'*Mais toi, ne veux tu pas,* **voyageur indolent,**
Rêver sur mon épaule en y posant ton front?'

I looked up at him from below so I could see right into his deep, dark eyes.

'I want to remember this day, Henri, so I can relive it when I'm lying in bed on my own. Isn't it good we've found each other? Twin spirits, having such a lot in common. Not just the sex, but listening to poetry, singing, splashing in the water and enjoying being with each other?'

Just at that moment we heard voices in the distance and, looking up at the towpath, could see a couple of figures walking in our direction. We separated and sat innocently next to each other as the two men carrying fishing tackle passed by behind us.

'*Bonne après midi, messieurs,*' we looked up and shouted.

'*Alors, continuez à vous amuser tous les deux, mes garçons.*'

'Carry on having fun, boys,' they replied, smiling down on us.

Cheeky buggers! How amazing to find such nonchalance, or was it cynicism? So bloody different from England.

'Come on,' he said, with a certain impatience, on his face, 'let's go to my place. My parents won't be back until later.'

We cycled through the village and out on one of the minor roads. His house was set back behind a lawn with pleached trees either side a rectangular pond, dead white, very modern, with a lot of sharp angles, glass and exposed concrete. Inside, it was all open plan. I'd never seen anything like it; it was all so bleak with almost no sign of anyone living here – no books or even magazines lying around, no colour anywhere except white, and only overhead lights with big ballooning shades. It had been designed by Henri's father and finished last year. I tried to hide my dislike of it. It could hardly have been more of a contrast to the château.

'My dad's a big fan of Le Corbusier. "*A house is a machine for living in*"', he said, as though that explained everything. I thought that idea was awful. I was within an ace of replying that I thought a house should be a machine for *fucking* in, especially with you, Henri.

We didn't linger and went straight up to his room. It was bleak, again, just a box, one big metal-framed window overlooking the garden with blinds, not even curtains. But there were a few hints of life: his desk with books, a chair with clothes piled up, and a couple of framed exhibition posters on the walls. One was for an artist I'd never heard of called Jean Dubuffet.

'They're not my choice,' he said, shrugging his shoulders. 'They're chosen by my dad. I wanted something more sexy, like this.' And he pulled a rolled-up poster from under his bed; it was James Dean, leaning against a wall with one knee bent, at his most irresistible come-hither.

'Let's have him up against the wall,' I said. 'We can lie back and fantasise in front of him.' After last night there was really nothing I couldn't say or suggest to Henri.

So down came the Dubuffet and up went James Dean, sellotaped sacrilegiously onto Henri's father's brutal white wall.

'He's so gorgeous,' I said, climbing onto the bed where Henri was sitting, propping myself up against the headboard. He moved over, putting his arm across my shoulder. James Dean's eyes were trained on the two of us aching to be seduced by his hypnotic allure.

Henri continued, 'Yeah, just imagine what it must be like, slowly taking off that casual leather jacket and T-shirt, then those sexy jeans. Do you think he's got any underwear on?'

The suggestion was enough to trigger an inevitable trajectory. In a trice I had Henri's shirt and shorts off him – to find he *was* wearing a jock strap.

'Wow! Henri, *what* a turn-on!' I said as I looked up at him and buried my face into the soft stretchy gauze-like material, feeling a rush as I inhaled his delicious sweat and piss. I let my tongue travel back and forth along the length of his tightly enclosed tumescence, licking and tasting the little wet glob which had just stained the fabric.

The moment was too good to lose; I had to capture it. 'Can I take some pictures of you: *style érotique*?'

'Let's make it *pornographique.*'

Reaching over for my rucksack to find my new Pentax, I quickly adjusted some of the settings. I got him to kneel among the ruffled bedclothes in front of me, full frontal, putting his hands behind his back, leaning his head to one side, but looking deeply and longingly into the camera like James Dean, licking his lips.

'My James Dean fuck-boy,' I said, taking the first shot. 'Move round so I can see the side straps framing your great arse.' He obliged with the ease of a professional model, looking sideways at me, mouth slightly open, eyes beseeching, giving me a babyish look of needfulness. Then he turned with his back to me, kneeling and leaning forwards, enhancing the size and roundness of his voluptuous bum, using a forefinger to open and reveal his beautiful boy-hole.

This was just too much temptation for a new boy like me. I cast the camera to one side, grabbing the elastic sides of his jock, trying to yank it off him, but he slapped my hand, insisting he keep it on, knowing how his tactics would bring me to a fever of lust. Both my hands went round to fondle his bum cheeks and plunge my middle fingers into his cleft, prising it apart as he fell backwards to lie flat on the bed. But he wouldn't let me go any further. He turned and lay on his back, raising his arms above him to hold the iron bedhead, exposing his pits. This time I pulled at his jock and at last he shifted to let me take it off him. Throwing back his head I took another shot of him as St Sebastian, writhing in fake-orgasmic agony. I watched mesmerised as his erection grew slowly of its own volition. Vaseline appeared from somewhere. Irresistibly, I straddled him, forcing him through my portcullis of pain, grinding and grinding him towards Valhalla. The Ride of the Valkyries had nothing on it.

*

My sweat was still dribbling off me as I rolled over to lie beside him, both of us facing each other, smiling into each other's eyes, now completely exhausted. I moved my hand to touch his face and caress his hair, kissing and gently exchanging each other's life-giving breath, our tongues meeting, sharing our juices, as though uniting in a final love-making coda.

As we withdrew it struck me that this time he'd been entirely in *my* power; his pleasure had been *my* gift to him, completely overwhelming him. I was pleased, almost proud, that I'd been able to do this for him: it was the first time in my life I'd ever consciously given such joy to anyone. But I asked myself, *where* had all this crazed priapic *wantonness* come from? Was it really *me* who had said such lustful words or choreographed such a frenzy? I could hardly believe it of myself.

I knew from just looking at Henri that he was incredibly grateful. He'd never say so, of course, boys don't, do they? But I knew it.

But he did say one truly wonderful thing.

'I don't need James Dean anymore, Frédi, I've got you. Having you here is better than a thousand movie stars.'

I just loved him for that. Did he really mean it? Or was it just the spur of the moment? What confidence this gave me! Maybe now I'd be able to do something *even more* wonderful for him next time, just to give him pleasure, to show him how much I wanted to please him.

I grabbed hold of his discarded jockstrap and used it to mop up our jizz.

'Can I take your jock home with me, to put under my pillow so I can smell it and wank over it when I'm on my own?'

'Of course you can, *mon Frédi*, just as long as you're thinking of *me* all the time. But I'm going to need something from you in return.'

'Like what?' I asked, as I lit us each a cigarette.

'I'll think about it,' he replied. 'But it's got to be something really intimate, something really *shocking*.' I smiled at the way this generic adjective had been appropriated by the French always to imply something sexual.

I suddenly had an idea.

'I don't know where I'm going to get the film developed, Henri. I'd probably be arrested if I took it to a Boots in England.'

'It's a pity, because Jacques's father is a photographer and Jacques knows how to develop films in their dark room. Anyway, I'm going to take some sexy pictures of you too, Frédi, just you wait.'

I put my arm round his shoulders as we both dragged on our cigarettes.

'So, my gorgeous new French *copain*, what are our plans for the next few weeks?'

'What would *you* like to do? You're our guest here in *la belle France*. That is, apart from taking your pleasure with me.'

I said I'd love it if he could show me some of the famous châteaux. Olivier had taken me to Azay-le-Rideau, but what about Villandry, which we could probably get to by bike? And maybe we could take a couple of coach trips to the others: Chenonceaux, Chambord, Blois?

'Of course, I'd love to show you *toutes les gloires de la France*.'

He grinned. Was he being ironic? I dared to hope so, and it gave me a sudden thrill.

*

The day after our James Dean-inspired tryst we took our bikes to Villandry. Henri led the way avoiding the main roads, through the rides and *allées* of a beautiful forest which had once been part of a great estate. At the château Henri proudly showed me the formal gardens, set out in the classic French style. I told him that the English did things differently and one day I'd take him to Parkworth to see a Capability Brown landscape where nature had been transformed by art to create a naturalism more natural than nature herself. A little intellectual conundrum I knew would appeal to his Gallic cerebralism.

For my part I was more interested in the interiors – all lovingly restored by an American heiress – the boiseries, tapestries and Empire furniture (in much better nick than Madame's). Henri preferred the portraits and hearing the stories of the past owners from the geeky but charming student guides. When I lost track of the genealogies I'd 'accidentally' brush up against him, discreetly pinching his bottom.

On our ride back, as we were deep within the forest, Henri signalled me to stop as we reached a wide clearing.

'You know, Frédi, we could come back here tonight while there's a full moon and I could show you something really beautiful. There are wild deer here but they're very shy and run away if anyone tries to come close. But there's a treehouse over there,' he said, pointing, 'from where one can see them as they come to drink at a pool just below. Would you like to do that after dark, tonight?'

'I'd do anything to be with you after dark, Henri. But yes,

what a lovely idea. Maybe we could have some fun in the treehouse while we're waiting for the deer?'

'But we needn't wait until then, Frédi. All this cycling has made me horny. What about right now? As a reward for your tutor?' It was an irresistible fantasy come true: pleasuring my handsome teacher up against a tree, deep in the forest, his balls in my mouth as he came all over my face.

We returned to the forest at about nine o'clock. We needed to be as quiet as possible even in the treehouse in case we frightened the wildlife. It didn't take long before a family of roe deer emerged nervously from the trees to drink from the pool: a proud buck sporting two antlers, followed by a furtive, protective doe and her two timid little fawns. The pale moonlight reflecting from the pool picked up their delicate, elegant movements, their fragile, slender legs, and the graceful articulation of their necks and heads looking about them for any sign or scent of danger. The slightest movement from me as I handed the binoculars to Henri must have spooked them; all four simultaneously looked up, startled and frightened, their ears pricked up and alert, before skipping away into the darkened woods.

*

Looking back now, after more than fifty years, the next few weeks seemed to pass like a dream of sensual delights. Henri would cycle over to the château after breakfast each morning in his shorts; we'd chat deferentially to Madame and then set off for the day, not returning until early evening. Olivier and Louis were delighted to have me off their hands, and it was obvious we were perfectly happy left to our own devices. Once at dinner Madame had said how pleased she was I had made a new friend, so *sympathique*, and from such a good family, at least on his mother's side. I reddened when Olivier's foot pressed against mine under the table.

We found the timetables for the buses to the châteaux. Madame usually gave us a picnic to take in our rucksacks, including her own delicious *pâté de lapin au cognac* and a bottle of wine. On the bus we'd head for the empty seats at the very back and sit close together. On our way home, after we'd finished the wine, Henri would rest his head against my shoulder (*he* was now the '*voyageur indolent*'), and I would clasp his thigh close to his groin. Just the touch, and its suggestiveness, often made us desperate to finish each other off. Once or twice we made it back to the ancient caravan, the scene of our first adventure. Otherwise, it was pot luck: once in his grandmother's garden shed in the village; another time – incredibly – in a deserted *tourelle* on the battlements at Chambord; and two or three times back in his room after I'd been invited to supper with his parents – fucking our brains out while our groans were smothered by the smoochy sounds of Charles Aznavour. The faint possibility of being caught must have added to the thrill each time. Sometimes we'd meet in the evenings at the bar in the village and then take ourselves off on our bikes into the woods or along the river again. We avoided my room at the château almost until the end, not wanting to compromise Madame who I'd grown to like very much, and she was, after all, *in loco parentis.*

We were becoming quite well known as an apparently innocent pair of friends, invited to tennis with Henri's neighbours, to go swimming at the pool at a nearby château, and to a bowling party with some of the boys and girls from the dance at the beginning of my stay. We'd always arrive and depart together, but of course circulate and chat with everyone pretending there was nothing special between us. But we'd be watching out for each other, exchanging little glances and smiles.

One day I suggested we visit the *marché aux puces* in Tours to search for some *objets* to decorate my forthcoming new room at Upton. I had been very impressed with the châteaux and their rich furnishings, seeing antiques with a new and critical eye. In the past I had taken old furniture for granted as the ordinary backdrop to everyday life at home where I knew we had a few good pieces. Now I was sufficiently inspired to foresee how my future room at Upton could express my newly found love for beautiful old things. It could become an extension of my personality, perhaps even providing the missing element that would make me 'different' and stand out from my peers.

Yes! The more I thought about it, the more it became a fixture; I wanted always to be surrounded by beauty – in short, to become an aesthete. But with a certain masculine style, not an obvious pansy's: ormolu and portrait engravings, rather than porcelain and flower pictures. Or maybe a bit of both. Either way, my surroundings would be a statement of who I was (or – more to the point – who I wished to become) and neither an avowal nor a denial of my Queerness. I'd be my own enigmatic self – keep everyone guessing!

I spied a pair of rock crystal sconces, then an ormolu Empire clock (the movement broken), followed by a pretty Limoges tea service decorated with sprays of violets; and, finally, an amazing group of six unframed engraved portraits of grandly bewigged gentlemen from the *grand siècle*, by a famous engraver, Pierre Drevet. (Later, Rosedale told me their significance. They cost a bomb to get framed properly when I got them home. In the end all the pictures – except one – followed me to all the places I've lived since. I even have a couple hanging in my study today. You may have noticed them, Sam.)

While I was leafing through a portfolio of watercolours – literally sitting in the gutter – the tall, muscled fellow in charge of the stand, probably early thirties, wearing shorts and a singlet and with long swept-back fair hair, must have made some kind of lewd remark to Henri. I could see a highly salacious expression cross his face, as he nodded at me sitting nearby on my haunches. I thought I heard him ask, '*Vache?... Ou chic?*' Henri smiled, and raised his eyebrows, and from what I could see, made him an equally lascivious reply.

Henri came over to me and said, 'Let's move on. That guy just asked if we wanted to see his Louis XVI *lit matrimonial* in his flat nearby. There's room for three, he said.'

'Wow! What cheek! But it might be fun! How about it?'

'*Non, mon petit ami!* Maybe if I get bored with you one day. But not while you're my *exclusive* boy-lover. And so I told him, quite pertly I hope, "That's kind, Monsieur, but not today, thank you – *nous, nous garçons aimons seulement les uns les autres*." We two boys love only each other.'

'Henri, that's just so sweet of you.' I was really moved and kissed him on the lips right there in front of our would-be seducer.

As we moved off, with my arm around Henri's waist, I looked back at the man. I gave him a big wink as I moved my hand to clasp it firmly round Henri's delectable manly arse. But I often wonder, even now, what I might have missed.

By this time Henri and I knew all the little places where we enjoyed being touched and loved. Our kisses were extraordinary: we could have spent hours just locked together, mouth to mouth, inhaling, breathing, drinking: we *fitted* so perfectly. Our lips had become sore and Henri's cheeks needed Nivea to prevent them becoming inflamed. I was entranced at the landscape of his body, the hardness of his torso contrasting with the softness of his skin. I loved fondling and licking his pectorals, his dark, hard nipples, inhaling the musky odour of his pits. He seemed obsessed with my neck, my left shoulder, under my arms, my thighs – biting them, exciting me and driving me wild. I learnt how blowjobs were more than just mindless sucking and face-fucking. They needed tenderness and concentration – exploring, touching, feeling, kissing and taunting that hypersensitive nerve. Henri had his own way of massaging my bum cheeks, relaxing me, stroking me with his tongue, driving me so close but knowing the exact moment when to move on. Then his fingers would probe deep inside me until they found that warm, soft, secret place. By now I'd be craving his full penetrations, moaning and whimpering as he took me hard and rhythmically, making me shudder and gasp.

I'd not had the guts to top him myself, although he'd never shown any inclination that he would stop me if I tried. Indeed, once or twice he'd given me encouragement and I had been within an ace of doing it, but like many seventeen-year-olds, I ejaculated too quickly. By now, however, I knew how to pace myself.

His casual remark to the stallholder at the market had so moved me by its honesty and spontaneity that I knew the time had come. I owed it to him to thank him for his lovely declaration.

That evening Madame insisted Henri stay for supper and keep me company afterwards, perhaps playing Scrabble in English and French, since they all had to go to a meeting and would not be back until late. Olivier – with his infallible pre-knowledge – gave me a wink as they departed.

We lost no time in taking another glass of wine upstairs to my room. I always loved our foreplay: sitting on the edge of the Empire bed, totally relaxed, touching, and saying flirty little things to each other. I had my arms around him, and we kissed again and again, at first on the lips, then in the special places as we undressed each other, our pulses quickening.

It was a transcendent moment for me. In that fever of lust, I felt I gave him everything I possessed, perfecting the intimacy we had forged between us. Instinctively I knew for sure that he felt the same completeness as me – our unity, our sharing, our communion – in an act of love. I'd come of age.

You may well ask, Sam, where was Paul in all of this? And the answer is that I hoped and prayed my beautiful virginal boy would be protected from all this promiscuity I was indulging in so wholeheartedly. The idea that anyone except me would ever do these same things with Paul filled me with horror and disgust. I loved him, with my heart burning within me as I remembered his beautiful face, his body, and heard his voice. But he was the future – if I could ever win him back. The present was here, with Henri.

*

I was very aware that the days left to me in France were running away fast. I hated the thought of leaving Henri but I knew it was inevitable. Were we ever going to see each other again after this summer romance, and if so on what basis? How was he going to fit in to my 'real' life back in England; how – if we were both willing – was I to accommodate both him *and* Paul into the framework of my life?

Before departing for the holidays my half-French friend Rosedale ('Roz') had suggested I visit him in Paris while I was in Touraine. I wondered if Henri should come with me; was there a danger this proposed expedition might spoil the little world we had created for ourselves, entering a different milieu, bringing in a third party from my 'other' life, even for a day? But if we were ever to become real, long-term, full-time friends and somehow integrated into each other's lives he would need to meet and engage with my friends, just as I had done his. Meeting Roz should be a relatively easy first step.

I sensed Henri was also feeling apprehensive. It was there in his eyes while I tried to convince him. Eventually he capitulated, and a date was fixed. Unfortunately – or maybe fortunately as it turned out – it had to be my penultimate day in France.

Roz was about a year younger than me, and we had overlapped in Junior House for just one term. He'd always been demonstrably friendly – and I'd reciprocated, aware that he was a bit of an oddball. His main 'difference', to which I was drawn, was his deliberate retention of his 'Frenchness'. I loved his slight accent – despite the fact he'd spent three years at a prep school in the Midlands – his urbane manner, and his stylish detachment from his peers whose boyish antics often seemed to bemuse him.

It was strange, though, that despite his 'Frenchness' he looked a perfect specimen of an Englishman. His features were quite fleshy and rounded, his complexion pink and healthy; given a periwig he could have passed as an eighteenth-century Anglican bishop. Later, as a thoroughly liberated undergraduate at Cambridge, he became an enthusiast of am drams and positively relished dressing up, preferably in drag. His impersonation of the eponymous heroine in *Charlie's Aunt* at the Footlights was talked about for years and years afterwards.

I'd learnt all about his family, his life in Paris and his grandparents in Normandy. His uncle was a well-known antique dealer with a showroom in Avenue Matignon where he would often go to help out in the holidays. In this way he'd become knowledgeable about French works of art, and back at school he would lend me his picture books about Louis XV furniture, Sèvres porcelain and Gobelins tapestries. My parents also enjoyed his precocious company when he stayed with us sometimes in London on his way to or from school. His charm was indeed beguiling and, later in life, was sometimes misinterpreted. I'm afraid your mother, Sam, thought he was too precious by half.

When Henri showed up in time for Madame to drive us to the station in Tours he was wearing a casual pullover and a pair of needlecord jeans. It wasn't a good omen. I should have warned him it would be formal. I was '*à l'anglois*' in my dark blazer, a yellow cravat and cavalry twills.

The Rosedales' flat was near the Invalides, so we merely walked the short distance from the Métro, me buying a big bunch of gladioli to present to our hostess. I'd met Rosedale-*mère* once or twice before when she'd appeared at Upton: very *chic* and French, short, dark, fragile like a Dresden shepherdess, with a disarming femininity, her smile and expressions faintly coquettish – completely different from all the mothers of my English friends. I always felt flattered that she obviously approved of me. Rosedale's younger brother, Martin, was also expected to be there.

The apartment was *belle époque* Louis XVI, all '*white paint with hortensias in blue enamel*' and big windows with balconies looking over the *esplanade*. We sat at the dining table very formally, with a manservant in a white jacket serving us, a white tablecloth and flowers, even finger bowls for the delicious peaches with which we finished the meal. Thank goodness I'd learnt from Madame de Ferrand how to peel them properly, using the special knife and fork with mother-of-pearl handles. Madame Rosedale insisted that we spoke French throughout (her own grasp of English was none too brilliant), and that we boys refer to each other by our Christian names. I'd never realised that Roz's was Théodore, which he allowed me to abbreviate to Théo while in France. Nor did he know that mine was Frederick (abbreviated for him to Fred, but not yet to Freddie, at least not for many, many years). His younger brother, Martin, who'd only just arrived at Upton, was forever known as Mini-Roz, poor boy.

Conversation was a bit stilted at first. Henri, I noticed, was looking uncomfortable from the start, even a little guarded among all the anglophilia.

'But why do the Brits send their children off to boarding school, away from their homes and families, with all that discomfort? It can't be good for them psychologically?' he asked.

'It's supposed to toughen us up so we can go off and run the Empire,' piped up Mini-Roz. We all smiled; I'd never credited him with much irony.

'It's supposed to make *men* of us,' said his brother, with a suppressed smile. 'And make us impervious to hardship and emotion. We're supposed to learn how to keep a stiff upper lip and never show the slightest weakness for anything, let alone *anyone*.'

I didn't like to say that the result was probably that it bred even stronger emotional neediness than if we'd been left at home. And that the system was absolutely guaranteed to confirm anyone with the slightest inclination to Queerness. Not that there was anything wrong with that, in my view.

Madame now pitched in.

'But,' she said, 'I'm never convinced by the so-called British *sang-froid*. I find that if you scratch the surface Englishmen can be very passionate and sentimental, just as much as we Latins. It's being in control that matters to them.'

I looked across at her; did this beautiful French lady have some interesting examples to tell me about? I'd love to hear more from her, although I realised it would have to wait until I was much, much older.

Henri confirmed Madame's enigmatic observation: *'Oui, Madame, je l'ai découvert par moi-même.'* 'Yes, Madame, I've found *that* out for myself.'

A glint of a smile crossed Henri's face. Madame gave him a sideways glance and then looked at me. *Oh goodness*, I wondered, *has she put two and two together?*

Mini-Roz seemed to anticipate an awkward moment and piped up again, in English but with an exaggerated French accent,

'*An Englishman takes time!*'

Roz and I almost choked suppressing our laughter. The little pipsqueak had obviously been listening to one of our gang's secret heroine-divas, Eartha Kitt, in his spare time. Madame and Henri just looked up bemused.

We were on our second glass of wine as we started gossiping volubly about the eccentricities of some of the monks, and then about my plans for my new room next term, Roz offering plenty of suggestions. Henri, I could see, wasn't really listening.

Over coffee Roz proposed we visit the Musée Nissim de Camondo as he said he knew it was full of things I would enjoy, and it had all been rearranged recently. I concurred enthusiastically and looked across to Henri, who just gave a shrug. *Oh goodness*, I thought as I glared at him, *please show a bit more enthusiasm.*

On the Métro, the three of us sat alongside each other, with me in the middle. Roz was talking in English at high speed, giving me some background to the museum's history. Was he deliberately ignoring Henri, on the other side of me, never even looking at him? I didn't like how things were developing and tried changing the subject.

I told them how I loved how the names of the Métro stations conjured up surreal images, allusions and associations in my hyperactive imagination which relished euphonic absurdities. One of my favourites was the bizarre juxtaposition, *Sèvres–Babylone.* What on earth could two such improbably named places, at the two extremities of history and culture, have in common? *Filles du Calvaire* – images of nuns in huge starched 'sailing' wimples escorting schoolgirls in 'crocodile' formations through the streets of Paris; *Abbesses* – a convention of eighteenth-century aristocratic nuns clad in black and white habits with diamanté crosses on their breasts; *Buttes–Chaumont* sounded wonderfully homoerotic and improper, maybe a place of assignation.

James Lomax

Roz thought it all highly entertaining, and offered a few more: *Gâité*, leaving little to the imagination; *Rue de la Pompe*, which sounded very grand in English, but was pretty pedestrian in French; *Plaisance* suggested sylvan frolics *à la Watteau*; *Couronnes*, perhaps where the court jewellers had their premises?

Throughout all this camp schoolboy banter, brought on by our mild tipsiness, Henri didn't even raise a flicker of a smile. 'What's *wrong* with you?' I felt like shouting at him. And then I realised: during our weeks together he had rarely shown the slightest sense of humour. He may be the hottest fellow I'd ever met, but as Pips had once said of someone else, '*he's much too serious for you*'. But, unlike Paul, Henri's seriousness was genuine, not just a mask for shyness. I would never have time to break that down; it's what would finish our relationship. A boy cannot live on lust alone.

I loved the little museum and its resonance with the *ancien régime*. Even as a beginner I could tell it was a total fake, but Roz persuaded me that was part of its charm. Indeed, it was the perfect choice for me as I'd be studying the French Revolution again next term and here was nearly everything I needed to visualise its cultural context. More subtly, it represented something of the *milieu de luxe* of some of the French artists and writers of the Third Republic in whom I was becoming interested.

Roz took me in hand, being the perfect and breathless guide to the furniture, the gilt bronzes, the chinoiserie tapestries, and the charming eighteenth-century pictures, including a lovely portrait of a beautiful but anxious-looking boy by Subleyras. He was in his element, bringing out a pocket torch as we went down on our hands and knees to examine some of the furniture close up. I wondered if we weren't making a public exhibition of ourselves, but the guards seemed to know him and let us carry on. Henri was evidently embarrassed, not enjoying it at all, and after a short time he disappeared. Of course, I knew it wasn't the works of art that he found boring and annoying. I wanted to go out to rescue him, but Roz didn't let up for a moment. Eventually, just as we were leaving, I found him sitting in the garden.

*

Angry, disappointed and dreading the inevitable confrontation, I waited until we were on the train and our compartment was empty before saying anything. I'd never been in this situation before and felt slightly panicky. Should I fire the first shot? Would an attempt at being sardonic be the right strategy?

'Did you manage to enjoy at least *some* of our expedition today?'

I'm not sure this conveyed sufficiently my disappointment at how he had behaved. Perhaps sarcasm would be more effective?

I continued, 'I got the impression you were just a *little* disappointed?'

'Not at all. Madame Rosedale gave us a delicious lunch and your friend Théo obviously knows *everything* about *objets d'art* of the eighteenth century,' he said, with more than a slight air of contempt, his lips pursing, and looking out of the window.

He paused before looking back at me and continuing in a voice that expressed resignation and sadness, 'No, I've had different emotions as the day went on. After lunch while you were gossiping about Upton, I became very jealous of how you share your friendships so easily and cheerfully among yourselves, all you English boys, cooped up together for months on end. I could see very clearly, Frédi, that Théo is very fond of you – probably more than you realise.'

Without blinking he carried on. 'And there's great chemistry between you. I'm afraid I felt very left out – the idea of my having to *share* you with Théo and all your other friends, none of whom

I'm ever likely to meet. Where am *I* in the queue for you, *mon "petit ami", Frédi?*'

I could feel his sarcasm and it pained me. I dreaded where this was leading.

'Then at the museum, I couldn't *stand* the way he monopolised you the whole time, showing off all his knowledge, making me feel worthless and stupid. I just had to go out.'

'Hey, Henri,' I said, 'I'm so sorry we seemed to be ignoring you. I never wanted you to feel uncomfortable. But Théo was being so enthisiastic.'

He looked up and shook his head. 'You should stick to him, you know. You both have very similar interests and attitudes. Yours is the sort of friendship that could last a long time.'

'Not like ours, do you mean?'

'I'm afraid not, *mon Frédi*. We've had a great summer but it's coming to an end and we're both going our separate ways. Maybe we can write to each other, and perhaps meet sometimes. But it's never going to be like this summer again, especially with this distance between us.'

He was silent a moment, staring at his shoes. Then he looked up at me, his eyes blurred.

'After Jacques dumped me, I swore I would never fall in love again. But then you came along, and just for a moment I thought maybe I could. But with us it's hopeless, I know.'

'Oh, goodness, I just can't bear to see you like this,' I said. I could feel my own tears welling up in my eyes as I reached to take his hand.

'I'm really going to miss you.'

For a moment I felt completely out of control, not just of *my* feelings, but how to comfort my dear friend. I couldn't bear to think I was the cause of jealousy – yet again – and this time between two boys with whom I imagined I had completely different relationships. It finally dawned on me that I needed to be much more aware of how I stood in the affections of my friends. It was good to know that I was prized; but, on the flipside, I now understood for the first time that it came with deep responsibilities.

In a panic I invoked an instinctive Anglo-Saxon pragmatism.

'We've had a wonderful few weeks, but – let's face it – both of us are still in love with someone else, aren't we? Someone neither of us have entirely given up on. Don't take it wrongly, but I know you're still pining for Jacques just as I am for Paul. Let's be honest with each other: both of us were thrown together on the rebound, weren't we?'

I tried to cheer things up. I reminded him that we had one last day together and still hadn't been for a swim in the river he'd told me about. I suggested we went there tomorrow.

If he had continued sulking I would have become really annoyed. But he agreed and the tension between us slowly dissolved, like an oppressive thunderstorm rumbling away into the distance. Yet we both knew that things were going to be different. I leaned across and stroked his knee and he took my hand and squeezed it. We smiled at each other wistfully, both of us in full knowledge that our self-created bubble had finally burst.

Olivier was at the station to collect us. Henri threw himself into the back seat of the car not saying a word. Having dropped him off first, Olivier asked if there had been a problem.

'You could say so,' I replied, not entirely sure I wanted Olivier's consolations right now, but he had me captive.

'You'll feel terrible for the next week or two, but don't close your heart just because your friendship has ended so inevitably. After I lost my first girlfriend, I reckoned I'd had enough of "love", thank you very much, but it didn't last long. There were just too many beautiful girls and opportunities everywhere.'

'Thanks, Olivier. I hope I'll get over it. I've had a wonderful summer here and I just hope I'll remember all the good things – the château, our visits, you, Madame, and Henri.' I wondered if I'd ever come back here – in twenty, thirty, forty, even in fifty years' time – and just what memories I would retain.

*

An air of melancholic finality seemed to pervade everything that last day. The de Ferrand boys were preoccupied with the imminent new university term while Madame announced that she'd been invited to stay with her cousins at Deauville for the tail-end of *la grande semaine*. She made up our last picnic for Henri and me and we cycled through the village to the big bend in the river where we could swim. Although it was still warm there was a slight breeze causing some early discoloured leaves to fall like stray confetti across the avenue.

There was already a handful of young people at the river so I guessed there would be no great intimacy with Henri today, or at least not here. It was only then that it struck me that he and I might never have sex together again. The thought made me want to take possession of him one final time, wrestle with him, pin him down and ravish him so hard he'd never forget me.

But instead, we changed modestly and enjoyed the agony of wading slowly into the freezing water, and then the shock of the first submersion. I loved watching the water running and draining over his body, the way his eyes dilated as his head appeared out of the water, and how he swept his wet hair back over his forehead. On my own body I loved the freedom of weightlessness, the cleanness of the water as it enveloped all of me, the new sense of alertness and the urge to keep moving. It was strange swimming in the clear fresh water, so different from the salty denseness of the sea. There was only a gentle current in the flow of the river – but enough to provide some traction against my energetic crawl and backstroke.

Henri had come with an inflatable beach ball and we started

throwing it between us, soon to be joined by a brother and sister who were vaguely known to Henri, and their energetic dog. Best of all there was a jetty from which we could dive, and ropes suspended from some of the overhanging trees enabling us to swing across, skimming the water.

We changed into dry swimsuits – our own, alas! – and lay on our towels on the coarse sand. I brought out a bottle of Ambre Solaire – oh happy memories! – applying some to Henri's back, around his shoulders, down the curvature of his spine as far as the small of his back, massaging it gently, then down the back of his thighs. I didn't care that I was getting an enjoyable and barely concealed hard-on. We lay on our fronts, sunning ourselves, not saying much, just watching the scene in front of us.

Then, suddenly, there was a voice from behind addressing Henri. We both sat up and looked round. There was a tall, fair-haired boy, very tanned, with sunglasses perched above his forehead, wearing khaki shorts and a loose summer shirt. He'd obviously just dismounted from his bicycle.

'Jacques? What a surprise!' said Henri, with just a note of reticence in his voice.

'We came back from Spain yesterday and I thought I'd ring to see how you were. Your mother said you'd be out here.' Was there something apologetic about his tone and careful choice of words? Only then he seemed to become aware of me sitting beside Henri.

Henri introduced me. Jacques looked me up and down with an air of Gallic insouciance probably meant to intimidate me. The scent of danger, of imminent violation of my rights, was almost palpable. I took an instant dislike to him.

Instinctively, I knew I had to make some kind of gesture of confrontation, there and then, to assert myself, signalling my role as Henri's former lover but still his protector.

'Henri has been telling me about you,' I said, as I put my arm across Henri's shoulder, letting it dangle over his pecs while I looked at Jacques in the eye.

I was within an ace of stroking Henri's hair or playing with one of his nipples right there in front of Jacques, but I desisted. I wanted Jacques to know that *I* knew about their previous relationship, but that Henri had moved on, and was now in control of his own life, free to choose his own lovers – of which I was proud to have been one. Jacques needed to work damn hard if he wanted Henri back again.

He glanced towards Henri who said nothing more. He moved his sunglasses to cover his eyes, nonchalantly inviting himself to sit next to us on a corner of the rug. They were both looking ahead of themselves, pretending to take an interest in the activities on the river. I watched as each stole occasional sideways glances at the other. I knew just what they were both thinking.

Something had to give. Henri turned towards Jacques.

'So how was Spain?' he asked, trying to sound indifferent.

Now it was up to Jacques to loosen up. He removed his sunglasses as he started to relate stories of the family holiday in Spain. It didn't take long before they were immersed in each other's gossip and news.

Jacques was certainly beautiful, but too blond for me. His body was just too bony, his bum too flat, his arms and legs too long. I couldn't help comparing him unfavourably with Henri's more rounded features, his dark and soft eroticism. I could never find Jacques desirable, yet he was the one who must have taught Henri all those lessons.

I was quietly seething at Jacques's presence; he hadn't been invited and here he was an intruder on this last occasion when Henri and I would be together. There was nothing I could do except remain aloof, almost imitating Henri's attitude with Roz yesterday.

We got out the picnic. As usual Madame had been generous with her provisions and there was enough for the three of us.

'Would you two like to come to the cinema this evening?' Jacques asked, perhaps trying to diffuse the atmosphere. 'I passed my driving test just before we left for Spain and can borrow my mum's DC for short distances when she's not using it.'

Without waiting for me to reply Henri spoke up. 'That sounds good. It's Fred's last evening so maybe we could go to a bar afterwards? What's the choice?'

What *I* wanted to say was that I didn't want to go to the cinema at all, let alone a bar afterwards. All I wanted to do was to vent my anger and jealousy by making love to Henri right here in front of Jacques to show the bastard what he had been missing, and that Henri was still mine at least until tomorrow.

They both agreed on Jacques Tati's new farce *Playtime*; as Jacques said, 'You'll see that not all of us French frogs are serious one hundred per cent of the time.' *Too late! Too late!* I thought cynically. How rare to find an example of Gallic self-deprecation, expecially in one so young.

Jacques left, having agreed to collect us later.

'Were you expecting to see him again?' I asked Henri, with more than a little suspicion in my voice. 'Were you pleased he showed up like that?'

He assured me it was a total surprise, and I could believe him. When they were last together, he told me, on a day just like this, he had announced that it was best they didn't see each other again, never giving a reason, just that he wasn't happy the way things were. Henri was sure he hadn't met someone new, but that his Catholic sense of guilt and shame had got the better of him. It had been bad enough to be dumped, he said, but almost as upsetting that Jacques had offered no reason, no apology, or shown any sense of remorse.

'And now he shows up again, wanting to see me. What am I to make of that?'

'He's obviously been missing you. "Absence makes the heart grow fonder", as we say in England,' I replied, beginning to see how this situation might turn out. 'Does he expect just to pick up where things were left off? What sort of relationship with you does he want or expect now? Do *you* want to see him again? After he treated you so badly? Do you love him enough to forgive him?'

He paused, then said with an apologetic but confident look across his face, 'Yes, I think I do. His magic is still there for me. I knew it the moment I saw him again. But I hate the idea *you* might feel betrayed, Frédi.'

'If you'd told me this before yesterday I would have been badly upset and angry. But we had our little discussion, didn't we, and agreed we must part, but with good feelings towards each other? I've never hidden from you the fact that I still love Paul who I'm praying may come to forgive *me* one day.'

'It's up to you,' I continued, 'but I'd take great care from now on that you don't get hurt again. You'll have to find out exactly why he walked out on you last time. And then get some sort of commitment that he's not going to do the same again for no reason. Can you trust him? Or is he the sort of fellow who'll go on doing it – breaking people's hearts without giving a damn? I hate to say it, but the chances are that it *will* happen again one day, so you'd better be prepared.'

I left my worldly wisdom, such as it was, at that, but I was secretly relieved that my responsibility for Henri had passed so seamlessly back to Jacques and, in a sense, to have been let off the hook so painlessly.

When they showed up later at the château to take me to the cinema I told them I'd decided not to go. My excuse was that it was my last night and Madame had made a special dinner. Besides, I needed to get up early for the train tomorrow. They took it well, with some polite protestations of course, but secretly I knew they were pleased to be back together; they had a lot of catching up to do and I would be in the way. As I gave Henri a tender hug, I slipped a little parcel into his hand.

'Here's my parting gift to you, in return for that charming article of clothing you gave me.'

I put the little tube of undeveloped film into his hand, and said quietly, 'Why not ask Jacques to develop the film with our *poses pornographiques*? He might be interested to see what we got up to.' Was there a tiny hint of revenge in my voice? If so, *tant pis*! 'I'd love some prints if they come out alright.'

With that I took my leave, turning round to run up the stairs before my tears became too obvious.

*

On my long journey home next day I tried to take stock of all that had happened during those weeks. I was already missing Henri, no longer able to look into those beautiful intense eyes and see them gazing back at me full of desire. But I felt happy for him that his true boyfriend had returned. I wondered how it would work out for them, but as my journey progressed northwards, I knew that a whole chapter in my life had finished. My mind kept turning to everything I had to confront back at home.

*

Just for the record, Sam, I did indeed return to the château about twenty-five years later. Bill and I had been together for about ten years and I wanted to show him the place of my first-ever holiday romance. We just turned up unannounced. Madame was there, almost blind, poor darling, with her daughter-in-law and a couple of grandchildren, but not the boys. She remembered me and we had a good chat. Otherwise not much had changed. The barn was still there of course, even the little bench where Henri and I had first snogged, but the caravan had gone! I was on pins to ask her about Henri, and in the end I just couldn't resist.

'Oh, yes,' she said. 'He's now Professor of English Literature at Tours, and we see him sometimes. Perhaps he learnt his good English when you and he were so friendly?'

I smiled inwardly; perhaps here was an unexpected legacy from our Summer of Love. I asked her to say hello from me when she saw him next. I wondered what *his* memories would be.

I googled the château just now. I see it's been given a complete facelift, almost unrecognisable, offering B&B at the most extortionate rates!

A bientôt.

Freddie

P.S. You may ask what happened to the photos taken on that memorable afternoon. Henri did indeed send me the prints, risking HM Customs and the Vice Squad. They were quite amusing, but not surprisingly, I had to bundle them away pretty quickly. They remained in an envelope at the back of my album, deliberately hidden from the other pictures I took of the châteaux. Every ten years or so I would take them out and look at them again, admiring myself so young and slim, and Henri forever so desirable. I showed them to Bill once; he was impressed. It was quite a compliment coming from him, a true connoisseur!

9

My dear Sam,

I sat on the deck of the Dieppe–Newhaven ferry, deeply inhaling the ozone, cleansing my lungs of the more earthy odours of France. After nearly three hours the sight of Beachy Head and the Seven Sisters loomed ahead through the sea mist. I knew them well from all those years at my prep school just down the road. I thought of myself at that time – a nervous, excitable, frightened, little boy. How different I was now; indeed, how changed even from the boy who had departed on the boat-train only a few weeks ago, so desperate to find love. In that short time I'd learnt many new things about myself and about other people. I'd discovered powers within me that I didn't know existed. I knew I had much to offer; no one was ever going to belittle me again. If Paul was going to leave me I knew I'd be capable of finding new lovers. But how transient would they be if I was always looking back for him, my first love?

As the ferry entered the harbour, I could see the little reception committee waiting for me on the quayside: your grandmother, your mother and Nanny. I was touched they were all there, and as we waved enthusiastically I realised how much I had missed them. When I saw they'd come in the Bentley I felt strangely humbled; was I yet another Prodigal Son returning to the straight and narrow after sowing my wild oats in France? A moment's recollection made me answer: no, I had no great need of repentance. They needn't kill the fatted calf just yet. I may have squandered my virginity but not my inheritance. I was merely returning home wiser and more experienced in the ways of the world and determined to look to the future with confidence.

We bowled along the coast road to the cottage. That evening we were joined by your dear grandfather.

There were a couple of letters waiting for me on my dressing table. I recognised a disagreeable-looking buff envelope – a bank statement – which had already been opened. I was pretty cross, and momentarily felt unmanned.

'Oh, but, darling, your father wanted to be sure that your new allowance had come through.' What a cheek! Fortunately there was nothing incriminating.

Thank goodness they hadn't opened the other letter. I recognised the bold, semi-italic script instantly, of course, and tore it open. It was postmarked a week earlier.

Freddie,

I thought I should write to you now that the holidays are nearly over and we're bound to run into each other soon after we get back to Upton.

I've had a pretty awful holidays, all the time thinking about how we left things that last day of term. I'm really sorry I took you by surprise and thumped you one, then went running off without any more explanation. I hadn't realised you felt as strongly about me as I did about you – and I still do. I should have let you explain yourself a bit more. Now I think I can understand what must have happened that night. I'm sorry I was so drunk after the play, but it was because I was trying to build up courage to say something nice to you after all we'd done together. So you can imagine how upset I was when I got to hear what you had done with R, literally behind my back. But now I can forgive you for falling for his charms, if – as you say, and I believe you – he was only a substitute for me. You're a free man, just as I am, and you have to do what you need to do. I just pray that your heart is still in the right place and we can move on together to somewhere brighter.

I hope your nose recovered from my buffeting. I'd hate to think I left a permanent flaw on your bonny face, my own Freddie.

With my love
Paul

Wow! I just burst into tears of pure joy. I had to sit down, my hands and body trembling as I tried to hold the letter steady, reading it over and over again, kissing it so that the ink began to run. But my agitation was such that I couldn't sit still. I began pacing the room, going to the window taking in deep breaths to fill my lungs. My head was swimming. I just wanted to shout as loudly as I could, 'He loves me! He's forgiven me! How wonderful is that!'

But I had to reply – and immediately. He might be expecting an answer and already be disappointed not to have had one. I fumbled in my bag to find one of the postcards from the Camondo museum – a detail from *The Gentlemen of the Duc d'Orléans* showing two be-queued old boys from behind, one with his arm around the other's waist. I scribbled quickly,

Got back from France this afternoon and just received your letter. All understood and SO HAPPY! A million thanks. Can't wait to see you. F

I had the presence of mind to put it in an envelope so the message wasn't available for all to see.

I tore down to the village on my bike just in time for the six o'clock collection, returning by the deserted back lane, meandering blindly all over the road like an out-of-control twelve-year-old, singing at the top of my voice, '*Can't take my eyes off you...*'

You may wonder, Sam, how it is that I remember these letters and messages verbatim. The answer is that I kept everything Paul ever wrote to me; one day you, or maybe someone else, will find them all in a box buried away at the back of the secretaire.

*

I seemed to be in a state of continuous exaltation for the next few days, counting the hours before I'd be back at Upton and with Paul. I was alternately nervous, obliging, solicitous, often with a glazed far-away expression, not concentrating or listening properly to anyone, entirely wrapped up in my own crazy happiness. People might have thought I was high on weed that I'd somehow smuggled back from France. I saw my parents glancing and smiling at each other while I recalled my time at the château, being very oblique about my new friend Henri. No questions were asked, but perhaps they hoped that some young woman had taken me in hand. After all, I wouldn't have been the first seventeen-year-old English schoolboy to have been deflowered in that land of all the senses.

I'd calmed down a bit by the time we all went back to London. These were the last few days before your mother and I had to return to our respective schools, and I had to put my plans into operation. The first was to engineer my mother and Nanny to come with me to Pontings department store to select the furnishings for my new room at Upton to become the embodiment of my new identity.

I'd inspected the room – little more than a cupboard – at the very end of last term. It was not in the main Ambrose block, but on Baker's Row, so called from being above the old school bakery, buried away past many small staircases and passages, overlooking a service courtyard. The barest essentials were provided and there was absolutely no room for anything more. Notwithstanding, I determined it should at least *suggest* luxury and sophistication, imitating some of the interiors of the châteaux I had seen in France. If it implied a Queer sort of taste, too bad! I was who I was, and I was going to enjoy it.

The key thing was on no account to give the impression of a lot of money having been spent; that would have been against the unwritten rule that disdained the flaunting of wealth in the more-or-less egalitarian world of Upton. My purpose was to demonstrate *taste*, not wealth; the game was to be nonchalantly self-deprecating. If pushed, one could admit to having tried to 'jolly things up a bit'.

I had rehearsed the shopping scenario in my head knowing I had to act in a determined way to avoid any argument about overdoing it from my mother or Nanny. I chose several lengths of ersatz silk damask in crimson and gold with which to clad the walls; a length of turquoise velvet to hang behind the bed and for two looped curtains for the little lancet windows; two matching and highly fringed bedspreads – one to go over the bed, the other for Nanny to split in two to form a draped canopy. Later, in the King's Road, I found a pressed-metal royal coat of arms in fake gold, which could be pinned over the bedhead. At home I claimed an old paisley shawl to throw over the decrepit armchair and a Persian rug, which would not be missed.

In the end my mother entered into the spirit of things and, once we were back home, offered me the *pièce de résistance*: a real tigerskin rug to cover the bedspread. The beast had been shot in India by my grandfather and was complete with head, teeth and claws. I knew it would be a sensation among my friends, and I rehearsed reclining on it, intoning the sexy little rhyme in a dusky drawl:

'Would you like to sin
On a tiger skin?
Or prefer to err
On some other fur'

Soon after this I had an almighty wet dream in which Paul and I had ejaculated over each other while wrestling naked on top of it.

Today you might describe my efforts as tremendously high camp, although in those days the word didn't exist, at least on this side of the Atlantic. My more polite friends would have called it 'theatrical' but my less enamoured confrères would have sniggered, calling it 'tarty'. I didn't mind, one way or the other. I knew perfectly well the monks would probably admire my originality and audacity.

I returned to school in some style, sitting with all my clutter in the back of the Bentley, my mother driving and Nanny beside her. We stopped for lunch at Cirencester where we bought an aspidistra. Nanny proved herself invaluable once we arrived, rigging everything up to my satisfaction. When at last they departed I felt ready to brazen it out with anyone.

*

Despite everything, I still felt half-apprehensive as I entered the dormitory for the first night's '*Miserere*'. My mouth went dry as I scanned the rows of boys standing beside their cubicles. There he was, on the opposite side of the room obviously looking out for me and breaking into a grin as I appeared. My heart was thumping uncontrollably, and I felt my eyes moist with joy. We nodded and smiled and even tried to mouth incomprehensible messages to each other, but I had to depart without having said anything. At Mass next morning he was about six rows in front of me. I spent the whole time gazing at the back of his beautiful head, his neck and shoulders, exerting all my will power for him to turn around so I could see his face again. Just as we reached the '*Agnus Dei*' he looked to one side furtively, then a full 180 degrees until he saw me and gave me a long, piercing look. Those angels were back at work.

It was only as he left breakfast that I had a chance to sidle up beside him before some of his friends appeared.

My goodness! He was more beautiful than ever: his face slimmer, cheekbones more prominent; the last remnants of that puppiness were gone. I could see immediately how he had grown by perhaps as much as an inch in the past few months, and his body had filled out in proportion. His jacket looked shorter at the back and tighter across his chest, his trousers fuller. Just the sight of him, even before he'd turned and given me a huge smile, had made me want to throw my arms around him. I whispered for him to come and see me on Baker's Row at the morning break.

I had no classes that morning and was on tenterhooks as the clock ticked slowly towards eleven o'clock. Then came a burst of voices in the passage and a loud thump on the door.

To my astonishment it was Rowse, looking spectacularly tanned and healthy, with his fat friend Marlow.

'Can we come in? We heard there's a new bordello just opened, and we've come to see what's on offer.'

Should I chuck them out straight away or let them stay for a few minutes to admire my décor? My vanity got the better of me. In any case Rowse had immediately thrown himself on the bed and was already fingering the fur rug. Marlow parked his large bottom on the only armchair. My other chair was wretchedly tucked under the desk and impossible to get out in time, so I had no option but to sit bolt upright at the far end of the bed trying to keep a safe distance from Rowse's wandering hands. I was fearful that Paul might arrive at any moment.

'Well, well, McNaughton, this *is* a cosy lair you've got here. It would be ideal for an occasional gasper – well off the beaten track of any marauding prefects. How about your letting us come here for a smoke sometimes?'

I started to remonstrate and was on the point of forcing them to leave. But Rowse was not to be deterred.

'There could be compensations, you know.' Then, in a whisper, 'We could continue where we left off at the end of last term. Why not?'

I looked at him in horror. Were the repercussions of that night going to follow me to the grave? Even if I wanted to erase the memory of it, was Rowse always going to be bringing it up, holding it against me, even blackmailing me like this?

'And I got this wonderful suntan this summer,' the wanton little whore went on. 'I could show you how I was wearing the skimpiest Speedos if you like.'

With that, he started to unbutton the top of his flies, then pull down the top of his pants. I could just see the start of his pubes and the contrast of the suntan with the whiteness of his midriff. I felt a movement in my crotch.

At that very moment there was a knock on the door. Without waiting for a reply Paul walked in.

'Hi, Freddie… What…What *the hell* is going on here?'

He looked in disbelief and fury, first at Rowse who was now desperately buttoning up his flies, then to me, then to Marlow.

'I can't believe what I'm seeing. Is this a repeat of last term, but now with the three of you?' he snarled.

'No, no, it's not what you think,' I pleaded.

'I was only showing McNaughton my suntan,' said Rowse, looking cowed and defensive.

'Yeah, you've got to believe us,' Marlow broke in. 'There's been no monkey business.'

'I *don't* believe you. My God, you're a little tart, Rowse. Can't you *ever* stop flaunting yourself? And you, McNaughton, why can't you grow up and say "no" occasionally. You've got a terrible reputation, you know. And as for you, Marlow, you're just a disgusting voyeur.'

'Hey,' said Rowse and Marlow almost simultaneously. 'What's it got to do with you? Why all this fury and anger? It's just a bit of harmless teasing.'

'McNaughton, *you* tell them,' he barked, his eyes flashing. 'I don't see why I should put up with this. I'm going to see Whiskers.' He slammed the door behind him.

'Go after him, Rowse. For goodness' sake tell him it was nothing. Tell him you only want to use my room for smoking, and I've said "no, never". *Believe me*, he's got his own reasons to be really upset. There's no time to explain, just *go, go, go*, or he'll do what he says.'

Rowse jumped up and ran out of the room. Marlow stayed behind for a minute.

I could hear Paul and Rowse shouting at each other in the passage, and then silence.

I was shaken. Whatever was he going to say to Whiskers? What difference would that make anyway, beyond having revenge on Rowse for 'stealing' me again, and on me for being 'unfaithful'? Anyway, what was the punishment for infidelity? Six of the best seemed hardly appropriate for a lover's tiff.

I felt utterly deflated. I'd been so looking forward to seeing Paul alone at last. I'd hoped to embrace him, maybe even kiss him properly for the first time. I'd taken all this trouble to make my room a place where we could be comfortable together and now it had all backfired. How I hated seeing him angry. He had really wounded me when he'd said I needed to grow up and had a terrible reputation; whatever did he mean?

The bell sounded for classes to resume. Lunch came and

went but I felt sick with anxiety. Then games – for me a reluctant cross-country run.

It wasn't until tea at 4.15 that I could slip a note into his locker. '**PLEASE** can we meet to discuss this morning's events: 8pm in Classroom XII. F'

I got no reply, but even so I showed up in the empty classroom, seating myself in the half-shadow at the back. After ten minutes of purgatory I was about to abandon hope when he came in, switching on all the lights.

He looked pale but calm. 'Sorry I'm late, Freddie. I've been having it out with Rowse. He's admitted it was all just a lark and of course there's never been anything serious between you. He won't be trying his little pranks on you again. My threat to go to Whiskers made him panicky. I didn't want to threaten him like that, but it seemed the only way.'

'Well, I'm really grateful, Paul. I know it must have looked terrible when you walked in.'

'I'm sorry if I'm so touchy about you, Freddie.' His eyes now were speaking volumes. 'I felt so let down at the end of last term. I really thought we had something special between us. All that time we'd spent together, all your little kindnesses, the way you'd been helping me with so many things. I thought maybe – in the end – you'd just been leading me on? Perhaps it was just a game for you? Maybe I didn't mean anything to you at all? And perhaps you really liked Rowse,' he paused, 'better than me? That's why I flared up.'

He held his breath before continuing, 'There, I've admitted it now, I was frantically jealous, and furious with Rowse of course. But it was *you* who I thought I could never forgive or want to speak to again. But then... in our showdown drama, you told me how much I meant to you, and how Rowse had almost thrown himself at you that night. So, during the holidays I tried to think about it from your angle. That's when I wrote you the letter, to say it was alright and that I understood.

'But then, my horror when I saw Rowse flirting with you so outrageously this morning...' He looked exasperated.

My own feelings were all over the place. *He thought I preferred Rowse to him?* How on earth could he? I tried to stay cool, looking at him full-on.

'I couldn't possibly prefer Rowse to you,' I said quietly. 'What I did with Rowse was the first time I'd ever done anything like that with *anyone*. And, if you must know,' I was sounding defensive again, 'it didn't amount to much. I was so drunk he had to throw me out.' Too late I remembered that it could have been the prefect's torch that had spooked him.

'So let's just leave it at that, shall we?' I continued. 'I'm really sorry to have been the cause of so much *angst*. There's been big misunderstandings on both sides. Now we know how we feel about each other. Nothing's going to stand in our way in future. Yes?'

'*Yes*. Let's shake hands on it,' he said, at last breaking into a big smile. For a split second I thought we were going to kiss.

We each brought forward our right hands to clasp the other's. But I was so elated looking at his happiness that I spontaneously brought my left hand over as well, to cover our interlocked palms. Instantly he did the same, so that for a moment we stood there, all four hands gripped together as we looked at each other. His felt warm and strong, and mine were still moist from all the anxiety. Apart from that brutal punch on that fatal day last term this was the first time we had touched flesh so deliberately, let alone held each other so firmly. Was the massive surge of relief I now felt coming from within *me*, or was it being transmitted from Paul?

'But, Freddie, there's something I need to put right after that punch of mine, and something else I want to show you when we can be alone together sometime very soon. Could we go on a longish walk at the weekend? I'm not in a fixture this Saturday. Perhaps you could take me to your favourite hideaway at The Rock? I've never been there.'

It was time to change the subject, to bring us back to earth. We talked about Rappy's new production of *The Winter's Tale*, which was to be the big set piece for Prize Day next summer. I asked if he was going to audition.

'He's already asked me to play Leontes. But I'm really not sure. It's such a big part.'

'Oh, but you must go for it,' I said, almost imploring him. 'Look, you're in the lower sixth form now, the only summer term you'll have at Upton without important exams. You should make the best of it. The part would suit you perfectly. Come on, I promise I'll help if you like, just as I did last term.'

He didn't need much persuading. 'Well, alright – but I'm going to make you keep your word.'

And then, to my delight, he asked if I was going to audition too. I had to tell him I thought my acting career had begun and finished with Antonio, but I'd be cheering him on from the wings.

*

With my anxieties now swept away it was possible for me to start enjoying my new room and the new self-identity I was trying to project with it. In no time, the rumour of its exoticism got round, and for the first few days of term the stream of visitors to my door was almost continuous. People started dropping in on the off chance to have a snoop around, sometimes while I was absent. Within the first forty-eight hours I even had a semi-state visit from Whiskers, the headmaster himself, who must have heard stories of an unlikely baroque *mise-en-scène* in his midst. He sat himself in the armchair now draped in its paisley shawl, giving a knowing smile as he looked around.

'I didn't know you had it in you, McNaughton,' he said, 'I always thought of you as having more, shall we say, *sedate* taste.'

'I've been visiting the châteaux in *la belle France* in the holidays, sir,' I replied with deliberate facetiousness. 'I thought I'd experiment. May I offer you a *tisane*? Or would you prefer Fortnum's Lapsang?'

'Some Lapsang would be most kind, and just a *nuage* of milk,' he said, as he made himself at home, adjusting his monk's cowl and dusting down his scapular.

'Nice piece of Second Empire Limoges, McNaughton,' he said, as I passed him the inaugural infusion. 'I hope Rosedale hasn't been leading you astray?'

'As a matter of fact, sir, Rosedale gave me a tour of the Musée Nissim de Camondo after we'd had lunch in Paris a couple of weeks ago.'

'Ah yes,' he said. 'One of the delightful small museums of Paris. Actually, I always thought it smelt a little too much of *new* money.'

That was an interesting view I hadn't considered before.

He looked around the tiny room and his eyes lit up when he spotted the Drevet engraving of Bossuet. He exclaimed, recognising the court preacher and theologian of the *grand siècle*, and told me that he kept the good bishop's *Discours* at his own bedside. I'd obviously struck a most un-monastic streak of envy in him. My heart sank as I realised I'd have to let him have it as my parting gift when I left at the end of the summer.

'But I haven't come just to admire your skills as a budding interior designer,' he continued.

'I've arranged for you and Herbert and Bickersteth to have your own History group with Dom Augustine. The three of you are doing resits so you can go at your own pace, rather than being held back by the second-year sixth formers.'

It was a truly amazing privilege to have our own private class with the greatly esteemed Gussy who taught only the most promising boys. But there was the additional bonus of being in close proximity with Charlie Herbert. He was the deputy head boy, captain of the 1st XI, six feet tall, with curly fair hair, perfectly formed in every particular, with chiselled Grecian looks and intensely blue eyes – a man of truly dazzling beauty. He looked, improbably enough, almost identical to the anglicised figure of the glorified and risen Christ, the centerpiece of Compton's great east window in the abbey church.

Yet I had known him since he was eight years old at prep school and was well aware that beneath this utterly convincing *bella figura* there lay a vulnerable boy who had lost his father as an infant and then his mother when he was eleven. Although famous for his success in winning the prettiest girls at teenage parties he was also perfectly aware of his hypnotic power among his schoolboy peers. Personally, and perhaps fortunately, I was never overwhelmed by his particular type of beauty; his flaw, as usual for me, was his blondness.

You may wonder, Sam, at our having almost Oxbridge-style tutorials or supervisions, three-to-one. But you have to remember that although Gussy had a PhD in Medieval History from Fribourg or somewhere about a hundred years ago, he had absolutely no qualifications to teach anyone, and was completely eccentric, like so many of the monks. Given half a chance, he'd go off on a tangent about some arcane subject, like Ultramontanism – about which he'd written a book – completely ignoring the curriculum. But we never complained. He'd somehow make it all absolutely fascinating, and we'd learn something completely off-piste every time. This whole approach to learning must have accounted for the school's success; I mean, from a relatively small establishment there were thirty Old Uptonians at Cambridge when I was there, and about the same number at Oxford.

With my love for now,
Freddie

10

My dear Sam,

I should have realised that my new room would become a 'safe house' for my more exotic friends. At the beginning I was happy to be their host. After supper they would pile in and I would cover the desk lamp with a scarlet polka-dot handkerchief, burn sweet-smelling joss sticks (later forbidden), self-consciously trying to create a world of decadent aestheticism. We'd drink Fortnum's infusions and listen to songs by Reynaldo Hahn on my Dansette while discussing negative capability in Keats. During the day we'd play operas by Donizetti or Bellini, sometimes at full blast into the service courtyard below – much to the delight of the Italian domestics. Rosedale once did a quasi-karaoke performance of the Mad Scene from *Lucia* imitating Joan Sutherland who we adopted as our diva. Just occasionally, to dispel any reputation for fogeyness, we'd turn up a raunchy number by Shirley Bassey or Dorothy Squires.

Were we being deliberately and provocatively counter-cultural? Yes – in part – is the answer to that! It was our way of asserting our identity as aesthetes, as Homos, as Catholics. It's not that we deliberately spurned our mainstream colleagues for their attachment to sport and popular culture; it's just that we saw the world in a different light.

My new identity and self-confidence was such that I became something of an agony uncle. I found myself listening to stories of my friends' love dreams, especially Pips's and Williamson's, and to a lesser extent Rosedale's and Galbraith's. Now I could afford to be detached, congratulating or commiserating as appropriate, but I continued to be amazed at the fickleness of their amorous intentions. They were mainly in the transitional stage; having once lusted over the heroes of the 1st XV, they were now craving favours from the lushes in the fourth and fifth forms. After each setback they'd find another walking vision, interpreting the merest friendly sign as a coded encouragement, refusing to believe anything else until the inevitable brush-off. They'd have been much happier to have found someone of about their own age like I had done.

I could only admire their relentless optimism. All the poor fellows were trying to do was to find someone to love and be loved by, or at the very least to have an object on which to project their fantasies. If they'd once had inner conflicts about their preference for boys, as I had, they had got over them by now and become reconciled or even complacent about their condition. Some, like Pips, positively revelled in it. At any rate, we took great consolation in knowing we were all in the same boat. Questions about morality, or legality, or even our future beyond Upton, were irrelevant in the bubble-within-a-bubble that we had created for ourselves. 'Coming out' to anyone beyond Upton was unheard of, especially to our parents; they 'just knew' – or would soon find out – about their sons, without having to be told. They might be disappointed, but they probably lived in hope that it was just a passing phase. Quite often they were right. No one, to my knowledge, had been disinherited. Indeed, some mothers – like mine, as I discovered later – were secretly pleased they would never have to surrender their boy to another woman.

When Paul became a regular visitor I'd steer the talk in different directions. I knew instinctively he could never be a core member of this group. It just wasn't his style. My friends took the hint early on. They could see for themselves how a real – perhaps unlikely – affair was developing right under their noses; to start with nothing was said and merely implied. But how they must have envied me!

*

It was a glorious Indian summer that year. Why is it always like that when we remember times of life-changing happiness? The colours in the shrubberies and woodlands were positively golden in the low, raking sunlight of the early mornings and late evenings. Fruit trees everywhere were heavy with apples and the hedgerows thick with blackberries. Cool breezes would scatter the fallen leaves across the pathways. When the rains came in a week or two they would turn to mush. Overarching everything was an urgent sense to enjoy the last days of the sun's warmth. Easter was a long way off.

Although our expedition to The Rock had been Paul's suggestion, I would have much to say to him too. As we made our way down the lanes, we must have looked the very picture of two boys supremely happy in each other's company – animated, laughing and giving each other affectionate glances – as though we hadn't a care in the world. Yet an eavesdropper might have detected a certain nervousness in our mildly stilted conversation. Neither of us wanted to make the first move or broach a subject that was uppermost in both our minds. Maybe we were both equally afraid of saying the wrong thing, spoiling the carefree atmosphere, or overstepping the mark. We talked about our holidays: Paul's trip to Brittany and my time in Touraine, not yet mentioning Henri. That hurdle would need to be tackled sooner rather than later.

I'd already discovered that Paul was in Dom Wilfrid's first-year sixth-form English group. Someone had told me that he had been asked – quite randomly – to read aloud Keats's *To Autumn* and had held the class spellbound by his rendition.

'Yeah,' he said, 'we're doing the Romantics. I really love Keats's imagery, the atmosphere and mood he creates with those words, so pregnant with... longing... music... melancholy...'

I told him how I loved Keats too – not just his poetry, but the story of his whole life, how he had died so young, so misunderstood, *'whose name was writ in water'*. How tragic was that.

'I'd love to hear *Autumn* from you, Paul. Couldn't you give me a private performance, when we get to The Rock? It should be just the right time and place to hear it.'

'Alright then. Anything for my best buddy! I know it off by heart by now.' He gave me a gentle punch on my chest, his eyes brimming over with smiles.

That truly broke the ice. I moved up close and put my arm over his shoulder. Should this be the moment for our first proper, tender kiss? But no, we both knew instinctively that we should save it; the field here was too open and we'd reached the stile where the narrow path would take us down to our eyrie.

The Rock was a sort of promontory forming a natural ledge or platform overlooking the bucolic Happy Valley. Immediately below us was the canopy of the trees clinging to the steep sides, and beyond were the small fields enclosed by hedges sloping down towards a stream. Sheep were bleating, their sound re-echoing across the narrow valley. One or two stone cottages had chimneys exhuming grey woodsmoke, filling the air with a sweet and crisp incense as it drifted towards us. An ivy-clad mill stood adjacent to the fast-flowing stream, gurgling and glinting in the autumn sun; and in the distance a white

Regency country house was silhouetted against a dark belt of trees.

The place was a popular destination for two groups of Upton boys, not entirely mutually exclusive. A handful of the sentimental-minded, like me, would come here to contemplate this vision of poetic sublimity, while others used it as a relatively safe haven for illicit cigarette smoking.

As we lay on the grass, propping ourselves up with our elbows, I took pride in pointing out the landmarks. I wondered if I should offer Paul a Gauloise from the case in my pocket. I'd continued with this brand because the smell and taste reminded me of those delicious after-moments with Henri. No, I decided, *not* today with Paul.

'So, are you going to recite *Autumn* for me?'

'Alright. I'll give it a try:

> *Season of mists and mellow fruitfulness!*
> *Close bosom-friend of the maturing sun...*'

From the very first words a shiver went down my spine. I just had to close my eyes to block out any sight, even of him, or any distraction, just to listen to his dark, languid, soulful voice, delivering the magical words so softly, with all the right cadences and inflections expressing every emotion from melancholy to eroticism:

> *'... And fill all fruit with ripeness to the core;*
> *To swell the gourd, and pump the hazel shells*
> *With sweet kernel; to set budding more,*
> *And still more...'*

right to the end, without a flaw, his words getting softer, quieter, almost tremulous, dying away:

'... and now with treble soft
The redbreast whistles from a garden croft;
And gathering swallows twitter in the skies.'

'Gosh, Paul, that's *brilliant*. How on earth do you do it?' I asked, stunned.

We were both still lying in the horizontal, and as I was speaking I shifted my head and shoulders to rest more comfortably against a tree trunk. It was almost as if this slight movement was an unspoken invitation for Paul to move too, stretching himself backwards, resting his head against my chest and taking my hand in his.

I felt my body give a silent gasp of joy, all tension and anxiety now replaced by the calm exhilaration of something indescribably beautiful happening to me without any effort on my part. After a second's hesitation I used my spare hand to start running my fingers through his hair; for how long had I dreamt of this? It felt thick, curly, luxuriously soft. With the tip of my index finger I stroked the nape of his neck; merely touching him made me shiver with pleasure. *If he turns round*, I thought, *I'll never be able to stop kissing him.*

Paul must have thought this the most natural, the most innocent thing in the world and he just carried on answering my question without even turning.

'Well,' he said, sweeping his spare arm in front of him, 'here it all is, right in front of us, autumn in all its glory.' He laughed. 'Just look: we've got Keats's "*barr'd clouds*", his "*soft-dying day*"... the "*stubble-plains with rosy hue*"..., even the "*full-grown lambs bleating from the hilly bourn*".'

He paused and turned around to look at me. 'I'm so glad you brought me here, Freddie.'

He took hold of my other arm and brought it round to place it over his chest. I hugged him tightly; we were so close I could feel his warmth under his jacket and longed to touch his skin, to feel his body, to caress and cover it in kisses. Nothing else in the world mattered.

I whispered into his ear, 'Is *this* what you want to put right with me, Paul? I think now's the time, don't you?'

He freed himself out of my tight embrace to lie sideways beside me, face to face, barely three inches apart. I reached out to stroke his cheek.

'*This* is what I mean by putting something right,' he said, lifting my hand to kiss it, then bringing his face even closer and pressing his lips against mine. It was the touch of an angel – so soft, tender, slow and restrained. I tasted his fleshiness, the roundness of his lips as mine opened to take his breath, finding his tongue, bathing in his warm sap. My whole body surrendered to the intensity of it.

'That's what I had to put right, Freddie. To make up for that bloody nose I gave you last term.'

'I thought it would never come.' I moved over to lie across him, taking his head in both my hands, looking into those deep, dark eyes now full of life and expectation. I had never felt so wanted, so exalted, so beautiful. The floodgates had opened. There was no stopping. Every square millimetre of his face was mine now. With every burst of passion from me he responded with equal intensity. There was no need of words.

I could feel his stirrings in his crotch lying against mine. I reached down to unbutton his shirt, to run my hand across his chest, and then to find his flies, ready to reach inside. I just wanted to give pleasure to every inch of him.

'No, no, Freddie. Not that. I don't think we're ready for that just yet,' he said, gently moving my hand away.

I rolled over on my side. 'Alright. I just want you to have everything you want of me. You just tell me.'

'This is beautiful enough, isn't it? I want this moment to go on and on forever.'

'That's fine with me. Let's stick to hugs and kisses. I'm happy with that. More than happy. *Deliriously* happy.' No, I wasn't being sarcastic or even disappointed. To prove it I gave him another long kiss on the lips.

We lay side by side. It seemed like an eternity, taking each other in, body and soul. Slowly my lust gave way to the sheer joy of holding him, knowing he was mine.

'Now,' he said, 'there's something else I want to show you, or rather it's something I want you to hear.'

'Go on,' I said, sitting upright and curious to know what he'd been holding back especially for me.

'It's another poem.'

'I can never listen to too many poems from you, you sexy bugger with a golden voice. Speak!'

He looked a bit shifty at that, as well he might; no one had ever complimented him like that before. Then he grinned and gave me another friendly punch on my chest. He said he'd been browsing in a secondhand bookshop in Harrogate during the holidays and had come across an anthology of American verse. There had been a bookmark still inside, at a page with one of Walt Whitman's poems.

'I thought of us immediately. I can't wait to read it to you.'

He brought out a slim volume from his inside jacket pocket and started to read. After the first few lines he put it down; he knew it off by heart.

> 'We two boys together clinging,
> One the other never leaving,
> Up and down the roads going,
> North and South excursions making,
> Power enjoying, elbows stretching, fingers clutching,

Arm'd and fearless, eating, drinking, sleeping, loving.
No law less than ourselves owning, sailing, soldiering,
thieving, threatening,
Misers, menials, priests alarming, air breathing, water
drinking, on the turf or the sea-beach dancing,
Cities wrenching, ease scorning, statutes mocking,
feebleness chasing,
Fulfilling our foray.'

I'd never read or heard of this poem before and was transfixed by the images as they flashed up in front of me, imagining, of course, the two boys to be him and me. But it was more than just a recitation; Paul was *performing* the poem, modulating his voice so carefully to express the meaning and sound of all those participles, gesturing minutely with his hands and using his eyes to glance over to me with changing expressions of defiance, tenderness… and sexy fun.

'My goodness, that's just wonderful. Those two fellows, I wonder who they were? And where did they come from?'

'I bet they were probably our age, run away from home, parents having thrown them out when they discovered they were more than just good friends – with hardly a bean in their pockets.'

'How do you think they met, where were they going?'

'*I* don't know. Do you think they had been in the army together, in the Civil War? Perhaps they were on the run, escaping court martial for their "indiscretions"? Or maybe they were from different sides?'

'Seems possible. But were they caught? What happened to them? Does anyone know?'

'I'd love to know. I like to think of them making their way west, not caring much about anything or anyone except themselves. What lucky fellows!'

'It's a pity Whitman's not on the curriculum. But can you

imagine Dom Wilfrid trying to answer our questions? He'd be spluttering about all over the place.'

We both laughed at the very idea of it.

'Could *we* be like them?' I mused. 'Couldn't we just drop everything and go off into the unknown, defying everyone and everything?'

'It's a lovely idea but somehow I don't think so, Freddie. At least not *yet*. But in our hearts perhaps we can be like them.'

'Yeah, I suppose that's better than nothing,' I said, unenthusiastically. 'But until then maybe this can be *our* poem, something we can share – our "national anthem". We could quote one or two phrases sometimes to each other. Even if only to remember this afternoon when we first kissed *properly*?'

'You really are *such* a romantic, Freddie. What a crazy, lovely idea! Anyway, I want you to keep the book. It's my present to you, for all you've done for me. But I'd love it if you would make a freehand copy of the poem for me to keep in my pocket – right here,' he said, pointing to his left breast.

'I'll treasure it like nothing else,' I said, as I kissed him again fully on his lips, then ran my fingers through his hair.

'I love it when you do that, Freddie. I don't think I'll ever get enough of your kisses. Wherever did you learn to be such a good kisser?'

'Like this, you mean?' I kissed him again passionately and greedily, deliberately ignoring his question. I could feel for myself how my passion was igniting him, making him want more and more. I just wanted to go on and on, giving him pleasure, all the time. If he was responding like this to my kisses how much more was he going to be blown away when he discovers some of the other skills I learnt from Henri?

Then Paul spoke first. 'But seriously, how is it going to work, though, if we're ever going to be… like… like those two fellows in *We Two Boys Together*?'

'Yeah, it'll be tricky,' I said. 'But we've got to be realistic. We can't go the whole way, at least for now. It would be terrible if we were expelled, or even worse. Imagine! I don't want to upset anyone – Dom Gabriel, my parents, Whiskers. They would all feel *so* let down.'

Paul was looking hard at a blade of grass and then lifted his head, snarling angrily, 'Why can't people just mind their own business. If they can't understand how we feel about each other, they should just leave us alone. We're doing no harm to anyone.' It came straight from the heart.

I touched him gently on the shoulder and looked at him in profile. 'Listen, we'll have to compromise for the time being at least. Let's stick to what we agreed just now. We can be "semi-celibate" best friends, can't we, with lots of hugs and kisses. Then no one can accuse us, or get us expelled. We can always steal away for moments like this.'

He looked up. 'Alright then. Until the right time comes, that's what we'll do. It'll be a pact between us. Come on, let's shake on it.'

We held out our right hands and the deal was done. 'Semi-celibate best friends,' we both said together, laughing. *Almost like being engaged*, I thought to myself.

'Anyway,' he said, 'you still haven't told me where you learned to kiss so passionately. Not with Rowse, for God's sake?' Suddenly his face went black.

'No, I never learnt anything from Rowse,' I replied with a degree of honesty. 'It's a long story. I'll tell you all about it as we walk back.' I realised time was passing and we needed to return.

We pulled each other up from the grass.

'Anyway,' I said, 'I need a piss right now – and I feel like aiming my piss at anyone who's going to prevent us being together or "*fulfilling our foray*".'

I got up and went to the cliff edge, undoing my flies. He

came up beside me. 'Me too,' he said, 'let's piss on them together,' as we yanked out our cocks.

Gushing over the edge we put our spare arms around each other and shouted into the abyss and across the valley: 'Piss off, all you bastards.' I cried, 'If you try and stop us.' 'Or anyone who tries to come between us!' Paul echoed equally loudly.

'It could almost be "*We two boys together pissing*",' I quipped, both of us laughing.

As we walked back through the woods I put my arm around his waist and after only a moment he did the same with his arm over my shoulder. We'd have made a different impression on that outside observer who might have watched us when we'd set out. When we reached the lane we disentangled, and for a few minutes as we ambled slowly and reluctantly towards Upton we linked our little fingers together. I smiled as I murmured, '*Fingers clutching*'.

But I couldn't procrastinate any longer. The moment had arrived for me to come clean about Henri.

'Now I've got something *I* need to come clean about which explains the kissing. I just hope to goodness it won't make you think differently about me, but I can't bear your not knowing.'

He looked at me apprehensively. I told him the whole story: how I'd met Henri, got drunk – alright not *that* drunk – had sex the first time, and became each other's *petit ami*; I flinched from using the word 'boyfriend'. I told him about our expeditions, our falling out after our visit to Rosedale in Paris, and how Jacques had turned up at the last minute.

When I'd finished, he turned and said quite calmly, 'Thanks for telling me all this. You needn't have done, I suppose. I have to say, yes, I really am a bit surprised. I honestly didn't think you had it in you. But I can see it's the reason for the big change in you since last term.'

I couldn't quite tell how he was taking it. Perhaps I needed to justify myself better.

'I'm really not going to apologise for taking up with Henri for a short summer romance. As we've discussed endlessly, I just didn't know if you'd ever take me back. I found Henri on the rebound, as he did with me. Anyway, I've learnt a lot about how to cope with other people's feelings, and a great deal about how bloody wonderful sex is too.'

He gave me a doubtful sideways glance.

'I'm still trying to get my head around all this. I told you before how I hate the idea of someone else climbing all over you – either Rowse or now this Henri – or you kissing someone else the way you do. Tell me the truth, did you go the whole way with Henri? And he with you?'

'Yes, we did. Both of us.'

'And how was it?' He stopped in his tracks and looked at me almost accusingly. I could see he'd gone pale.

'I have to say it was amazing. It just seemed to come naturally to us. We both wanted to please the other, and the giving and the taking just seemed to fall into place. We had a great time, I'm afraid. He taught me an awful lot of things.'

We walked on in silence. *Oh, goodness*, I thought, *this is going to be another big test for him*. Which way would it go? What else could I say to persuade him that the affair with Henri was in the past, that it had nothing to do with him?

'Alright, Paul,' I said, trying to anticipate him, 'I can understand how you might be feeling. But let me just say that throughout my time with Henri I never, ever, forgot *you*. Once I even called out your name when we made love, and he didn't like it at all.'

Still no response from him so I continued, but now speaking softly,

'I've been waiting for you all this time. If you walk away now, I just don't know what I'd do. I think it would be the end of me.'

He looked at me, but I just couldn't read him.

I played my last card.

'But there's *one thing* I've never done with anyone, and I won't do until the right person comes along. And that person is going to be *you*, Paul, and I know it'll be the greatest thing in the world when it happens. I've never fallen asleep with someone I love in my arms, and woken up with them still there beside me. I'm saving that exclusively for *you*.'

'Oh goodness, Freddie. You've really put me on the spot.'

I should have felt bad about the agony I was putting him through, almost blackmailing him. But I couldn't; this was a do-or-die situation.

We parted in deepest silence once we got to the side gates – he to Ambrose, me to Baker's Row.

*

Here was yet another crossroad, with Paul in the driving seat giving no indication which way he would turn. Would his feelings for me be strong enough to dispel his jealousy of Henri, if that's what he felt? Was he shocked at what I'd done, or merely surprised? How loyal would he be?

I was well aware I had never probed him deeply about his feelings towards other boys or men; it had simply never come up. Perhaps I had dreaded what he might say. For now, though, it seemed that all his feelings were exclusively for me. I could hardly believe my luck compared with my loveless exotic friends. But if that was the case, how much worse for him were my infidelities and failings, first with Rowse and now with Henri? How hurt he must be, how traduced he must feel. I wanted to kill myself for causing him misery or distress. What a worthless piece of shit I must be in his eyes.

But then came the letter, written in guarded terms, no doubt in case it ever got into the wrong hands. I have it here in front of me.

F,

I'm so grateful you told me all that stuff the other day. I can't pretend that the things you told me weren't a surprise, but now I've had time to think it over. I can see Henri was a one-off and must have answered a real need for you at the time. Anyway, why should I judge you? At that time I had no claims over you. But after all the things we did and said to each other at The Rock, it's different now, isn't it?

Let's stick together and do – and don't do – as we agreed, at least while we're under the roof at Upton; let's hope we can last out and things can be different for us when the right time comes. I've never felt like this about anyone before and I'm having a really hard time with you, Freddie. I just want us to be happy. But I need to trust you.

P S

I felt a huge sense of relief – almost the same elation as when I'd had his first letter of forgiveness only a few weeks ago. How generous he was! How understanding! He rose even higher in my estimation, if that were possible. No, he wasn't just a beautiful face; he had a beautiful soul as well. Really, I didn't deserve any of this; I had to be the happiest boy in the world. We would be together now – on *his* terms, and that was fine by me. It was more than I had ever dared to hope.

*

During the rest of the term our relationship eased into a certain 'normality' but never became stale. We both had work to do. Paul was in the school 2nd XI hockey team, and he had his ongoing rehearsals for *The Winter's Tale*. For myself I was determined to make my body as beautiful as it could ever become against the day when we would eventually make love: I redoubled my efforts at cross-country running, and – rather against the grain – joined a gym group, with surprisingly good results. Anyway, I needed to get into trim before we set off for St Moritz in early January.

As time wore on, I made it clear to my other friends that my hospitality on Baker's Row was not unlimited and my room was no longer the CEP or Confessional for Ephebic Passions as some wag had christened it. I wanted it to be a private sanctuary for Paul and me. He'd often come while I was working at my desk, and throw himself onto my bed lying on top of the fur rug with his book, going over his lines for the play, letting me hear them when he reckoned he needed an audience or a prompt. When he'd finished I'd go over and lie next to him and there'd be a bit of rough and tumble. We'd kiss and say nice, stupid, boyish things to each other. Our kisses were glorious and hot, and when one of us put his hand on the other's thigh we'd let it rest there for a moment, making us both horny, but then the other would remove it gently. Paul would murmur, 'Not yet, Freddie, not yet. Remember, we're saving it up.' Not surprisingly, there was a lot of jerking off in private this term. Henri's gift now came into its own. A salty-chlorine kind of smell seemed to cling to the fur rug much of the time.

How were we able to get away with it? You have to remember the age gap was not so obvious now that Paul was in the sixth form, like me. It was to their eternal credit that the monks, especially Dom Gabriel, obviously trusted us, and we, in our turn, made sure there was nothing for which they could take exception. For example, according to the rules, Paul should have obtained permission from Dom Gabriel every time he wanted to visit my room on his own, but I'd managed to extract a blanket approval for him to come at any time as he needed a private space to rehearse his big part in *The Winter's Tale*. Dom Gabriel had paused and put down his pipe, saying to me with more than a hint of suspicion,

'Can I trust you, McNaughton?' He obviously knew much more than he had been letting on, and *he* knew that *I* knew.

I'd replied, looking at him straight in the face, 'Yes, sir. Please take my word for it.'

It was even more reason for us – me in particular – to honour our pact. Once – and he must have done it as a test – he made an unexpected visit to my room on some flimsy pretext, barely knocking on the door before marching in. He found Paul lying across the bed reading the play and me ensconced at the desk with Robert Blake's new biography of Disraeli. 'Ah!' he said, with an ironic smile. 'The very picture of scholarly endeavour!'

Instead of encouraging Paul to mix with my more exotic friends, I tried steering him towards my more high-powered 'mainstream' circle. For a short while he was obviously my protégé, but in no time he was on an equal footing with most of them. Strangely, I felt the opposite to jealous, taking a real pleasure seeing him become the perfect Renaissance prince beginning to tower over these less noble satellites. An early move was to engineer his election to the evening sessions of The Conclave, which had now acquired a reputation for being quite highbrow.

At the first session he attended, Woronsov had read out a piece from *The Guardian* about the imminent repeal of the Sexual Offences Act. He asked rhetorically why the age of consent had been set at twenty-one. Why not sixteen, as it was for 'normal' boys and girls, or even thirteen as it had been in France until the war? And what did 'in private' mean anyway?

'And *what*,' he asked, as though he were in a courtroom, 'is the legal position if two boys, both supposedly "under-aged" at seventeen, were found together?' He said this looking straight at me.

'Would *borstal* be able to cure them or teach them a lesson?' he demanded sarcastically.

There was an embarrassed silence followed by a po-faced discussion, which concealed a lot of unstated anxieties. A sudden fear crept over me. Until now I'd been aware of the so-called criminality of Homo activity but never thought it would apply to *me*. Woronsov continued his indignation with a certain rhetorical flair, asking why there was one rule for Heteros and another for Homos. We all agreed on the unfairness of it all and succeeded in persuading our hero Dom Edmund too.

It's interesting, Sam, that another leading light from The Conclave went on to become a famous human rights QC and yet another a Lord of the Supreme Court. Woronsov himself went on to become the CEO of a worldwide Catholic charity despite living openly with his long-term civil partner. Little did we know!

Throughout this session Paul didn't say much; I wondered if he thought he'd joined a secret cabal of Queers determined to rule the universe? But shortly afterwards he proved his credentials by reading out a piece from *The Tablet* about the Pope's latest encyclical on Catholic Social Teaching, and then leading the discussion. I'd lent him a pamphlet on the subject, myself having come to the conclusion that it was the only worthwhile alternative to all the failed political ideologies. Dom Edmund was hugely impressed, and for Paul it was another breakthrough.

On the very last day of term Dom Gabriel called me into his study. I had my suspicions as to what it was about, and I was right: he was making me a house prefect from next term. He said he'd been impressed with my new self-confidence and reckoned I could be a benign and civilising influence on the house. *At last*, I thought irreverently, *I'll be entitled to a smart double-breasted black waistcoat and coloured handkerchiefs for my breast pocket – symbols of my dizzying new status.* Things seemed to be turning out well. My father was so pleased with me that he increased my allowance to £120 a year.

But there was sadness too as I had to say farewell to Pips, who was leaving. He'd no need to resit his A-Levels, having just taken the Christchurch scholarship exam and dazzled them at the interview. The result was a foregone conclusion. We kissed goodbye on our cheeks and swore we'd be meeting up just as soon as he got back from his travels. He'd become fascinated with oriental rugs and had persuaded his parents to let him go overland to Afghanistan and Persia (as it then was). When he got home he was going to start importing them and have a stand in Portobello Road. I just hoped he didn't get up to too much mischief along the way.

'I want to make my first million before I go up to the House, darling. I might be able to entertain you there in a bit of style.'

He did too.

*

The Christmas holidays were particularly eventful that year. Pippa – your dear mother – and I were invited to several teenage dances in London. These had been part of our social landscape for many years, but were now becoming increasingly smoochy and finishing later and later. But, strange to say, the whole druggy thing hadn't hit our nice upper-middle-class world yet; all that was still a couple of years off.

I didn't exactly dread these occasions, but they were a source of some anxiety as there were few girls who I could even pretend to fancy, nor many who seemed to fancy me. As a defence against suspicions, I made it my business to be amusing and attentive to them all almost indiscriminately. Thus I became known, among their mothers at least, for being 'reliable', and among some of the girls as quite good company. I was especially kind to the shyer ones, those who may have been dragged along to the parties reluctantly, and were probably still besotted with their ponies. Most of the slightly older ones, of course, wanted something much more adventurous: boys who were definitely NSIT (Not Safe In Taxis) or even more. Rather gallingly, and more than once, I overheard myself being described as 'Pippa's brother'.

The person I got along with best of all was my good friend Miranda, a big and busty girl with a happy, round face of freckles, frizzy reddish hair and a bit of a chin, but a big smile and an equally big personality. She was a brilliant mimic, and we would fall about laughing at the same absurdities. We always seemed to end up together at these parties and people even began to talk about us in the same breath. She and her parents would be coming with us as part of the big party to St Moritz after Christmas, together with her mate-ette Christine.

Away from these nocturnal events I began to explore the museums and galleries of London on my own. I had been inspired by Rosedale's effortless *sprezzatura* in Paris and I determined to make myself just as suavely erudite and discriminating. Once or twice I went with my mother and the experience gave us an unexpected new bond.

I decided I loved the English rococo style best of all. At the V&A I was drawn to the shapeliness and rich colours of the Chelsea gold-anchor vases, the exuberant carving of the Chippendale furniture, and the ultra-naturalistic chasing of the Lamerie silver. I saw how they shared the spontaneity of Hogarth's paintings in their earthy, witty *joie de vivre*, which made me smile and *enjoy* them. The French equivalents at the Wallace, which my mother preferred, I found cold and affected and somehow could only *admire*. I reserved judgement on Bavaria and Spain.

For paintings I found myself gravitating to the Venetian and Florentine portraits. At the National Gallery I was spellbound by Titian's early *Portrait of a Young Man* from the Halifax Collection. This dreamy fellow, not much older than me, was not conventionally handsome, but beautiful nonetheless: sensitive, wistful and intelligent, the very picture of melancholy. What heartfelt agonies was the poor soul going through, I wondered? Was he pining forever for an unreachable loved one, or remembering the long-lost love of his life?

I doubled back across the galleries to compare him with the Florentine prince by Bronzino whose image had risen up in my memory when I had first seen Paul in the dayroom just over a year ago. I dreamt about how I would bring these two portraits together if I were the curator, contrasting the two of them in juxtaposition, with a tantalising gap between them, seeing how they would respond – even speak – to each other. The young Florentine – Paul – full of youthful coolness, looking directly out of the frame, his expression forthright yet hiding a touching vulnerability. How this would contrast with the Venetian – me – with his far-away, melting gaze! I bought a postcard of the Titian and sent it to Paul, with the oblique message, '*Orsino?* or *Antonio? F.*'

*

This year's visit to St Moritz was the best ever. At last I'd become quite proficient at skiing and felt pretty good about myself accompanying my father on some of the more advanced runs. Foreign exchange restrictions had been lifted so *après ski* became more adventurous. It was good fun having Miranda and Christine with us.

I had been summoned for my interview at Cambridge on the day after we were due home. Unfortunately, I went down with a high temperature just before our departure and had to remain behind for a few more days, sending a telegram requesting a postponement. It might have seemed quite glamorous in the circumstances, I suppose, suggesting I was an injured sporting hero. I hope I didn't disillusion them by failing to show up with my leg in plaster. My conversation with the admissions tutor seemed to be mainly about our preferred ski resorts. As I was gathering my coat to depart, he came out with it:

'Shall we say three straight As in your retakes and you're in?'

That brought me down to earth; obviously it wasn't going to be a walkover. For the very first time I wondered whether I'd get in to Cambridge as everyone expected. It was a real wake-up call. I certainly didn't have an alternative plan. I really had to get down to work – no more time-wasting. There was too much riding on it.

With my love,
Freddie

11

My dear Sam,

It had been during these Christmas holidays, '67–'68, that Pippa and I persuaded your grandparents it was high time we returned all the hospitality we'd received from our friends over the years.

Once we'd established the principle, we pointed out that if we gave a dance soon after Easter it could, after all, double up as a slightly early eighteenth birthday party for me, and as a sort of 'pre-deb' dance for Pippa. We'd all begun to realise that she was likely to be drawn into the fringes of the London deb scene in a couple of years' time, however much my father baulked at the idea.

You may well be surprised at our blithe expectation that our parents would lay on something like this for us. We knew they were not particularly well off compared with some of our schoolfriends' parents. But we argued that to throw a full-scale deb dance in London in a couple of years, with a band, and a disco and all the trimmings, would cost a fortune – far more sensible, therefore, to be ahead of the game and host something on a smaller scale a year or two earlier. Perhaps a big cocktail party at the club would eventually suffice for your mother's Coming Out.

After much discussion we decided on the Hyde Park Hotel, which we knew well from a number of shindigs there in the past. It had a large, elegant ballroom with full-length mirrors down one side and French windows overlooking the park on the other. A date during the Easter holidays was booked.

There was no real precedent for this kind of 'in-between' party, so we had to invent an untried protocol. Today I suppose it would be seen as a sort of upmarket school prom, the difference being that the McNaughtons had to pay for it all! To make it appropriately 'grown up' we decreed that everyone was to come in evening dress: boys in dinner jackets and girls in long dresses. There would be dinner parties at private houses across London beforehand so that people could get to know each other in advance, and then come on to the party in taxis. Those living outside London would need to be found places to stay overnight.

Top of *my* agenda, of course, was that Paul should not only be invited, but that he should stay with us on Campden Hill, *with me, in my room, in my bed.* In this context, away from Upton and the constraints of our pact, we might finally share something wonderful with each other. If it didn't happen now, would it ever happen at all?

I greatly approved your mother's choice of Jane Hilton as her house guest. They were best friends at Ascot, and I'd decided a long time ago that I liked her after staying with her family in Suffolk. The two of them couldn't have been more different: Jane was fearsomely intellectual and well read, always ready for a spirited argument about life, death and everything in between; your mother would look on amused and slightly bewildered and then say something apposite and witty, and the two of them would fall about in giggles.

There would be about a hundred boys and girls coming, mainly from the usual extended Catholic cousinhood and including a fair contingent from our two schools. I had no serious fears that Paul would look out of place by being one of the youngest; his maturity and good looks would get him anywhere, if only he knew it. But it took my firmest resolve with my parents to insist on him being my chosen house guest rather than being landed with an out-of-town cousin.

*

The Lent term began, and to my great regret I had to vacate my niche on Baker's Row. As a house prefect, I was entitled to a much bigger room in the main Ambrose block, although it was a little closer to Dom Gabriel's study than I would have wished. The opportunities for intimate meetings with Paul were going to be more difficult but not impossible. Dom Gabriel had trusted me; maybe, I reflected, one of the reasons he'd appointed me a prefect was to demonstrate to the wider world how close friendships between two boys of slightly different ages could be tolerated, even approved of, if they were genuine and kept in control. Perhaps by putting me in a position of responsibility he knew me better than I did myself – that I would never compromise my loyalties. Something like this could never have happened in any other house except Ambrose.

One of my first duties was to meet my new 'fag': the junior boy who – under Dom Gabriel's new regime – had himself chosen me as his fag-master. In his well-meaning naivety he couldn't have foreseen some of the consequences of this apparently more enlightened practice.

I was indifferent as to who might choose me, not knowing, let alone seriously fancying, any of the new boys coming up from the Junior House. I had no expectations when I was called into Dom Gabriel's study to be introduced to the fourteen-year-old Nicholas Jones. I'd noticed him briefly in the line-up for the '*Miserere*' and at the first assembly, but now I could see him at close range I was immediately taken by the sweetness of his person and his disarming manner. He was quite short, slender, fair-haired, and with a flawless strawberry and cream complexion, like an English rose. His beseeching eyes were a matchless sapphire, but without the slightest hint of coldness. As we shook hands he blushed and looked down, obviously very nervous and trembling slightly. An arrow was being fired at me from somewhere not so far away.

Gosh, you lovely boy, I thought.

'How do you do, sir,' he said, with a rather quaint formality, extending his hand. His voice had obviously broken, but probably not so long ago.

'There you are,' said Dom Gabriel, putting down his pipe. 'I'm sure you two will get on famously. Jones has a great talent at drawing and is learning the violin. Oh, and he's volunteered for the Confraternity of St Stephen so you must bear in mind he'll have duties as an acolyte or thurifer and serving at Mass.'

Jones blushed again, and my heart went out to him; he would need very gentle handling. I resisted the temptation to say, 'Yes, you'll look absolutely adorable in a white alb and swinging a thurible. Like an extra in the Ghent Altarpiece.'

As we walked towards my room, feeling thoroughly chuffed to be accompanied by the prettiest of all the fags, I told him I hadn't finished setting it up yet. I asked if he would begin hanging the pictures and damasks and unpacking some of my things.

His eyes lit up. 'Oh yes, sir, I'd love to help,' tilting his head slightly to the side as he made eye contact with me. It was only the first in his battery of seductive little mannerisms.

It gave me a definite jolt to be called 'sir' by someone of my own background, if not my same age. But a voice inside me said, 'For goodness' sake, don't let it go to your head.'

'Maybe you could start by fitting the hangings along the walls. They're probably not quite wide enough to cover the whole area but just see what you can do by spacing them out. And then we need to hang the Drevet prints. Could you get started now? I have to go to a meeting to work out the duty rotas.' I had toned down the décor slightly; Nanny's elaborate bed canopy had not survived the transition from Baker's Row.

I was mildly concerned that my requests might seem overdemanding, but the boy had not shown the slightest reluctance, in fact the reverse. Many a 'normal' fag would have greeted them with a monosyllabic grunt.

When I returned I found the room transformed. Jones had hung the damasks, alternating them in crimson and gold, so that they covered both the long walls with equal spaces between them and he was now hanging the pictures. He had found some picture wire and was hanging them in such a way that they nodded forward at a slight angle from the wall; it all looked pretty smart.

'Jones, you've done a great job here. Well done. It's almost as good as a professional. Wherever did you learn how to do this?'

'I quite enjoy hanging pictures, sir. My father has some watercolours at home and we have to change them round every six months because they shouldn't get too much daylight. I like to help the gardeners with the hanging and arranging.'

I later discovered this was quite a famous collection representing all the classic English artists, which Jones himself would inherit one day.

I asked if he would make coffee for me and a group of friends after supper.

He gave me a charming smile, just opening his lips enough for me to see the perfect row of white teeth. *'I'll look forward to that, sir.'*

I felt astonished at his remark, and at the same time deeply flattered. This was hardly a fag's normal attitude when asked to give up some of their precious free time. In response I allowed him a flicker of a smile.

In the days that followed we got into a certain routine. Jones was assiduous in calling in after breakfast to make my bed, finishing the task by covering it with the by-now famous fur rug, tidy away my pyjamas, and take my shoes away to be polished. After lunch and supper he would make coffee for me and any of my friends who had called in. In return I would give him my copy of *The Times* after I had finished with it each evening, and he would borrow my *Country Life* and *Apollo* magazines, to both of which I now subscribed with my increased allowance. I enjoyed seeing him read them conspicuously, reclining in a window seat in the dayroom.

I noticed that he seemed a quiet boy, never trying to draw attention to himself in any way. But he was obviously self-conscious of his prettiness and hated how older boys admired him to the point of teasing him. I once witnessed his face grow dark after a couple of seniors walked past giving him a wolf whistle. I had intervened and made the offenders go and report themselves to their housemaster. I hoped to goodness the lad would become immune to such attentions. He seemed much more relaxed with a select little group of contemporaries, although at this stage he wasn't their leader. Neither was he obviously a great games player, but went along dutifully wherever he was required. I had noticed him on the football and hockey pitches in his shorts and long stockings; there never seemed to be the slightest trace of mud or dirt about him.

Whenever he saw me in public and away from the context of his fag duties he would give me a nervous glance and then blush and look down at his shoes. Sometimes at morning assemblies, I was aware he was looking towards me for a fraction of a second too long, and I'd acknowledge him with a smile.

Towards the end of term I noticed an additional degree of attentiveness creeping into his usual routines. For instance, he took it upon himself to start tidying the papers and books on my desk, doing so very carefully so as not to disturb anything I might be working on. Had he been reading my diaries and letters? Then one afternoon I returned from a walk to find a small bunch of primroses arranged in a tooth glass on my desk. A few weeks later there were some daffodils. I had thanked him but said nothing more.

Throughout all this we had been on good terms, but very polite and formal. On the last day of term I asked him to stay behind for a minute after lunch.

I motioned for him to sit on the bed where he propped himself up with his back against the wall, supported by a cushion, his legs dangling over the front. He had grown during the term and his trousers now hung a little too short for him. There was a flash of pinky-white skin between his socks and trouser turn-ups.

'I'd just like to thank you for all you've done for me this term, Jones,' I said. 'I've really appreciated it. You've been a model fag.' I gave him a smile.

He looked down at his hands on the fur rug and started to play with it in his fingers. Then he looked up a little tremulously.

'Thank you, sir. I've really been happy to help you this term. It means a lot to me.'

Oh God, I thought to myself, *where is this heading?*

'I've asked Dom Gabriel if I can stay on as your fag next term, sir. I hope that's alright.'

'That's absolutely fine, Jones. In fact, it would be ideal. You've probably got used to my little ways by now,' I said, keeping up the smile.

'Oh, yes, sir. But I do enjoy being able to come into your room and helping you.'

My goodness, you lovely lad, I thought, *I just want to eat you up.*

'Well, here's something as a small token of thanks.'

I handed him the customary ten-shilling note and he put it away in his pocket book. I just knew from the way he looked at it that he would never spend it.

'Can I just ask you one favour, sir?'

'Of course, what is it?'

'Can I take a photo of the room, please? I'd love to show some of my friends from the other houses what it's like.'

I agreed, and a few minutes later he returned with his new camera. He fiddled around with the settings and I moved away so he could get a wide-angle shot.

'Oh, no, sir. You must be in the picture too. Please can you just lie on the fur rug and look into the camera.'

I did as I was bidden, lying sideways across the rug, my head supported by one arm while the other was draped over a bent knee, a bit like Isaac Oliver's miniature of Lord Herbert of Cherbury, giving the camera the full-on gaze. It seemed a bit forward and suggestive, but maybe that was just what he wanted. For a split second I remembered fondly another photographic session, less encumbered, not so long ago.

Of course I was hugely flattered that a younger and very attractive boy obviously had a big crush on me. But I determined to remain as cool, even aloof, as best I could. Thank goodness it was the end of term. With luck he'd return in a month's time with his affections redirected elsewhere. If not, I knew he might become a distraction for me, maybe even a temptation. I sensed Eros was hovering around ready to make a stab, but this time I had my shield up.

With my love,
Freddie

12

My dear Sam,

We now come to an event that your mother will remember very well, although even now I wonder how much she knew what was going on behind the scenes. Try asking her one day!

The Easter holidays 1968 were upon us and there was much activity preparing for the dance. I should also have been revising for my exams but instead I was spending a lot of time daydreaming about Paul and how we were going to spend our time together. Maybe, at last, we would say the L word to each other.

You may ask why we couldn't keep in touch by phone. The answer was that we only had one telephone at the cottage – and that was in the hall, so there could be no privacy there. And in London it was the same, although there were three extensions, but it was hardly conducive to exchanging little intimacies. In addition, my father was a stickler for scrutinising the bills. He insisted that if we had to make trunk calls, we must do so in the cheap period after lunch. It all sounds archaic in the extreme, but that's how it was.

*

I was straining to catch sight of Paul at the barrier at King's Cross. As he came into view everyone and everything else became a blur. I loved seeing him walk towards me in his glad rags with such maturity and confidence: green tweed jacket, Viyella check shirt with some dark rust in the pattern, picking up his auburn-brown hair, a smart yellow paisley tie, grey flannels and brogues – the very picture of the country boy in London, and I the town boy in my blazer and cavalry twills. Today you'd call us a couple of young fogies.

'Hey! It's brilliant to see you, Paul.'

'You're looking great, Freddie,' he said looking me up and down, his lashes moving slowly and seductively, his lips quivering into a smile. I could barely resist kissing him there and then but had to make do with a lingering, manly handshake.

I took his bag and we made our way to the Underground. Sitting opposite each other on the short bench seats, we were not able to speak because of the noise. We just looked at each other, smiling meaningfully, sometimes trying to look away, but then being drawn back magnetically to study each other head to toe. Once or twice we moved our legs so they touched for a fraction longer than necessary. I could feel my blood pressure rise.

Strolling down Church Street I explained the scenario.

'The other two fellows coming to dinner are Herbert and Waybrook, and the girls are Tessa's friend from school, Jane – terrifyingly bright – and some skiing friends, Miranda Gardner and Christine Cooper. Miranda is a lot of fun. But I warn you they're both on the prowl.'

'*Really?*' said Paul, smiling leerily.

'Yeah,' I continued. 'So be careful not to lose your virtue to them, at least not tonight. They got me drunk last time we were in Switzerland. I'd been put to bed almost unconscious after a boozy party. They both came creeping into my room wanting to deflower me as a threesome. I was too blotto to oblige.'

Oh God, I thought, *should I really let on about that?* I laughed nervously.

'Sounds interesting.'

I raised my eyebrows in an attempt to be enigmatic.

We passed a florist's and he dashed inside to have some spring flowers to present to my mother. I just thought, he doesn't need to be told *anything*; he's going to fit in beautifully. Mama will *love* him.

I let us in with my latch key and we went up to my bedroom on the second floor. He went straight over to look out of the window. We were on a level with the top of a Japanese acacia, which filtered the view towards the small block of flats opposite. I walked across and put my hand round the back of his neck and stroked his ears. As he turned, we kissed, lips to lips. We clung to each other, laughing, as I steered him over to my bed where we both perched, arms entwined, then falling backwards, holding each other tight.

'At last we're together and not having to feel bad about ourselves,' I said. 'Our pact is suspended, isn't it, if we want it to be, while we're here, away from Upton?' I was sitting upright now as he lay back in the horizontal with his hands casually joined behind his head.

'But what about your parents?'

Was he getting cold feet, trying to find an excuse to be cautious? I reckoned I needed to be determined. 'Look,' I said, 'this is *my home*, believe it or not. If I can't be comfortable or happy here with the person I want to be with more than anyone in the world, what sort of a home is it?'

I could feel myself getting wound up. I tried to sound calm. 'I know my parents love me and want to see me happy, even if *this* isn't what they expect of me. What I really want over these couple of days is for us to show them how much we care about each other, how happy we are when we're together. You've got to call me "Freddie" at every opportunity. No one outside the family does. They should twig soon enough. I know they'll want the best for us. You'll see.'

'I can't help thinking you're being a bit optimistic, Freddie. I'm still not sure about *my* family. Anyway,' he continued, looking around him, obviously wanting to change the subject, 'I love your room. It's very *you*. The green wallpaper goes very well with the antique furniture.'

I told him I'd wanted to be more adventurous – just as I'd been at Upton – but somehow all the inherited things I had to contend with had defeated me.

'Which of these two rather narrow beds is yours?'

'It's the one you're lying on right now, you sexy little bugger. It's only ever had one strapping lad in it at a time, but that's going to change tonight, isn't it?'

'I'd say so.' He lifted the pillow from behind his head and hugged it with both arms, giving me a saucy smile. 'It's what we've been waiting for, isn't it?' he murmured quietly in my ear. 'It's going to make *everything* complete for us at last.'

I felt relieved I hadn't misinterpreted things.

'You know you're almost as seductive as Rowse when you look at me like that,' I said, trying to be ironic, but perhaps slightly unwisely. I saw a flicker cross his face.

We couldn't delay any longer and made our way downstairs. Off the landing on the floor below I knocked on my mother's bedroom door, calling out,

'Can we come in, Mama? Paul's arrived and would love to see you.'

'Of course, darling. Do come in.'

She was seated at her secretaire in the recess beside the chimney. The full-length nets were billowing slightly in the breeze.

Foo-Foo, our aged and bad-tempered Pekingese, descended imperiously from his tuffet and waddled over to snivel at Paul's shoes, looking up at him and giving a short little bark. He was already famous amongst my exotic brigade, of course, if only on account of his outrageously camp name.

I bent over and waved a finger at his dribbling snout, telling him to pipe down. Paul stroked his ear without eliciting much enthusiasm. When he saw there was nothing on offer he heaved himself back to his place of honour, regarding us from thence with oriental disdain.

My mother had evidently been writing on little cards, which I could see were the place names for the dinner party.

'I'm delighted to meet you again, Paul. What lovely flowers, thank you so much,' she said, genuinely pleased.

She was looking *très chic* today, I thought, and clearly Paul was impressed too. Until a few years ago she had had long golden-blonde hair often done in a Veronica Lake style, but now it was morphing into a distinguished silvery grey in a shorter perm. Despite her intermittent and mysterious 'illnesses' her figure and pale complexion were still much admired, and, given her height, she always made an impression whenever she entered a room. This afternoon she was in a grey cashmere twinset with pearls, with a pleated skirt – perfect for showing her fine dancer's legs.

'It's been so kind of Freddie to invite me for these few days, Mrs McNaughton. It's a real treat for me as I don't get to London very often.'

I could see he was slightly flushed making a special effort to be charming and succeeding brilliantly.

It was thrilling to hear him use the diminutive of my name. A glimmer across her face suggested she'd noticed. My little plan might be starting to work. She knew perfectly well that none of my friends ever called me anything except 'Fred'. Maybe she might even mention it to my father.

We briefly discussed the *placement* arrangements she was proposing.

'Paul, I suggest you sit between Pippa and Jane. I'm sure you'll charm them both. And, Freddie, I thought you'd better go between Jane and Miranda. For goodness' sake do remark on how Miranda has lost so much weight. Her mother persuaded her to go on a diet to try and lose half a stone just because she's coming to our party.'

'Oh, that's a shame,' I said, genuinely disappointed. 'I rather prefer girls to be nicely rounded and shapely. It usually means they're more fun.'

Too late I realised I might have been a little tactless.

'Well, do at least try and *sound* encouraging, darling.'

She continued, 'Now, you two boys had better hurry up if you want Nanny to find you some tea. Freddie, please could you give her the flowers and ask her to find a vase from the pantry. I'll come down later to arrange them and put them in the drawing room.'

The so-called nursery was in the semi-basement, off the passage between the dining room and the kitchen, thus geographically separate from the main rooms. It had been redecorated quite recently, this time at my suggestion with William Morris wallpaper and curtains. Its main feature nowadays was a big mahogany radiogram, a boxy black-and-white TV set and an ancient but recently reupholstered sofa. Pippa had insisted on a couple of trendy beanbags for the floor. The cupboards hid all our ancient toys and games, many of them not looked at for years.

We ran into Nanny in the basement passage.

Did you ever meet her, Sam? She'd been with us for over fifteen years by then and was now in her early fifties. At the beginning she'd been Pippa's nanny, but had stayed on as de facto housekeeper after our mother began to be ill. She had a pretty face, with freckles and kind, dark eyes. Her previously jet-black hair was going grey and she was becoming 'stout' as my father described her. Alas, she wasn't all that bright although full of common sense, totally reliable, devoted to us, and to your mother in particular. Having come from rural Wales, she loved living in London and being a part of our lives. It was only years later that I developed a lingering guilt that we might have taken advantage of her all those years.

I introduced Paul, who gave her another of his winning smiles. 'Hello, Nanny. Master Freddie here has told me a lot about you and how you spoil him rotten.'

I don't think she was quite sure how to take this boyish quip, coming from this handsome lad who she had only just met. What right did he have to call me Freddie? Was he being condescending with her? Trying to be funny? He must have sensed he had overshot a certain boundary after she responded with one of her rare withering looks. He was going to have a lot of making up to do. I came to the rescue.

'You see, Nan, you've become famous for all those homemade cakes and scones you send me at Upton. Sometimes we use them as currency, instead of money. Yours go for a high premium so you're pretty popular among my friends. Anyway, what's on the menu for tonight?'

'I don't know about *my* baking, but tonight you're having *her* smoked salmon roulade, chicken casserole and crème brûlée,' she said pointing in the direction of the kitchen with a slight sneer.

She didn't really get on with Mrs Drake who was the exact replica of Mrs Bridges in *Upstairs, Downstairs* and still treated her as though she were an Edwardian nursery maid. She was obviously miffed she wasn't making our dinner herself.

'If you boys want some tea and cake you'd better stick to the nursery as you can see we're busy down here.'

We heard a *boom, boom, boom* coming from the right direction. Going in, we found it was Engelbert Humperdinck's latest number blasting out from the radiogram. Not really my kind of thing nowadays, but I'd learnt to put up with it cheerfully.

Your mother looked a sight with her hair having been tied up laboriously by Nanny with dozens of rags, to be released at the last moment to reveal a cascade of curls and ringlets. As we entered the room I noticed how the two of them eyed up Paul.

When the record finished I introduced them, and by the time Nanny appeared with tea we were well away talking about the dance, who else was coming and who we thought might hitch up with whom. My fears that your mother might start to exercise her siren charms on Paul were unfounded; she was back again with Robert Waybrook, while I knew Jane was hoping to get lucky with one of her brother's friends.

Nanny urged us not to linger. Up we all went, Pippa and Jane first, to purloin the shared bathroom, which led off the passage between our two rooms. They seemed to take an interminably long time over whatever they were doing. My room had a washbasin, so Paul stripped off his jacket and shirt and started to shave still in his vest. I loved the faint smell of his body odour, and watched him from behind, moving his arms and tilting his head as he applied the razor, seeing his wide shoulders move under the white cotton and his arm muscles flex and then relax. After he'd finished, he turned around, drying his face with a towel, giving me a big grin. I threw him my dressing gown for him to go for a quick bath. How I fantasised hugging and smelling this garment for days after he'd left.

Ten minutes later he returned. Was he going to discard the dressing gown and reveal himself naked before me as he started to dress? Instinctively – from years of communal changing for games – he cast it off. For a split second, standing there full frontal, he gave me a wicked grin, before turning around to start dressing.

I sat on the edge of my bed, clad only in my underwear, admiring his graceful, almost balletic, movements like a voyeur at a private performance. He was even more beautifully proportioned since I had last seen him naked: more developed and toned but without having lost that sensual fleshiness I so admired. I loved the new little humps of his pectorals and the way they accentuated his dark nipples. His torso tapered elegantly to his hips, his rib cage barely visible beneath the taut skin. There was a sweet little dusting of hair between his pecs and in a line down to his belly button. His legs and thighs had become stronger, more meaty and shapely, delicately softened with a dark downy gauze. Thick black pubes formed another natural V shape above his cock. As he turned again to slip on his vest I was struck numb at the beauty of his plunging spine, the curves and creases of his bum, their fleshy cheeks and enclosed valley. The whiteness of his underwear was the perfect foil to his golden skin, making it glow with health. Everything about him seemed to articulate life, movement and beauty.

I had to concentrate hard to minimise my mounting tumescence and grabbed the dressing gown, fleeing to the bathroom. There was no time for a wank; it would probably have finished me off for the evening.

When I got back Paul was almost dressed, standing at my dressing table, fiddling with his shirt sleeves. I discarded the dressing gown and, deliberately imitating his earlier nonchalance, strode over naked to the chest of drawers to find my own clean underwear. I could feel my cock taking on a life of its own and become an embarrassment unless I could smother it in a pair of briefs. I just had time to put some on, but still no vest, when he looked up.

'Could you give me a hand with my cufflinks, please, Freddie. My uncle's lent me his very best gold ones with his monogram, but I can't get them through the slits in the sleeves.'

'Of course I can,' I said as I went over to my Prince Charming making a big fuss over his finery. He must have noticed the profile between my legs.

He stretched out his arms for me to feed the links through the sleeves. As I was finishing the second one, giving it my full concentration, I was aware that his spare arm was hanging loose between us. Then, totally unexpectedly, his hand moved across to cup my bum cheek, pulling me closer towards him. What a moment! What an invitation! I turned my face to kiss him. But there was a knock at the door, the most unwelcome sound in the world.

'What is it?' I bellowed. It was Pippa. 'No! You *can't* come in.'

'Come on, hurry up, you two. We're going down to the drawing room. People will be arriving in ten minutes.'

I turned to Paul.

'Later, Freddie, later,' he said, softly and smiling. How *cruel*, and how only vaguely promising those words sounded. But then, 'I think we're ready, don't you?'

My heart leapt. 'Of course we're ready. 'Semi-celibacy' can go to hell!'

Something new had happened; a brake had been released. A moment's erotic complicity had taken us from neutral into first gear, propelling us inevitably towards an exciting and unknown destination. We were no longer barely-boyfriends, bound by a pact; now we were soon-to-be-lovers entering a whole new world. There could be no more inhibitions.

He donned his jacket and looked at himself in the full-length mirror.

'Do I look alright?' he asked.

'You bloody little peacock,' I said, feeling an even greater freedom to tease or flatter him, say just what I liked to him. 'You know you look more than alright, you look totally gorgeous. Move over. I'm going to look equally fantastic too.'

In truth it should not have taken me long; I was perhaps more used to the ritual. But just for the sake of prolonging our togetherness I moved slowly and deliberately. He watched me, smiling, as I put on my stiff-fronted shirt, tucking it under my trousers and lifting the braces over my shoulders.

'Now it's your turn: can you help me with my bow tie, please?' He came up close and with a look of concentration straightened out the two wings. It was another delicious moment; no one except my father had ever done this for me before. I ran my forefinger down his smooth cheek and savoured his aftershave. 'What's that you've got on?'

'It's the new Eau Sauvage my mum gave me for Christmas. Would you like some? It's quite sexy and fruity.'

'Yeah, let's be twins.'

'I'm going to smell you all over tonight,' he purred, as he dabbed it around my cheeks and neck. How I just wished we could go on like this forever, kissing, kissing, kissing.

We stood beside each other in front of the mirror. Yes, we really did look *quite something*. Two boys, nearly men, but trying to look like men, in our black and white outfits, so flattering and masculine.

'You know what this reminds me of?' he said, putting his arm over my shoulder and looking into my eyes in the mirror.

'Tell me,' I replied, returning his gaze.

'*We two boys... together clinging...*'

'Ha!' I said. 'Yes,

Up and down the roads going
North and South excursions making...'

'I can see it's going to be more like "*Up and down the staircase going*", in this house,' he said, laughing.

'"*Up and down our love-nest going*" might be more romantic,' I said, giving him a kiss before taking him by the hand and leading him to the door.

By the time we reached the drawing room I had hardly started to cool down. I didn't seem to be aware of my familiar trappings or conscious that they mattered or even existed. I was living on two different levels: one the zombified world of the here and now surrounded by all the familiar people and things; the other a world of anticipated bliss with Paul. I seemed to have gained a kind of superhuman strength, like being on speed, prepared to spend the entire evening being sociable, patient and kind to anyone and everyone, however difficult, boring or ugly they might be – but in the full knowledge that tonight, at last, I would be in the arms of my lover.

My parents were waiting, both in their evening gear: my father in his dinner jacket and my mother in a glamorous long black dress entirely covered in glittery silvery sequins. It must have cost my poor father the earth. On the grand piano were the family photographs, and among them a vase with Paul's flowers. Maybe it represented the bridge between my two worlds.

The plan was for the oldies to remain upstairs in the study with supper brought up to them on a tray by Nanny, leaving Pippa and me to host the young people below in the dining room.

My father had given me strict instructions about the drinks: the girls were to be encouraged to have Coke, the boys to be offered a very weak Bloody Mary as the 'house cocktail'. If they proved awkward, there was a bottle of white wine in an ice pail.

Herbert and Waybrook arrived separately, both resplendent in black and white, but – to my intense annoyance – both were wearing low-slung double-breasted brocaded waistcoats, Herbert's in a shiny silver, Waybrook's in a rich crimson. Why on earth hadn't *I* got one of those? It went straight to the top of my next birthday present list. What they must have thought of Paul being in the party, let alone a house guest, a mere lower-sixth former, and both of them school prefects, can only be guessed.

I suspect they were just mildly amused. Both were famously impervious to boy-crushes.

Miranda and Christine arrived together, escorted by Miranda's mother, as large and voluble as her daughter. The two girls were both in strapless long dresses showing a great deal of cleavage: Christine, slim and intense, in electric blue; Miranda, curvy and jolly, in a showstopper in emerald green. I was glad to see that her attempted diet hadn't been very successful, and told her so, quietly, later.

'That dress is far too grown-up for a girl of her age,' said my mother, later, obviously put out. 'I don't know what she thought she looked like.'

'Much too revealing,' agreed my father, with a sly smile, as they ensconced themselves with their private supper in the study. Nanny had plenty to say about those two girls later.

Pippa was in a sleeveless black empire-line dress, making her look at least nineteen, and Jane in a pale blue silky affair.

I had laid the dining table with special care earlier that afternoon and cleaned all the silver myself, including the candelabra and our wonderful Georgian centrepiece, a sort of Chinese pagoda, surrounded with baskets and little dishes full of fruits and chocolates specially chosen and arranged by me. The colour theme was crimson: the curtains, the Bokhara carpet, the tablecloth and napkins. Everything – the mahogany furniture and even my ancestors in their portraits – looked wonderfully rosy and warm in the flickering light of the candles. I prayed it wouldn't be too overpowering for a group of older teenagers who had probably never been in such a formal ambience without the company of adults before. The two waiters, hired from Searcy's, had shown up in the nick of time.

I needn't have worried. As we were finding our places around the table Miranda broke the ice. Looking at the centrepiece, she put one hand on her hips, wiggled her bottom and thrust out her bosom, drawling in a magnificent imitation of Mae West, '*Peel me a grape, Beulah*', pointing a crooked finger towards my artful arrangement of the fruits. I picked out a single grape, grabbed a knife and pretended to be peeling it before popping it into her mouth. Everyone fell about laughing at this little performance, and from then on the banter and conversation flowed seamlessly – gossip, future plans for the summer, post-mortems on recent parties and theatre visits – back and forth across the table. The subject of exams, less than two months ahead, was off-limits.

I watched Paul from the corner of my eye as he joined in the conversation each side of him. Miranda must have seen my glances and cleverly shifted her eyes down to notice my crotch without moving her head.

Quietly, so that only I could hear, she did another Mae West number: '*Is that a gun, or are you just pleased to see me?*' '*Or him?*' she added. But she gave me a saucy smile as if to say, 'Don't worry, your little secret's safe with me.'

But she soon turned her attention to Charlie Herbert, my impossibly *soigné* aristo friend, who had the measure of her in no time, flirting and making her melt – not difficult, given his looks and irresistible charm. Next to me, on my other side, Pippa's friend Jane was asking what books I'd been reading recently. She was deeply into *Karamazov* and planning a trip to Russia with her parents. I said I had just started Huysmans's *A Rebours* and finding it rather creepy, but was hoping to visit the Moreau museum in Paris next time. We agreed we loved the *fin de siècle* and would be persevering with Proust over the summer.

Paul leant across the table. 'Tell us about the painting over there, Fred,' pointing to the group portrait of the family hanging above the sideboard. Thank goodness he wasn't using my diminutive in front of *this* crowd.

'As you can see it's *la famille McNaughton* in the drawing room upstairs. There's my mother in a crimson evening dress playing the piano, my father in his mess uniform standing on one side. He's looking down, rather disapprovingly, at me seated on the carpet playing with a model Airfix aeroplane, and Pippa playing with Foo-Foo.'

I continued my little lecture. 'It was painted by my aunt Mary, who's a professional – my mother's sister, the mother of the two Scarisbrick boys. The older one, James – you'll remember him at Upton, went up to Oxford last year – is coming tonight. It was my aunt's first attempt at a group portrait. A bit of an experiment.'

'It's a clever composition,' said Paul.

'A bit like a modern-day Zoffany or even a Sargent,' said Jane.

'But I can't imagine you making an Airfix aeroplane, Fred,' said Paul, with a teasing smile on his face. 'How successful was it? You're not exactly the most practical fellow, are you? Was it a case of artist's licence?'

Everyone was watching as I winked at him. 'I can be very dexterous with my hands given half a chance. You just try me,' I replied. *Touché.*

'Butter wouldn't melt in your mouth in that picture,' he continued, returning my wink. 'And I *love* your little blue shorts and that splash of yellow in your tie.'

Gosh, I thought, *where does all this undisguised flirtiness come from, Paul? Has the Bloody Mary gone to your head? Or*, it occurred to me in a flash, *are you teasing me deliberately, laying claim to me in front of this crowd, here on my own turf? If you are, I don't mind, not one bit. Let them guess.*

'That was my favourite tie,' I replied. 'Yellow, with little brown horses jumping around on it. I refused to sit still unless I could wear it. I wish I still had it.'

Miranda weighed in. 'It's a great picture, but somehow you don't all seem very *connected*. Both your parents look as though they're about to go out for the evening, leaving you two behind to play on your own in the drawing room.'

'Nanny should have been there too,' I said. 'Perhaps just entering the room from the door at the back, telling Pippa and me it's time for bed. Like the artist in that picture by Velasquez.'

Things were going swimmingly by the time we had finished our crème brûlée. My father appeared at the door saying: 'Five minutes, everyone.' The girls scurried to the loo while the boys went upstairs to hang around in the hall puffing away on cigarettes. I went back to the kitchen to thank Mrs Drake; the place looked as though a bomb had hit it.

In twenty minutes we were at the hotel, making our way up the pompous white marble staircase with its vast scrolling carpet cascading towards us. At the top, the ballroom's wide double doors had been thrown open. The room had been beautifully decorated with coloured lights festooned across the big French windows giving onto the park. Moving, twinkling traffic could be seen through the trees beyond. Around the dance floor there were groups of little tables with candles and gilt chairs. Suspended from the ceiling was a rotating glitterball throwing out sparkling stars.

Your grandparents, your mother and I stood at the top of the stairs to greet everyone as they arrived. I soon became aware that this was, of course – and not even vicariously – *their* party as much as mine and your mother's. They were the most glamorous people there, no doubt about it: she at her most Marlene-esque, in her slinky full-length sequins and a huge, fluffy white fox-fur tumbling from her shoulders; likewise, your grandfather was at his most Errol Flynn-like, muttering that the boys ought really to be in white tie and tails as they would have been in his day. My generously hand-picked school contemporaries were there of course, all in their dinner jackets and at last looking (and mostly behaving) like mature adults. They'd made a big effort, tidied up their hair, piled on the Clearasil, and doused themselves with aftershave. Old Spice, Brut and Eau Sauvage wafted enticingly through the air.

Although your mother's friends were mainly a bit younger, mostly her own age, they looked equally grown up. They met each other with excited squeals, admiring their new long dresses and allowable makeup: foundation, mascara, lipstick, a touch of powder. They had their hair 'up' for the occasion revealing their slender white necks. One or two had beehive arrangements with big bows in them, the effect more Dusty Springfield than Marie-Antoinette (slightly common, I thought). Others wore it back-combed with diamanté alice bands. A few even had the very latest bobbed Mary Quant style. Nanny had come along too, of course, not just to watch from the sidelines but to be available in the Ladies' loo to help with any little crises.

The DJ knew just how to handle it, beginning with some sprightly numbers to get everyone onto the dance floor, like 'Ob-La-Di Ob-La-Da' by The Marmalade. He varied the music so that there was something for everyone to enjoy and move with, however terrible they were at dancing. It was a great year for music, from Amen Corner's 'Bend Me, Shape Me', Marvin Gaye's 'I Heard it Through the Grapevine', Stevie Wonder's 'Shoo-Be-Doo-Be-Doo-Da-Day' and many others. The Beach Boys, The Beatles, The Rolling Stones were all at their peak; and there were wonderful ballads: Mama Cass', 'Dream a Little Dream', Dusty Springfield's 'I Close My Eyes' and Dionne Warwick's 'Do You Know the Way to San Jose'. My favourite of course was Andy Williams's slow, slow 'Can't Take My Eyes Off You'. My goodness, if only I could have had Paul in my arms when that was being played.

From time to time there would be a pause, and people would move over to the little gilt chairs, or stand around finding a drink from the weak white wine cup or lighting up a cigarette. I noticed one or two couples walk out onto the terrace overlooking the park and the lights beyond, no doubt for some light dalliance. Then the music would start again at a different tempo, with most finding someone new to dance with, or – more often – alongside. There was an unwritten rule that no one should hog a single partner for the whole duration. According to tradition, the boys were on their honour to change their partners frequently and not to let any of the girls, however plain, feel left out.

I reserved the last dances for Miranda and Christine, knowing that the lights would probably be turned lower by then, the music slower and the mood smoochier. I wanted to see if they would make a move towards some heavy petting. I'd be intrigued, but not too worried, to see how Paul dealt with this.

Sure enough, by this time Paul had hooked up with Christine and was holding her tightly. She seemed transfixed with him as their cheeks touched and she put her arms around his neck. He held her with one hand against her back, which he stroked discreetly, tantalisingly close to her bum. It certainly looked as though she was doing most of the work, which gratified me. For my part, I let Miranda take me in hand, pressing me close to her ample bosom, her face against my cheek, then her lips seeking mine. She smelt very nice and everything about her was soft and plump and comfortable. For a moment I teased her by seeming reluctant to succumb, but I yielded with a friendly snog as she guided my hand down the gap in the back of her dress. We both knew we were just play-acting. Somehow in all of this I managed a sideways glance towards Paul; we caught each other's eyes.

It was getting close to 1.00am and the lights were turned up as the music got faster and a couple of favourites were played. Then the double doors at the end of the room were thrown open and 'breakfast' was announced; there was kedgeree, sausages, bacon and scrambled eggs laid out on the sideboard for everyone to help themselves and take over to the tables. The happy sound of champagne bottles being opened (more likely Asti) was greeted with applause. After twenty minutes or so the DJ made his final announcement: a conga, to round off the evening. So we all lined up, clinging to each other's waists and set off round the ballroom, down the grand staircase, up the other side, back into the supper room and on to the terrace.

We were the last to leave, of course, and finally we clambered into two taxis. My parents suggested a quick post-mortem and coffee in the drawing room. This time my father offered us boys Black Russians but, rather pointedly, not the girls (who didn't smoke anyway). We sat around comparing notes about who had been getting along with whom. Pippa had broken the rules and been with Robert Waybrook almost continuously, greatly to the disappointment of her many admirers.

When reprimanded by my father she made only the faintest semblance of an apology.

'I'm sorry. Anyway, Robert and I are going ice-skating tomorrow evening with Jane and Charlie.'

Apart from that, it was obvious the party had been a great success. No one got too drunk, no drugs were on offer, and everyone went home in one piece. We later discovered that a few teenage romances had been born.

I was desperately on edge to get to my room with Paul. Everyone seemed to be taking forever to say their goodnights. There was a lot of idle chatter between the four of us as we went upstairs, me leading the way. Passing my parents' bedroom Paul gave me a quick pinch on the bum. I turned around to smack his hand. Jane was following and I'm pretty sure she saw what was going on; Pippa was further behind and oblivious to anything.

Once safely inside the room he pulled off his bow tie and threw himself onto my bed, propping his head up with one hand and looking at me with smiling eyes that seemed full of expectation. I came to sit beside him, leaning over to kiss him and gently started to remove his jacket.

'Go on then, Freddie, I'm all yours.'

I pressed him back against the pillows, unbuttoning his shirt, tenderly kissing every inch of his flesh as it became exposed. We stood up while I began to undress him. I would have loved to rip off every item of his clothing in a frenzy, but his invitation was so deliciously seductive I just wanted to prolong every moment, slowly revealing, touching and caressing his beauty, all the time looking into each other's eyes. The sight of him like this was almost too much to bear. He really was all mine now.

Everything I'd learnt from Henri came back to me as I knelt to take him. My instinct was to keep on giving, giving and giving as I saw him writhe and gasp in my power. I became more assertive, making him incapable of resistance. How I wanted to prolong all the pleasure I was giving him! Looking up, I saw his face contorted ecstatically. But it must have been too much, too soon, for him: he groaned and trembled as he came over me in great waves and gushes.

The poor darling boy had to lie back on the bed, exhausted. He had his eyes closed and I knew he'd had enough for this, his first time. I couldn't ask any more from him. For a split second I wondered if I had violated the most sacred temple on the planet. But when he opened his eyes and smiled I knew it had been just the opposite; I had sanctified it with my love. With his sublime face in both my hands there was only one thing to say as we kissed again and again:

'My beautiful, beautiful boyfriend, Paul. I love you. I love you.'

He looked back straight into my eyes. 'I love you too, my wonderful Freddie.'

We fell asleep with our arms around each other, two peas in a pod.

With my love,
Freddie

13

My dear Sam,

We slept well that night.

The next thing I knew, daylight was filtering into the room from under the curtains. I was waking slowly, my body aware of Paul's closeness, his touch and warmth as we lay together. We had untangled during the night and now I was lying on my side against his back with one of my arms hanging unconsciously over his hip. I had a magnified view of the back of his head, the outline of his haircut, his ears, the beautiful curve of his shoulders, the nape of his neck.

I listened to his quiet breathing, gently inhaling our lingering effluvium from last night. My body was tingling with a sensuous laziness, slowly morphing into lust. I watched closely to see his lashes begin to move, his eyes open slowly, and his muscles start to tense. As he turned to face me, my hand reached for his groin, feeling him grow at my touch. This was surely the greatest thing in the world: to have made love and slept blissfully in the arms of my boyfriend – now my lover – and to wake with him still so close. I moved as if to climb onto him, to hold him closer.

But there was the sound of someone rattling on Pippa's door next to oours. It was Nanny. I heard her go in and I nudged Paul.

He leapt across into the adjoining bed, which had remained completely undisturbed.

A minute later Nanny swept in. 'Morning, boys,' she said cheerily, having at least knocked on the door, but without waiting for an answer. She went straight over to the window to draw back the curtains before looking over to the two beds, seeing our heads peeping over the covers.

'Really, boys, you might have been tired last night, but at the very least you could have hung up your trousers.' She looked askance at the debris strewn across the floor, picking up the clothes and hanging them over a couple of chairs. Did she have suspicions? She knew perfectly well how uncharacteristic it was of me to be so untidy.

'Breakfast in twenty minutes. The girls have gone down in their dressing gowns but you'd both better get dressed. The Major wants to see both of you before he leaves for the office.'

This sounded ominous. Had the noise of our love-making been heard in my parents' room, immediately below us?

Despite all our exertions last night I wasn't in the least tired. On the contrary, I felt completely awake and alert, bristling with energy and ready for anything.

My father was deep in the *Financial Times*, and the two girls silent and looking distinctly wan. My mother, of course, was nowhere to be seen.

I poured out some coffee for Paul and me and asked in a general sort of way what were the plans. Pippa reminded me that she and Jane were due to go ice-skating at Queensway in the evening. There was an implication that Paul and I would not be particularly welcome.

My father put down the paper, took a final mouthful of his coffee and asked, 'Would you two boys like to join your mother and me at the club for supper and go on to see *The Charge of the Light Brigade* this evening? It's just opened in Leicester Square.

The reviews here are excellent. It's with Trevor Howard and John Gielgud.'

'Oh, Dad,' I said, 'that sounds lovely.' It was a totally unexpected offer, although not quite what I had in mind. But instantly I knew it would be an ideal opportunity for my parents to get to know Paul better. I gave Paul a nod for him to reply to my father.

'Thank you, Major McNaughton. I'd love to see it, especially since I'm studying the Crimean War as a special subject next term.' Paul knew exactly how to handle my father, just as he did my mother. Pippa probably thought he was being a bit of a creep.

'Good lad,' said my father, probably for the first time really taking notice of him and showing enthusiasm for meeting him. My father had read Military History at Cambridge and spent twenty years in the Royal Artillery, so this was a special subject for him too.

'I'll be interested to see how they replicate some of the innovations to field guns which were used at Sebastapol for the first time. Some of them are still in the museum at Woolwich, you know.'

'Oh, really?' said Paul, giving every indication of being interested. I hoped he'd be storing up these and other titbits for little asides in his A-Level essays.

'Let's see what they make of it in the film,' I said, anxious not to get bogged down in a discussion on nineteenth-century artillery.

We were left with the girls. There was a consensus that we'd head towards Kensington Gardens for some fresh air, calling in at Biba in Church Street, and then to the London Museum in Kensington Palace. If we felt like it, we could go into the State Apartments. Then maybe take in a knickerbocker glory at Derry and Tom's roof garden, and go on to Harrods in the afternoon.

It was a well-rehearsed scenario which Pippa and I frequently enacted with our friends when they came to stay.

On our way upstairs I called in to say good morning to Mama, leaving Paul to go on ahead.

She was sitting upright in bed, her shoulders covered with a cashmere shawl, her breakfast tray obviously finished with, no doubt expecting me to remove it, saving Nanny the job. Breakfast in bed was part of the price she had exacted from my father when she had been more or less obliged to leave the job she loved at Sadler's Wells just before I was born and join him in his peripatetic army life. To her credit she knew perfectly well how lucky she was and did at least have a sense of humour about it.

She said my father had just rung to say he'd booked four tickets for the film.

'I could take us in the mini and with luck we should find a parking place in St James's Square if we're not too late.' The challenge of finding somewhere to park in the West End and exchanging information on the subject was almost an obsession with her.

'Oh,' I said, looking disappointed. 'Please, *please* can we go in the Bentley. It's so much more comfortable, especially if there will be four of us on the way home. It would be such a treat.'

I didn't add that it would give me such huge pleasure to sit in the back of that luxurious limo holding hands with Paul in the dark. The deep leather seats were supremely comfortable, their smell combining deliciously with the whiff of the little cigars my father smoked. With the polished walnut finishes, soothing deep carpet and pale suede linings one felt totally cocooned against the world. The sense of well-being was enhanced by being slightly higher off the road and able to look down imperiously into other people's cars. In retrospect, it might have been a metaphor for my own life up to that date.

She caved in easily to my pleadings.

'Alright, darling, but you know how I really don't like driving it in London. But I'll do it for you and Paul as a special treat as you're going back to Upton next week. Now be sure to be back here and ready to leave by six.'

Giving her a kiss on the cheek I thanked her and took away the tray.

'I hope you're not trying to "show off" to Paul too much,' she said just as I reached the door. My plan was going well; I had wanted her to notice how I was so attentive to him. Had her maternal instinct begun to guess at our relationship?

'No, Mama. But you must admit it's quite stylish for us fellows to be driven around London by such a glamorous lady-chauffeur.' I knew my little cheapskate flattery would please her.

'Fiddle-de-dee. Off with you,' she said with a smile, starting to get out of bed.

*

It was a fine spring morning as we set off down Church Street. Our first stop was Biba, the ultra-trendy new shop that was enjoying a big success with its daring clothes for girls: mini and maxi dresses, strapless or backless, often with huge quasi-Art Nouveau patterns. For men there were the unisex trousers and frilly shirts in psychedelic patterns and colours. Their accessories included ethno bags, scarves and hats. The shop itself had bare floorboards, big aspidistras, open clothes rails and just the one long mahogany counter. Its transformation from the premises of Messrs Nichols, the former royal grocers – by appointment to the ancient princesses at the Palace opposite – had been total. The girl assistants, if and when they could be found, were indistinguishable from the customers.

Pippa and Jane were in their element, heading straight for the rails, yanking out the dresses, skirts and blouses, holding them up against themselves, laughing and putting them back again, not *quite* in the same place they had found them. Despite being disparaging about the merchandise I was quietly admiring of their range of low-slung crushed-velvet trousers and tight-fitting open shirts. Maybe I'd come back next holidays and throw caution to the winds. Paul was taking an interest in a very beautiful turquoise silk scarf of a vaguely Indian paisley design. He put it down after he'd seen the price.

Getting rather bored, we sat opposite each other in the long window seat looking out on to the street. Stretching out our legs in front of us, Paul with one knee bent, our backs were supported against the window reveals. I had a sudden recollection of the first time I had plucked up courage to speak to him when he was sitting like this in the window seat at Upton. I remembered my exaltation after we'd parted. Nothing had changed, yet everything had changed; then I had been in awe of his beauty and conscious of my own inadequacy. It was the same now; I still couldn't stop gazing in wonder at this semi-recumbent boy-god as he looked out of the window, his head partly in profile against the light. What *had* changed was that he had responded, and found me worth his attention, even his love. Yet I was conscious that we were only at a beginning and our future was in the hands of providence.

He must have sensed I was watching him as he turned and smiled. *My goodness, how I desire and ache for you; everything in me is just crying out for you. I desperately need to touch you so that I can come alive, for you to electrify me once more. How can I possibly wait until tonight to explore again every nook and cranny of your body, slowly and lovingly, smothering every inch of you with kisses, over and over?*

The urge to reach out and touch him was so strong, and yet so dangerous, that I had to stand up and look away. Going across to the counter, I found the turquoise scarf he had been inspecting and bought it without opening it out. I wanted to give it to him there and then, just to see his face light up in delight. *But no*, I thought, *don't rush it. Relish that prospect for now, pace yourself, give it to him at the right moment.*

This was the London of the Swinging Sixties, Sam. Kensington wasn't quite the same as Chelsea, but close enough at the centre of things. Your mother of course had thrown herself into the *zeitgeist* from the first moment she could: miniskirts, fishnet tights, then – heaven forbid – hotpants, and all the rest of it. I was more hesitant. Remember, I was now a self-identifying aesthete and was a bit doubtful of its general tastefulness or where it was all heading, let alone hippies, the Maharishi, and all that.

Eventually Pippa and Jane gave up their rummagings and we all left. Passing the block of flats where T.S. Eliot had lived, we walked through the pedestrian passage into Kensington Gardens.

The entrance to the museum was on the north side of the Palace, so we turned into the Broadwalk, and then past the sunken Dutch Garden, with its terraces ablaze with tulips and the fountains gushing forth elegant sprays from the tanks. We made a detour through the bowered walkway under the overhanging pleached laburnum with their festoons of yellow blossom just coming into flower and dangling above us. How wonderful to be alive, and here, walking side by side with the boy I had loved for so long, praying that one day he'd feel the same about me. To my intense surprise he jumped up and dislodged an overhanging chain of blossom, hanging it round my neck like an Indian wedding garland.

'Freddie, you are… amazing!'

It was my turn to do the same for him. As I looped it over his shoulders I murmured in his ear,

'*One the other never leaving...*' before we both burst into laughter.

Could this exchange have been our very own *matrimonio segreto*?

As we approached the museum, I became aware of my little group's expectations of me as their host. I relished the chance to show off my insights into some of my favourite objects just as Roz had done for me in Paris. I'd always enjoyed the costume collections, especially the fantastic court dresses of the mid-eighteenth century, with their wide hoops and dazzling 'bizarre' patterns in brocade picked out in silver and gold tissue. The pleated 'sacks' at the back, running in a single flat piece from the neck to the floor, gave them an ethereal elegance straight out of Watteau's *fêtes galantes*.

The men's court suits, slightly later, were just as showy, albeit more subtle: cut-away three-quarter-length coats in deep blue or crimson velvet, the open borders and cuffs embroidered in silk with lily-of-the-valley, narcissi and forget-me-nots. Their ivory satin waistcoats overflowed with bees, butterflies and beetles flying between sprays of cornflowers, lilies and carnations. What dandies they must have been!

'If only we could have gone to the party last night dressed like *that*,' said Jane. '*And* I would have had lots of black beauty spots specially dabbed on my cheeks to give out hidden messages,' she added, giving a flirty smile over to Paul. Typical of her to know about this little trick of the Georgians.

'Me too,' I said. 'I'd love to dress up as the wicked marquis from *A Tale of Two Cities*. Next time, let's make it a fancy-dress party.'

Then she drew attention to some tiny ladies' shoes, incredibly narrow, with little block heels and pointed toes, covered in embroidered satin, each with a huge silk pom-pom.

'How... how... *unbelievably* sexy!' gasped Paul. I was so pleased he was enjoying all this artifice as much as me.

We sauntered down the Broadwalk towards the High Street. At Derry's we took the Art Deco lift to the famous roof gardens, choosing to sit at a table at my favourite spot in the Alhambra Garden with its shady cloister. When the knickerbocker glories arrived we gasped in wonder: the tall fluted glasses were filled with separate layers of whipped cream, meringue, ice cream, syrups, liquid caramel, strawberries and topped with a sort of custard and a cherry. As we attacked them the colours slowly merged into each other creating the effect of freakish sunsets.

I watched Paul as he dipped his long spoon into the delicious, sweet *mélange* and lifted it to his mouth. I could see the instantaneous pleasure on his face as he gorged on this viscous confection, closing his eyes and groaning with satisfaction.

Just you wait 'til tonight, I thought.

'That was *délicieux*,' he said. I was intrigued to hear him imitate this little eccentricity of mine – my habit of suddenly bringing out a *mot juste* to express something that would sound utterly banal if said in English. People who didn't understand me called it an affectation, and the way I had overdone it in my first term at Upton had not been appreciated by everyone. Now we were four years on, and everything was different. Paul was learning from me that he could adopt such little mannerisms without compromising his own personality. I had a disciple.

We piled onto the top of a No 9 bus, passing the Albert Hall and Memorial, the latter somewhat jaded in those days. Getting off at Knightsbridge, we took the shortcut to Harrods, stopping en route at the Espresso Coffee Bar for a sandwich and a coffee – an insipid pale brown affair served up in a trendy see-through perspex cup and saucer. It wasn't my style, but it was cheap enough after the expensive glories at Derry's. Pippa and Jane were in seventh heaven. Once inside the huge shop, the girls went off to the new boutique, 'Way In', on the top floor.

'What about a haircut, Paul? Shouldn't we get ourselves into shape before going back to Upton? Otherwise we'll be at the mercy of the school barber. They do them really well here.'

He looked a bit reluctant, but I persevered. I'd noticed more than once that he was rather fussy about his hair.

We navigated our way through the marble-clad bank with its rows and rows of green leather benches in which elderly ladies up from the country would meet their friends (I often thought of Miss Marple), then through the food hall with its Art Nouveau tiles, to the rear of the shop and the softly carpeted men's clothes department. We lingered among the hopelessly expensive suits, sports jackets and shoes, which were out of my range, even with my £120 a year.

I spotted an amazing full-length suede coat entirely lined in mink, with a great luxurious mink collar. I beckoned to an assistant and made Paul try it on. Turning up the collar behind his neck, the fur framed his head like a halo, softening his features angelically, making him utterly tempting – to be kissed, stripped naked and pleasured, slowly at first, then harder and harder, making him writhe orgasmically, still swathed in fur. My hands were trembling as I looked at the price tag: '1,000 guineas'. Gladly would I have robbed a bank just for a few moments of ecstasy. Maybe one day I would become a rich sugar daddy, giving my pretty boyfriends expensive beautiful clothes to make them even more desirable. I'd rather enjoy that!

Fat chance, as it's turned out!

The assistant remained impassive but was evidently moved to say, quietly and discreetly, as he was helping Paul out of the coat,

'Have you ever considered modelling, sir?'

Paul looked at him somewhat astonished. 'Er, no. Why? Do you think I'd be any good?'

'It's just a thought, sir. But if you did consider it, you could try contacting this gentleman who is an agent and always on the lookout for new faces.' He produced a business card out of his pocket.

'Thank you,' said Paul, with all his instinctive disdain, putting it away without even looking at it, 'but I don't think I'll have time for any of that.'

I watched this exchange in sheer disbelief. How dare this man pounce on my boy like that? What an appalling thought: my hard-won lover being ogled at in magazines or even on a catwalk, for God's sake, by countless strangers. Thank goodness he'd been so dismissive. But it made me anxious whether he would always be able – or even want – to defend himself against the advances of predators.

He went over to look through the trays of neck ties. They were arranged by colour, spread out in fan-shaped formations. I saw that he had chosen one, but by the time I reached him it had been wrapped up in tissue paper and slipped into a glossy bag.

'Can't I see it?'

'No… too late… sorry,' said Paul, playfully hiding the bag behind his back. 'Maybe later.' I thought of trying to wrest it out of him but desisted out of respect for our surroundings.

We descended into the barber's shop in the basement. It was a strangely clinical space, but I had always enjoyed the subtle and deliciously masculine smell of hair oil mixed with an unidentified eau de cologne. We sat in adjoining seats.

'Good afternoon, young gentlemen,' the first barber announced, taking hold of a pile of white linen. 'Short back and sides, sir?'

'*Certainly not*,' I replied, with more than a hint of annoyance at his familiarity. The very idea of it! I was intensely proud of my – to me – beautiful light brown lustrous hair, which I wore *à la mode* just over my ears and swept sideways across my forehead.

'Only joking, sir,' he said. 'What can I do for you?'

The barbers were two late-middle-aged old boys, beautifully

mannered and manicured, wearing wraparound aprons and their own hair smoothed down with oil. They brought forth freshly laundered white linen sheets, opening them with great flourishes, covering us almost completely to the floor. Small white towels were then tucked in under our collars.

They did it all with great delicacy; I suspected they were in seventh heaven with two handsome posho boys completely in their hands for the next half an hour. I looked over to Paul; from his smile I guessed he was thinking the same.

First came the shampoo. After he had tested the hand shower until it reached exactly the right temperature, I leant forward into the basin while he let the soothing water run through my hair. He massaged a sweet-smelling shampoo into my scalp, kneading my hair gently, then rinsing it while the water drained away. He dabbed it dry as I sat upright.

While my hair was still damp, he combed it approximately into its rightful shape, parting it at the side. Out came the scissors: clip, clip, clip as they attacked first the sides and then the top of my head. The whole operation was such an intimate one: the proximity of the man, the nature of what he was doing, and my complete helplessness almost strapped to the chair.

When we dismounted and after being brushed down, I looked across at Paul. What a transformation! The floppy locks over his forehead had gone, exposing a wide and clear brow, which I had seen only once before, on the day I first spoke to him and had teased him. It was an amazing improvement; he looked different, an ephebe suddenly morphed into a young man.

'Wow, Paul! You've shorn your boyish locks.'

'Yes, after last night I thought I needed a makeover. The new me.'

With my love,
Freddie

14

My dear Sam,

That eventful day was by no means finished!

Returning to Campden Hill, Paul and I dashed to the top of the house to occupy ourselves in the bathroom while the girls played their new records in the nursery. I immersed myself in a bath while Paul, stripped down to his white briefs, washed and shaved in the handbasin opposite me… *two boys together.* The hazy scented humidity reminded me of that other time when I had first seen him in his naked godliness in the showers at Upton. Now he was looking at me through the steamy mirror as I lay immersed in soapy foam, transfixed by his shapely back. I just wished he'd been there in the bath with me – next time maybe. As I arose out of the water, the bubbles running off my body, I let him rub me down with a towel. I felt like a mannequin as he made me turn around, rubbing down my back, my bum and up my arse. He was enjoying it as much as me. As I faced him he dabbed at my chest, making me lift up my arms, and then my thighs and legs. His playful massage of my cock had the desired effect on both of us.

*

We found Mama in the study – beautifully turned out in a plain navy suit with a slightly nipped-in knee-length dress, and a jacket with a wide white collar, white piping, and large white buttons down the front. She was holding a white patent leather bag. I felt proud she had the Hermès scarf I'd given her last Christmas draped round her neck.

I let Paul sit with her in the front of the car. I wanted to see how the two of them would get on; and, more immediately, to admire how his expensive new haircut now sculpted his head. Perhaps it was too formal; if only I could tousle it, scattering it with tiny particles of gold to make it sparkle.

Paul could sense how my mother loved driving this great limo from the first moment she inserted the key into the ignition on the walnut fascia and turned the engine over softly. There was just a gentle purr and an effortless movement as we glided away from the curb. It was an S-type Bentley, already a few years old and had been inherited by my mother recently from her rich bachelor uncle.

As we cruised silently towards the High Street, Paul asked polite and intelligent questions, expressing astonishment at its petrol consumption of fifteen miles to the gallon; and disbelief at the way the silver-plated initial B on the bonnet was continually being stolen. She was always unnecessarily apologetic about it all, but insisted the car was worth maintaining as it was 'holding its value'.

With a cheeky smile Paul reminded her, 'Freddie said you'd used the car to smuggle the cider into Upton for our party after *Twelfth Night* last year.'

'That was very naughty of him, making us break the school rules. But I agree you all deserved a treat, especially after *your* wonderful performance, Paul. I remember it very well.'

'That's so kind of you, Mrs McNaughton. Freddie and I really enjoyed being in the play and that's where we got to know each other.'

'I hope you're going to be doing some more acting while you're at Upton. I got the impression you could take on some more demanding parts.'

Paul told her that he'd been roped into *The Winter's Tale*, blaming me for persuading him.

'But Freddie told me *you* were on the stage too,' he said, turning the conversation away from himself.

'Oh, that was a long time ago – during the war and just after.'

'I'd love to hear about it all, Mrs McNaughton. What an interesting life you must have had.'

'It was all a lot of fun, but could be rather hazardous with the theatres remaining open throughout the Blitz and the Blackout. We'd stay in full costume and makeup between matinees and evening performances going for high tea at the Old Vienna. Then there were the after-parties in Jane Shore's suite at Claridge's.' She looked across at him with a wistful smile. I knew what she was thinking: *you'd* have been a big hit with all that crowd.

My goodness, I said to myself. *She's never told me any of that. The after-parties at Claridge's sound a whole lot better than our sordid little thing at Upton.*

We drove into St James's Square. There was much reversing and manoeuvring to get the great barouche into the last remaining parking place. Paul jumped out and made all the right signals to Mama to ensure a perfect fit.

The club had recently been rebuilt after war damage, and although intended for military and naval officers, ladies and guests were permitted in the drawing room and dining room, both of which had the atmosphere of a family hotel. My father was waiting for us seated on a low chintzy sofa, happily browsing through the latest issue of *The Gunner*. I always thought he looked more relaxed here than he ever did in his own house. As we entered the room my mother paused, as she always did, looking around her, and, seeing my father, went over to greet him. He immediately stood up, his face lighting up as he kissed her on the cheek and his eyes moving over her to admire her slender figure, and her smart and flattering outfit. He gave Paul a genuinely friendly handshake.

We sat at a corner table in the dining room overlooking the square, my father taking charge of the ordering, recommending the pre-theatre menu. As he never failed to remark, at 10/6d a head it was pretty good value: grapefruit cocktail, roast chicken, and ice cream or fruit salad.

'Not very exciting, I'm afraid, but very reliable.' Once we'd all agreed, he turned his attention to Paul.

'Tell us a little more about your family, Shipton. Freddie said you live in Yorkshire and that your uncle's a consultant.' I was taken aback that he was calling Paul by his surname, a practice I thought had well and truly died out. He was obviously trying to be courteous in an old-fashioned sort of way, but really he mustn't do that anymore. I would speak to my mother. Likewise, I knew he was trying not to sound too inquisitorial, but at the same time wanting to know some of the background of this boy who was obviously occupying such a big place in his son's life.

'Yes, sir. We live a few miles north of Leeds and my uncle works there at the main hospital. My mother – well, she looks after my sister and me and my grandmother. She's also a painter and does watercolours of the Yorkshire Dales, using her maiden name.' He mentioned her name, maybe hoping it would spark some sort of recognition. I had forewarned my parents that any discussion of Paul's father was off-limits.

'It must be a perfect place for sketching. We have some friends in Harrogate but haven't seen them for years. But how old is your sister? Perhaps she should have come to Freddie's party?'

'Oh, that's a kind thought, sir. But she's two years younger than me – very keen on ponies, not into boys yet.'

'That's sure to happen any day now, believe me,' my mother interjected with a hollow laugh. She paused before continuing, 'I wonder if you're related to the famous model with your mother's maiden name?'

'Oh yes,' said Paul, smiling. 'My mother's sister. She was quite famous in her day – used to be all over the front pages of *Vogue*. But she retired years ago.'

My mother looked at him admiringly.

'She certainly was the *chicest* woman in England – and with a famous eighteen-inch waist.' She paused and smiled. 'Yes, I think I can see a family likeness.'

I'd never heard about this lady before and wondered why Paul had been so secretive about her. I was thrilled to think I'd introduced my parents to someone related to someone quite famous. Maybe I'd get to meet her myself one day. I'd have to start searching the back numbers of *Vogue* and *Tatler* piled up in the garage at the cottage.

My father expressed himself more guardedly, giving Paul an unusually long glance and a knowing smile, followed by a 'Well! Well!'

Paul attempted a weak laugh.

My father continued in a more characteristic mode. 'And how are you enjoying London? I'm glad to see you've both had your hair cut.' He looked at us both approvingly.

Paul took it on himself to give a résumé of our activities.

I'd never seen him improvise a long soliloquy before, but here he was, a natural actor, giving us an entertaining account of all we'd done today, not being deliberately facetious or stagey, but with little ironic asides and turns of phrase, keeping us all in tucks of laughter. Beginning with a description of Tessa and Jane let loose among the confections at Biba, then the outrageous court shoes at the museum, followed by the sight of the knickerbocker glories at Derry's, and finishing with the barbers at Harrods offering us short back and sides. They were loving it. I interjected from time to time, almost like the chorus, to make it a two-hander.

But then it was left to me to relate the story of his being propositioned as a male model. For a split second I wondered just how funny they'd find this episode, but to my relief my father burst into a loud laugh, and I saw him look Paul up and down as if to say: yes, it might be a very suitable short-term career move for a good-looking fellow like you.

'You and your aunt could make it a family business!'

Paul feigned a certain modesty.

I was overjoyed that they were obviously warming to him. I could foresee no difficulty in his being accepted into my small band of friends who came to stay with us regularly. I watched my mother assessing him according to her own very feminine ratings, giving him high marks for his confident masculinity, his charming voice, his relaxed attitude, his general tone. I could hardly believe this was the same shy, diffident boy with whom I'd fallen in love at first sight just eighteen months ago.

My mother glanced over towards my father and said,

'Freddie, your father and I have been thinking about the summer holidays.'

Oh, goodness, I thought, *they've been plotting behind my back.*

My father continued,

'We're going to be driving Pippa out to Montreux to her new school in September, and then continue for a short holiday in Italy.'

'Sounds nice for you,' I said rather sarcastically, trying to make them feel guilty as I guessed I wasn't included in their plans.

'We'd be away for about ten days. But of course, we don't want to leave you high and dry at home on your own before you go up to Cambridge in early October – that is, assuming you're offered a place!'

It flashed across my mind that I wouldn't mind *at all* being left on my own for a couple of weeks with the run of Campden Hill and the cottage.

'We wondered whether you'd like to spend the week at the cottage on the sailing school course, and ask a friend to join you? Nanny would be there, and Foo-Foo, to look after you both.'

'Oh,' I exclaimed. The fact was that I 'didn't mind' sailing, without ever seriously admitting that I positively enjoyed it in case that led to unwanted commitments. It always seemed to involve so much faffing about before one could get going, awkward small things needing instant replacement, or the wind in the wrong direction, or the tide being too high or too low. Let alone being stuck in the cold and rain, even if everything else was going well. However, under the right conditions, I quite enjoyed it. I was very used to our Albacore, which I could handle perfectly well on my own.

'You know what the sailing school's like, darling,' said my mother. 'It's not exactly a school at all. It's just a good way of going out with a few others, with someone in charge to make sure you don't capsize every five minutes.'

I looked across at Paul. He was concentrating on his food.

'Well, Paul,' I said, 'what about it? How would *you* like to be my class-mate?' trying to feign indifference in front of my parents, but my heart racing.

'That sounds a really nice idea,' he said, looking up with a big smile across his face, pretending to be surprised. 'But I'd have to ask my mother. I'm not sure if she's made any plans for us all to go away yet. But I would love to have a week's sailing at the cottage, especially with Freddie.'

I gasped inwardly. Those last three words were quite a bold declaration. How would they take it?

He looked at me, and I looked at him, just for a second, both of us trying to hide our smiles and obvious thrill. My mother saw it all.

'It should be fun for you both there together,' she said. 'There'll still be quite a few people around. You can see what they're doing in the evenings after Nanny's fed you. You'll have the bicycles so you'll be able to get about. There might be something on at the theatre in Chichester. You should find plenty to do.'

'I tell you something else, Freddie,' said my father. 'If you manage to pass your driving test before then, you could use the mini while we're away. But only within a ten-mile radius of the cottage.'

'Thanks, Dad. That's a great incentive.' Indeed it was; the possibilities of escapades with Paul opened up before me as never before. *No law less than ourselves owning, sailing, soldiering, thieving, threatening...*

Paul broke through my silent imaginings. 'Perhaps, Mrs McNaughton, you would be kind enough to write to my mother with your generous offer so she knows it's not just something I've dreamt up.' It was all agreed, the subject was changed, and we made our way to the cinema.

Concentration on the film was impossible. The thought of Paul being with me, almost alone for a whole week later in the summer totally preoccupied me. Sitting next to him in the dark we were at least able to brush our knees together. Anything more tactile would have been too risky. But I had a lovely semi-hard-on for almost the whole two hours.

It was quite late when we left the cinema, and – just as I expected – my father suggested we call in at Fortnum's Fountain for Ovaltine before going home.

Once we were seated he asked Paul if he had found the film helpful. He replied that he'd now understood some of the personal motives of the main protagonists in the war.

'Have you read Cecil Woodham-Smith's book *The Reason Why*? It's a real page-turner,' my father asked.

'No, I haven't, sir. I'm not sure it's on our book list.'

'Well, you really should. I can lend you my copy if you like.'

Heavens, I thought, *my father really* must *approve of Paul if he offers to lend him one of his favourite military history books.*

Paul then went on to say how I had encouraged him to cross-reference widely in his written work. Seeing the film had given him plenty of ideas for enlivening his interpretation of the Crimean War. I wondered what my father must have thought of his son becoming his friend's self-appointed mentor.

'I heard, sir, that you were in the battle for Hong Kong in 1941. I'd really enjoy hearing about it from you, and the aftermath, if you've got time one day.'

For a split second I thought if Paul might be going too far. But he must have been feeling genuinely comfortable to risk asking them such personal questions. I'd never had the nerve, or even much of an inclination, to talk to my father about his experiences during the war; he'd never volunteered to tell us, after all, and I'd always assumed he simply didn't want to remember it.

I backed him up, saying, 'Yes, Dad, I'd love to hear about it – properly – from you.'

He looked across the table at both of us sitting side by side.

'Well, alright,' he said after a momentary pause. 'But I need a bit of time to put my thoughts in order. It was such a long time ago. Maybe when you come and stay with us next time, Paul, we could get out some maps and photographs and talk about it then. It wasn't the greatest moment in the history of the Empire, I'm afraid. That's another reason why not many people care to remember it.'

I felt a surge of affection for my dear father. What a wonderful man he was – how self-deprecating! I'd heard from others how he'd suffered appallingly as a POW and been severely punished for at least one attempted breakout, but he'd always made light of it and his natural resilience had seen him through. I knew he'd make a great job of explaining to Paul and me the tactics of the invading Japs and the heroic resistance of the Brits, the Canadians and Indians, not to mention the Hong Kong Chinese. He had a way of explaining things, which had made me so proud when he'd given such a clear and concise talk to The Crucible last term about the principles of investment. He was so understated, so heroic, so *correct*. He'd have made a brilliant prep school master and role model.

We drove back to Campden Hill through the lamplit streets, via the Mall and Buckingham Palace, past the smart shops in Knightsbridge with their glaring window displays, past the Albert Memorial and the front of Kensington Palace, and then up Church Street. In the intermittent darkness in the back of the Bentley I laid my hand on Paul's upper thigh, leaving it there for the whole journey. I remembered fondly the effect this little tactile intervention had had on both Henri and me sitting on the back seats of the buses in France last summer. It never failed then, or now.

We sat with Tessa and Jane briefly to hear about their adventures at the ice rink before heading upstairs. Paul took my dressing gown and went straight for a bath. I couldn't resist picking up his briefs, stroking them and then lifting them to my nostrils. Yes, I had known this delicious odour of him last night; it was him alright, however faint – unique, pungent, rich, slightly earthy. Next thing, I was wearing them. They were deliciously tight.

I heard him leave the bathroom and quickly took them off, and was just lifting them again to my nostrils as he came in. I'd thrown back the blankets and was lying there stretched out fully naked, playing with myself.

'Hey, don't start without me,' he smirked, as he threw off the dressing gown and climbed in beside me. Tonight, maybe because we were less tired than before, we seemed more at ease, less in a hurry, keen to be more daring.

'Come on, Paul, now it's your turn to do whatever you like with me.'

He was evidently not going to hold back as I enjoyed the virile strength of this, my rugby-playing lover. He was kissing me fiercely on my mouth, then my nose, my ears – playing with the fleshy curves and licking the lobes. As he reached below I had to make him calm down, remembering how Henri had dealt with my own wildness the first few times. I had to show him the art of tenderness in giving as well as receiving such intimacies. He was trying too hard, and I had to concentrate not to come, gently urging him to move to other areas of my body. I turned over, and arching my back, inviting him to stroke and explore. Feeling his touch like this made me want to cry. But my mounting lust didn't allow me to remain the bottom any longer. There was one place on his body that I was desperate to take possession of at last. This must be the moment. I turned over again and firmly grabbed his legs to put them over my shoulders as I delved to find the precious orifice. But then I held back. This was going to be Paul's first time and he'd be tight as hell. Stupidly, I had nothing to help us. No, I really couldn't bear to hurt him however careful I was.

I just had to say it. 'Paul, I can't do any more, not tonight. I'm not sure we're ready… I'm so sorry.'

'Don't worry, Freddie. Let's stop it there.'

So, instead, we obliged each other.

Now it was all over I reached out for a pack of cigarettes and lit one for each of us as we lay there, silently gazing at each other.

'We'll have the summer to do whatever we like,' I whispered.

'Yeah. I'll do anything to please you, Freddie. I know I can trust you completely.'

He closed his eyes and a celestial smile covered his whole beautiful face as he fell asleep wrapped in my arms.

*

I woke first again next morning, my body pressed right up against him. I stirred and stretched as carefully as I could so as not to wake him, but despite my efforts he began to move.

'Sorry, my beautiful lover boy,' I said. 'I didn't mean to wake you. You look far too happy and content just lying there with your face so relaxed. I just want to go on seeing you so peaceful.'

But Nanny was rapping on the girls' door again. It was the signal for Paul to move before she came bounding in. This time we'd been more careful in putting away our clothes.

In the dining room my father was finishing his breakfast.

His greeting was accompanied by an enigmatic look at me, and then at Paul. Did we look unnaturally happy and sprightly for two teenage boys at this hour of the morning?

'I've left the book I promised you on the table in the hall, Paul. I hope you enjoy it. You can let us have it back if you're able to come to the cottage in the summer.'

'Thank you, sir, it'll be perfect reading for my long train journey home later today.'

My father stood up from the table and glanced across at me, and then to Paul, his smile looking perhaps a bit forced. There was something not quite right about him, although he was polite enough as he held out his hand for Paul to shake. Had he and my mother been talking?

With my father now safely gone, Pippa and Jane appeared, both wearing the fishnet tights and miniskirts they'd bought from Biba the previous day, their faces thick with makeup and mascara. There weren't many smiles from either of them quite so early in the morning.

I broke the awkward silence by telling them that Paul was probably coming to stay in September.

'So it'll just be the two of you?'

'And Nanny and Foo-Foo,' I said, laughing.

'That'll be nice for you all,' said Jane, with a giggle, looking knowingly at Pippa.

This made no impression on Paul who concentrated steadfastly on his boiled egg. But my reaction was to shout at them, mentally, if not aloud, 'God, you bitches! It's alright for you to go canoodling with Charlie and Robert, why can't we have some fun too?'

'Anyway, we're going shopping in Carnaby Street before Jane has to take the train home,' Pippa continued.

Paul made his polite goodbyes to the two of them as I did, and we made our way upstairs. As we passed Mama's bedroom, I knocked on the door. She was sitting up in bed, reading the papers, her shoulders draped again in her cashmere shawl. The breakfast tray had gone. Paul made his formal little speech of thanks.

'It's been very good having you for a couple of days, Paul. You were a big hit with the girls, you know, everyone asking who this Richard Burton lookalike was.' I recognised a tiny suggestion of coquettishness in her smile.

Paul blushed. 'You're only the second person who's ever said that to me,' he said. 'Freddie was the first, almost the first time I met him.'

'With you as the young Richard Burton, and Freddie looking more and more like Anthony Perkins every day and my husband the spitting image of Errol Flynn, we've almost become an outpost of Hollywood here,' she joked.

We went upstairs for Paul to pack. After closing the door, I went up to him and took him in my arms saying, 'You realise this is the last time we'll be alone together for months now? After all this, how are we going to get through next term, until we can be together at the cottage?' I hugged him and looked into his face.

'We'll manage. Let's just hold out for one more term, "*arm'd and fearless*".'

'I know you're right, but the next few months are going to be bloody hard.'

'Look, I've got something to help you think about me,' he continued, bringing out the Harrods bag. 'It's for you, for your birthday, to show you how much I've loved being with you.'

It was a yellow tie with little brown horses.

'Hey! How wonderful. It's my favourite tie from when I was a little boy, in the portrait,' I gulped, momentarily overcome.

Pulling myself together, I said, 'Funnily enough, I had the same idea myself,' and I walked over to the chest of drawers to fetch the bag with the turquoise silk scarf I had bought at Biba. 'I know you liked this too, and it complements your natural colouring.'

'Hey, that's beautiful – how thoughtful, and *special* of you.' He opened the little parcel and unfolded the scarf to admire its full pattern. 'I'll really, really treasure this.'

'I'm going to wear your tie right now,' I said, as I took off the dull stripy thing I had on.

'And I'll do the same. But *you've* got to arrange it round my neck for me, Freddie.' I opened his top two shirt buttons and tied the scarf in such a way that it billowed out loosely but unobtrusively.

He moved over to the full-length mirror and I stood behind him with each of my hands on his shoulders. We looked at each other. His scarf didn't look at all incongruous with his green tweed jacket and check shirt.

'My God, you look brilliant in that, you gorgeous fellow,' I said, and imagined to myself how he might be in a couple of years' time.

We went to say goodbye to Nanny who was having coffee in the kitchen with Mrs Eccleston, the daily. Mrs Drake hadn't yet arrived. I told her that Paul would probably be coming to the cottage in September.

'It'll be good to see you again then, Paul. By the way where did you get that wonderful scarf?' she said. A little blush crossed her face. Nanny, like all Welsh spinnies, had a secret crush on Richard Burton, and she'd obviously transferred this to Paul.

'Oh, Freddie gave it to me. It's from Biba.'

Nanny looked at me, surprised. I was not particularly famous for acts of spontaneous generosity.

'Oh, it's just a little thing, but I thought it suited him.' I tried to cover my embarrassment.

Then she noticed my new tie. 'I don't think I've seen that tie before either, Freddie.'

'Oh yes you have. I'm wearing it in Aunt Mary's portrait in the dining room. Paul found it for me yesterday. It's my eighteenth birthday present from him.'

I knew that she'd spill the beans first to Pippa and then to my mother. *She* would then tell my father and the whole family would know about this unexplained exchange of gifts. How would I face them all? Well, why not let them get used to the new and generous Freddie and the good influence his inseparable young friend is having over him?

We walked up Church Street together, slowly, side by side, towards the Underground. I had never felt like this before, both elated and sad at the same time: elated because we'd shared so much intimacy; but sad too, because it would be impossible for us to be like that again for months. And there was still something left undone.

At King's Cross, filthier and smellier than ever, we found the Leeds train and I walked beside him as far as the carriage door.

'It's like *Brief Encounter*,' I said, with a hollow laugh, trying to suppress my sadness. 'Although the station's not as steamy these days.' Then I lowered my voice.

'But my heart's as steamy as it ever can be, just looking at you, Paul.'

'Bugger all these people, I'm going to kiss you, Freddie McNaughton,' he said. 'Let's pretend we're French or something.'

Casting caution to the wind, he brought his face up close, intent as I imagined on pressing his lips against mine. But just at the crucial moment he moved his head a fraction so that his kiss fell on my cheek and mine on his.

Drawing back, I found myself saying involuntarily, '*Bye for now, gorgeous.*'

'All aboard,' shouted the guard, blowing his whistle, 'including you young gents.'

With my love,

Freddie

15

My dear Sam,

Those momentous holidays were capped by a surprise phone call from Dom Gabriel the day after Paul left.

'I'd like to make you Head of House next term, McNaughton. It's your last at Upton. Are you up for it? But before you answer, I'd better come clean. As you may know I was going to appoint Fanshaw, but his parents are sending him to Italy for the next few months before he goes up to Oxford. You're next in line.'

'My goodness, sir, I'd no idea I'd be in the running. But of course I'd be honoured to lead Ambrose next term.' My instantaneous thrill had been followed by a minor sense of deflation at being considered second best. A discreet ploy of Dom Gabriel's to offset any potential big-headedness. As if!

'Good. I'm very glad. Well, you know the drill. The younger boys will be looking up to you as the model of a perfect Catholic gentleman, and all that implies. I'll expect you to lead from the front.'

'Of course I'll do my best not to let you down.'

'I've noticed you over the past few months. You've grown in stature, become much more confident, more assured and – dare I say it – more responsible. You seem to bring out the best in people. I know you're not the greatest sportsman, nor even much of a team player, and I don't expect you'll change. But I know you'll put your shoulder to the wheel now, for the sake of the house. Anyway, it's time we had someone a bit different like you. You'll be a good ambassador for us.'

Another small grey cloud passed overhead; was I being chosen *just* because I'm 'a bit different'?

'Oh, and by the way, Dom Augustine says you should submit that essay on Disraeli for the School Essay Prize. He thinks you'd be in with a chance. It's worth £50, you know – to spend on books, to set you up at Cambridge,' he said, adding swiftly, 'or anywhere else, of course.'

I felt dazed as I put the phone down, almost as though I'd just woken from a long dream. After such a rollercoaster of success and failure my school career would be ending on a high after all. But almost immediately I was diverted by the image of myself wearing that ultimate symbol of status and cool. With the studied nonchalance that I hoped was becoming the public hallmark of my new style, I made the call to the school tailor to order my new dove-grey double-breasted waistcoat.

My parents were genuinely thrilled. On the face of it their faith in me had paid off at last. My father increased my allowance to £150 a year, backdated to January. 'I don't want you to stint yourself, Freddie. I want you to be able to be generous – to yourself and others. But for goodness' sake be discreet.'

*

My public début came with the first night's '*Miserere*' routine. All eyes were on me as I accompanied Dom Gabriel with the asperges bucket. Taking my cue from him, I acknowledged each of the boys with eye contact and a smile or gesture of recognition. A surprising number reciprocated happily while the usual suspects feigned indifference. Behind it all I could feel Paul's powerful gaze following me as I circulated the dormitory. When at last we reached his cubicle he was looking at me steadfastly, expressing something I'd never seen before: admiration, almost adoration. I felt humbled to be in the presence of his celestial judgment; it was all I'd ever wanted.

Immediately following the '*Miserere*' I chaired a meeting with the other house prefects in Dom Gabriel's room; he pretended not to be there, sitting in the corner smoking his pipe and reading a book. My performance needed careful handling as two of the existing prefects, Thicknesse and McPherson, probably considered themselves passed over. The other four were new and needed a pep talk about sharpening up on some of the old laggards but to go easy on the new boys. Top of the agenda was the make-up of the house sports teams for that term. Without any prompting Paul was voted captain of the 2nd XV for rugby.

Next morning, at the first assembly, I announced the team lists and was surprised at how genuinely enthusiastic I sounded as I commended the players. To stamp my authority at this early stage I chose the thorny issue of the house record player, laying down new rules on the permissible volume at different times. To make an immediate and popular impact I instigated a high-powered weekly Ambrose Quiz as a fundraiser for the African orphans. As things turned out, this was to be my lasting legacy; it continued long after I left and was extended to the whole school, making hundreds of pounds each year for the charity.

Paul came to see me in my room at the mid-morning break.

'You never told me you were going to be Head of House, you secretive bugger.' We were back on planet earth again. 'By the way, you look fantastic in that waistcoat. It makes you look...' he paused, smiling and looking me up and down, '... *so masterful*.' And thanks for making me captain of the 2nd XV.' He gave me one of his playful punches on my chest.

'Nothing to do with me,' I said. 'The choice was obvious. It didn't even come to a vote. You'll be captain of the 1st next year – when I come and cheer you on, gaping at you in your shorts as a venerable Old Uptonian.'

He snatched a kiss from my lips, at the same time as tickling my right ear lobe. My God, he tasted and smelt so delicious. With just the slightest touch on his bum I traced the outline of his briefs but withdrew my hand quickly. He needed to know that our pact was now more important than ever.

*

Nicky Jones was evidently taking some reflected glory in my new status. I noticed how he seemed to have become the unofficial leader of his small group of friends; I'd often see them all sitting together in huddles, mostly chatting and laughing amiably. I was conscious of his increased attentions; he seemed to love hanging around me, full of little unsolicited gestures, watering my new aspidistra, polishing the crystal appliqués, and making sure my ormolu clock was keeping proper time. When I indicated that he was becoming tiresome he would take the hint and disappear. Then I was sorry I might have disheartened the boy. Once or twice I'd agreed he could stay alone in my room after I'd left.

The real date of my eighteenth birthday fell a few days before the exams and was therefore kept very low key. But Nicky produced a stunning hand-drawn birthday card, on a folded sheet of A4 art paper, done in pen and ink in his own very personal style: finely drawn, precise and detailed, touched in with watercolour. In the background was the whole south elevation of the abbey church, with the tower at the crossing and the cloisters in front. In the middle distance was the great lawn, and in the foreground, off centre to the left, one of the giant cedars. Sitting on the grass under its shadow were two boys, one with his back supported against the tree reading a book, the other lying beside him propped up with one elbow. He was looking sideways at his neighbour with his own book evidently discarded beside him. It had more than a touch of Tristram Hillier's surrealism: clear shapes, long shadows, a limpid sky. An indeterminate animal skull was placed prominently in the foreground with the motto: *Et in Arcadia Ego.*

He had written on the inside: '*To F... Happy Birthday... From N 14*th *May 1968*'.

It was heartbreaking; I felt truly sorry for the dear lovelorn lad. I'd become very fond of him, but I dreaded the confrontation that must come sometime soon. It would require the greatest tact on my part. I'd been there myself, after all, but in my case providence had been on my side. Many senior boys would be tempted to indulge the situation, taking advantage of a younger boy's vulnerability. But I was engaged elsewhere.

When he called in next morning I didn't acknowledge him and continued reading my exam notes.

But after only a moment I couldn't go on being so unkind. I put my notebook down saying, 'Thanks for the card. Your drawing has really come on beautifully.' I took hold of it in my hands and studied it admiringly. 'You've got the perspective absolutely right.'

He took it off me. 'Yes, I think it's the most ambitious thing I've ever done. It was quite difficult getting the scale – balancing the buildings, the trees and the figures. It took quite a few sketches to get it right.' There and then he propped it up on the shelf above the gas fire, turning his head a little to the side as he looked at it again.

'I think it's the nicest card I've ever had from anyone,' I said. 'But who are these two boys under the tree? And what's this skull doing at the front?' I asked. I knew perfectly well but reckoned he should explain himself.

The boy blushed to his roots and turned as if to leave. 'Oh, nothing in particular, just compositional devices… but thanks for the compliments, sir.'

*

Things came to a head a few weeks later. There was a day's holiday for Corpus Christi and most of the school had gone into Cheltenham after High Mass in the morning. The coaches were due to return by six o'clock, in time for the great eucharistic procession through the monastery gardens and into the church. My great-grandmother's most spectacular gift to the abbey – the McNaughton Monstrance with its four concentric rings of diamonds, emeralds, rubies and sapphires surrounding the Glory – would be held aloft by the abbot for all to venerate. The canopy would be supported by the four most senior school prefects, including me.

I had decided not to go into Cheltenham. I needed time to prepare a short talk with slides on treasures of the Wallace Collection for the élite XX Society, which I was giving jointly with Roz in a few days' time. Only a small number of boys had remained behind, although I had noticed Nicky was among them. Presumably this was because he would be one of the two thurifers this evenings and required for rehearsals.

After lunch I went on a short cross-country run to shake me up and make me feel virtuous. I'd long since given up hope that such activity might be a cure for sexual deviancy, but the habit had stuck.

Returning to my room I opened the door and there, to my intense surprise, was Nicky.

He was standing beside my bed, with his trousers down to his ankles, pleasuring himself with one hand and holding my pyjama bottoms against his nose with the other. He was erect and evidently about to explode. Looking up as he saw me, he instantly dropped the pyjamas and desperately tried to pull up his trousers. His face had gone scarlet.

'What on earth... are you doing, Jones?' I asked, sounding shocked and disapproving.

Here was the confrontation I'd been dreading.

'Oh, sir, I didn't realise you'd be back so soon. I'm so sorry, really, really sorry.' He collapsed into the chair, his shirt still sticking out from his trousers, his collar and tie askew.

He buried his head in his hands and started blubbing. 'Oh, Freddie, you won't go telling anyone about this, will you? I'm just so ashamed. I'll be expelled, I'll have to tell my parents...'

I've never been able to see anyone in tears without melting. My astonishment turned to sympathy.

'No of course I won't,' I said softly. 'I'd never do anything like that.'

'Thank you, sir,' he said. 'But surely you must know how I feel about you by now. I'm just so desperate and unhappy. I can't bear the idea of your leaving here forever in three weeks and I'll never see you again. I just wanted to feel and touch and... well... *smell you*... close to me.' He said this pointing to my discarded pyjamas.

Drawing up the other chair I sat down, bringing it close to him.

'Isn't it time we spoke to each other properly, face to face?'

'Freddie,' he said, the poor boy was so flustered, '... I... let me just tell you... I've loved and worshipped you, ever since I first saw you in the distance while I was in Junior House. You were so tall, so elegant and handsome, so kind, and so different from everyone, I couldn't wait until I could be your fag when I moved up to Ambrose. Maybe I might get to touch you, or even kiss you. But it's always been *you and Shipton*. You're always together. I keep watching you both and I just know there's no room for me.'

I pulled the chair a bit closer to him. 'Look, Nicky – can I call you Nicky as you've called me Freddie? – I do know all this. I'm not unobservant. We all remember that time you spilt coffee all over Shipton's trousers. Everyone knew it wasn't an accident.'

We both smiled at each other as the atmosphere became more conspiratorial. I continued,

'I really *can* understand how you're feeling right now.' *But do you really?* I heard a little voice ask.

'I know it's no help saying so, but you'll soon forget about me and find someone else. If not tomorrow, then sometime soon – believe me. You probably hope against hope that I can love you too. I'm sorry but I can't, but that's not because you're not a lovable and attractive – in fact *the most lovely* – boy. It's just that I'm destined for someone else.'

I thought he was going to burst into tears again, so I dragged the chair even closer to him and brought my right hand over to caress his arm ever so gently.

'Can I kiss you – just this once?' he said, looking at me through his distress.

I said nothing but moved my face closer to his. In a second he had pressed his lips against mine, finding my hand to hold and squeeze. With my other hand I clenched his thigh just below his crotch. But he was too fast, too anxious, and moved his face away almost at once, closing his eyes.

For two pins I would have taken his head in both my hands again and kissed him softly and longingly, making him open his mouth to find his tongue, to breathe deeply into him.

But no, no, I said to myself, *no more. I can't trust myself to stop. I could give you so much pleasure, Nicky. I'd love to see your sweet face light up, you're so desirable, but it must never happen.*

As I withdrew, he smiled. I knew things had gone way beyond his wildest dreams. Thank goodness he seemed to have recovered.

'Alright, that's enough now. You'd better get going.'

But he was taking his time to pull himself together. 'Thank you, Freddie... I love you so much... You're so understanding and kind... It's been wonderful just to be with you.'

Then he added, disarmingly, 'I know we'll never do this again, but can we exchange a little gift or something as a souvenir to remind us of the time we've had together these past two terms?'

'I'm not sure that's such a good idea, Nicky. It'll just prolong things, won't it, and probably make you unhappy. Besides, you've got the photos from last term.'

He looked terribly disappointed. 'I would so love something personal and intimate to remember you by, something I could hold on to when I think of you. There'd be no harm in that, surely?'

'Well, alright,' I said reluctantly, yet again a total sucker to his sweet pleadings.

'I know,' he tried to sound spontaneous, but I could tell he'd rehearsed it, 'when you leave after Prize Day could you give me this pair of pyjamas so I could lay them out on my bed at home, pretend it was you, and make love to you, and smell and taste you? And then put them on, imagining you so close to me?'

I was really quite overcome, and needed to think quickly. 'I'm not going to say yes, Nicky, but if you happen to find them accidentally discarded in the waste-paper basket on the last day of term I won't stop you. Are you sure you haven't been dreaming about this already? Weren't you going to nick them anyway?' I tried not to smile.

'No, honest,' he said, looking at me imploringly.

'You realise they'll have my name tab sewn on them,' I said. 'If your mother found them she wouldn't know what to think, finding you've stolen your fag-master's pyjamas.'

'Don't worry,' he said. 'I'll keep them hidden away where no one except me will ever find them.'

'So, what would you like from me?' he continued, looking at me in a way I had never seen before.

In a moment of inspiration, I said: 'Have you ever done a self-portrait?'

'No, I've never tried that, but I suppose I can always have a go.'

'Could you do one for me?'

As he left my room I felt massively relieved I hadn't taken advantage of the boy. It would have been so easy; I could have enjoyed his complete surrender. But before I began to fantasise, I had to see Paul, *right now*, to assure myself of *his* beauty and his love for me, look deeply into his face, hear his voice, to be touched and held and kissed by him.

It had been a near miss.

With my love,

Freddie

16

My dear Sam,

I had not become involved in *The Winter's Tale* since persuading Paul to take the part of Leontes, but I got to hear about its progress at second hand. The play was an ambitious new departure not least because it was a joint production with St Mary's, the Catholic girls' boarding school nearby. The preparations and rehearsals had been taking place over the course of three terms, involving much to-ing and fro-ing between the two establishments. Despite all the complications involved, the production was being hailed as a model for collaboration between single-sex schools.

The play was one of the set books for English A-Levels that year – another good reason for its choice as the 'official' school play. I had grown to love it: its fairy-tale world threatened by evil; love and fidelity overcoming jealousy and sin; the curative power of time; the contrasting worlds of court and country; and, overarching everything, the sublime language and imagery in which it was all expressed.

I attended some of the rehearsals, sitting at the back of the theatre. I'd marvelled at everyone's efforts at this long and difficult play. Paul's part demanded a wide range of emotions from insane jealousy and anger, to sorrow, grief and humility, often in long soliloquies and dramatic dialogues. How on earth could he do it? It was a world away from his part as Orsino in *Twelfth Night* last year. It required massive skill, memory and emotional control, not to mention maturity.

All I could do was watch, or if we were together, hear his lines whenever he wanted a prompt. Sometimes he would take a copy of the text with him while we lay on the grass under the cedar, just as we'd done last summer, or we'd just sit with it in my room in the evenings. As always, it was the power and subtlety of his voice that carried all before it, its deep sonorous quality, capable of a thousand inflections, so mesmerising and expressive.

*

Exams over for another year, the Prize-Giving Weekend and Festival arrived at last. By five o'clock on the Saturday all the exhibitions, workshops and activities had finished so as not to clash with the performance.

As it gathered momentum I sensed that I was not alone in witnessing, indeed becoming part of, something truly remarkable. Every time Paul made an entrance all eyes were drawn irresistibly towards him as though he were radiating a powerful magnetic force. Some latent power was transfiguring him into somebody entirely different from the young man of Ambrose whom, in my imagination, I had once identified as a melancholic, lovelorn, Renaissance prince. He had played that limited role to perfection last year, satisfying all the fantasies I then had about him. Now he was incarnating the vastly more complicated but ultimately heroic king. Yet the words he uttered seemed merely *sounds* to me, almost irrelevant. I knew them as well as he, having rehearsed with him so often, but now it was like watching an opera in a half-understood language – Italian or German. They belonged to someone else, a man supposedly three times Paul's age, articulating emotions he could never have felt.

It was unnerving to feel so small, so humbled, in the presence of such objective greatness. Did I feel resentful that I had to share this revelation with everyone else in the audience? On the contrary; I felt intensely proud and elated because I knew for certain that this boy, this young man, loved me and belonged to me and me alone. I was the only person present with a total claim on him, knowing every sinew of his body and every shadow of his soul, anticipating every inflection of his voice, every blink of his eyes, every gesture and move he might make.

The audience were on the edge of their seats until the very end when, electrified by a gasp from someone in the stalls, Hermione descended from her pedestal – alive, no longer a statue! As he embraced her, Paul transformed this tale of human sinfulness into one of love and forgiveness triumphant. The catharsis was palpable, both on stage and among the audience, as he turned graciously to the faithful Paulina:

> *'Lead us from hence, where we may leisurely*
> *Each one demand, and answer to his part*
> *Perform'd in this wide gap of time,*
> *Since first we were dissever'd.'*

*

The after-party was very different from the last occasion. This time it was held in the theatre foyer. Parents and guests were invited, although mine skipped it and returned to the cousins with whom they were staying nearby.

Paul, high on adrenaline, introduced me again to his mother and uncle, saying, 'You'll remember my friend Fred McNaughton from last year? He's the one who's been helping me get through all this and who I'm going to stay with in September,' giving me a smirk and one of his mock punches in my chest.

His uncle, short and tweedie, hair receding, was affable and friendly; his mother, tall and dark, was where Paul had got his looks: the eyes, the complexion, the nose. She smiled in a resigned sort of way while his sister Claire looked at me uncomprehending. I was relieved almost immediately by Rappy who engaged them with a plan for Paul to go on a young actors' workshop for a fortnight during the holidays. I sidled away, glad to have met them again. But I knew I'd need to work hard to become accepted as easily as Paul had been by my own parents.

*

Next day, Sunday, there was to be High Mass at ten o'clock, at which all parents and boys were expected, filling the nave and transepts and even the gallery chapels of the abbey church. This would be followed by prize-giving and speeches in the theatre and a buffet lunch in the main refectory. I had indeed been awarded the Essay Prize and would have to give a short speech of thanks. Later, in the afternoon, there would be the usual running programme of events. After tea all the boys departing by car with their parents would leave, while those destined to go home by train, and the cast of *The Winter's Tale* performing at St Mary's that evening, would spend a final night at school before being bussed to Stroud station next morning.

Paul and I could only be together for a couple of minutes after breakfast when he came to my near-empty room.

'You were brilliant last night,' I said, embracing him, running my fingers through his hair. 'I just don't know how you did it. You had everyone eating out of your hand. You're such a hero.'

'I'm so glad you enjoyed it. I did it for you really,' he said, taking my hand and kissing it. 'You helped me such a lot. But gosh, it was hard work! I'm still reeling from it. Anyway, we're going over to St Mary's straight after lunch to have a rehearsal there, so we'd better say goodbye now.'

We kissed again, and hugged, both of us holding back our feelings.

'I just can't wait 'til I see you again in a few weeks. Just stay well and think of me sometimes, if you can.'

'Of course I will, Freddie. I'll be thinking of you *all* the time. It's funny that today is the end of our time together at school. After this everything is going to change and we can become real lovers.'

He paused. Looking dreamily out of the window, and then turning to me, he said,

'Do you remember that first time we spoke, when you interrupted me reading *Antony and Cleopatra* and I tried to give you the brush-off? But you persisted, ever so gently. Thank goodness you did! Who would have thought we'd end up like this today?'

I gazed at him, drinking in his beauty and the love he was directing at me. My voice nearly cracked when I whispered, 'We've everything in the world to look forward to, Paul, this is just the beginning, *"fulfilling our foray"*.'

*

I'd managed to dispose of most of the contents of my room at an auction in the dayroom: the damask hangings, the Limoges, the clock and appliqués from Tours, the aspidistra and its stand, and the Persian rug. They netted me just £5. I 'bequeathed' the fur rug to Paul as he would be setting up his own room next term. It had become quite famous in its way, and I wanted everyone to know by its presence in his room that he was my nominated 'heir'. Perhaps it would continue to provoke an occasional smile on the lips of boys who lay on it caressing its sensuous pile.

Despite the sale there was still much to stow away in the boot of the Bentley when my parents drove it round to the side door: my trunk, the Drevet portraits (minus one) and a couple of boxes of books and ephemera. Nicky came up to help me, looking nervous and sad. We took the first things down and I introduced him briefly to my parents. Both of us returned upstairs to collect the remainder.

He closed the door behind us and came over to hug me from behind. Of course I was going to miss him but I had no intention of letting him kiss me again on the lips, even today.

'Come on, Nicky, let's be sensible. Anyway, you can look in the waste-paper basket now,' I said, disengaging myself.

'Your pyjamas!'

'Yes – and they *haven't been laundered.* Isn't that how you wanted them, you little perve?'

I didn't tell him that I'd unpicked the name tabs, so carefully sewn on by Nanny when they were new.

'And now I've got something for you,' he said, producing a sealed white envelope. 'Don't open it now. Wait 'til you're on your own and then...'

At that he turned and left the room.

As we drove away, me in the back seat, my father driving and my mother beside him, I found a way of opening the envelope unseen by either of them.

It was his self-portrait – a half-length, his figure dominating the entire foreground. He was looking at me full frontal, his creamy white flesh naked to the waist, showing his adorable shoulders, delicate arms and slight chest with his tight rosy nipples, such as I had only seen once. He had done it in pen and ink, with delicate washes, emphasising his fair hair, pinkish face and deep blue eyes. He looked quite intense, with his red lips apart showing his white teeth as though about to speak. Truly, he looked like everyone's ideal boy-lover: an English angel in the slave market in Rome – *non angli, sed angeli* as St Gregory had said, so knowingly. In the background was the tower of the abbey church, with two boys sitting under a cedar of Lebanon again, the motif of his birthday card. This time there were little butterflies hovering and flitting over them. No animal skull anywhere. Over in the top left corner he had drawn a symbol, which at first I couldn't make out; it looked slightly heraldic. Looking more closely I realised it was half a heart, a demi-ogee, and, in the centre, piercing it, was a little arrow tip. He had signed and inscribed it: '*To Freddie with love from Nicky* Au revoir *July 1968*'.

'Was that your fag who helped you down with your baggage?' asked my mother. She obviously hadn't been listening when I introduced him. Or perhaps I had been too vague.

'Yes, that was Nicky Jones. He's been such a big help to me.'

'Seems a nice boy, darling, I hope you thanked him properly.'

'Oh yes, Mama, I think he was very satisfied.' I smiled to myself, but then felt desperately sad.

'Very pretty boy,' interjected my father looking at me from the driver's mirror. I felt myself blushing but looked back at him in the mirror. 'Yes, I suppose he is really,' I answered.

Then I caught his eye again; he was trying to suppress a smile. *He* knew alright; he hadn't had an all-male education for thirteen years for nothing, even in a more innocent age. I returned his smile with a grin of my own, well out of view of my mother.

With my love,
Freddie

17

My dear Sam,

Now at last, after five years in formation, I had joined the illustrious ranks of the Old Uptonians. I took great pleasure in ordering my new stripy blazer, boater and tie with the OU colours and looked forward to wearing them with flair on the right occasions. You will laugh, probably thinking I looked like an extra in a musical comedy, or someone out of *Brideshead*. I'm sure I still have the outfit here somewhere.

The next few weeks were an agony waiting for Paul's arrival in early September. I should have been far more concerned about the imminent results of my A-Level retakes but I had a premonition that they would somehow be alright. I had no alternative plans if I was turned down for Cambridge, only a vague idea that I could probably get into Durham or Exeter if need be. Nowadays it makes me squirm to think of my sense of exceptionalism!

As usual, it was almost impossible for Paul and me to keep in touch by phone. Rappy had succeeded in persuading his mother to send him on that short residential course for aspiring actors, after which he was going to Brittany with his family again. Sometimes I had visions of him with his fellow students, beguiling them with his beauty and talents. I'd feel a pang of jealousy in case any of them took a shine to him. How would he react? Would his head be turned, at last?

Your mother would not be returning home from school for another few days, so I was pleased to have some time on my own in London before we all went down to the cottage. In another couple of weeks we were both due to spend a fortnight near Grasse at the farmhouse of one of her schoolfriends. I put a brave face on this, anticipating all the adolescent caperings in which I'd be expected to compete. I cheered up a lot when I heard Miranda was going to be there at the same time.

After supper on my second evening back at home I was helping Nanny clear away the dishes when my father indicated for me to stay. My mother had already departed upstairs.

He went over to the sideboard and brought out a decanter and two small glasses.

'Here, Freddie, let's have a glass or two of port. It's quite a decent one – 1963 Graham's. I think you'll probably get used to it at Cambridge. It's a very agreeable way of entertaining your friends after dinner. But for goodness' sake always, always, decant it first. Otherwise it's undrinkable. That's one of the first things I learnt when I went up in '34.'

I hadn't bothered with port until now, thinking it an old person's drink – visions of old Mrs Drake in a snug bar with a port and lemon. But sipping this delicious vintage I could see how it could become addictive.

'Tell me,' he said, 'what is your good friend Paul Shipton hoping to do after he's finished at Upton? By the way, your mother and I thought he was superb in that Shakespeare play.'

My eyes lit up at the mention of Paul's name – and my father noticed.

'Oh, he was quite chuffed at how well it went down with everyone. He's thinking he might take up acting as a career after Cambridge.'

'I'd forgotten he was hoping to go to Cambridge too. Which college?'

'Trinity, I think. That's where his uncle went.' I tried to sound vague; I knew perfectly well.

'Not Powis then?' My father shot me a direct and almost threatening glance. I felt myself becoming heated. I tried concentrating on my wineglass, twisting it on its stem, making the dark fluid revolve in the bowl. Where was this leading?

'No. Not Powis.'

'Well, it'll be good you'll overlap for two years while you're there – *if* you both get in, that is.

'Look,' he continued, getting serious, 'your mother and I both like Paul very much and think he's a very talented and charming young man. We're really pleased he's coming to stay at the cottage while we're away. But, you know, these very close – and dare I say it – *intense* friendships between boys are fine while you're away at school. But they should be allowed to fade away before too long, before they become unhealthy. You follow me?'

'But, Dad,' I said, suddenly shocked and fearful, my face flushing and my mouth going dry, 'Paul is my best buddy. We do everything together.'

'That's just what I mean,' he said. 'And that's all well and good. But what your mother and I want is for you to start exploring the world a bit more now that you've left school. Find out what else is out there. You've got to spread your wings, Freddie. Move on.'

He was trying so hard to be circumspect. I was on the edge of my seat, certain that something awful was coming next. How on earth could I explain to him that my vision for the future was for Paul and me together, inseparable, forever?

My father must have seen my bewilderment and struck home his advantage. 'So, we want to make a bargain with you. Paul is very welcome to come and stay as planned, but before he arrives we want you to visit an address in Seymore Place. I've made an appointment for you to see a certain young lady called Suki. She comes highly recommended. In fact, we *insist* on it. And by the way, you're not the first; I discovered that Colonel Waybrook and Sir Peter sent Robert and Charlie there as part of their eighteenth birthday coming-of-age presents. Separately, I hasten to say.'

He tried to chuckle to diffuse his obvious embarrassment. 'So your appointment is for 2.00 tomorrow afternoon. I can drive you there myself if you like. I hear it's about the best place of its kind in Mayfair. Here's the £50 you'll need.' He handed over a wadge of £5 notes.

My God, I thought. *This can't be happening.* The very idea of it appalled, even terrified me. How was I supposed to react?

I had to think on my feet. If I refused, I would need an excuse. The one they were probably expecting, even dreading, was for me to own up to being a Homo, to 'come out', as we say today. Were they trying to force the issue? But I just wasn't ready for all that now, if ever. But there could be no question of giving up my longed-for week with Paul; what would our future be otherwise?

Alas, I was helpless, and would have to go along with their beastly plan, however painful it was going to be, hoping to God I would survive the trauma. Maybe one day they would understand what a high price I had paid to keep the love of my life.

'Oh! *Alright then*,' I said, trying my hardest to sound surprised, maybe pleased, in some confused sort of way. But at least I could make a protest, pretending to take the moral high ground without sounding prudish.

'Although I'm not at all sure about the morality of this – after everything I've been brought up to believe, and at such huge expense *for you*, Dad. Anyway,' I continued, trying to sound scornful, 'it seems a pity you've got to pay for it. And there's no need to drive me there, thanks. I'll take the bus to Marble Arch.' I didn't want him to think I'd shirk it.

'Oh, come on, Freddie. It's not that bad, surely. In any case, I'm told the girls there are very understanding and used to looking after young men like you.'

Whatever did he mean by *that*? I wasn't going to ask further. Either he imagined I was still a virgin, or else a Homo needing to be sorted out.

'Have another glass of port, for goodness' sake, Freddie.' His relief was palpable; he had probably been dreading a negative reception to his proposal and an unwelcome confession by me, even a scene. He poured us each a full measure from the decanter. 'Now, tell me what you think about reading Law when you get to Cambridge. You'd have to start eating your dinners at the Inner Temple if you decide on the Bar…'

Lying in bed that night I felt pained that my parents were resorting to such a low trick, in effect blackmail, if they wanted an admission from me. I'd heard about boys being treated by their fathers to a session in a high-class brothel when they were eighteen. Maybe everyone just laughed it off as no more than a check-up at the doctors, or some kind of rite of passage. But now I knew my own parents had deeper worries about me. Did they seriously think I could be 'cured' before my deficiencies became irreversible? Perhaps they imagined they were doing me a favour, or even that I would enjoy it.

Tossing and turning in bed my pain turned to anger. I wasn't going to let them off scot-free from this experiment. If I did this thing for them tomorrow, then, in return, if not revenge, I was going to reaffirm myself as a Homo by getting laid as soon as possible afterwards by a man. Goodness knows I would need some consolation after enduring something so profoundly false to my nature. I would find myself a man – an anonymous man, the first one I fancied. My natural fastidiousness could go to hell. The hook-up could be somewhere just as sordid as a brothel: a public lavatory – the one in Notting Hill Gate I'd often seen shifty-looking men hanging around outside; or the Cornet Cinema where I'd been groped by men in dirty raincoats when I'd been younger; or a pub. There need be no emotional engagement, nothing disloyal to Paul. Maybe I'd even pay the fellow with some of the money intended for the prozzie and get my own back on my parents that way.

Sitting on the bus on the way to Seymore Place I had a mounting sense of dread, almost akin to the anxiety I used to experience before going back to prep school at the end of each holidays. On the doorstep and just before pressing the bell I wondered if I should flunk the whole thing. But my pride got the better of me; I reckoned it need be no more painful than a visit to the dentist.

The girl, Suki, was certainly 'understanding' right from the start, and she needed to be. My fear was probably very obvious, although at first I tried to hide it by a certain nervous machismo. She was pretty and blonde, perhaps in her mid-twenties, slim, with small breasts and narrow hips, softly spoken and elegantly turned out. She could almost have passed as an ex-deb, the very last person anyone would recognise as a prostitute. But my confidence crashed as she began her foreplay and I found it impossible to get aroused. The one thing I had been dreading was to see her naked. Instinctively she knew what to do with me and put a mask over my eyes. She told me to imagine she was a beautiful and eager boy as she took me in hand. That seemed to work, and at the last minute she helped me complete the job. But it was all so laboured compared with the frenzied abandon Henri and I had thrown into the experience. As I was leaving, I was in two minds to ask her how it had been with Charlie and Robert, but then thought better of it. She gave me a kiss on the cheek and invited me to return if I found my inclinations were changing. She could show me another trick or two, as she put it.

I felt massively relieved it was all over and that I need never do that again, ever. It was entirely down to Suki that it had not been more of a trauma. And then, for a brief moment, I wondered how it might have been if I had been offered someone the polar opposite to Suki – someone dark, voluptuous and mysterious. Now, *that* might have had some potential.

I heard my father returning at about six o'clock, and went downstairs to his study, closing the door firmly behind me.

'Well?' he said, dropping his copy of the *Evening Standard* on his desk.

'Well... I've been. You'll be pleased to hear that everything's in working order and you could potentially become a grandfather.' It was a half-lie, I knew, but good enough. 'And here's the £5 change as there was a discount before six o'clock.' I was trying to sound defiant. I'd given up the idea of spending the change on a rent boy as part of my revenge; I should be capable of pulling a man without any outside help.

His expression changed to one of genuine thankfulness. 'Well, Freddie, I'm glad to hear it and I won't ask any more of you. Now of course you must have Paul to stay just as we'd planned. If you two are going to stick together at Cambridge, and even later, that's fine by us.'

I think this was meant to be a half-apology. Maybe he realised how distasteful it must have been for me and even admired me for having gone through with it. Perhaps also his conscience was salved that he'd done his fatherly duty and that was the end of his responsibilities. Only now it occurred to me that it had probably been my mother's idea.

Thank goodness my grandmother was coming to dinner. Any further awkwardness was avoided as we all listened to her complicated plans for the summer. Afterwards she presented me with my grandfather's gold cigarette case as an eighteenth-birthday present. I felt I had earned it after proving today that I could ensure our family's dynastic survival – if absolutely necessary. My father drove her back to South Kensington and my mother went to bed early. I disappeared to watch television in the nursery with Nanny.

With my love,

Freddie

18

My dear Sam,

It's been a while since my last letter. I've needed some respite after recalling that time at Seymore Place. Here comes the antidote.

That night I planned my tactics. In the morning I'd go shopping at Biba for all the provocative gear I'd need. Then come home to change and go on the prowl. I'd start at the Irwin Arms off Bayswater Road, colloquially known as the Cock and Cushion on account of its heraldry. I knew there was no guarantee of success there at lunchtime, of course. Hampstead Heath or Soho in the evening would obviously be much better. But that was impossible in the present circumstances. If it didn't work there were the alternatives.

After a late breakfast, purposefully avoiding my father, I went in to see my mother propped up in bed reading the newspaper. She looked up at me blankly, taking off her reading glasses. It was our first *tête-à-tête* since the Seymore Place incident, but I had no intention of referring to it even by implication.

'What are you doing with yourself today, darling?'

I felt the thrill of being deliberately evasive, if not downright mendacious.

'I thought I'd go shopping for some summer clothes and then perhaps head for the National Gallery this afternoon.'

'Good idea. But do remember, Freddie, that you look best in *dark* colours – even if it's summer. Navy suits you best of all. I'd love to join you at the National Gallery, but I'm having lunch with Aunt Helena.'

Hurray, I thought to myself.

I strode purposefully down Church Street. I had remembered Biba's crushed-velvet trousers from last Easter; now I looked through the rack: pink, crimson, bottle green, purple (ugh!), even navy. I tried on the navy pair. I was a perfect 28 waist and 32 leg and found they were wonderfully tight round my groin and bum. Being provocatively low slung they were crying out for a wide belt with a big buckle. I had to have them. I'd need a shirt of course and found just the ticket: a silky, wide-collared navy number, covered in small white polka dots. At the same time, for more respectable occasions, I couldn't resist the white linen suit in which I fantasised myself as my new hero, a reinvented Robert de St Loup on whom I was developing a big literary crush.

I went on to Barkers and bought some quite tasteful Bermuda shorts suitable for the cottage but turned tail to get home as soon as possible. Fortunately there was no one about. I made sure I was spotlessly clean, inside and out, before changing into the new pants, deliberately omitting any underwear, and looked at myself in the full-length mirror.

What a transformation! The tightness ensured a definite profile below the belt buckle. A bit much? No, definitely not for what I had in mind. Turning around I admired my *derrière*; my bum looked deliciously appetising, even if I say it myself. I left the top three buttons of my shirt open to allow a glimpse of my downy chest, and backcombed my hair out of its usual style, letting it flow loosely. If I couldn't pull a bloke looking like this, I never would.

'You bloody little whore,' I said to my reflection. 'You should be charging for this. You could make a fortune. Well, maybe...'

With that determined attitude I left the house, still unseen, and made my way to the Cock and Cushion. If I encountered any astonished glances en route I would just smile sweetly.

But there was one more job to do. I had brought with me a crimson watered silk hanky, previously worn in my breast pocket when I became a house prefect. I had a better use for it now, as I stuffed it into my left backside pocket, just hanging out to be visible. Pips had told me that the colour of the handkerchief and the location of its exposure gave out coded messages indicating availability and preferences. I couldn't remember the details but hoped I'd got it right.

With only a moment's hesitation as to whether to go for the saloon or the public bar I pushed open the door to the latter. It looked and smelt appropriately sordid: a squelchy old carpet, stained lincrusta wallpaper, a slight pong of disinfectant and urine mixed with the clinging fug of cigarette smoke. Behind the bar there were a couple of short-cropped boys in singlets and the tightest imaginable short-shorts showing great arses when they turned around, bending over to fetch drinks or reaching to fill glasses. Sitting or standing around at the copper-topped tables were about a dozen men, talking and drinking, with one or two playing darts. I was aware, and amused, that all eyes were on me as I walked towards the bar. Several – most, even – stopped speaking or drinking for just a moment longer than necessary as I came into view. Maybe I'd be in luck.

I paused to decide who to stand next to at the bar. One of the men, a ginger who was obviously on his own, turned again in my direction, at the same time lifting his glass to take a drink. As he put it down he took me in in a single sweep. He blinked twice with a slow flutter of his lashes, took another swig from his glass, and turned away. For a moment I felt disappointed, if not resentful. Didn't he fancy me? What an insult! (You have to remember I was still hopelessly green about the protocols.)

Undeterred, I moved confidently into the space beside him, leaving a discreet little distance between us – room to manoeuvre in case he or I changed our minds.

I looked straight ahead trying to catch the barman's attention while asking myself if I wanted to go with this gingery fellow with the fluttery lashes? I reckoned it was *my* prerogative to decide; after all I might be in serious demand as the new chick in a room full of horny older cocks. I looked round: most of the men were young and passably handsome, some a bit rough and probably working class, with longish hair, muscly arms and hairy chests under their singlets; a couple were older and fatter, holding forth waving their hands around, wearing gold bangles and chains (not for me!); and there were a couple of threateningly beautiful Black boys watching the others expectantly. Now *they* might be fun, but what on earth would I talk to them about?

I weighed up my neighbour again with a mixture of caution and interest, seeing his profile as he leant against the bar. He was shortish, early twenties, with a rather sweet and very round head, close-cropped hair, small ears, which somehow stuck out in the horizontal, and a cute body encased in a tight sports shirt and pair of blue shorts that showed off his plump bum and nicely shaped downy thighs. Yeah, I reckoned he'd do.

I ordered half of lager and a cheese sandwich. How should I engage with this guy? Who makes the first move? Last time in Bournemouth it had been me and Pips who'd been chatted up. This fellow looked at me once again with his big green eyes without smiling, and then shifted his gaze into the half-distance. Was he playing hard to get? Was he interested? Was he deliberately winding me up?

As my drink arrived I thanked the barman and turned blandly to my neighbour.

'It's not very busy here today.'

'No,' he replied, turning to me, looking at me straight in

the face, smiling at last, 'but 'tis T'ursday lunchtime and the art college has broken up, so it's not surprising, to be sure.'

Of course. He was Irish, with that lovely soft accent.

Sam, you'll just have to believe the conversation that follows. It seems extraordinary, but even now in my dotage I can recall it fairly accurately.

'Is this your local?' I asked, feeling the ice had broken.

'Well it might become so. I've only been living round here a couple of weeks and I'm trying out some of the pubs. I like it here 'specially in the evening. The folks are much more friendly than in the other places down Church Street.'

'I agree. I love sitting out in the garden in the summer,' I lied.

'Do you live nearby?' he asked. 'I can tell you probably do,' he smiled provocatively.

I blushed a little, aware of the tease. 'Yes, we've lived near here for a long time. What about you?'

'I came over from Ireland a month ago to work at the hospital now that I've qualified as a midwife.'

'A midwife?' I exclaimed. Oh God! Did I sound patronising?

'Yes, there aren't many male midwives, I know, but I'm one of them. I love little babies,' he said with a twinkle in his eyes, as he put his arms together moving them from side to side, imitating a cradle. There was something definitely *not* very macho about this gesture. Perhaps I'd struck lucky.

'Oh, that's nice,' I said with a laugh, taking a gulp from my glass.

At this point my sandwich appeared. 'I'm going to sit over there. You joining me? Are you having a sandwich?'

'I'll join you, but I've already had something to eat, thanks. By the way, I'm David.'

'Not Dave?'

'*Certainly not*,' he said with a look of feigned disgust. 'I'm not one of those Irish navvie types.'

'Oops, sorry!' I said. 'I can see that. And I'm Fred.'

'Not Freddie?'

'Not until you know me *a lot better*.' To my amazement I managed to say this, turning towards him with a suggestive little smile of my own, followed by a slow flutter of my lashes. I was learning fast.

'OK, fair enough.' Just for a second he looked at me sideways with a semi-comical expression as if to say, 'I know just what you mean.'

We sat side by side on the bench behind a table, chatting away about nothing very much, him telling me about Ireland and how he had come to start work at St Mary's 'where all the *royal* babies are born, don't you know'.

I had to own up to having just left school and awaiting my exam results before hopefully going up to read Law at Cambridge. How could I have been such an *ingénu*, giving away everything at the first throw!

'Oh, but I'd hoped you were at least *barely legal*,' he said, with a cheeky smile.

'I was eighteen two months ago, so I can go anywhere and do anything I like now,' I said with a little *faux* pout.

'Yes, there are *lots of things* you can do *perfectly legally* now,' he rejoined, 'but there are still some things that you definitely *can't*. Are you sure you're only eighteen? Did I hear right, or was that twenty-one?' He put a hand up to his ear.

Oh God, I thought, *I've messed this up.* 'No, no,' I said, laughing, 'of course I meant twenty-one.'

'I bet that's what you tell all the boys,' he whispered.

This has *to be an invitation*, I thought. *Great! I'm being seduced! How bloody wonderful and flattering.*

I continued, 'Yes, I'm looking forward to *lots* of new experiences.'

Oh, goodness, I wasn't being very subtle.

'A nice boy like you can have plenty of fun, now you're twenty-one. Let me get you another drink.'

As he leant forward at the bar, resting his elbows on the surface and one foot on the rail, his bum cheeks assumed a coquettish asymmetry. For a split second I imagined ripping off his shorts, taking hold of his arse and groping its squashy succulence. His shirt was only partly tucked in, and I could see quite clearly a hint of pink flesh above the elastic belt of his briefs. He turned around and caught my gaze, giving a cheery little wink. He *knew* I'd be looking at him.

He brought us over a pint each. I had to admit I wasn't used to drinking much in the afternoons. He said he never did usually except that today was his day off. He ought to be looking for somewhere permanent to live since he was only in the nurses' hostel for the next two weeks.

But he showed no sign of wanting to move, and so we prattled on. It was almost as though there were two parallel conversations: a tantalisingly amorous one with our flashing eyes and smiley lips, and a mundane one with our voices. It was my turn for a round.

After nearly an hour the pub began to empty. Any residual nervousness had long since vanished and I was feeling pleasantly hazy and ready for anything. The novelty of being made mincemeat by this cheeky Irish chappy was entrancing. He had moved slowly but discreetly closer towards me on our two-seater settle. Our legs were under the table; twice they had touched and neither of us had shown any inclination of shifting them. They touched again a third time, and now he began a gentle rubbing movement, thigh against thigh, shin against shin. At the same time his hand went under the table and moved imperceptibly onto my groin. With his very first touch against the soft pile of the velvet my whole body went into spasm, tingling all over, twitching in anticipation. Within a moment I could feel myself getting bigger, uncontrollably, and made worse by the tight constraint. If one of his fingers moved even an inch further something might explode involuntarily. He was obviously enjoying my agony.

'Tell me what you're looking forward to, now you've come of age,' he said quietly and cheekily. Our parallel conversations seemed now to converge. His charm was completely irresistible.

'I'm up for anything really. Anything *you* can show me?'

Wherever did I find it in me to say *that*?

'Frederick!' he said, in a camp little attempt at sounding shocked. 'Are you trying to *lure* me into your trap? I don't know *what* you mean. I couldn't possibly lead a nice boy like you astray, *to be sure.*'

'Actually,' I said, assuming an affected tartiness, 'I wouldn't mind *at all.*' I must have been three quarters drunk.

He looked at me as if to say: 'OK, posho boy, I don't mind taking you in hand. Let's have a bit of fun.'

But instead, he said, 'Well, now the pub's closing, why not come back to my hostel for some coffee and we can think of what to do next. It's only around the corner.' I felt another delicious twitch under the crushed velvet. Was I going to hold out?

I had to walk slowly and carefully as we ambled towards Notting Hill Gate, crossing into the Villas and then into one of the side streets. I became aware of our difference in height; I must have been a good two inches taller than him. I suddenly imagined myself the tall sinuous Adam, an innocent alone in the Garden of Eden, and he the rounded, luscious piece of forbidden fruit, ready to be devoured, dangling in front of me, being offered by an invisible Eve. How I wanted to surrender to the temptation, to gorge on that plump, fleshy ripeness. Then – it was almost as if he could read my thoughts – he suddenly put his hand around my bum and squeezed it. My body shook with delight.

'Hey,' I said, 'stop it… here… you naughty *Oirish* boy.'

He answered by blowing me a pouty little kiss.

Seeing someone coming round the corner he withdrew, leaving me gasping.

Reaching the hostel – a crumbling white stucco house, indistinguishable from all the others – he let us in with his latch key. I followed behind him, mesmerised by the way he sashayed up the stairs.

It was a sad, rather bleak little room, with a window overlooking the back, not much bigger than mine at school. As soon as he'd closed the door he came over to give me a long, juicy kiss on the lips, putting his hand round my bum again stroking it gently. Another thrilling jolt passed through me head to toe.

'Coffee first?' he asked, with a lecherous smile.

I sniggered. 'Yes please, to sober up. Milk and two sugars.'

'I'll be back in a minute.'

While he was out, I looked around the room. It was a much-needed chance to cool down. There was little evidence of David's personality. On the table, which must have served as a desk, there were a few dreary-looking textbooks: *Practical Midwifery*, *Advanced Gynaecology*, etc. Then on the table beside the single iron-frame bed there were a couple more: *A Room in Chelsea Square*, with a marker in it, and below that a pile of magazines – *Men's Health*, *Body Building for Men*, and a French one, *Poses Plastiques*. I picked up the first two and started thumbing through them. They were full of obscenely overdeveloped men showing off their muscles, wearing miniscule posing pouches. Not quite my style. The French one was more subtle and erotic; the men seemed less self-conscious and almost contemptuous of the camera as they lay together in close proximity, naked but with the crucial parts artfully obscured. Here and there an innocuous hand was about to touch a neighbour's thigh. The next move was obvious but left implied. I was transfixed.

David reappeared. 'Oh, I see you've found the art collection,' he said, putting down the mugs of coffee. 'Which of the guys do you like best?'

'Phew! I like the French ones,' I said. 'I've never seen anything like them.'

'Well, you wouldn't,' he said, 'coming from a nice English family. I bet you never imagined such books existed?' He sat down beside me on the bed.

'Well actually, there's a grubby little shop in Wardour Street, near the striptease joints where I saw some on a back shelf,' I replied, trying to sound worldly-wise.

'I've got one or two more to look at when I'm feeling lonely.' He opened the drawer of the bedside table. '*Voilà* the secret library. Some hot guys there, to be sure.'

We flicked through the pages. I gawped at the men doing even more porno things to each other than when I'd photographed Henri last year. I tried to hide my amazement, not to say shock, by making catty remarks about the models.

'Now let's put these schoolboy things away,' he said, taking the last one out of my hands and returning them to the drawer. They'd fulfilled their purpose.

He smiled cheekily as he turned around and reached his hands up to my face to give me a tender and sensuous kiss. My response was much less subtle as I rammed my tongue down his throat and used my left hand to grab at his groin.

'Let's get all this fancy stuff off you,' he said, standing over me while I lay sprawled across the bed. I let him slowly untie my scarf and unbutton my shirt as he put his hand onto my chest. I helped him unbuckle the belt, and pulled the velvet trousers down to my knees. I enjoyed seeing his admiration.

'You *naughty*, *naughty* boy, going around Kensington like that with no underpants on. What were you thinking of? What would your nanny say? Now I've discovered your little secret can I call you Freddie?'

'Yes, *now* you can,' I said. 'It's only for family, but I let my lovers call me that too. But there have only ever been two and a half of them.' I sat up to give him a huge kiss on the mouth.

'I'm very privileged,' he said, quite genuinely and without the slightest hint of sarcasm.

'Now, what are we into?' he asked.

'Pretty well everything. You show me. No holds barred, I hope?' I said, trying to sound as though I knew it all. 'What about you?'

'Whatever comes naturally.'

'Now that sounds *really* nice,' I said with a lewd little smile.

'I think you liked what you saw? You can start from there if you like.'

He let me strip him off, slowly, smiling seductively as I fumbled with his buttons, yanking down his shorts to reveal the cutest pair of briefs. *What* a delicious little bundle he had! He turned over on his knees, splaying himself and allowing me to explore those hidden parts of him, lapping my way in: his little groans were meant for me as much as him. He turned over, raising his legs as he lay back, showing me another entrée.

Reaching across to his bedside cupboard he took out a small brown bottle, unscrewed the top and lifted it to his nose, closing one nostril. After inhaling and holding his breath for five seconds, he passed it to me. As he leaned back on the pillow his mouth was agape and his eyes dilating wildly, spreading himself even more broadly for me.

Wow! The five-second rush left me reeling with the euphoria. Vast reserves of energy came welling up from deep, deep inside my belly, aching for release. I pushed the bottle under his nose, and then mine, for a second, third and fourth huff. His muscles were falling away completely as he urged me on with unspeakable obscenities. My hips were thudding against him, rhythmically and forcefully until I'd filled to overflowing that great, empty, inviting abyss.

*

We lay together side by side, sweaty and still a bit dizzy from too much poppers, hands stroking each other's thighs. It took a moment before the thank-you kisses and happy smiles. I reached for one of my French cigarettes and gave him one.

What happens now? Should we start all over again? If he made the first move I'd be more than happy, although I could feel a slight headache coming on.

'Come on,' I said. 'What about some fresh air and a walk in the park? Have you explored Kensington Gardens yet?' I half hoped that he'd say he had other things to do. On the other hand, I'd have been hurt if he'd gone cold on me so soon.

'No, I've been waiting for a nice guy like you to show me round,' he said, so sweetly and with a wide smile. I was touched. Only later I discovered this wasn't the whole truth.

But a distant alarm bell rang, reminding me to go steady. I'd told myself this was not supposed to be the beginning of anything emotional or any kind of relationship. I had to tread carefully; heaven forbid I find myself in another triangulation.

We walked back to Notting Hill Gate and along Bayswater Road, entering the park opposite the Coburg Hotel. I pointed to the Broadwalk. 'This is where Queen Mary used to be taken for a drive in her last years. No one else was allowed through the park in a car.'

'Spoilt old cow,' he said, 'what right did she have for special treatment?'

'Well, she was the Queen's grandmother, after all,' I replied, somewhat taken aback at his overt republicanism. He'd seemed so proud of working at the hospital where all the royal babies were born.

I told him the story of when I was about one year old and being given an airing in my pram with my then-nanny. As Queen

Mary's great barouche approached, so I was told, it stopped, and a lady-in-waiting rolled down the window, motioning for us to come closer. The Queen looked out of the window, and since I must have been unbelievably adorable, she gave me one of her rare benedictional smiles, saying, 'What a *delightful* little boy.'

'I'm sure she won't be the last old queen to admire you, Master Freddie,' he said, giving me a wink.

Gosh! How I enjoyed these little flatteries of his. Of course he was only teasing but how nice it would be if he was forecasting a lifetime of un-serious amorous adventures? How should I reciprocate a compliment like that?

We walked along the path parallel to Bayswater Road commenting on the immaculately maintained borders just becoming kaleidoscopes of colour and pattern. At Lancaster Gate we wandered onto the Italian Terrace with the fountains splashing and glinting in the sunlight. David pointed out the famous 'cottage' behind Queen Anne's Alcove. It hadn't taken him long to suss it out, he admitted with a knowing smirk. I duly noted this useful titbit for future reference.

He had brought a camera and now asked a Japanese passer-by to take a shot of us both, standing in front of one of the marble urns. Just before he closed the shutter I put my arm over David's shoulder and moved my head against his so that they were almost touching. He reciprocated by giving me a pinch on my bottom making me laugh at the crucial moment.

We wandered slowly towards Peter Pan's statue where there were lots of small children all playing around the bronze hillock with the fairies, rabbits and mice, with Peter standing at the top blowing his pipe.

David was in his element, transfixed at the sight of the children playing so happily. They were crawling about all over it, stroking the animals and trying to climb to the top to sit next to Peter himself. At one point it looked as though a little four-year-old girl had overreached herself and got stuck. David rushed forward to lift her off and presented her back to her mother. The little girl was told to say 'thank you' to the stranger. The sulky little thing looked as though she would have preferred to stay there.

We strolled down the avenue of immense elms towards the Statue of Physical Energy. The majestic trees were looking at their healthiest, their shady canopies creating bright moving mosaics across the pink gravel.

'You really love children, don't you?'

'Oh yes,' he said. 'I've three brothers and three sisters at home, all younger than me. A good Catholic family, to be sure.

'I've helped my mum and dad bring them all up ever since I can remember – bathing them, playing with them, helping them with their homework. My youngest sister, Bernadette, had her fifth birthday last week. I sent her a special London doll for her present. How about you?'

'Just me and my sister who's two years younger than me. My dad is a Catholic, and I suspect my mother, who isn't, put her foot down about having any more after Pippa was born.'

'So you won't know what it's like being part of a big family. I've got sixteen uncles and aunts. Lots of them are in England or America. We all keep in touch. 'Tis lovely.'

'You're so lucky. I've never had to be responsible for any small children or anything else for that matter. Life seems to have been organised for me by other people ever since I was born.' I sighed. 'I'd love to have someone to look after.'

Then I turned to him and said: 'What about you? Wouldn't you like to have kids of your own one day?'

He looked rather sad. 'There doesn't seem to be too much chance of that, does there?'

'Well, why not? Imagine yourself, as a midwife-dad, delivering your own baby!'

'That's how I think every time I see one pop out. It's why I chose to become a midwife. But, Freddie, how would *you* like to be a dad? And what names would you call them?'

'I've never thought about it until now. I think I'd call the boy James, quite a masculine sort of name without being too alpha, and the girl Lavinia after my grandmother – such a pretty name. But then, there's the question of *how*!' I added, giving a sad little smile, remembering yesterday's test of endurance.

'No, Freddie, don't get too carried away. You're a Queer, like all of us. When you're old and rich you can always be "the bachelor uncle", taking your nephews and nieces to Paris for the first time, or the ballet, and paying their school fees!' He laughed, as I imagined myself shepherding a brightly scrubbed pair to a ballet matinée at Covent Garden.

We continued towards the Albert Memorial.

'Wow!' said David. 'What a wonderful building – but is it a *building*, or *what*?' I told him the story of how it came to be built, the climax of an 'Albertopolis' stretching all the way to South Kensington. I told him that the prince had been originally covered entirely in gold leaf.

'How flattering!' he said, eyeing up the dishy prince. 'Looks like he deserved it. Come on, let's take some more photos.'

We posed under the big groups at each corner. The figures were too high up to be within reach, but I made David stand under Africa giving a lascivious grin at the half-naked Black slave boy with sexy bangles round his arms and ankles. It was all so carefree and relaxed, our behaving completely irresponsibly like boys – perhaps, as I reflected later, my natural default. Would I ever feel as *liberated* as this with Paul? The words of our poem flashed in front of me:

Cities wrenching, ease scorning, statutes mocking,
feebleness chasing...

The thought of Paul made me feel guilty. It was he who should be with me, here, right now; David was a mirage, a substitute.

'Look, I'm afraid it's getting late,' I said. 'I need to get home as we've got my great-aunt coming to dinner and I'll need to change before anyone sees me like this. Let's head towards the Palace and cut into Church Street.'

He became rather quiet as we walked along the Flower Walk. There were children running along beside us.

'So what are we going to do now, Freddie?'

'David, you know I really can't ask you into the house. How on earth would I explain you?' *Oh God, I've put this so badly.*

'So now you're just going to dump me, are you? Having had your wicked way with me, I'm to be thrown to one side and forgotten?' He sounded genuinely hurt.

'Oh, David, no! No! I'm so sorry, that's not at all how I want you to feel. I didn't know I'd be meeting such a great guy today.' How I hated to think I might be wounding him.

'I know, Freddie, it's not much good. You're just eighteen and only just starting in life. I'm twenty-two and going my own way in the world. You've been a lovely mate, despite dumping me like this and being so posho.' He sounded resigned. 'It's best we don't meet again when there's so much against us. Let's try and remember this lovely afternoon and what a great time we had.'

I wanted to take him, hold him and comfort him there and then, but he carried on walking straight ahead. I wondered how many times this same scenario had been played out with him before: a one-night stand followed by a disappointing goodbye. Had he been searching for love when he'd seen me? Or was it all just a big game, cruising for vulnerable young guys like me, then manipulating them into feeling guilty? I needed to learn things fast.

We crossed the Palace forecourt, and went through the passageway into Church Street.

'You could get a 27 bus here and it'll take you up to the Villas direct.'

'But I want to stay with you 'til we reach your home.'

'Alright, of course, that'd be lovely.' Yet a ghastly thought occurred to me: what if he made a scene on the doorstep, just as we were trying to part? *No, I'm sure I can trust him.*

As we rounded the corner I said, 'Well, here's where I live – and that's my bedroom.' I pointed up to the window on the second floor. 'Think of me there on my own tonight.'

'And you think of me in that pokey little room in the hostel,' he replied.

'Oh, I can't bear it. Let me give you a hug.' I glanced round, and no one was in sight, so we embraced and I gave him a kiss on the lips, then dashed up the steps to let myself in without looking around.

A minute later and alone in my room, I parted the nets and just caught sight of him walking slowly back towards Church Street. Oh God, I felt so sad that I was letting go of someone for whom I'd begun to feel a real affection and with whom I had shared so much. I recognised it as the same feeling I had had when parting from Henri so inevitably last summer. Once again, inadvertently, I had allowed myself to fall for this fellow to whom I had given myself so eagerly. Was this going to happen every time I went out to find satisfaction? And did this count as 'infidelity', or worse, being 'disloyal' to Paul? I tried to persuade myself that David didn't mean much to me. But he *did*; I couldn't evade my feelings.

A few days later, just as we were about to set out for the cottage, an envelope came through the letterbox. It was just addressed to 'Freddie'. Pippa took it down to the nursery.

'What's this?' she said. 'And who addresses you just as "Freddie"?'

I opened the envelope and there were three photos: David and me together at the Italian Terrace, and the ones showing us separately at the Albert Memorial. On the back of each he'd written '*F & D July 1968*', and underneath a big X enclosed in a circle.

'Let's have a look,' said Pippa, almost grabbing them from my hand. Before I could get them back, she'd turned the first one over and seen the message:

'"F & D"?' she said. 'I know who F is, but *who's* D? Anyway, he looks rather a nice little fellow whoever he is or was.'

'He's a *very* nice little fellow, as you call him, just a new friend I made a few days ago, that's all.'

'Is he as nice as Paul? Would *he* approve of your making strange new friends?' She was mocking, and being cruel, but only playfully, or so I hoped.

'Don't you dare say a single thing about this to anyone or I'll rat on you next time I catch you out with Robert.'

*

Why did I seem to fall in love so easily? Was this going to be my Achilles heel and my undoing for the rest of my life? Was there room in my heart for more than one lover at a time?

Why do these things come to test us?

Fondest love,

Freddie

19

My dear Sam,

You may ask whether the famous riots, the *événements* of spring '68, had produced any obvious changes in France since the last time I'd been there. The answer is no! At least not to my innocent eyes. Nothing across the Channel ever seemed to change very much. At the Singletons' farmhouse near Grasse everything seemed timeless – suspicions of lavender wafting through the air and the cicadas croaking their throats out. Some schoolfriends of your mother's were there too, and we spent our time swanning about the pool, playing tennis in the cool of the evenings, and being ferried around to lunches and evening parties. It sounds idyllic, but despite my best efforts I'm afraid my heart wasn't in it.

After a couple of days we were interrupted by a couple of unbearably cool boys from Appleford. They showed up, uninvited, in a beaten-up old VW and immediately started flirting with the girls and directing events. The tables were turned somewhat when Miranda appeared soon afterwards, more buxom than ever, and the two of us soon outpaced the Applefordians. One afternoon, while the others were at the *Festival du Jasmin*, we lay beside the pool, slightly tipsy, and I told her *everything*. She'd guessed already, of course, and thought it was all wonderful. I felt good having a confidante of the opposite sex. But where was she when I needed her later on?

My results arrived. I had achieved only two As and a B, instead of the three straight As that Cambridge wanted. But somehow I couldn't quite believe they'd turn me down. My father, back at home, did some fancy footwork and, after a couple of days' suspense, all was well; I was given a place at Powis, his old college, to read Law and to start in October. Family honour had been saved, albeit by a whisker.

*

I had failed my driving test a second time, so my plans to impress Paul with the mini had to be abandoned. Somewhat humiliatingly, I had to take the bus into Chichester to meet him off the five o'clock Sunday train. The rest of the family, except Nanny and Foo-Foo, had departed for Switzerland that morning. I detected a general sense of tiredness, almost *tristesse*, in the air, as though nature was telling the rest of the world that it was time to go home. The next few days belonged to me and Paul.

Sitting on the top of the empty double decker, I felt lightheaded with an unfamiliar sense of liberation. *At last* I was free – free to share the cottage with Paul, just the two of us. Welling up inside me was that old urge, to give, give and keep on giving to Paul – everything, crazily, extravagantly, lavishly. And conversely to take, take and take from him, greedily, rapaciously, anything and everything he wanted to give me. I daydreamed that these next few days would become forever locked in our memories, to be remembered in years to come as a golden moment, suspended eternally in time, neither of us ever changing or growing old. I was beginning to understand what I'd heard: that you discover things when you're eighteen that you'll never find again. I wanted to keep them now and hold them forever.

Until today, I realised, I had been no more than a guest in my own home, and in truth had only ever behaved like one. Not that I felt at all resentful – far from it. I knew my parents loved me unconditionally, as I did them, even if they didn't fully understand me and hoped I would grow into their own image and likeness. But one day I would make a home of my own, just like the cottage over these next few days, to share it with the person I loved. It would be recognisable, even familiar, to be sure, with echoes of all I'd inherited, but it would be different. Neither better nor worse, but different.

For now at least we should be able to enjoy the warmth of the late summer and the freshness of the sea while out sailing each day. Later there would be tennis or croquet, and after supper we could join the others at their houses or on the beach. At night and early in the mornings we'd make love just as our instincts took us. And then we'd curl up together in my narrow single bed, falling asleep in each other's arms.

At the last minute I had to think on my feet when Nanny announced, 'I thought I'd put Paul in Pippa's room. There'd be more space for him and his things in there.'

Suppressing a surge of panic, I said as coolly as I could manage, 'Oh, Nan. Paul won't be bringing much. He'll be fine in my room in the twin bed.'

I waited at the barrier, straining to see him as his train emptied. There he was; my heart leapt as I saw him among the crowd. My God, how I loved that boy – still my Renaissance prince, even more handsome than ever, taller, more graceful, his face thinner, his hair thicker, his forehead wide and noble. As he waved and walked towards me, his face lit up, his beauty eclipsing everything and everyone else around him. I raised my arm in greeting, taking his bag, looking into his face, my body quivering with delight and expectation.

'Welcome to Sussex-sur-mer,' I said loudly and cheerfully,

and then, more quietly, as I stretched out to hold his forearm, 'My goodness, it's so good to see you, Paul.'

'Just the two of us now, Freddie, and for the next ten days! How great is that!' He was laughing, briefly putting his arm over my shoulder.

'My feelings exactly. Except that I've got to share you with Nanny, and Foo-Foo, and you know she's got a secret crush on you. So, don't you go breaking her heart!'

Or mine either, I thought. On that subject I asked him how he'd got on with his fellow actors at the summer school.

'Oh, there were some *rather nice* fellows there,' he said, playfully, trying to wind me up. I felt a moment of fury, entirely dissipated by his next remark, delivered with a sarcastic smirk. 'None, of course, as nice as my best friend Freddie.' He gave me a jab in the ribs; what a little flirt he'd become!

We took the bus back to the cottage, walking the short distance down the empty lane from the main road, the two of us linking our little fingers. I was thinking how beautiful to be able to do this here so openly when from behind there came a discreet toot making us jump and disconnect. A huge Rolls-Royce had crept up on us silently. I recognised it as belonging to Keith Richards, of the Rolling Stones, who owned the ancient moated manor house at the end of the lane. The limo pulled up beside us. At the open window on the passenger side was the smiling face of Anita Pallenberg. She gave us a little wave and leaned out, saying in a thick German accent, not without its attraction,

'Hi, Freddie. Who's your dishy friend?'

I was lost in confusion, but managed to say, 'Oh, hi! This is Paul who's staying while my parents are away... Paul, this is Anita... and Keith... our neighbours.'

Keith Richards, at the wheel, looked inscrutable and waved before putting his foot on the accelerator. Anita just managed to blow a kiss, shouting,

'Have a great time together, boys!' They cruised on silently down the lane.

'Blimey, Freddie, you never told me we'd be living next to one of the Stones. Do you think they saw us holding hands?'

'I'm sure they did, lover boy. But don't worry, they're hardly going to report us to the fuzz. They're not the only unconventional ones round here.' The previous year, of course, their house had been raided and they'd been hauled up in court for possessing drugs. It had been an international *cause célèbre*. Since then they'd built a high wall around the estate.

Paul greeted Nanny with a big hug and kiss on the cheek, making her blush and fluster. I led the way up to our room, trembling but utterly confident in anticipation. With the door closed behind us, he leapt at me like a wild thing as I lifted him off the floor holding him close against me, my hands under his thighs, mouths locked together, tongues desperately finding the other's. A moment later, as I tried to put him down, we both tumbled onto the bed, laughing, now kissing more gently, hugging, clasping, caressing. I don't know how long we were like that; it seemed an eternity. All prohibitions had expired. We were full-scale lovers now, free to do anything and everything we wanted.

'Come on,' I said, sitting on the edge of my bed. 'I want to see you change into a pair of sexy shorts.'

I watched with unblinking voyeurism as he took off his trousers revealing his snow-white briefs contrasting, as always, so beautifully with his golden skin and the curves of his thighs. It was too much.

'Cum 'ere,' I said, in the commonest and most lustful way I could summon.

He stood in front of me as I sat on the edge of the bed. I was thrilled as my admiring touch made him hard. But knew enough to stop it there.

'I'm going to get all *that* out of you later, you hot bastard,' I said. 'You'd better save it up for me.'

'I've been saving it up for weeks, Freddie boy, just for you. So be prepared. I hope *you* have too.'

After I'd shown him round the house and the garden as far as the tennis court, we found the spare bike I'd dusted down for him. Setting off along the back lane we passed the village green, the little row of shops and the church. Beyond that we took the private road leading to the houses giving directly onto the beach, ignoring the 'Residents Only' sign.

'*No law less than ourselves owning,*' I shouted to him as we dashed past. He tinkled the little bell on the handlebar in response.

Reaching the wide greensward immediately in front of the long sandy beach we stopped to take it all in, our bums raised up off the saddles. Ahead of us, the wide embracing sea reached out to the horizon where it met the huge late-afternoon sky. It was interrupted in the middle distance by the great bulk of the Isle of Wight, an immense and dark Leviathan emerging from the deep. A couple of liners or container ships were making their way dimly up the Solent. Closer to, a few sailing boats were flying downwind through the water.

The tide was some way out, leaving behind big shallow pools. Their stillness was disturbed by dogs splashing and shaking themselves, their owners silhouetted against the dark foreshore. The sea was looking nervous, with a half-hidden rhythmic swell suggesting it could erupt into a bad temper at a moment's notice. It was constantly changing in colour, depth and density from deepest blue, to palest green, then to grey. Fast-moving sunbeams, like searchlights, kept breaking through from behind the clouds, their rays sweeping unpredictably across the water as though trying to find something elusive but then giving up and switching off. The surge of the waves, foaming with spray as they hit the shoreline, was slow and almost hypnotic – *whiiiish, whaaaash* – all the more audible as it was carried along on the breeze. We inhaled the ozone, invigorating our bodies with its salty freshness.

To the left of us the beach stretched eastwards in a wide curve as far as the horizon, backed by small dunes and spiky tamarisks. The sands were broken up at right angles by the long timber breakwaters. To our right the beach continued barely a short distance to the end of the headland.

I thought I'd better exercise my role as host and factotum.

'Let's ride along the greensward towards East Head where the harbour joins the sea. There are some brilliant views from there looking inland towards the Downs. You can see all the little creeks and islands that we'll be exploring this week with the sailing school.'

We cycled along the smooth grass verge, passing the houses set back behind their gardens. They were a strange architectural mixture: either quaint but quite large Arts and Crafts part-time family houses, all tile-hung and half-timbered – one of them belonging to my uncle and aunt, the Scarisbricks – or ultra-modern cubic blocks with vast and unsuitable extensions and picture windows. And some utterly hideous pre-war bungalows, which ought to be demolished.

'Hey, it's really beautiful here,' said Paul, as we reached the end, and he paused to survey the whole 360-degree vista. The views to the north took in the spire of Chichester Cathedral, and beyond it the line of the South Downs behind Goodwood. Beside us, at the entrance to the natural harbour, lay the Solent and the Isle of Wight looming beyond, varying in visibility and density every few minutes.

'What a fabulous place your parents found here, Freddie. We don't have anything like this in Yorkshire.'

I told him I was looking forward to the day when he could show me the Dales, the Moors, the ruined abbeys, the country

houses, not to mention all the people '*nowt so Queer as folk*'. I
ended with a leery smirk. He poked me in the ribs,

'I'm not sure I'm going to share you with *that* lot.'

Nanny had made us a supper of shepherd's pie followed by
fruit salad and ice cream, and we all three sat together in the
kitchen. Paul was in his element answering Nanny's questions
about his sister with little dashes of humour – where she was at
school and if she had any boyfriends yet. I produced a couple of
bottles of beer for us. Nanny, famously, 'didn't drink'.

'You boys have to be up early tomorrow. I promised your
mother, Freddie, that I'd have you out of the house by nine
o'clock as the school starts at half past. I'll have bacon and eggs
on the table for you, and sandwiches for your packed lunches.
Shall I wake you in the morning?'

'Oh, no, Nan, don't bother, we'll make sure we're ready in
time.' Paul and I looked across at each other suppressing our
smiles and happy memories of Nanny nearly catching us *in
flagrante* back in April.

After supper we all did the washing-up together and then
the three of us sat on the wide sofa in the sitting room to watch
Nanny's favourite weekly TV programme, *Sunday Night at the
London Palladium*. I had been growing tired of its charms but of
course we humoured her and pretended to enjoy the crooners
and entertainers while she got on with knitting my Christmas
pullover.

After she'd said goodnight I opened another bottle of beer
each and we moved up close to each other, making ourselves
comfortable as he lay against me, watching TV, then slowly
touching and kissing. We had a lot of catching-up to do after
weeks of abstinence. It soon became obvious we'd better get to
the bedroom fast. This time we were prepared.

That night we consummated. I wanted to stay inside him
forever.

*

The sailing school was based in the neighbouring village, just twenty minutes' bike ride away. Our time was spent in the Firefly dinghies in the care of instructors, mainly university students making a bit of pocket money – handsome and healthy boys with bleached hair and bodies glowing from weeks' exposure to the sun and sea.

I still recall those few days as a dream of ethereal images: the joy of being with him in this new setting, seeing his face and hair in the sun and wind, the splash of water on his legs, the elegant turn of his instep in his sailing shoes, the way his arm muscles stretched and then relaxed as he tugged on the sheets as we went about; and then his anxious concentrated look while he was at the tiller, balancing the boat against the force and direction of the wind.

There were about fifteen other boys and girls with us on the week's course, three in each boat with an instructor. Thus Paul and I had another student with us each day. One I remember was a sweet young girl called Diana, very quiet and nervous, but we soon made her feel she was part of our little team. Our destinations varied; East Head with its sand dunes was our favourite, where we could moor at lunchtime and bathe in the sea, still deliciously warm. Alternatively, there was Bosham, Birdham or Dell Quay. There was plenty of variety, and we were lucky that the weather, the tides and the wind always seemed in perfect alignment.

At the end of each day our exertions had made us quite tired, but after cycling back to the cottage, a shower (only once together, memorably, while Nanny was out), and some tea and cake, our strength revived and we would always have a set or two of tennis. He usually won, but I was never far behind. After supper we'd cycle down to the beach to join some of the other students and instructors, getting mildly sozzled on beer and cider, exchanging stories and gossip with our confrères. After the second or third time someone brought out a guitar and I couldn't resist announcing that Paul was a dab hand with it. In his typically modest way he gave us a few samples from his repertoire, including – especially for me as he said later – 'Can't Take My Eyes Off You'. I gazed across at him, our eyes meeting in the gloaming.

One night when there was a full moon we stayed late on the beach after the others had gone. Since the tide was high we threw off all our clothes for a midnight swim, splashing and chasing each other in the water, me diving beneath the surface to grab his legs in an underwater rugby tackle, he trying to catch me as I sped out to sea in my powerful American crawl. Then we embraced lustily standing in the water, our mouths locked together, groping and stroking each other, our lips and saliva tasting of salt. I got out of the water first, grabbing my towel to dry myself. Just as he was approaching, I took hold of his and started running along the deserted beach, waving it in the air, forcing him to run after me, stark naked. I let him catch me up and rugger tackle me onto the sand. But I still held on to the towel so he was forced to lie on top of me to extract it from me, laughing and cursing all the time.

'*On the turf or sea beach dancing...*' I reminded him as we rode our bikes home in the moonlight.

Best of all was falling asleep in each other's arms in my narrow single bed after making love, our bodies locked together as one. Sometimes we'd use the floor for our love-making, pulling out the other mattress covering it with a rug, the McNaughton tartan no less; it soon began to smell deliciously of our sex. I'd be taking it with me to Cambridge to throw over my bed in my lonely digs. Always, always without fail, we made love face to face, consuming each other with our eyes. Any other way would be unthinkable. I swore to myself I would never do this with anyone else unless I truly loved them.

I discovered his great weakness. He absolutely loved to hear little sexy endearments whispered in his ear, sometimes in French or Italian, as we kissed lying naked. Or I'd invent new nicknames for him, affectionate or obscene depending on our mood. The result was always the same: he'd curl up and then stretch his whole body in sheer pleasure; and the next thing he'd be on top of me. He'd sometimes play the whore for me: lying on his tummy on the bed, his head turned and looking at me sideways, legs erotically splayed out, his bum moving up and down irresistibly. I'd stand over and finger him as he made tarty suggestions in a whiny little Cockney voice, pretending to be a delinquent rent boy; it made me randy as hell.

We'd wake several times in the night because of our closeness, and there would be more kissing, cuddling, playing and loving. We explored every possible way of giving ourselves completely to each other, utterly confident, gentle, loving, sometimes a little playfully rough. Our oneness had transformed us; we had become fused together, neither of us just ourselves alone. Were we the only two boys in the whole universe who had found such intensity, reaching out into infinity, alive in each other's body and soul?

*

One afternoon, I think it was on the Thursday, I was with Nanny in the kitchen washing up after our tea and cake while Paul was fetching the tennis rackets and winding up the net.

As she was putting the things away she looked me straight in the face.

'Freddie, you know, I've never seen you looking so *well*, or so *happy*, in all the years I've been with you.'

I gave her a kiss on the cheek, and quietly whispered in her ear and with a big smile on my face, 'Oh, Nan, I think you know why, don't you?'

She smiled back, but just a little wistfully, with a tiny hint of sadness in her eyes.

'Yes, I think he's the nicest of all your friends I've ever met. I just hope it all ends up alright for you both, that's all.'

*

Paul was staying until the Tuesday when my parents were expected back, so we still had a few more days after the sailing school had officially finished. It was wonderful lying in bed together postcoitally all Saturday morning, then spending the rest of the day in the garden, sunbathing, reading and idly chatting. At Paul's suggestion we took Nanny to the pictures in Chichester as a thank you, and, as we hoped, to secure her future discretion. The choice was between *The Killing of Sister George* ('Ooh! Not those horrid lezzies, thank you very much') or *Oliver!*. It was a foregone conclusion. She loved it, especially having a chance to put on some slap, nick some of my mother's perfume, and being escorted by two tall handsome boys.

We'd been invited to lunch on Sunday after Mass with the Scarisbricks whose house was on the beach near where we'd had our midnight swim. You'll remember, Sam, that your great-aunt Mary was the portrait painter who did our family group. David, my mother's brother, was a solicitor with fingers in lots of suspicious pies as my father put it. We'd heard that James, the eldest of their two sons would be there. Rod, the youngest – the one whom Paul had played opposite in *Antony and Cleopatra* and *Twelfth Night* – was away on an exchange. James had left Upton last year and was reading History of Art at Oxford. I'd heard he'd been spending part of the summer as a volunteer with the National Trust at Parkworth. I had an inspiration.

'Why don't we get James Scarisbrick to take us round Parkworth on Monday? We could go over by bus and have lunch there.'

'Great idea. I've heard it's packed with good things.'

I assumed that Paul would accompany me to the little Catholic church in the village before we went on to lunch on our bikes. But I thought I'd better check.

'You've no problems with going to Mass then, Paul?'

'No. Why ever should I, *or we*, Freddie?' He was almost frowning. 'We love each other, don't we, if that's what you're worried about, and that can't be a sin, for goodness' sake.'

'Yes, of course. You're dead right,' I replied. 'It's just that I used to have qualms about it, but I'm over all that now.' I paused. 'I still feel bad I haven't been to Confession for a long time, though.'

'Why do you need to go to Confession?' He looked surprised, and then added, 'Unless it's for nicking my towel the other night and making me run starkers all over the beach. C'mon, Freddie. "Jesus had his St John", as someone once said – and I've got *my* Freddie and you've got *your* Paul.'

And with that he cast off his bike. For my part, I really couldn't bring myself to go up to Communion as I was still unshriven since my encounter with David. I wondered which was the worse 'sin': the sex, my infidelity, or dumping David so heartlessly?

Lunch *chez* Scarisbrick was a buffet laid out on the terrace of their walled garden, bounded by a moongate giving onto the greensward and the beach beyond. It was quite a big gathering and evidently the Pimm's had been flowing generously even before we'd arrived. James was there in his stripy OU blazer; it was just as well I wasn't wearing mine. I'd come in my white linen suit *style St Loup*, Paul in a less conspicuous seersucker jacket. I'd noticed how James had acquired a new air of urbane nonchalance since he'd gone up to Oxford and wondered if it was a passing affectation or a sign of genuine maturity.

He greeted us with a weak smile and poured us drinks. He clearly knew the score; I'm sure I detected a whiff of jealousy as he looked me up and down, and then Paul. I enjoyed a moment of wicked *schadenfreude*, knowing he'd obviously *love* to have a boyfriend as handsome as Paul at his side. It was a pity for him; I liked James, and if he could bring out his latent and mildly camp sense of humour a bit more often, peppered with touches of irony, he'd be quite a catch. Pips had once said to him, flirtingly,

'Drop a hairpin, darling. You never know your luck...'

As it was, I took great pride introducing Paul to my uncle and aunt, and then to my cousins and their friends. I didn't need to feel possessive. Here we were, 'great friends', as we used to say, in a party with no questions asked, nothing threatening, nothing judgmental.

James's younger sister was there with a couple of her schoolfriends who were staying nearby and with whom we exchanged friendly banter. But after a while I felt the pull from a gaze somewhere beyond the terrace. In the middle of the garden there was a large ornamental pond in the centre of which was a fountain in the guise of a bathing beauty of the 1920s, water gushing miraculously from a shell in her hands. Sounds a bit kitsch, I agree, but it was just about tasteful. I looked across and saw a couple of older gents sitting on the low parapet, both quite distinguished-looking and slightly overdressed. The taller and slimmer, perhaps younger, was wearing a nautical cap with some sort of insignia, the other a panama.

James evidently saw that our conversation with the girls was flagging and intervened. 'Let me introduce you both to Peter and George over there. They're staying with us tonight before going to their house in France tomorrow,' he said, steering us in their direction.

We stood in front of them as we were introduced. I could see in their eyes that same over-long suggestive look that I'd noticed on the older men in the pub near Bournemouth with Pips. It expressed a certain eagerness, mixed with envy, inviting us to reply with a certain complicity. Or we could answer with a look of total indifference, or even contempt. For a split second I wavered, but then chose complicity and smiled back; why should I not enjoy the admiration of these old boys? At the very least they'd be interesting and might be fun to play along with. Paul glanced at me and followed my lead. He was beginning to know the score.

We seated ourselves one of us each side of them, Paul next to the panama and me next to the cap. It transpired that one of them was an antique dealer with a showroom (not a 'shop', heaven forbid) in Mount Street, the other an academic, now on a sabbatical writing a book on Tiepolo. The panama was James's godfather and an old family friend; the cap had been in the navy with my uncle during the war. For me they were no enigma; I realised I'd never again have any difficulty identifying another 'Friend of Dorothy'. Even so, I felt they deserved a certain deference and neither Paul nor I quite liked to probe too deeply about how they'd come to share a house in France.

But conversely, and perhaps under the influence of the Pimm's, they were being just a little *too* enquiring in their questions to us. I noticed a few smiles exchanged between them as I explained we'd been at the cottage together for the past week, and been for a midnight swim 'in the altogether' a few nights before, very close to where we were now sitting.

'Oh, for the lost innocence of youth!' cried the panama with fake-queenie histrionics.

'I'm not so sure about the lost innocence,' I said under my breath, but audible enough, 'actually it was a lot of fun.' The Pimm's was definitely taking over.

'Well, if you boys want any more midnight swims you can always come and stay at our little place just over the Channel,' he said. 'It's only twenty minutes from Cabourg and we've got a big *floodlit* swimming pool. The "altogether" might be less invisible but not unwelcome!' He looked me up and down.

All four of us were enjoying this increasingly louche repartee when James came over.

'What's all this about your "little place across the Channel"?' he said as he joined us. 'It's not "little" *at all*. Don't you believe it, Fred and Paul, it's a *huge* seventeenth-century château with twenty-six bedrooms, stuffed with works of art that haven't yet made it to Mount Street.'

The panama made to reply in mock deprecation. 'Well, it *has* to be quite big. You know how we like to have lots of young people to stay all the year round. You've been, James, with your friends. Anyway, you two fellows are very welcome anytime. Come for as long as you like. Even better if you can play a hand at bridge.' I duly made a note of this essential social skill with which my parents had lamentably failed to equip me.

I asked James if he could show us round Parkworth next day.

'Monday's actually my day off and the house is closed to visitors, but otherwise it's not inconvenient at all,' he laughed sarkily, but then added, 'No, of course I'd be happy to show you both round. I'll call for you at half past nine in my old banger, shall I?'

At the end of our bibulous lunch there was a consensus that a swim in the sea was required if only to sober us up. There was a half-timbered cabin used for changing and then we all dashed across the beach and plunged into the water. The older members, including the two elderly gents, walked to the edge to cheer us on, and then sat with us on the reclining seats on the greensward, Paul and me in our Speedos. I rather enjoyed their watching Paul apply the Ambre Solaire to my back – yes, that stuff again – starting with my shoulders and working his way down to my thighs, my calves and my feet.

*

If I'd felt any ambivalence towards James it vanished completely next day as he took us through the great house, now empty of visitors. He was the perfect guide, pointing out all the masterpieces with small anecdotes, prompting a discussion rather than a lecture. We took in the van Dycks, the Titians, the Claudes, the Turners, the Grinling Gibbons and the extraordinary collection of ancient and modern sculptures. Paul loved the views from the windows over the Capability Brown parkland; 'We are mocked with art,' he said, quoting one of his lines from *The Winter's Tale.* James was obviously enjoying himself, not least when he held out on the obscure iconography of La Guerre's vast mural *The Apotheosis of the Duchess of Somerset.*

I was in raptures at the White and Gold Room. With its carved boiseries, eighteenth-century furniture and portraits, it reminded me of the châteaux I'd got to know so well last year. But my eyes were drawn to the towering gilt mirrors between the windows. Their carved frames consisted of a series of elongated interconnected S-shaped curves, interspersed with deeply carved luxuriant C-scrolls, all overlaid by cascading leaves and flowers. An ultra-realistic basket of fruit, including a split watermelon, peaches, plums and a couple of aubergines, was within reach in the centre of the frame at the bottom. I was sorely tempted to stretch out my hand to stroke them, but was restrained by James. At the top, on each side of a sort of pagoda, there were two dragons with outstretched wings flapping wildly and squawking furiously at each other, clearly with lustful intentions.

'I wonder what them two dragons are up to?' I asked, with a pretended innocence, not very successfully. 'What are those funny stiff things projecting from their underbellies? Are they about to give each other a good time?'

'Typical of you to notice that, McNaughton, you perve,' my cousin's nonchalance disintegrating rapidly as he defaulted to surnames. 'Instead, you should be admiring the Serpentine Line, all those scrolls and curves – the Line of Beauty as Hogarth called it – "*which leads the eye a wanton chase*". I can see it's leading *your* eye astray alright, McNaughton. Actually, we always thought the frames were made by Chippendale, but the other day I discovered in the archives that they're by one of his rivals.' Slightly typical of James, I thought, to make a boring, self-enhancing claim using the first person singular.

The frames may or may not have been by Chippendale, but I was in awe at the way they invited one to go on and on *looking*, keeping the eye in continuous movement with its sensuous lines and suggestive eroticism. In a split second I recognised it *exactly*: those elongated, elegant, concave and convex curves, the voluptuous scrolls – my God, it was Paul's *derrière* all over again – or was it David's or Henri's? – inviting me to stroke, fondle and make love to.

*

We took James to the Egremont Arms for a late lunch. He deserved it.

'Come on then, tell us what it's like at Oxford. What have you been doing with yourself?'

'Oh, it's been alright.' He sounded not entirely enthusiastic.

'It took quite a bit of getting used to, not being in the Upton bubble anymore, now surrounded by people from different backgrounds. None of the tutors are anything like as eccentric as the monks at Upton. There's no equivalent to Rappy, or Gussy or Whiskers. No, I haven't joined the Bullingdon, if that's what you're wondering – much too rowdy. And I strongly suggest you don't join the Pitt Club at Cambridge, Fred, at least not until your third year. They're such a waste of time and money.

'The best thing, though, is the four-month Long Vacation. I went on a road trip for two months with Charlie Hardcastle, a sort of Grand Tour, before coming here as a volunteer. We did Spain, Portugal and Italy in that old banger of mine – going everywhere and seeing everything from Mafra to Lecce. We'll be doing *Mitteleuropa* next summer.'

I looked across at Paul. Visions of unending togetherness in exotic and beautiful places flooded my imagination: weeks and weeks of great art, great sex, sunshine, heat, red wine and poetry… It was intoxicating just to think about it.

'Come on, what about it, Paul – next summer? Just taking off and going from one amazing place to another?'

'Like the guys in our poem? "*Up and down the roads going, North and South excursions making*", he replied, his eyes wide with pleasure and expectation. 'Maybe we'll get to do some of those other things too – "*Cities wrenching, ease scorning, statutes mocking, feebleness chasing*". It's a great idea, Freddie, you're always such a dreamer. Let's just do it.' He gave me one of his mock punches.

James had no idea what we were talking about. He brought us back to earth.

'Better get your driving test first, McNaughton, and a car, or you won't be going anywhere. And I strongly recommend you call in at Peter and George's in Normandy for a few days at least. They'll give you a very good time, give you introductions to all kinds of interesting people and tell you where to go. You could learn a thing or two from them, especially you, Fred.'

I must have looked squeamish at the idea, so James laughed.

'Don't worry, they won't pounce. They're a pair of dear old queens, been together for thirty years and rather enjoy being discreetly closeted. They like their guests to be elegant, well-spoken young men, like you two. But when they get down to it they're much more interested if you can make up a foursome.

'For bridge, that is,' he added hurriedly, trying hard not to laugh.

He paused. 'Anyway, this afternoon if you fellows want to go for a walk round the lake, I can do with spending a couple of hours in the archives. Shall we meet back at the car at half past four?'

Paul and I let ourselves into the park from a gate near the church. It was like entering another enchanted world. Within minutes of taking a winding path through a small wood, the view opened up and we found ourselves overlooking sweeping lawns interspersed with small clumps of trees, and here and there a magnificent solitary chestnut. In front of us was the Upper Lake, an irregular sheet of water, enlivened with little sparkling wavelets as the breeze disturbed its inky darkness. We climbed a short hillock where there was an open circular temple and looked across the lake with the house to the side and the range of the South Downs in the background.

As we stood there admiring the beauty of it all, an unexpected breeze brought a slight chill to the air, and an unfriendly touch of autumn took hold as the sun disappeared behind a cloud. A few dry and tarnished leaves fluttered to the ground to lie at our feet before blowing away. All the colour in the landscape was being sucked out.

'Oh goodness, Paul, suddenly it's autumn. I can just *feel* the melancholy coming on.'

'Yes,' he said, 'I can feel it too. Remember last year when we went to The Rock and I recited Keats to you? Somehow it didn't seem quite so bad then, did it? Maybe because we were still finding out about each other and had everything to look forward to. Now it seems different. You got edgy when I recited a few lines from *Autumn*. But *Melancholy* is even worse,' he smiled wanly.

> *'She dwells with Beauty – Beauty that must die;*
> *And Joy, whose hand is ever at his lips*
> *Bidding adieu; and aching Pleasure nigh,*
> *Turning to poison...'*

'Oh, no, Paul. *Stop!* That's enough! Don't say any more. Don't let's even think about what's going to happen after tomorrow.'

'But, Freddie, you mustn't think like that. Autumn's a lovely time. Think of buttered crumpets for tea, crackling log fires, and looking forward to Christmas.'

'Yes, there's all that, I grant you. But that's not really the point. I'm going to be starting all over again in a few weeks at Cambridge. I'll tell you now, I'm very anxious about it. Worst of all is being apart from *you*, lover boy.'

'Hey! Don't be like that. We're going to be seeing each other. You'll be coming over to Upton after a few weeks and you've promised to trek up north before Christmas. And with luck I'll be at Trinity next year.'

'Yeah, that's what I'm hanging on to. But also I'm really anxious that I've been pressured into reading Law. I've no idea if I'll be any good at it. Nor being in a completely new place again, with a bunch of people I might have nothing in common with.'

'Go on with you. You should be brimming over with confidence. You told me Whiskers had written on your last report, "We expect great things from him", and so do I, Freddie.'

'But you know, I've a terrible feeling I may have peaked too early, as they say. Being made Head of House and getting the Essay Prize might be the best I'll ever do in life.'

'That's nonsense. Sure, you acquitted yourself brilliantly, but that's only the beginning for you – for us. I was so happy for you getting the prize – knowing that you belonged to *me* and no one else when you gave your speech in front of all those people.'

'I felt exactly the same when you were performing as Leontes. Everyone in the audience must have felt they knew you through and through, but none of them – except me – could have understood how you had *become* that part.'

We tried to block out any more melancholic feelings for our last night together. It was the most loving of all, full of attentive playfulness with each other, and then overwhelming passion. There wasn't a single millimetre of each other's bodies that we hadn't caressed or made love to. We both knew all the little places where little spasms of delight and pleasure could be given and received. More than ever, I felt I was emptying myself entirely to him, my very lifeblood entering his. Never had we felt so completely to be just one body, locked together, giving life to each other. This surely was our destiny now being fulfilled, loving each other like this for eternity, two boys together lighting up the great vault of heaven like Castor and Pollux. We needed each other for our very existence; if we ever separated, we would vanish into the great black hole of uncreation.

*

Early next morning the weather broke. After breakfast we had to pack up as my parents were returning direct to London and I probably wouldn't be coming to the cottage again until next spring. There was a lot of baggage so the three of us, plus Foo-Foo in his cage, piled into a taxi and boarded the train at Chichester.

The journey was beastly, lashing rain outside, cold and draughty inside. Paul and I sat opposite each other: he with one of next year's set books, *The Portrait of a Lady*, me with *Learning the Law*. My God, how tedious that was. From time to time we looked up over the tops of our books, exchanging delicious eye contact; once I even managed to mime a kiss. Nanny was deeply ensconced with Mills and Boon, with Foo-Foo snoring away beside her. At Victoria we made our farewells, he to King's Cross and Yorkshire, Nanny and me to Campden Hill.

Throughout this whole idyllic week there was just one nagging conscience-pricking thought that kept rearing its horrible head, beckoning me to confront it. Yes, you've guessed: *when* and *how* was I going to tell Paul of my encounter at Seymore Place, and more importantly, with David? But did I really need to tell him, I kept asking myself? It'll be sure to foul up everything. But was I being dishonest in remaining silent? On the other hand, what business was it of Paul's? Is it *ever* possible to promise total fidelity? In the end, I'm afraid, I was a coward and said nothing. It's haunted me the rest of my days.

With my love,
Freddie

20

My dear Sam,

I had another ten days in London before I was due at Cambridge. I used the time to keep busy, but I kept thinking about Paul now back at Upton – what he'd be doing, where he'd be. He wrote me the most wonderful letter, thanking me for everything: being his host, and his lover. I have it here in front of me still, and even now, especially now, it moves me so much that I can't bring myself to transcribe or share it. I'm sorry.

His mother had confirmed that I should come and stay with them in Yorkshire for a few days before Christmas, which set my heart racing. He'd been made a house prefect, with his own room, and was thinking of me every time he smoothed down my fur rug now strewn across his bed.

I enrolled on a week's touch-typing course and took extra driving lessons with a test at the end of the week in deepest Neasden, which, to my amazement, I passed. Alas, there was no question yet of my having unlimited use of the mini – let alone the Bentley.

My good friend Williamson – now in our new context to become George – was also going up to Powis to read Law. It was decided he would stay with us overnight before Mama drove us both up next day. That evening we reasserted our counter-culturalism by dressing up in our dinner jackets and going to *Carmen* at the Coliseum and then to dinner at Quaglino's. Whatever must our fellow diners have thought of two eighteen-year-old boys together at this well-known venue for hetero trysts? Your grandparents, Sam, showed a wary amusement.

Like James's first experience at Oxford, I found my first few weeks at Cambridge difficult, not to say bewildering. Because I had been awarded my place so late in the day, I was given a room in one of the small hostels in Panton Street near the station – truly the fag end in the hierarchy of the college's lodgings. It was a ten-minute bike ride to the college, and even longer into the heart of the university. There was absolutely no chance of being able to deck it out like my room at Upton. I might be able to do something creative when I moved into the college the following year.

I was also at sea with my new subject, having barely opened a book on Law. It was obvious my heart wasn't in it, and I became resentful when I discovered it was almost impossible to change. Nor did I find it easy to engage socially with the undergraduates from different backgrounds with whom I seemed to have been thrown together. Despite my best efforts I found myself seeking out the thirty or so Old Uptonians who were at different colleges. I felt infinitely more relaxed and at home with them. George was being much more adventurous, making it clear he wanted to go into politics eventually. He started speaking in debates at the Union and I followed in his shadow by joining CUCA briefly. My sense of loyalty prompted me to volunteer as the Catholic Chaplaincy's college rep.

Where were the girls, you may ask, if not for me, then at least for the heteronormatives? The answer: out of the thirty or so colleges all but four were male only. In addition, there were only four women students at the university reading Law in my year, with 200 men. The most glamorous one, blond and deb material, took up with the son of a peer within the first week and never looked back; the next was plump and plain but good fun – we became friends; the third was Jewish and only looked at boys in skull caps; and the fourth was a fifty-year-old wife of a don at Emmanuel, hoping to go into Parliament. Are you surprised that Queerness continued to flourish not far below the radar?

I was finding it all a massive anticlimax.

I kept some of the photos of Paul and me in the top drawer in my desk. There were the ones taken by Pippa, showing us reclining on the sofa side by side after the dance; another taken by Nanny with us setting off on our bikes for the sailing school; and then, the best one, taken by our sailing companion, both of us sitting each side of the tiller being held masterfully by Paul's left hand. We were looking straight into the camera, laughing and looking completely natural, the wind just ruffling our hair. It was so beautiful I put it into the silver frame I bought at an antiques stand in the marketplace. I kept it hidden, and would bring it out when I was on my own, and recite our poem quietly:

> '... sailing, soldiering, thieving, threatening...
> air breathing, water drinking, on the turf or the sea-
> beach dancing...'

My one consolation was the prospect of a weekend visit to Upton after about six weeks to see Paul. My mother had promised to lend me the mini if I went with another driver. George agreed to come too, and we set a date.

Just a week before we set out, an urgent letter arrived. Paul hadn't mentioned it before, but he had been having pains in his right leg for most of the term and been unable to take part in many of the sports he so enjoyed. No one had been able to diagnose the problem. Latterly he had started to feel sick and nauseous and been confined to the sick bay with frequent high temperatures, loss of weight and increasing pain in his leg. He was going home for the rest of the term, where he would be looked after by his family and undergo tests at his uncle's hospital.

What on earth was this? How could he possibly be ill? We had been together so recently and there had been absolutely nothing wrong with him. The idea of him, always the picture of health, suffering in any way disgusted me and made me feel ill myself. George, who by now knew all about my obsession with Paul, looked pretty glum about it. He hardly improved my mood by saying that it could be the start of something really nasty.

What on earth could I do? I needed confirmation and, for God's sake, some sort of reassurance. Ringing him wasn't so easy as there was only one coin-operated telephone at my lodgings, in the lobby, making conversation audible to the whole world. Nevertheless within an hour of receiving the letter I made the attempt.

His sister Claire answered. My negative impression of her when I'd met her first was confirmed when I pressed her for details. 'He's coming home later today,' was all she said, 'and having his first tests at the hospital tomorrow.' I gave her my number and asked if she or anyone could ring me when they had any news. I didn't get the impression she had either written down the number or that she could be relied upon to ring me back, or even leave a message. My heart plunged with frustration. I found it difficult to remain polite.

'You *will* do that for me, won't you,' I almost snapped.

'Alright,' she said, almost dismissively.

George and I decided to make the visit to Upton for the weekend anyway, travelling down to London on the Friday and collecting the mini. The late November weather was appalling, gales and rain storms and weekend traffic making the journey miserable. That evening Dom Gabriel told me that Paul's pains had begun almost immediately at the beginning of term, slowly getting worse. The whole of Ambrose had been shocked when he'd had to be sent home. I wondered then if that overwhelming sense of melancholy at Parkworth hadn't been a premonition after all?

We took three of our friends for a convivial lunch in Painswick, all five of us piled into the mini, Dom Gabriel having given his reluctant permission. I tried hard to hide my broodiness.

The person I definitely wanted to see, however, was Roz. I knew he was hoping for a place at Magdalene next year. I found him in his room and was pleased to see that he had been the successful bidder for my ersatz-damask hangings at the sale at the end of last term. They looked splendid, covering one wall, while the other had a machine-made tapestry, '*very* late Aubusson', as he said, cleverly imitating someone I couldn't quite identify, possibly Kenneth Clark.

'I'm looking forward to seeing you at Cambridge next autumn, Roz,' I said as I sat on the edge of his bed.

'Yes, it's all a bit daunting, but I'm hoping to read History of Art, although I'll have to do Archaeology and Anthropology in the first year. Studying indigenous peoples and admiring their feathers.'

'Hey, you can't go saying things like that at Cambridge, you'll be thrown out.'

But he wasn't listening as he put his hands up above his head, fingers outstretched and waving them from side to side, wiggling his bottom.

'Is that the Josephine Baker *Banana Dance* from the Folies Bergère?' I asked, in stitches.

'No disrespect intended,' he answered, finally giving way to a broad grin. My God, how he was changing, although I'd glimpsed this irreverent side to him before.

'Anyway, what are your plans for next summer?'

'I don't have any at the moment, except that I want to go on my travels. Things aren't very happy at home.' He looked dejected. 'My parents might be splitting up. I want to keep out of the way if I can.'

I said how truly sorry I was and what a blow this must be for him and his brother. I wished I could have expressed more sympathy but it was a situation I could hardly envisage and had no experience of. I admired how he seemed so stoic. It was clear he was going to take his mother's side in what had become a messy situation.

To change the subject, I asked how we might meet up while Paul and I were on our big European road trip. Entirely characteristically he suggested it should be somewhere memorably expensive, like Florian's in Venice, the Café Greco in Rome, or the Sacher in Vienna.

'Done,' I said, stroking his sleeve and looking at him with a surge of affection.

George and I drove back to London that same evening, dropped the car off at Campden Hill and took the late train back to Cambridge. I was getting increasingly restless in anticipation of a message, or at least something, from Paul.

*

And the very next day there was a letter from him. As I picked up the envelope in the hall I noticed his handwriting had changed; it seemed uncertain and trembling, like an old man's. I opened it in trepidation.

> *Dear Freddie,*
> *I had a biopsy last week and they've identified cancer in the bone marrow of my right knee. It's too late for radiation treatment – they're considering other options or possibly amputation.*

Something within me just died.

Then, in a panic, a massive sob welled up and I blurted out, '*No, no, no!*' My beautiful, beautiful lover to be mutilated in this way, his body hacked away like a piece of meat!

I felt sick as I thought of him having to endure this terrible ordeal. In a daze I sat on the stair, bracing myself to read the rest.

> *I'm being kept on drugs to help with the pain but they make me very tired so I can't write much. Next week I'll be going into the General Infirmary where they can monitor my progress (or lack of). It would be great to see you and I'll get Mum to let you know when it's best – even if you can make it just for the day.*
>
> *Paul*

There were no big expressions of affection this time. Why not?

I ran upstairs instantly to write my reply. It would be going against the grain but I felt I should be guarded, using expressions of fraternal sympathy rather than heartfelt passion.

> *My dear Paul,*
>
> *You can't imagine how upset I am to hear your news and how much I feel for you at this terrible time. It is unbearable to think of you in pain – I can only pray they are keeping you as comfortable as possible and are doing everything to find you the right treatment. Of course I'll come to see you whenever you say. There's so much I want to tell you, but it'll just have to wait.*
>
> *You're always with me in my thoughts and prayers.*
>
> *Freddie*

*

It was nearly the end of my first term, thank goodness. Any effort I may have made in my studies had dissipated since I first heard of Paul's illness, and I had skipped several lectures and even one supervision. It wasn't looking good, and I was called in for an 'informal chat' over a glass of sherry before Hall one evening by my Director of Studies, a burly Scottish bachelor, an ex-rugby blue now famed for his Sunday morning bagpipe playing in the squash courts.

'How are you getting on, McNaughton? Is studying the Law everything you thought it was going to be?'

'To be truthful, sir, I've found it difficult to get my head around some of it.' I proceeded to lie, 'But I think I'm on top of it now. I rather enjoy Criminal Law and Contract, but find Roman Law a bit tedious, and it's not easy to navigate the English Legal System and its procedures.'

I didn't have the courage to admit that, quite frankly, I was hating it. It had failed utterly to grab my imagination: comparing the manumission of slaves under the Twelve Tables, or at the time of Gaius, or under Justinian; let alone considering the proposed reforms to the Scottish Juvenile Courts. I'd been reading Proust all summer, for goodness' sake. The Law seemed a complete waste of my time when I could be doing much more interesting things like spending more time in the Fitzwilliam Museum. *That*, I now realise, Sam, was – without doubt – my problem.

'Well, if you take my advice,' he said, 'I'd make sure you attend *all* the lectures without fail. It saves such a lot of time to hear everything explained in person rather than having to study it in a book and which you could do anywhere.'

'Yes, sir, I apologise if I've had to skip some in the past few weeks. You see, I've had some very bad news that a friend of mine is now obviously dying of cancer.'

I suddenly realised this was no exaggeration. It was the first time I had articulated my deepest fear and it brought tears to my eyes. I managed to control myself but gave a very deep gulp.

'Oh, I'm very sorry to hear that, McNaughton. Is he,' he paused, 'a very particular friend?'

'Yes, sir.'

'Well, then you must take as much time off as you need to see him and look after him. If it looks as though you need to postpone taking your Tripos Part I for another year, I can see what I can arrange.'

I thanked him but said that I hoped it wouldn't come to that.

As I left his rooms I wondered at the kindness of this old boy who could so easily have made things difficult for me. But, despite his offer, I feared the reaction of my parents; I was conscious that my father had probably budgeted for my three years as an undergraduate, but almost certainly not for the expenses of a fourth year if I had to postpone. Would they understand? Maybe. But I hated to think that my lack of resilience would be seen as a step backwards in their hard-won estimation.

*

Two weeks later the Christmas vacation began. I had telephoned Paul's home several times in the hope that I could speak to him, or at the very least hear some news. They had been patient with me, but Paul was still in hospital. Eventually I got a promise that they would ring me if anything changed. I was on tenterhooks all this time: sleepless nights, grumpy by day, going for tearful walks on my own in the park, cutting invitations to Christmas parties – just waiting to hear something, anything.

There was just one piece of good luck. I had a win of £1,000 from my Premium Bonds, part of my godmother's legacy years ago. In the face of much opposition, I bought a secondhand Triumph Spitfire, two-tone cream and brown, with its own stereo system for cassettes. I felt proud as I drove it up Church Street and parked it outside our house. There was no question of taking it to Cambridge of course. Nevertheless, I could start planning my expeditions with Paul as he convalesced, and next summer's Grand Tour, speeding down the continental autoroutes.

It was just a week before Christmas when the phone call came. It was Paul's mother to say that he was responding well to treatment and feeling much better. He would be coming out of hospital on Christmas Eve. He'd love to see me if I could come up to Leeds for the day by train. The Infirmary was not far from the station.

I had to contain myself from cheering loudly down the phone at her.

'I'll be there tomorrow,' I said.

For the first time in weeks I had a decent night's sleep.

The Brotherton Wing was a wonderful example of 1930s Deco. In contrast to all the neighbouring soot-encrusted buildings it was all gleaming white Portland stone and metal-framed wraparound windows. It faced a big public square set up with a Christmas market, which I could only presume came to life after dark. Just then it looked pretty desolate with only a few stragglers wandering through the half-open booths and the noisy merry-go-rounds devoid of customers.

The Irish nurse accompanied me to his room. 'Yes, we're so pleased with Paul's progress. The doctors have even said he might go back to boarding school next term.'

We reached his room, and before going in I looked through the window in the door to see him propped up against the pillows lying on top of his bed in his dressing gown, reading a book. My heart was thumping in anticipation.

'Freddie! You've come at last!' he cried as he looked up and a sparkle came into his eyes and a smile across his face. I had never heard my name called so sweetly or excitedly before, nor anyone's face so transformed as I appeared.

'Paul, it's fantastic to see you... Thank you, sister,' I said, desperately wanting her to go away.

I had been fearful of seeing him gaunt, thin and ill, but instead here he was, almost his usual self. Admittedly his golden complexion looked a few degrees paler and there were rings under his eyes, but his voice was just the same, only a little slower and drier.

I went around to the side of the bed and drew up a chair. With the nurse gone, I gave him a kiss on his lips, stroking his chin with my fingers, then putting my hand into his and keeping it there.

'You're looking good,' I said, beaming at him, trying to find the right words.

'They're treating me really well here. I'm a whole lot better than I was. You shouldn't have seen me a month ago. There's no more talk of amputation, at least for the moment.'

'Thank God for that,' I exclaimed, massively relieved. 'Anyway, whatever happens, I'd go to the ends of the earth to see you, wherever you were, and however ill you were. You know that.'

As he was telling me how he had fetched up here, I looked around. There was a wheelchair parked in the corner of the room and above the bed various medical contraptions, none of which seemed to be attached to him. There was a television set at the end of the bed, flowers in vases and cards on the windowsill. To my amazement (but why should I have been amazed?) on his bedside table there was a familiar-looking photo of the two of us together.

'Hey!' I said. 'Happy memories! I've got the same pic of us beside *my* bed at Cambridge.

'... *Up and down the roads going...*' I quoted.

'... *Ease scorning, statutes mocking, feebleness chasing...*' he replied, laughing.

The noise of the Christmas market and the merry-go-rounds and dodgems could be heard faintly in the background. Now they seemed less sinister and intrusive.

'You're obviously having de-luxe treatment here,' I said.

'Well, it does help that my uncle is one of the consultants.'

I asked if it was true he'd be returning to Upton next term. He said the doctors were so pleased with him that they were prepared to take the risk. He might have to be in a wheelchair, but certainly not all the time. Anyway, he wanted to be there with his friends. He was already missing his classes. They'd been sending him stuff to look at already.

I pointed to the book he had beside him on the blankets. 'I see you've got *Comus* on the go. Honestly, what sort of a fellow reads *Comus* in bed, let alone in hospital?'

'Well, I was rather enjoying it, since you ask,' he replied, mock-defensively. 'A little allegory on the superiority of virtue over vice is just what I need right now to cheer me up!' He gave me one of his now-familiar lascivious grins.

'Actually,' he continued, 'I really think I prefer reading plays to anything else – alright so this is a masque – although it's nothing like seeing them in the theatre, let alone acting in them.'

'Seriously, do you think you'd like to take up acting as a career?' I asked.

'I'm coming round to it. Of course, it would mean switching to read English. And then there'd be years of training at drama school after that. It's all a bit risky.'

'But you know how good you are with words, Paul. Rappy's productions have been a great starting point. But, anyway, you must know by now that it's your voice that will make your fortune. Although the face will help too, I suppose. And there are all those other bits of you too, which your fans might come to drool over once you get into films.' I groped at him playfully over the blanket.

'What about you?' he said. 'You could always get a job as Anthony Perkins's understudy, 'specially if they did a stage play of *Psycho*.'

I disclaimed any ambition in that department. We laughed, and I continued, 'But look, the struggle's the same for everyone. I'm going to have to spend two or three years as an articled clerk or a barrister's pupil in Chambers. Somehow I've got my doubts I'll ever get that far.' I really didn't want to go into it all now.

'Anyway,' he said, 'I want to hear all about Cambridge, your new car and how you've been getting on, and what it's like. I hope you haven't been leading boys astray wearing those crushed-velvet pants of yours.'

In truth, I *had* taken the pants up to Cambridge and once or twice gone out in them with George to prop up the bar at the Tickell Arms, just to see what effect they had. I was sufficiently encouraged, although I'd chosen not to pursue things. Nor did I want to admit yet that I'd been to a couple of late-night parties where marijuana joints had been passed round. They had made me feel incredibly uninhibited and, more significantly, romantic and horny. I wondered how Paul would respond when he got the chance. I hoped I'd be with him when that happened.

Right now I didn't think it right to let him know my real feelings of disappointment. So I burbled on about my new car and how we were going to go everywhere in it next summer. I told him about the dons, the characters, the student demos last term. My *pièce de résistance* was the story of how I almost knocked Prince Charles off his bicycle on King's Parade when I had braked too quickly on mine in front of the Copper Kettle.

The nurse now came in.

'I'm going to disturb you two gentlemen, I'm afraid. Paul needs his medication and has to rest for half an hour afterwards.'

'Why don't you go out and have a ciggy or something, Freddie – or have a look round the Christmas market and come back at half past three? I've got something to give you.'

I went out into the square and wandered round the stalls. It was already getting dark and the coloured Christmas lights were helping to cheer things up. It was such a relief to have seen Paul looking so recovered and not the emaciated corpse I had been dreading. Maybe he would return to complete health after all; perhaps I could encourage a miracle by organising a trip to Lourdes with some of our mutual friends?

I suddenly realised I hadn't got him a Christmas present. Here was my chance.

Among all the tinselly things, handmade ornaments and artisanal preserves on offer, there was one stall that was selling small-scale antiques, bits of silver, jewellery, old china and lace. On a shelf at the back I spotted a small sculptural group of two boys – obviously a copy of something classical. They were both stark naked, one with his arm over the other's shoulder, the other with his arm raised as if in defiance. My God, it was us! I asked to see it.

It was bronze, about eight inches high – quite heavy, warm to the touch and wonderfully tactile.

'How much?' I asked, in some trepidation.

The old boy behind the counter took it from me, turned it over, then gave me a smile.

'Two quid for you, young man. It's a bargain.'

I felt a slight panic; that was all I had in my pocket right now. But I *had* to have it.

'I'll give you thirty bob for it,' I said, trying to look cool. 'It's for my friend,' as if that would make any difference.

He sighed and shrugged his shoulders.

'Alright then. But only for you, young sir.'

I was relieved, and let it show. 'Thanks a million,' I said. 'He'll love it.'

I asked if he had a sticky label I could use to write a message to fix on the underside.

'Don't let it obscure the signature,' he said, pointing to the inscription, 'F Righetti, Roma 1792'. 'It might make your fortune one day.'

I had to think on the spot. The space was very small. I wrote,

My Dearest P
Happy Christmas 1968
'One the Other Never Leaving'
With all my love F

The man found me some grubby secondhand Christmas wrapping paper and I crossed the road back to the Infirmary.

'Here's your Christmas present, Paul, hot from the market,' I said handing him the oddly shaped parcel.

'Don't tell me I've got to wait 'til Christmas Day before I can open it?'

'No. It'd probably be best if your family didn't see it. At least not on Christmas Day. They might think it was ever so slightly Queer,' I laughed. He tore at the paper, slowly exposing the figures.

'Wow, Freddie,' he said. 'They're just like *us*... two young guys together... completely brazen about themselves!'

'*Just* like us!' I repeated with a different emphasis and laughing. I was thrilled to see how captivated he was.

'Thank you so, so much. I want to be able to see them from my bed and think of us together. Can you put them on the shelf over there, opposite my bed.'

I did as I was bidden and went back to sit beside him. Both of us looked silently at the little group. After a minute he said,

'But *I've* got something for you, although I'm afraid it's not really a Christmas present.' He was opening the drawer in the bedside cupboard and took out an envelope.

On the front was written in his own hand, 'For Frederick McNaughton. To be opened in the event of my death and BEFORE my funeral.'

I knew that something outside my control was about to unfold. 'My God, what's this, Paul? It looks a bit melodramatic.'

'Don't open it now, whatever you do,' he said, raising his voice.

He went on, now avoiding my eyes and looking into the middle distance: 'You must realise, Freddie, I've been thinking of the worst of scenarios. It's possible, maybe probable, that I'll die any time soon now. They've only been able to stabilise the cancer in my leg. It's very likely to spread and reappear somewhere else and get out of control. Amputation will probably be too late, God help me.'

I had been dreading him speaking these very words, desperately hoping there would be no need. But now he had. For a split second I felt helpless, dumb with sadness and fear. I was unable to say or do anything.

I tried looking into his eyes. But he was deliberately still gazing into the middle distance.

He turned and reached out to hold my hand. 'You're going to have to be as brave as me, because you'll be left behind and have to get on without me. But I don't worry about you too much. I know you'll find someone else to love.'

I looked up, really hurt, almost shocked. 'Paul, how could you think of such a thing? You know *you're* the only one for me.' Then, even though my voice was parched, I blurted out in desperation, 'I... I... just don't know how I'm going to live, or what the point of living will be...'

I could barely hold back my tears. It took an agonising five seconds before I could pull myself together. I was only making things worse.

He shook his head gently and continued. I was finding it difficult to concentrate.

'Inside that envelope is a note for you and, very importantly, an instruction about something I want you to do for me when the time comes. It's *really important*, not just for me, but for you, and everyone else like us. We've been incredibly lucky, Freddie. We've had an easy ride. But it's not the same for everyone. I've told my uncle you've got a task to perform, but he doesn't know what it is. He knows he's got to contact you, wherever you are, when I die.'

'Paul, I just so hope I'll be *with you*, for goodness' sake, if and when that moment ever comes… but all this sounds so very calculated.'

'Yes, it is, I'm afraid. I've been thinking about it for weeks, and I want nothing left to chance. But they really *are* my instructions, Freddie, and I don't want any excuses for not fulfilling them.'

'Of course,' I said, putting the envelope into my breast pocket.

Something within me now compelled me to close the curtains of the internal window, and put a chair against the door to prevent anyone disturbing us. Paul looked sideways at what I was doing with a smile. Silently I climbed into the bed beside him, taking his face in my hands, kissing him on his lips, then his nose, his eyes, his wonderful forehead. I pressed my body against his, my legs caressing his thighs as I smothered his neck and shoulders with more kisses. He returned them tenderly but passively. I realised how tired he must be.

We lay side by side, my arm over his shoulder, his head against my chest.

'Can't we stay here now, beside each other, forever, just like we were this summer?' I said. 'If only I could share some of your pain with you, some of your illness I'd be so happy. I just want to die here with you.'

Silently he turned to face me, his eyes watery with unshed tears. For what seemed like an eternity we just looked at each other, saying nothing. As I stroked his hair, I remembered that first vision of him appearing out of that hazy sunshine in the Ambrose dayroom only two years ago.

'I'm remembering the exact moment when I first saw you, and knew instantly that I loved you, Paul – that first assembly in September two years ago.'

'Yeah, I remember you looking across at me,' he smiled. 'I could tell straight away that you were obviously a nice fellow, but I didn't know how to take it. I'd never been looked at like that before.'

He paused and then continued, 'I wondered how long it would take you to seek me out. And then when you did, I was reading *Antony and Cleopatra* in the window seat and you tried to chat me up. It was all very flattering, but I was still uncertain about you, let alone your intentions. If I'd been a bastard, I could have taken you for a complete ride, like Rowse.

'But of course I didn't. After that, it was a slow burn. Once I let go my suspicions, I could see you in a different light. You were so kind helping me with my work, and then with *Twelfth Night*. I came to realise how you really cared about me. How could I have been indifferent? I found myself looking forward to seeing you, and whenever I did, I just loved being with you. I began to notice some of your other lovely features – your gentle smile, your kind eyes, and the endearing and funny way you talk.' He traced a finger over my eyes and my mouth.

'But then, when I heard you'd been groping with Rowse I found myself insanely jealous. That's when I realised that I loved you, Freddie McNaughton. In the end I had no option but to forgive that little dalliance, and then all that stuff you got up to in France. Anyway, perhaps it made a man of you while we were apart, and you learnt some useful transferable skills!' He laughed.

'From then on life just became better and better. Everything I did I wanted to share with you, and I savoured every minute we were together. Our week at the cottage was the pinnacle of my life, you know. Were two fellows ever so happy?'

This was so lovely to hear. But a black thought flashed through my head: now I'll *never* be able to own up about Seymore Place and David. It would break his heart. But I could do one thing.

'You've got to know, Paul, that I've always been loyal to you. Even if I've been unfaithful, I've never stopped loving you. I can only pray you've always forgiven me and always will.'

'Of course, Freddie. Don't ever doubt it.'

My God, I thought. *How completely trusting he is. I don't deserve such unconditional love. How can I ever live up to it?*

There was a knock on the door. I sprang off the bed to move the obstructing chair. It was the nurse again, come to check Paul's temperature.

'Freddie, you'd better get going or you'll miss your train.' Oblivious of the nurse I bent over him and gave him a kiss on his lips, not a kiss of passion, but something pure, with love and tenderness. He held me by my arm as he looked straight into my eyes: 'Goodbye, dearest Freddie,' he whispered, 'I'm always thinking of you. You've been the love of my life.'

'*Bye for now, gorgeous,*' I just managed to say as my eyes filled with tears.

Next I had to make a dash for the door or else I knew I would explode. A short way down the passage I slumped against the wall and just let it all flow out. At that very moment the nurse appeared from out of Paul's room. She saw me looking utterly helpless, screwed up in grief. Instinctively she took me in her arms and did her best to comfort me.

'Come down to the staff room, love, and let me make you a cup of tea.'

I shook my head and wiped my eyes.

'No, it's really kind of you, sister, but I've got to catch my train. The trouble is I don't know if I'll ever see him again.' I looked up into her kind Irish face.

'To be sure you will, love,' she said. 'We're doing all we can for him, and he'll soon be fine.'

I wasn't convinced.

That was a terrible day, Sam.

With my love,

Freddie

21

My dear Sam,

The journey home on that cold, damp train seemed interminable. I was restless, walking up and down the passage, chain smoking, then stopping to look out at the starless night. How must Paul have felt when he was first diagnosed? Just now he had seemed so calm, even resigned, with no sense of panic. I was lost in admiration at his inner strength and courage. But was that only for my benefit? I just wished I could be close to him, to comfort him, nurse him, and attend to his every need. But I was useless, and ashamed of being so. All I could do was pray for a miracle.

Christmas came and went. There was no St Moritz for me this year. My parents were going there in March and with a different group of friends. Your mother was at school in Switzerland anyway, and they reckoned I should arrange my own skiing trips now that I was eighteen. In any event I was hardly in the mood for it. Instead, I went back to Cambridge a few days early in the vain hope of catching up.

Paul's remission at least allowed him to return to Upton at the beginning of the new term. Alas, after only three weeks he started to feel unwell again, spending days at a time in the sick bay, returning to the school, and then back again to the sick bay. We managed to speak on the phone a couple of times, but his voice was weak and it was difficult to have any privacy, both of us using payphones. He was determined to stay among his friends for as long as possible and positively refused to be taken back home, saying that Upton was the place he wanted to be. I had a couple of sprawling letters from him, but they were almost illegible and sometimes incoherent. I just wept as I held and kissed them.

Why wasn't his family making any attempt at staying in touch with me, letting me know how he was? Whenever I phoned I only ever received evasive answers, almost rude, usually from his sister or the housekeeper, making me feel I was pestering them.

One morning in the third week of February, after over a week's silence, I knew I couldn't wait any longer. I had had a bad night in which I heard Paul calling my name so tenderly, just as he had when we had lain together every night at the cottage. He was somewhere very close but invisible. Even when I woke and cycled into college I could hear his voice.

It was a bitingly cold, wet and windy day. I found a phone box near the marketplace. It looked and smelt as though someone had just wanked in it.

His sister answered.

'Hello, Claire. It's Fred McNaughton, Paul's friend again. Have you any more news?'

There was a pause before she answered faintly, 'You haven't heard?'

'No?' There was another pause.

'Paul died three days ago in the sick bay at Upton.'

Blood rushed to my head. Everything blacked out. My tongue could barely move except to moan, 'Oh my God, Claire! How... *terrible... terrible... terrible...* I'd no idea.'

Before I could say anything more she continued with that coldness in her voice, which I'd heard often before: 'Mum and

Uncle David were with him and I'm going down for the funeral the day after tomorrow with my grandmother, aunt and cousins.

'By the way, we found that present you gave him. We weren't impressed *at all*. It explained a lot about you two.' There and then she hung up on me.

I staggered out of the phone box in a daze, oblivious of where I was or where I was going. I managed to find a filthy bench to sit down, despite the driving rain. My gut felt completely empty as I put my face in my hands and just wept. Paul was no longer here, *really gone*, forever. There was nothing whatever I could do about it. I would never see him again, never hold him, never touch him or be touched by him. It was so final, and I hadn't even said goodbye. Had he asked for me? I couldn't believe for a minute he had forgotten me; maybe he had been too ill... I was shaking and sweating, beginning to feel sick. I desperately wanted someone to talk to.

My grief turned to anger when I remembered that Paul had instructed his uncle to contact me when he died as I had some kind of task he wanted me to perform. Why hadn't he done this? Then, in a flash, I understood what Claire had meant by her snide remark. They must have guessed about our relationship, perhaps when they'd found the statue with my careless message written underneath. They must have drawn their own conclusions before confronting Paul. How had he handled it? I hated myself for not being there with him when, or if, there had been a showdown.

This galvanised me. If the funeral was the day after tomorrow and at Upton, I needed to be there. I would see his family and take their accusations. I phoned my mother and told her the news. I said I was coming to London to collect my car to drive straight to Upton. She tried to commiserate. 'He was a good friend for you, Freddie. But cheer up, darling. You've known about his condition for a long time. You'll get over it.'

For the very first time I felt angry and exasperated with her.

'For God's sake, Mama, don't give me that. Will you *ever*, *ever* understand that he was a million times more than just a good friend? How can I ever, ever "get over it" as you think?' I put the phone down on her.

Now I think of it, that was very hurtful of me. I only hope she forgave me. After all, she was only trying to console me in her own way. I'm sorry, Sam, I know how fond you were of your grandmother.

I went back to my dismal room in Panton Street and pulled open the drawer in my desk to find the envelope Paul had given me in hospital. Sitting down, I prayed for strength before opening it. There were two messages, just as he had said. The first had a formal instruction, obviously a copy of an original document.

> In the event of my death I wish my Requiem to take place at Upton Abbey. My executor, my uncle, Dr Gerald Shipton, has been made aware of this.
>
> I also wish that my closest friend Frederick McNaughton should read the poem by Walt Whitman, We Two Boys Together Clinging, *at an appropriate moment during the Mass.*
>
> Paul Shipton
> 1st December 1968

Our poem! Of course I must! But how was I going to achieve that? But right now, it was more important to open the next message.

> My dearest Freddie,
> By the time you read this I will be gone.
> I thank God every day that He put us together. We were

obviously meant for each other from the very moment we came into being. But it was your fearless determination that made it happen, Freddie. All I can say is thank you, from the bottom of my heart, for your unconditional love, your kindness, generosity and patience. My meeting you and responding to your love has been the purpose of my existence and my place in Creation. I don't feel my short life has been pointless; I came into being in order to love one person only – you – and I've been loved by you in return. What more could anyone ask? There's so much more we could have done together, but even so I firmly believe we've fulfilled our destiny, 'our foray'.

I've asked you to read out our poem at my funeral. I know you'll agree that we must tell the whole world what we were for each other. No more subterfuge. It'll require a lot of courage to stand up there, but I'll be right beside you.

*You'll grieve for me, of course, but I don't want you to close your heart and walk away from future relationships. Instead, I want you to be open to find someone else to love and take my place; he will be out there somewhere, and you must search for him actively while you're still young. Whoever you end up with you'll have my blessing from heaven. I hope you'll still be together when you're both ninety-five and can still say our poem, but using the words 'We two **old** boys...!'*

Goodbye, Freddie, my dearest, first and only love.

Paul

1ˢᵗ December 1968

P. S. I'm enclosing the copy of our poem which you wrote out for me, do you remember? It's my legacy to you. Use it to read out at my funeral.

No one had ever written or said anything so beautiful to me

before. I threw myself back in my chair and closed my eyes. I imagined him writing these words in hospital in the twilight hours, having looked back over the course of his short life.

*

But now I had my task to perform and there was no time to linger. I gathered some things together and almost ran all the way to the station, jumping on the first train to London. Mama and Nanny were at home, both looking very concerned. Nanny's eyes were red; the poor darling had obviously been crying. She gave me a tearful hug, whispering, 'He was such a lovely boy, Freddie. You must be so upset.' My mother was more worried about my driving such a long way on my own. Finally, she offered to come with me. I tried to hide my consternation; this was something I couldn't possibly share with her.

I found Dom Gabriel's number. 'Of course it will be good to see you, Fred. I'll make sure you have a room in the guest house. Supper in the monks' refectory is at seven. Do come and call on me any time later this evening. We can talk then.'

I raced off towards the A40. The whole journey was another nightmare of wind, rain and cold. *My God*, I thought, *how inappropriate is this wretched car*. I hated it. I'd bought it for Paul and me, for us to share, to celebrate and be happy. *Now it'll never happen, it's pointless*. I swore I'd sell it at the first opportunity and get something bog standard instead.

Meanwhile, Paul's instructions needed a careful strategy. I was beyond caring what people would think of the poem or its implications; no one was going to stop me if I could only reach the lectern at the right moment during the funeral. Afterwards people could think whatever they liked. I knew perfectly well that Holy Mother Church still had her protocols, which forbade any deviation from the prescribed rubrics at funerals. Substituting the poem for one of the official readings would require approval from the abbot. I had to speak to him urgently.

Then, how was I going to stand up to Paul's family? They must have known that I had a role to play at the funeral and yet they'd failed to contact me. If I was generous – and maybe in the circumstances I should be – the explanation might be that Paul's instructions had slipped their mind. Alternatively, I wondered, did they want to exclude me from anything more to do with him?

I wondered again how they had responded to the discovery of our relationship. Had Paul been forced into admitting it after they'd found the bronze statue and seen my message? Or had he chosen voluntarily to admit everything? How had they taken it? Had they understood? Given Claire's apparent attitude, perhaps I should expect the worst, and be prepared for their accusations that I had corrupted Paul of his innocence, perverted him and led him into eternal damnation. Maybe they intended taking revenge tomorrow, threatening to denounce me to the school, to the police, to my own parents, making me face prison or borstal? Reciting the poem might incense them even further.

In which case, *too fucking bad*! *Tant* fucking *pis*! I'd be perfectly honest with them and admit everything. In my mind, *they* were the guilty ones, betraying Paul's trust by concealing his death from me in defiance of his wishes. Nothing, but nothing, was going to prevent me from reading the poem and declaring our love to the whole world.

I arrived in the pitch dark. I had once loved this place, but I wasn't so sure now, especially as I was very obviously a guest, and in the unfamiliar monastery at that. I just had time to wash and run down to wait in the cloister outside the monks' refectory before supper. I knew the procedure was that all new guests should make themselves known to the abbot when he appeared.

I hung around in the deep claustral shadows as the monks slowly foregathered. I was not sure who the abbot was these days, but I knew he would be distinguished from the rest by a pectoral cross. At last, a familiar figure with white hair appeared, wearing a gilded Maltese Cross on his chest. It was Dom Placid! I bowed to kiss his ring.

'No, no, dear boy... please... none of that. Stand up so I can see you. Why, it's my old friend Freddie. How good to see you again! I think I know what brings you to Upton,' giving me a gentle embrace.

'Yes, thank you for letting me come, Father, but it's a little complicated. Can I have a word with you after supper?'

'Of course you can, dear fellow. Meet me right here immediately after we've finished.'

Supper was conducted in silence while a novice read aloud in purest RP to the assembled sixty monks: first the Gospel of the Day; and then from an 'approved' book. It happened to be the first pages of Evelyn Waugh's biography of Edmund Campion describing the grotesque deathbed of Queen Elizabeth I – she who had caused the martyrdom of my sainted ancestor. I had to concentrate hard on my cauliflower cheese and chips, followed by an apple, while I rehearsed inwardly what I had to say to Dom Placid.

After the meal I followed him upstairs to his sitting room overlooking the floodlit cloister.

'Tell me how I can help,' he said, having filled our cups from a cafetière.

'You might remember when I came to see you a couple of years ago when I was troubled, having fallen in love with another boy?'

'Yes, I remember it very well,' he replied.

'Well, Father, that boy was Paul Shipton whose funeral we will be having the day after tomorrow.'

'Yes, I know that,' he said, looking at me with deep compassion in his eyes.

I was taken aback. 'How ever could you have known, Father?'

'Don't ask me too closely, Freddie, but I gave Paul the Last Sacraments just three days ago. He was trying to be calm, but I knew he was anxious. I heard his last Confession and gave him Communion, after which he became much more peaceful, almost serene. As I was leaving, he asked me to pass him the photograph on the bedside table. It showed you both together. As I put it in his hands, he kissed it. Something prompted me to give you *both* my silent blessing and Absolution.'

I was astonished and looked away; he must know our whole story! He had used his powers of forgiveness to absolve us. There was nothing to prevent Paul's ascent into paradise.

After a pause he asked, 'But how has it been for you, Freddie?'

'It's been the worst thing I've ever had to endure in my short and very protected life, Father. It just got worse and worse. At first I could hardly believe it when I heard he was so ill; we had been together this summer, enjoying so much, the two of us... together. Then when I learned they might have to amputate one of his legs I just despaired – to think that the love of my life, the most beautiful person in the universe, would become *mutilated*! And then when I heard – so unexpectedly – that he was dead, and I had not been with him or seen him, it was unbearable.'

I looked ahead of me out of the window but could see nothing as my eyes had watered up. Dom Placid leant forward, resting his elbow on the arm of the chair and put his hand over his face. He was evidently in tears too, but didn't want me to see it. We both remained silent for a moment.

He looked up. 'Dear Freddie, what a terrible thing for you. These great sorrows usually happen when we are so much older, when our lives have run their course, and maybe we can deal with them better. I can't possibly explain why our Heavenly Father has called Paul home so early in his young life. All we can say is that it is His will and there is a purpose to it. It might be just a little comfort for you to remember that message from St Paul: "*Love never comes to an end*". Your love for each other will endure forever in your immortal souls.'

Hearing his words, I felt genuinely consoled. At last I'd been able to share my grief with someone else. Maybe I could get through this, after all.

'But here I am, Father, with a special request. Before he died, when Paul was in hospital, he told me he had something important he wanted me to do. He left his instructions for me to find after he was dead, so I only discovered them this morning.

'He wants me to read out a poem at his Requiem – a work that was very personal to both of us, almost a declaration of how we felt about each other. He wanted the whole world to know about us, leaving behind no secrets or shame so that he could rest in peace.'

I paused, amazed at my audacity so far, but bracing myself for the rest. 'I know that there are strict rules about the liturgy for funerals, but can I beg you to let me carry out Paul's wishes?'

The dear man had been listening carefully and showed a flicker of apprehension as I finished speaking.

'I'm sure we can accommodate Paul's request. I will be the chief celebrant at the Requiem. The whole school will be there, and we are making it a very big, very public, affair. As well as being a great send-off for him, it's an opportunity to show the boys how much we value each one of them while they are in our care. And also it's a chance for them to show their appreciation of Paul, with all of us praying together for him as his community.'

Yes, I thought. *This is something bigger than just me and* my *private grief. This is something I have to share with everyone. This is why Paul wants me to read the poem.*

'Now I'd better see the poem you are proposing.'

I handed him the hand-written copy I'd made for Paul.

The abbot took out his spectacles and began reading it out aloud, slowly, with his soft Irish accent giving it a lovely musicality, which I hadn't encountered before.

"Tis a very beautiful poem, to be sure. I can understand how it might express the special times you had together and your hopes for the future. It contains nothing that should offend anyone. If only everyone could understand that the love between two people, whoever they are, should always be celebrated as a gift from God.'

After a pause, he carried on, 'But it's brave of you to put yourself in the firing line of anyone who might be surprised or pretend to be shocked. But you must go ahead with my blessing.'

He continued, 'I'll tell the MC and the organist so they will be in the know. Otherwise it will be a secret until the very last minute when everyone will be expecting the "*Dies Irae*". Instead, they'll see you walking up to the ambo, no one knowing what's going to happen next.' He gave a smile.

'Thank you, Father. That's so good of you to be so understanding. I really hope it isn't going to be awkward for you.'

I continued, 'You know, when we spoke about this two years ago, it may have been prophetic, but you said I might be called upon to perform an act of heroism one day for Paul's sake. I suppose this is it?'

'Yes, it will be heroic, because you'll be telling the whole world that two boys can love each other, just like everyone else. If people refuse to understand, it's *their* problem. "*Who are they to judge? Who are we to judge?*" So, go on, as your good poet says, and be "*arm'd and fearless*", and prepared to stand your ground.'

*

I walked through the dimly lit cloisters and into the school to see Dom Gabriel. I was so relieved by what Dom Placid had said as his words began to sink in. At best I thought my request might have received a grudging acceptance from whoever was in charge. I had no idea that it would be my old friend and that he would be so affirmative, so positive, so understanding. *This is meant to be*, I thought, *it really is.*

The corridors were empty and silent as this was the time for evening prep and the boys were supposed to be working either in the classrooms or in their own rooms. Taking the shortcut across the moonlit quad, I made my way to Dom Gabriel's door.

He was smoking his pipe with his head deep in a book as I entered.

'Is this a good moment?' I asked.

'Of course it is, Fred. It's good to see you, come in and sit down.'

'Thank you for booking me in to the guest house at such short notice,' I said.

'Not at all. Of course I knew that you would be coming to Shipton's funeral,' he sighed. 'We've all been affected by his death in our separate ways. Normally we would ask that a boy should be taken home in this situation, but he was very determined to stay at Upton as long as he could. Everyone felt it would be cruel to take him away from the place he loved. You and he were very close, I know full well.'

Why dissemble any more? 'Yes,' I said, quietly, 'I loved him with all my heart. He meant everything to me.' I felt tears welling up in my eyes again.

'And I'm sure, in fact I know, *you* meant everything to *him*, Fred. I watched how he matured during the time you and he were such good friends. You really brought him out, you know. What an attractive boy he became! Such a great example for everyone! That's the reason we are giving him a spectacular departure – to show how much we *all* cared about him.'

I could see Dom Gabriel's eyes beginning to water, and he looked away towards the wall as he finished his little speech.

But no, I was not going to say any more to him, or to anyone else for that matter. The full revelation of our relationship can wait.

'Are Paul's family here?' I asked.

'Yes, I believe they're staying with relations nearby. His sister and other family are due tomorrow. Straight after the funeral they'll be accompanying the coffin to the crematorium and then going home.'

He fiddled with his pipe as he continued, 'This Requiem will be the last big liturgy in the old form. Immediately afterwards the abbey church is closing for six months while all the changes are being made. The high altar is being moved to a new platform in the transept, the abbot's throne is being taken out, and all the rush-bottomed seats in the nave are being replaced with modern benches. And all the liturgies will be in English in future.'

I gasped. 'Sounds pretty drastic… in fact *absolutely dreadful*,' I said, momentarily aghast, forgetting myself and feeling no need to be deferential towards everything Dom Gabriel said any more. 'Thank goodness Paul's Requiem will be something he would have recognised.' *Oh God*, I thought, *this isn't just the end of Paul, but the desecration of all that beauty. What madness must have taken hold of the place.*

I returned to my room in the guest house thinking how Paul had known all the sounds and smells, the nooks and crannies as intimately as me. But with his loss and all the changes being proposed it could never be the same again. I didn't feel I could ever come back.

*

Next morning I rose at five o'clock and sat in the nave of the abbey church while the monks sang Matins and Lauds in the choir. It was very dark, with the whole church illuminated only by the two flickering candles far off on the high altar and by the vertical shafts from the lanterns suspended above the choir stalls. There were no books provided for guests to follow the psalms or prayers, but I was not bothered. The effect of the Latin plainchant was soothing and peaceful, and at the same time strong and powerful with its repeated rhythms and simple melodies.

At first my prayers were only for Paul, that the Lord would be merciful to him. I had known him through and through and for me he was as perfect a human being as could be. Wasn't that enough? How could he be excluded from the kingdom of heaven?

And then I prayed for myself, thanking my Heavenly Father for having given Paul to me. How providential had been that September morning when I first saw him, the opportunities I had been given to become his friend and his lover. Yes, maybe I had been predatory and shameless in my pursuit of him at the beginning, but he had always been free to pull away at any time. I could feel no guilt there. My sin lay in failing to live up to his rightful expectations of me, my infidelities, and always assuming his loyalty. He'd never put me through the agonies I had inflicted on him.

Then I thought of Paul in glory in heaven. I prayed that he would protect me in the years to come, be with my guardian angel to prompt me in the right ways, to prevent me from disasters. I hoped I would always feel his loving presence in all that I did in the future. The Lord only knows what would happen to me, but my deepest hope was that I could join Paul in my own glorified body in our heavenly home.

*

That morning I couldn't bear the prospect of attending the early school Mass; I wouldn't be able to tolerate all that adolescent anarchy. So I kept to my room, and went to the monks' breakfast at eight. An hour later I went and sat in the nave for the conventual sung Mass; apart from the monks in the choir there were about six other people in that vast building, sitting apart from each other in the first few rows of the nave.

Dom Gabriel had explained that the coffin would be received into the abbey church for the special Vespers for the Dead at six o'clock that evening. It would rest on a small catafalque in the crossing with candles and prayer desks surrounding it. Everyone was welcome to attend this liturgy, and to pray beside the coffin until the church was closed after Compline at nine o'clock. It was hoped that many boys would do this, even if they had barely known Paul.

In the meantime, I stayed in my room in the guest house until lunchtime with the monks. Afterwards I took a walk through the lanes to The Rock, imagining Paul with me, talking and laughing with him – to the place where we'd first kissed, made our pact and he'd first read our Whitman poem to me.

I jumped over the short wall that led into the wood overlooking Happy Valley. There was The Rock, but now the canopy of trees beneath was bare, revealing the whole valley below wreathed in a smoky mist.

As I approached, I heard voices; it was just my luck that someone had got there before me. But as I descended the small path, I saw who it was: Nicky Jones and another boy whose name I could not remember.

'Well, well,' I exclaimed. 'It's Nicky Jones.'

He looked almost as astonished as me. 'Freddie! I can't believe it's you. I thought you'd be coming for Shipton's funeral, but didn't expect to see you here.'

It was strange. The bloom had gone from his pretty little face, but the sweetness of his voice and his disarming little mannerisms were undiminished. Not quite the fallen angel yet.

'This is my friend Mills. He's in Gasquet House.'

'Hello,' I said. The boy was obviously the same age as Nicky, the same height, but dark, almost swarthy. He looked at me with a certain shiftiness and only a glimmer of a smile. Had Nicky told him about our encounter last summer?

'Are you two here for a gasper? Here, have one of mine,' I said, bringing a packet of Gitanes out of my pocket.

Mills brought out his lighter – one of the new throwaway French ones.

I looked across at the valley, so bleak and lifeless in its winter garb. 'I've come here to remember the time when Paul and I recited Keats and Whitman poems together on this very spot.' At least, I thought, Nicky should be able to understand.

'Wow!' he said, and I saw him put his arm round Mills's waist. 'What a *romantic* and lovely thing to do. Would *you* do that for me, Mills?' He wasn't being sarky. The two of them were obviously an item.

And at that moment I felt my heart burst, the tears welling up, coming from the very deepest part of me. I just couldn't control them. 'Oh God, I just can't bear it. How am I going to live now?'

Nicky was obviously overcome too, and put out his arms inviting me to embrace him. I wept on his shoulder as he tried to comfort me by stroking my back and my neck. How ironic was this: Nicky consoling me just as I had tried to do the same for him only nine months ago.

At last, at last.

With my love,

Freddie

22

My dear Sam,

I walked back from The Rock with Nicky and Mills. I was touched by the way they were obviously so fond of each other and I said a little prayer that their relationship would endure.

Tea in the monastery refectory was surprisingly convivial, with the monks circulating and chatting among themselves and guests almost like a cocktail party, awkwardly balancing cups and saucers with biscuits and cake. Several asked how I was getting on at Cambridge. One or two gave me genuine commiserations knowing that Paul and I had been so close. *How will they take it tomorrow when I recite the poem?* I wondered. *How many will understand? How many will wish me and him in hell?*

I had a short talk with Whiskers who told me that the Mass would be in plainchant, although the boys' choir, the *Scuola Cantorum*, had been practising the Allegri '*Miserere*', which had been requested by the family. Ah! At last they've shown a bit of inspiration, I thought. Six Ambrose prefects would be the pall bearers bringing the coffin into the abbey church this evening at Vespers. Tomorrow, after the funeral, six School prefects would bear it out again to the hearse. Vespers this evening was entirely optional for the boys but tomorrow the whole school would be at the Requiem.

At quarter to six, the abbey's great bell began to toll, slowly and almost ominously, reverberating throughout the church and echoing over the moonlit landscape. It sounded so different from the usual benign call to prayer. The catafalque had been prepared with a Persian rug laid on the stone floor, a draped trestle, surrounded by four tall candlestands. I found a place close by. The church was almost half full.

A few minutes before six, a silent procession emerged from the central door in the south crossing, making its way up the middle of the nave. A cross bearer, a thurifer and two acolytes followed by the abbot in a cope and then the monks, in pairs with their cowls covering their heads. They reached the west door where they waited in expectation.

The double doors were thrown open and the sound of cars drawing up on the gravel outside could be heard. I saw the six prefects go into the forecourt and a few minutes later enter the church, carrying the coffin on their shoulders. As the procession started to move up the nave the cantor began:

In Paradisum deducant te angeli
In tuo adventu suscipiant te martyres
Et perducant te in civitatem sanctam Jerusalem.

May angels lead thee into Paradise,
May martyrs receive thee at thy coming
And lead thee to the holy Jerusalem.

The monks and choir continued antiphonally:

Angelorum te suscipiat,
Et cum Lazaro quondam paupere
Aeternum habeas requiem.
Gloria patri…

May the choir of angels receive you
And with Lazarus, who once was poor
May you have everlasting rest.
Glory be to the Father...

The sweetness and simplicity of it was tearing at my heartstrings.

I stared at that polished, gleaming box as it came ever closer towards me in the procession. Inside were the remains of all that I had ever loved and all that I had never said goodbye to. I felt my knees giving way and had to sit while all around me were still standing.

A small group of figures clad in black had followed immediately behind the coffin. They now took their seats in the front row. I recognised Mrs Shipton instantly, wearing a black mantilla, and presumed the lady accompanying her, in a wide-brimmed black hat and veil, making her face half invisible, was her sister, the famous ex-model. Next to them were Dr Shipton, and Claire in a white mantilla.

Vespers for the Dead now began. Each psalm, each antiphon, had words of such poignancy, gathering in intensity as we prayed for Paul. They expressed insistently our faith in eternal life: *Requiem aeternam... Ad Dominum cum tribularer clamavi... Levavi oculos meos in montes... De profundis clamavi at te, Domine!... In conspectu Angelorum psalmam tibi...* We weren't just *remembering* Paul – how minimal and pointless that would be – we were *praying* for him, for goodness' sake, begging God to show His mercy and admit him into paradise. The plainchant was mesmerising: insistent, simple and eternal. If God really dwells in beauty he had to be here, now, and listening.

The readings, the '*Magnificat*' and the blessings all followed. The monks then filed out in procession. A couple of novices brought out six prayer desks and put them around the catafalque. A great silence fell across the shadows.

Now it hit me again: this was the last time I would be within touching distance of Paul in this life. I needed to be close to him, almost to guard him. I fell on my knees at one of the desks, covering my head in my hands. There were others standing nearby, but I paid them no attention. As I prayed for him, I spoke words of endearment too heartfelt for me to recall now.

After a few minutes I felt a tap on my shoulder.

I looked up. It was Paul's uncle, Dr Shipton. He nodded and made a sign that he would like to speak. I looked at him, trying to hide my reluctance. We walked slowly into the semi-darkness in the north aisle of the nave. He turned, and to my surprise put out his hand to shake mine silently. We walked slowly on, passing the wall monuments of deceased abbots.

As we neared the west end I stopped and turned. I wanted to be the first to speak.

'I must apologise, sir, that I haven't been able to say how dreadfully sad I feel for all Paul's family. You must have had the most terrible few months.'

'Thank you. Yes, it has been the worst time of our lives for us, and exhausting both emotionally and physically. But I'm sorry, too, that we couldn't keep in touch to let you know of events. We know how very fond you were of Paul.'

'And I still am,' I cried out, just a little too loudly. 'I really can't believe he's gone. For me he will always be alive, if only in my heart. But, sir, I need to ask you. Why didn't anyone tell me that he was so close to death? Did he never ask to see me? I would have come at once. Why did I have to find out for myself?'

'Yes, he did talk about you, Fred – a lot. He had a photo of you beside his bed when he died. But we decided not to call you because we thought it would upset both of you too much. You would have been shocked to see him so ill, and he would have been distressed to know he was seeing you for the last time. And besides, it all came on so suddenly.' All this sounded pretty feeble to me. I was exasperated but powerless.

He must have known that more was needed.

'But, I can understand how you must feel, knowing him so intimately as you did, although many might *not* understand.'

He turned to nod vaguely in the direction of Paul's mother and sister, and then looked at me sideways, his eyes full of sympathy. He obviously didn't want to say much more. There must have been a backstory, which I was not sure I wanted to hear.

'And after this is over, Fred, we want to draw a line under it all. We should all move on, always remembering Paul and praying for him of course, but not letting our grief overwhelm us forever. In some ways he was very blessed in dying so young, without having to endure all the difficulties of a long life. We can remember him always in the full bloom of his beauty and youth.'

He continued, 'So what I am saying is that, after tomorrow, Paul's family want to be left in peace, and not be visited by anyone who knew him. Do you understand that, Fred?'

I did indeed understand. I was not to visit them nor communicate with them again. What's past is past, and they only want their own private memories. That excluded me who had loved him as much as they had, but differently. Now they had discovered the truth of our relationship they wanted the memory of it blotted out forever. As far as they were concerned, I was never part of his story. Perhaps they felt they had been deceived by us.

'I will honour your wishes, sir. But I can't feel the same as you. I just want to be reminded of Paul all the time. He was my family too, you should know, and all of ours here. He will live forever in my heart and in the memory of all his friends at Upton. But I won't be troubling you anymore.' I said this with as much disdain as I could muster and was about to walk away.

The doctor was obviously touched by what I'd said and turned to me again saying, this time gesturing towards the nave,

'If you take my advice, you should get away from all *this* once tomorrow is over. I'm not sure that all the intensity and claustrophobia of this place is good for you. You need to escape, go away – a long way away – not necessarily to forget, but to see what else the world holds for you. I get the impression you've been far too protected here and at home. Unless you move on, take a risk in life, you could get stuck here and – I'm sorry to have to say it – never grow up.'

I was so astonished at his words that I had no time to answer before he shook my hand again and moved away, saying that he had to collect the others. How could someone I had barely met speak to me like this, taking such a liberty in giving me advice such as only my father had the right to do? Yet I couldn't take exception to anything he'd said; there was no criticism, he was very calm, and it came straight from the heart. It was almost as though Paul had been speaking to me through his uncle, confirming everything he'd said in that letter.

I went over to the south aisle and back to the prayer desks by the catafalque. I saw Paul's mother and aunt join the doctor walking towards the side door at the west end about to leave. Claire was the last to move, and as she did so she caught sight of me in the semi-darkness on the other side of the crossing. The look of contempt that she threw at me was accusing, judgmental and condemning – all in one. But I felt no shame; instead, for a moment, I was sorry for her.

I couldn't face any supper so went back to my room for a coffee and a cigarette and to ponder what I had just gone through. But I was restless; my place was surely at Paul's side, tonight of all nights.

At nine o'clock the bell tolled for Compline, the last Office of the day, a gentler sound, and the monks drifted in to take their places in the choir. There was no procession but the boys still at the prayer desks moved to the front of the nave. There was silence. It was pitch dark, all the lights were extinguished, and the only chinks in the vast dimness were from the sanctuary lamp far away above the high altar and the four candles round the coffin.

The cantor began, this time in English:

'*O God, come to our aid,*

And then came the response,

O Lord, make haste to help us.
Glory be...'

There followed a hymn, and then the Psalm 90, the most consoling of all the psalms:

'*He who dwells in the shelter of the Most High*
And abides in the shade of the almighty says to the Lord:
"*my refuge,*
My stronghold, my God in whom I trust..."'

And, towards the end... I knew what was coming and could not prevent my tears welling up once again as the words took over. It was my Heavenly Father speaking to *me* of Paul,

'*Since he clings to me in love, I will free him;*
Protect him for he knows my name.
When he calls I shall answer: "I am with you",
I will save him in distress and give him glory.'

I could barely take any more. A light went on for the reading, and then was switched off. The '*Nunc Dimittis*' was sung and the monks made their way to the majestic statue of the Virgin and Child in the south crossing. They formed a semi-circle to sing the '*Regina Coeli*'. The abbot sprinkled them with holy water, and then the half-dozen remaining boys and me.

We took our leave as the novices extinguished the candles around the catafalque, leaving the church in complete darkness.

It had been a trying and exhausting day, but even so I found it difficult to sleep. In my dreams Paul was here, there and everywhere: we were acting in *Twelfth Night*, but both of us were making up our soliloquies and dialogues as we went along, not making much sense, or knowing how to finish them. Then I was lying on his chest my tongue tickling his hard nipples, making him squirm with pleasure. Or we were having knickerbocker glories on a bench beside the sea, but the creamy splodge I was wiping from Paul's lips morphed into something else and I woke up finding I had drenched myself involuntarily. I had to get out of bed to clean up, feeling ashamed, tonight of all nights. I kept waking, but the dreams kept coming and I didn't want to stop them.

With my love,
Freddie

23

My dear Sam,

Now came the morning of the funeral. I rose again at five o'clock and entered the church as the monks were assembling for Matins. The candles beside the coffin had been lit. Once more I knelt at one of the prayer desks.

The liturgy was similar to the previous day but this time, in my agitation, my attention kept wandering. I determined that I would escape immediately after the funeral. Thank goodness there was to be no wake and that the family would be leaving immediately afterwards.

Coffee was all I could take for breakfast. After which I removed all my things to the car in readiness for a quick departure later, pausing there for a cigarette. At ten minutes to nine the great bell began to boom out over the rooftops of this little self-contained city-state. This time it was with even greater solemnity than at Vespers yesterday – crashingly loud, but more slowly, continuing for a full ten minutes. I found a place in the nave a few rows from the front but well away from the family.

As the boys started to arrive, taking their places in the

351

body of the church, I was moved by how sombre many of them looked. There was hardly any ragging or resentful slouching with hands in pockets; they seemed fully aware of the occasion. For most of them this had been the first time they had encountered death at such close quarters, let alone of one so near to them in years. Dom Placid's words began to ring true; this spectacle was for all Paul's communities – the boys, the monks, his family. I had my part to play for sure, but it was only one of many. If it were possible, I needed to be objective; the time for my private grief had passed. Now I had to share my love for Paul with everyone.

I saw Roz approaching and made a gesture for him to sit next to me. He was the one person I knew I could rely on. He touched my arm and said quietly, '*Sois courageux, mon cher ami.*'

The thirty-strong *Scuola Cantorum* processed silently in twos from the sacristy to take up their position in the north transept. After the great bell's last echo had died away there was total silence across the whole church. I'd never experienced such a sense of collective anticipation, least of all among my usually restless peers. A massive shudder reverberated through the church as the bolts to the double doors at the back of the south aisle were opened. The procession emerged, advancing up the centre of the nave.

The cantor's unaccompanied voice rang out the antiphon in a pure, almost ethereal tenor:

'*Asperges me domine hyssopo et mundabor...*'

The choir and monks continued, antiphonally,

'*Miserere mei, Deus, secundum magnam misericordiam tuam.*'

At the head of the procession was a magisterially tall, fair-haired boy clad in a white alb carrying the gleaming processional cross. Behind him, similarly radiant in white, came the thurifer, vigorously swinging his Gothic censer, clouds of the sweetest-smelling frankincense enveloping him. It was Nicky, and beside him was his Mills, holding the boat-shaped receptacle for the dry incense. Then came about thirty black-clad monks in pairs, with their heads covered by their cowls, beginning with the youngest novices, ending with the eldest and slowest. They were followed by two matching acolytes bearing candlestands with burning yellow candles.

Bringing up the rear were the celebrants in black velvet vestments: the deacon in his dalmatic, Whiskers himself; the sub-deacon in his tunicle, Dom Gabriel; and then the abbot, Dom Placid, in his chasuble embroidered with *opus anglicanum* worked by the famous seamstress-nuns of Southam. He seemed frail and vulnerable as he almost hobbled to keep up with the rest. Despite his evident discomfort there was a sweetness of expression in his face, and – paradoxically – a nobility in the way he wore his mitre and grasped his crozier. In his right hand he was waving the *aspergilium*, spraying us all with holy water as he moved forward. Mackenzie, now the head boy, was beside him, almost supporting the aged priest, wearing a black gown over his regulation suit and holding the silver holy water bucket.

How well I knew every word of the '*Miserere*', which now followed, now chanted in Latin. All those night-time performances in the dormitory had had their effect.

As the monks took their places in the choir, the rest of the procession moved forward into the sanctuary. There was a pause while the abbot and celebrants ascended the final steps to incense the altar. At last he intoned the opening words of the Introit in his old man's quavering voice:

'Requiem aeternam dona eis Domine'

The Mass then proceeded on two different levels. The party at the high altar recited the *'Confiteor'* to each other, and then went to sit – the abbot on his throne, the others on stools each side of him. The rest of the congregation sat as the choir began the *'Kyrie'*. Paul would have wanted it like this: grand, masculine and austere.

We reached the Epistle: the sub-deacon read from 1 Thessalonians. The choir struck up the Gradual *'Requiem eternam...'* (again), and, after a pause, the Tract:

'Absolve Domine, animas omnium fidelium
defunctorum...'

This was my signal. I looked ahead at the altar as I walked slowly past the crossing, bowed and ascended the steps to the right-hand ambo. Everywhere the sense of surprise, even astonishment, was palpable; boys were waking up, shifting in their seats and murmuring to their neighbours.

I stood in front of the lectern, seeing the whole school in serried ranks in the nave and aware of the choir, monks and celebrants close behind me. All my nervousness vanished. I paused for at least five seconds. I was in complete control.

I knew the poem off by heart, of course, so had no need to take my steady gaze away from the whole assembly, but it was the images of Paul that I saw rising up in front of me:

'We two boys together clinging,
One the other never leaving,
Up and down the roads going,
North and South excursions making,
Power enjoying, elbows stretching, fingers clutching,
Arm'd and fearless, eating, drinking, sleeping...'

Here I paused, deliberately, before declaiming the most crucial word of all with as much defiance as I could muster:

'*LOVING.*'

Then another pause before continuing,

'*No law less than ourselves owning, sailing, soldiering, thieving, threatening...*'

The visions were so strong and came flooding back; there we were, dressed up to the nines, standing in front of the mirror before my eighteenth, my arm over his shoulder, saying nice, sweet things to each other; then lying in the grass next to him, overwhelmed by his beauty, his closeness, and the sound of his voice, so rich, so gritty...

'*Misers, menials, priests alarming, air breathing, water drinking, on the turf or the sea-beach dancing,*

Cities wrenching, ease scorning, statutes mocking, feebleness chasing...'

The last line now was crucial; it was imperative that everyone should understand that our love had been consummated. We were complete; our foray into life had been fulfilled. The words had to be said slowly – *andante* – not accentuating the word 'our', but ensuring it was not lost or blurred when read between the alliterations.

'*Fulfilling our foray.*'

I remained at the lectern for five seconds of eternity. The silence was vast.

I was about to move when I heard someone behind me begin to clap. I looked round; it was Dom Placid, smiling benignly. His gesture looked for a moment as though it might remain his alone. But it was taken up by a boy sitting close to him. It was Nicky, the thurifer, the fag who had loved me. And then, as if by contagion, others started clapping, followed by a few more, until the whole school in front of me was clapping and some cheering. The noise was like thunder reverberating through the choir, the transepts, into the furthest ends of the nave.

The euphoria was almost tangible. Instinctively, I realised that Paul knew this would happen; I had been his instrument to proclaim what we had been for each other: he – we – had been totally validated. That was why I was here; there was nothing more for me to do.

I just managed to contain myself as I walked slowly back to my place. This time there were tears of joy, not grief. I felt the impact of hundreds of pairs of eyes bearing down on me and felt nothing but pride in my total transparency. But as I reached my seat I stumbled and bent myself forward with my head in my hands, tears falling silently. Roz put his arm over my shoulder. I fell back onto his chest until I was able to dry my eyes and look up. The echoing tumult died away as the choir began the Sequence.

My heart was pounding so violently, making it almost impossible to concentrate as the Mass continued. I regained semi-consciousness when the boys went up for Communion and the choir began Allegri's '*Miserere*'. Ah! Those agonisingly pure, angelic voices rising in great arches, dissolving in the vault of heaven, taking Paul's soul with them; then descending again to comfort us here on earth. I was shaking again. I had never heard anything so beautiful, so humble, yet so full of sublime hope.

At length the abbot and his depleted procession moved from the sanctuary to the crossing for the Committal. With the deacon and sub-deacon holding each side of his cope, he circumnavigated the catafalque, incensing it vigorously while the choir sang the '*Nunc Dimittis*'. Just as they had finished, and while the sweet-smelling clouds were still hanging in the air, a burst of winter sunshine came flooding into the church from the south clerestory. All the shadows seemed to vanish as the golden light swept up the nave to the crossing, the choir, to the high altar, even the side chapels beyond, penetrating even the innermost recesses. Last of all the great east window became a blaze of light. The central figure of Christ in Glory, swathed in purple and ermine within His golden mandorla, was impossible to look at without being blinded.

As suddenly as it had appeared the light vanished, and we were plunged back into the greyness of an English February morning. But everything had changed. The time for weeping was over. An everyday sense of normality slowly permeated the crowd. Murmurs of conversations between the boys could be heard. We had returned to the world of the living. The school prefects lifted the coffin onto their shoulders to process down the central nave, followed by the family. The west doors were opened, and the coffin was placed into the waiting hearse. A minute later the crunch of the gravel signified the departure of the cortege.

It was all over. There was nothing more I could do, nothing more to be said.

I was still half numb as some of my near contemporaries came over to shake me by the hand, giving me a word of encouragement and a sympathetic smile. I saw Rowse approaching but I was too tired to bristle or feel on guard. He had changed; as he'd matured he'd lost his cheap prettiness and today he was pale and drawn. He put his hand on my shoulder and looked me in the face, saying,

'We're all really sorry, Fred.'

Then I remembered and thank goodness I had the guts to respond, 'Thanks. Yeah, you went back a long way. You'll miss him...'

Roz stayed beside me. The novices were already dismantling the catafalque, moving the prayer desks and changing the altar frontal. When nearly everyone had left, we walked down the north aisle to the west door. He continued silently beside me to the car park. The fresh air and brightness added to my sense of being in an unknown, foreign place.

Then it came to me how all our senses – sight, sound, smell, touch and even taste – had converged this morning in an immersive work of sublime beauty. But we had not been mere spectators as though in a theatre. Everyone present had been part of it, giving it an extra dimension, life and meaning.

It must have been this sudden clarity that prompted me to burst out:

'That was extraordinary. It was like a glimpse into heaven – a unique moment when eternity seemed to reach down to earth to claim Paul. Just for a moment I thought I was witnessing his ascent into glory.'

I paused. Was I sounding ridiculous? But I knew I could count on Roz at least to understand as I struggled to find the right words.

'It was like… like… a sort of… *apotheosis*.'

'No, you don't sound ridiculous at all, Fred. You're not the only one. I think everyone was aware of a moment of transcendence. But, you know, it was *you* who made it happen by reading that poem. It changed everything. We've learnt the most important lesson of all: in the end, all that matters is to love and be loved. You and Shipton have shown us that.'

He continued, 'Look, I know you'll be feeling terrible right now, but you can count on me. Why not come and stay with us in Paris in the next vacation if you want a break. It's only a month away.'

I wanted to hug him.

'That's a lovely idea, Roz, or should I call you Théo from now on?' I said with a wisp of a smile. 'Let me think about it. I really don't know what I'm going to do. I'm just completely exhausted.'

*

A few months later a parcel arrived for me. It contained all the letters and postcards I had ever sent Paul, and the bronze statuette of the two boys, which had traduced us; it's here in front of me as I write this – Castor and Pollux. There was nothing else.

The rest you probably know, Sam. At Easter I took up the offer from Roz – now and forevermore Théo – and went to stay with him for a week. He was incredibly kind, but I kept thinking how Paul would have loved being there too.

I was in a bad way back at Cambridge, but George helped me scrape through the Tripos Part 1. By then I'd decided that the Law was not for me; I wouldn't be returning. In my own mind Cambridge had always been contingent on Paul being there too. I had to confront my parents; they were disappointed but not angry. They understood everything all too well by now, although nothing was ever said – at least not for years and years.

I met up with Théo again in the summer and we spent three months together, travelling all over Europe in my Spitfire and blowing the rest of my Premium Bond win. We stayed with Peter and George in Normandy who were perfect hosts and gave us some wonderful contacts in Italy. For the next ten years Théo and I were best friends and for a short time he even became my beloved Ted.

I found I had to keep busy. I went into the City and made a small packet in the Barber Boom, enough to buy my own flat, and later get me through the Courtauld. There was a lot of monkey business in those years, I'm afraid, but it was all pretty heartless – although there were some exceptions. Somehow, despite everything, I managed to cling to the faith, at least as interpreted by Dom Placid. A few years later I came north and eventually hitched up with Bill before the AIDS thing became endemic, thank goodness, and we stuck together for the next thirty years. When he died three years ago his passing was sad, of course, but more natural; we'd had our ups and downs, done everything we could ever do, and been everything to each other. But in all those years I never forgot Paul. He was always there, always seventeen, eternally beautiful. Maybe, as time went on, he became a lost mirage, an ethereal vision of perfection that had once been mine and real.

Then, fifty years later and out of the blue, came that encounter at the Gallery.

A lot of water has passed under the Calder Bridge since I began these letters a couple of years ago, Sam. *Non sum qualis eram.* I am not as I was.

Now, of course, I have my Giles.

Enough said.

With my love,

Freddie

Epilogue

From Samuel.Burton@xxxx.co.uk
To Giles.McNaughton-Harbord@xxxx.ac.uk

Date 26/6/2025 08.30

Hi Giles,

Emma and I have finished reading all Uncle Freddie's letters at last. Sorry it's taken so long. I haven't shown them to my mother – I'm afraid she would probably want them destroyed.

It was a total revelation to learn about his early life and the loss of his first love. It obviously affected him deeply, changing him from an immature, perhaps rather spoilt boy into the man we thought we knew and loved. Behind that cheery façade there was a deep hinterland of experience which we had no idea about.

TBH I'd completely forgotten he promised to write to me. But once I started reading the letters I became rather upset that he decided not to send them! Once he got started he must have had cold feet, but continued anyway, hoping they'd all be found after he died. Did he think I'd be shocked? Or that I wouldn't understand the world in which he was brought up? Let alone his struggles around issues of faith, loyalty and identity, which were so important to him?

But no. I think the reasons went deeper. I suspect he had doubts as to whether we – his blood family – should be the rightful heirs to such a personal and intimate story. In the end he must have realised that you – the last love of his life – were his real 'family'. Am I right? That must have been why he made you his heir.

No hard feelings! It's what he wanted.

So we feel you should be the rightful custodian of these letters despite their being addressed to me. Their obvious home is his Queen Anne secretaire – which is now yours. You should keep them there among the family papers, just as he wanted. In the end they were probably written for you as much as they were for me and for posterity.

I'll be sending them back to you tomorrow by Recorded Delivery.

But let's continue to be friends. We would love it if we could become part of your new extended family, if you will let us. You're always welcome here when you come to London. Uncle Freddie's legacy means we'll be getting a bigger house where there will always be a spare room for you to stay. Although you may have to put up with two noisy children wanting to climb all over you! They'll probably start calling you 'Uncle Giles'!

With our love,

Sam

Independent graphic designer
https://www.samburtondesign
Follow me on Facebook, YouTube

ACKNOWLEDGMENTS

Writing my first novel – this fictional memoir – in the eighth decade of my life would not have been possible without the help of many kind people. I am especially grateful to Michael Langan for gently bringing me down to earth in the early stages and helping me shape the initial concept. His suggestion that I try to answer the question, 'But what did it *feel* like?' was a game-changer. To Leonora Rustamova I am forever thankful for sticking with me and finessing the final drafts. I shall always remember her kind admonition, 'You don't have to *explain* everything!' To my classmates at Swarthmore, Leeds, I am indebted for their sympathetic encouragement; and to my fellow scribblers in our Rogue Writers online group for their solidarity and support. Among friends who have given me the benefit of their advice are Tony, Alan, Liz, Jane, Andrew, and of course my own Tony.

At Troubador I would like to thank Kelly Coombs, Meera Vithlani, Beth Archer and their colleagues for their professionalism.

Despite all the help I have received from friends and professionals over the past three years, I am aware that there are many shortcomings, which are entirely my own.

I am grateful to Picador for permission to quote from

I hope 'Upton' is still as beautiful and inspirational as ever. Much has changed and the scenario enacted in these pages could never happen there today: attitudes are different, the monks have left, and the place is now co-ed.

There never was a Paul Shipton or a Freddie McNaughton.

ABOUT THE AUTHOR

James Lomax was born in Surrey and brought up in London, Somerset and Sussex. Despite having a degree in Law from Cambridge and training as a chartered accountant he became an art historian and museum curator. He has written extensively, mainly on eighteenth-century decorative arts. This is his first novel. He lives in the Yorkshire Dales with his civil partner.